Good Bait

Good Bait

John Harvey

PEGASUS CRIME

NEW YORK LONDON

GOOD BAIT

Pegasus Crime is an Imprint of
Pegasus Books LLC
80 Broad Street, 5th Floor
New York, NY 10004

Copyright © 2012

ISBN: 978-1-60598-378-3

10 9 8 7 8 6 5 4 3 2 1

Printed in the United States of America
Distributed by W. W. Norton & Company, Inc.

Oakley Hall
1920–2008

May his work live on.

1

The face looked back up at her from beneath the ice. Dead eyes, unblinking, their focus defused as if through bottled glass. Off to one side, a small covey of ducks, uncomprehending, shuffled this way and that. In places, Karen Shields thought, the skin would have stuck fast: the forehead, the bridge of the nose, the chin. Little doubt the substance that had pooled close alongside the head, then frozen, was blood. That wanker, she thought, the artist — what was his name? — a small fortune for slicing animals in half and shoving them on display, pickled in formaldehyde.

Officers in protective clothing were cordoning off the path that ran down between the ponds with tape, no urgency now, time theirs to take. A brace of early runners stymied in their tracks, hats and gloves, jogged up and down, looking on; Karen could see their breath bobbing in the air.

When the call had come through she'd fumbled uneasily awake, mobile falling between her fingers and down on to the bed.

'Hey!' A shout as she leaned her elbow against something soft in the shape alongside. 'Hey! Go easy, yeah? Chill.'

She had almost forgotten he was there.

She spoke briefly into the phone then listened, the man beside her moving grudgingly to give her room, whatever was tattooed between shoulder blade and neck starting to fade into the natural darkness of his skin. She wondered if she would pick him out again in a crowded bar. If she would want to.

'Twenty minutes,' she said into the phone. 'Thirty, tops.' No way she was leaving without a shower.

'What's all the fuss?' the man asked.

Scooping up his shirt and trousers from near the end of the bed, she tossed them at his head. 'Dressed, okay?'

She arrived as the Crime Scene manager and his team were assembling: no agreement as yet on the best way to free the body from the ice. Someone from the Coroner's Office would decide.

Where the ground rose up beyond the pond's edge, threads of trees were laced against the sky. Christmas in four days. No, three. Presents bought for her family in Jamaica but still not sent. Come spend it with us, her sister had said, Lynette, the one in Southend with the twins. You don't want to spend Christmas on your own.

'Ma'am.' Without his helmet, the young PC barely topped her shoulder. 'The Chief Super, he wants a word.'

Karen looked up.

Burcher was standing on the broad slope of path that led on to the Heath, beyond the point where the route for entry and exit to the scene was marked. Overcoat unbuttoned, green wellingtons protecting the trousers of his suit, pale yellow gloves. Detective Chief Superintendent Anthony Burcher, previously with Covert Intelligence and now head of Homicide and Serious Crime Command. Twenty-four Homicide teams under his control, one of them hers.

'What the hell's he doing here?' Karen asked.

No reply.

Burcher stood with one glove removed, as if he might want to shake her hand. Waiting for her to come to him.

'All under control?'

'Sir.'

'No idea yet, of course, who . . . ?'

Karen shook her head.

'Yes, well . . .' His gaze slipped past her, attention caught for a moment by something at the farther side of the pond. 'I was in the area, last night, friends. Picked up the call first thing.'

There were more people gathering now, peering interestedly before being moved on: cyclists on their way to work, solitary walkers, joggers, people with dogs, too many dogs. The gravel was deeply freckled with frost.

'Much on your plate right now, Chief Inspector?'

Her plate. Oh, yes. A double murder for starters. Holloway. Mother and child. The mother only seventeen, little more than a child herself. Battered, then stabbed: edge of a stool, underside of a saucepan, a kitchen knife, whatever had been to hand. The child, a girl, suffocated with pillows, three years old. The estranged father had been seen hammering on the door of the flat two days before. 'I'll kill you, you bloody bitch! Bloody kill you!' The neighbours had heard it all before, shut their windows fast, turned up the volume on the TV, made yet another cup of tea. Karen had seen it, too. Too many times now. Inadequate men unable to cope without anger, lashing out. Family life. The police were, as the phrasing went, anxious to speak to the father, Wayne Simon, in connection with both deaths.

So far there had been sightings in Sheffield, Rotherham, Leeds. Rumours he'd slipped abroad. Karen would still not be surprised to find he'd strapped himself into his car in a lock-up somewhere, sucking down carbon monoxide; either that or hanged himself from a length of flex; walked off the edge of a cliff. Beachy Head, that was popular. More often than not, it was what they did, men like that, men she despised, too cowardly to face the consequences of their actions, the way they'd lived.

More recently there'd been a shooting in Walthamstow. All the appearances of a drug deal run sour. The teenage victim gunned down as he ran. Some disagreement still as to how involved he had been, mistaken identity a possibility, the family swearing by his good name – a lovely boy and loving son, a grade A student, college place secured. So far, there had been two arrests, both men – Liam Jarvis and Rory Bevan – released, insufficient evidence to charge.

Before that a fatal stabbing in Wood Green. An argument over nothing that had ballooned from threats to fists, fists and boots to knives. By rights it should have been handed over, lock stock and barrel, to Operation Trident, which dealt with violent crime in the black community, but since the new government had taken power Trident's resources had been cut and they were already overstretched. Sixteen murders in London the year just ended, none of the victims older than nineteen.

'Enough, sir,' Karen said.

'Handle this yourself then, or . . . ?'

'A reason why I shouldn't? Sir?'

Something interested him near the toe of his boot. 'See how it develops, but at the moment I can't see any need . . .'

'Need?'

'You know, delegate. Reassign. Besides . . .' Inclining his head towards her, he smiled. 'Can't go on plundering the minority thing for too much longer. Good result now, not go amiss. Been a while.'

'Which minority thing is that, sir? The gender minority or the black?'

'Either. Both. You choose.' The smile had disappeared.

Fuck you, Karen thought, the words unsaid.

Burcher heard them nonetheless, read them in her expression, her stance.

'Don't let me keep you, Chief Inspector.'

A magpie startled up raucously from a branch as she walked away.

Back down at the pond, they were gingerly breaking the ice in a broad circle around the body, preparing to float it closer to the shore.

All the way back to the office it nagged at her, a good result, not go amiss. Knowing it to be true. She remembered the first time she'd been introduced to him, Burcher, some function not long after he'd been confirmed in post; the way he'd looked at her, appraisingly, so much prime meat.

She'd seen the victim's face freed from its frozen mask before she'd left, the last drops of moisture caught along his upper lip, hair that curled against the nape of his neck: a young man's face, eighteen at most. Younger. The body stripped naked before immersion. Two knife wounds in his back, either one deep enough to have punctured his lungs. Bruises. Other marks. The second finger of his left hand missing, severed below the knuckle. Expediency? Identification? A stubborn ring?

At the last check there were no mispers that matched, no worried parents, lovers, brothers, aunts. Not his. Within an hour, the details, such as they were, would have been passed on by the Press Bureau to the media. Some Riz Lateef wannabe on work experience with BBC London News, shivering in front of the camera and hoping her make-up hadn't smudged and the cold wouldn't make her nose run. If nothing new had emerged by the end of the day, they'd release the victim's photograph in time to catch the dailies, maximum exposure, pray no natural disaster or ministerial cock-up shunted them off to the bottom of page six or eight.

On the computer screen the images were strangely bleached out, so that the face resembled something sculpted, cast in plaster: Roman, Greek. An altarpiece. A minor god. All colour gone from his eyes.

Karen remembered his eyes.

His eyes had been blue.

2

Christmas came and went. Karen spoke to most of her close family on the day itself – mother, uncle, aunt, a smattering of cousins – trying not to count the cost of calls back and forth to Jamaica; talked to her sister later, reining in her impatience while her nieces vied with one another over never-ending litanies of presents.

Mid-afternoon, she sat herself down in front of the TV, a bargain meal from M&S assembled on her tray, a decent red to wash it down. New Year's Eve she went for a meal in Exmouth Market with four of her girlfriends, then on to a club near the Angel; not for want of offers, she was home by half twelve, in bed before one alone, reading a book. There'd been a time, not so long ago, when if she hadn't pulled she'd have reckoned the evening a failure.

God, girl, she thought, you're getting old!

January kicked off with sleet, then rain, then snow, then sleet again. At night it froze. Coming down the steps from her front door her first full day back in the office, she'd almost lost her footing, had to grab hold of the railing to avoid going headlong. The pavement was like a skating rink, ice packed solidly along the kerb's edge. Fresh snow fluttered, moth-like, in her face as she walked. The latte bought at Caffè Nero had lost most of its heat before she even reached the Tube.

Photographs and a description of the Heath victim had been passed on to the Met's Intelligence Bureau before the holiday for possible identification. Since when, nothing. Karen had emailed the Intelligence Bureau's Co-ordinating and Tasking Office from home and chased up her request. Co-ordinating and Tasking Office – it sounded like something out of *Bleak House*, the boxed set of which her sister had sent her for Christmas. Automatically generated, a reply had bounced back by return. This office is currently closed.

At her desk her stomach rumbled; coffee aside, no breakfast. Maybe she should give Mike Ramsden a call: Ramsden, for years now her bag man, aide-de-camp, her sergeant-at-arms. Mike, if you're coming in, you might stop off at Pret and pick up one of those egg and tomato baguettes. Pain au something while you're about it.

She wondered if he'd spent Christmas alone like her or whether he'd found company; Ramsden, who seemed to be permanently between wives, usually other people's.

Pushing back her chair, she walked to where the detailed map of the area where the body had been found was pinned to the wall.

The road from the Whitestone Pond down towards South End Green allowed access to that side of the Heath at several points, none of which – Karen had found this almost impossible to believe – were directly covered by CCTV. The only cameras on that stretch of road belonged to private individuals intent on protecting their valuable property and focused accordingly.

'Most of them locked up and shuttered,' Ramsden had said in disgust. 'Wintering in fucking Mustique.'

As far as they'd been able to determine, the actual killing had taken place off the path to the north of the pond: traces of a struggle that had been brutal and swift, branches broken, hard earth kicked up, filaments of blood that had proved, discouragingly, to be the victim's own and nothing more.

There was no sign of the victim's clothes in the immediate vicinity; stripped from his body, they'd likely been bundled into bin bags and burned or else been transported to some far-flung field, a contribution to the national landfill.

The area around the pond had been fingertip searched, bins, drains, bushes, everything. The pond itself had been drained. Thirty-one large bags of debris to be sifted and listed; at the last count, seventeen were still in storage, slowly festering. She had asked for volunteers to sort the remainder — no overtime, just a sign or two of her endearing love and respect — but with half the world still on holiday, takers were few.

Through the square of window, the sky was a resolute grey. The snow had faltered to a halt.

Perhaps she would call Mike Ramsden after all. They could get miserable together, curse the world.

Even as she was thinking that, the phone rang at her desk. 'Mike?'

It was Gerry Stine, Intelligence Support. Karen listened, made careful notes, confirmed the information and thanked Stine profusely, wishing him the happiest of new years. After checking against UK Border Agency records, he had come up with a name. Petru Andronic. Country of origin: the Republic of Moldova. Date of birth: 27 November 1994. Seventeen years old.

Almost unbelievably for someone his age, he had no account traceable on Facebook or any of the other social networking sites, nor on Twitter. Even more remarkable, an initial check of the major networks failed to register him as the owner of a mobile phone: presumably he used a cheap prepaid model or, if the need arose, borrowed a friend's.

Karen shook her head: the Republic of Moldova. She didn't think she even knew where Moldova was. Not enough to point to it on a map. She had heard of it, at least. Or was that Moldavia? The same country, different names? You say Moldova and I'll say Moldavia.

She looked again at her notes. Andronic had applied for a student visa in the summer of the previous year.

She speed dialled Ramsden's number.

The background noise suggested he was engaged in a one-man Status Quo revival.

'Leyton High Road, Mike, you know it?'

'Back of my hand.'

The college was squeezed between a discount DIY store and a halal butcher's and, even though it was doubtful the new term had started, a dozen or more putative student types were standing around on the pavement outside, heads down, plugged into their iPods and MP3 players; smoking, most of them, occasionally stamping their feet but otherwise feigning not to notice the extreme cold.

A narrow corridor led to some narrow, uncarpeted stairs. *This college is fully recognised by ASIC*, read a poster on the wall, *the Accredited Service for International Colleges*. The *No Smoking* sign had been decorated with the smiley face of someone enjoying a large spliff. *Please do NOT bring food into the building* had been handwritten on a sheet of A4 and pinned alongside.

There was a door on the first landing labelled *General Office*, another poster, purple and gold, fixed to the wired glass: *OTHM* in big capitals — *Registered Centre for the Organisation of Tourism and Hospitality Management, supporting the tourism and hospitality industry throughout the world.*

'Who'd have thought it?' Ramsden said. 'The centre for tourism and hospitality, here in downtown Leyton.'

The woman behind the desk — middle-aged, spectacles, brown hair dislodged on one side from the combs intended to secure it in place — scarcely glanced up from what she was doing. 'If you want to enquire about courses, enroll a student, prospectuses are all online. Keeps the print costs down. Application's the same.'

No immediate reply, she half-turned in her chair. There was another door behind her: *Dr D. G. Sillet, College Principal*.

'Is it the gas? It's not the gas? Gas and electric? Public utility bills, all paid, direct debit, straight from the bank. If payments are delayed, I'm afraid that's not of our doing.'

Karen took out her ID and placed it on the desk.

The woman shook her head and another strand of hair slipped astray. 'I've told them till I'm blue in the face, we've all told them, don't block the pavement outside, it constitutes a public nuisance. But do they listen?' A small grunt. 'Do they understand?'

'Petru Andronic,' Karen said. 'He was a student here.'

The woman removed her glasses and looked them up and down. Ramsden in well-worn leather jacket, stomach resting easily on the belt of his jeans. Karen, thanks to her boot heels, taller by a couple of inches; black trousers that accentuated the length of her legs, black woollen belted coat, sweater, scarf loose about her neck.

'Was he?' the woman said.

'Apparently. He applied, at least. Summer of last year.'

'Ah.'

'Ah?'

'Many apply. Few are chosen.' Pleased with that, she allowed herself a little smirk.

'Keep records?' Ramsden asked.

'Of course.'

'Matter of minutes, then, if that. To check.'

The door to the inner office opened and a man stepped through, late forties, balding, a suit that had been to the cleaner's too many times.

'Mrs Dawes?'

'The police, Mr Sillet, just a routine inquiry.'

'Very well.' He paused, a moment, no more; a quick glance towards Karen and Ramsden, an inclination of the head and he was gone.

'Busy man,' Ramsden observed.

Mrs Dawes' fingers clicked briskly on the computer keyboard. 'Yes, here we are. Andronic, Petru. Date of birth, November 27th, 1994. Passport number. Date of entry. Place of residence in this country. He applied to take three courses: ESOL, Administration and Office Skills, Computing and ICT.'

'ESOL?'

'English for Speakers of Other Languages.'

'Of course.'

'According to this, he was offered a place in September, September last, but never seems to have enrolled.'

'Is that unusual?' Karen asked.

'Oh, no.'

'And in that event what happens?'

'We send a letter to the address we've been given. After that, a follow-up, if necessary, warning the student that unless the place is taken up by a certain time it will be forfeited and offered to somebody else.'

'And that would have happened in this case?'

'I assume so.'

'After that? If you hear nothing after that?'

'We're obliged to inform the UK Border Agency of his failure to attend.'

'Which you would have done?'

'We take our responsibilities seriously.'

'Give or take the odd gas bill,' said Ramsden quietly, an aside.

'I'm sorry?'

'Nothing.'

September, October, November – by the time the Border Agency had been informed, Karen thought, Petru Andronic didn't have so very long to live.

'His details,' she said. 'UK address and so on, you can print us out a copy?'

No sooner said, almost, than done. The address was in Green Lanes, off St Ann's Road. She knew the Salisbury pub.

3

The main street was awash with Kurdish and Turkish bakeries and cafés; mini-markets whose stalls, laden high with fruit and vegetables, stretched down across the pavement towards the kerb. Windows advertised cheap calls to Africa and the Middle East, secure ways of sending money home.

'My old man brought me here once,' Ramsden said. 'Up the road from here. Dog track. Harringay. Couple of years before it closed down. I was still at school. Tucked a fiver into my top pocket. See how long it takes you to lose that.' He grinned, remembering. 'Couple of races. Three, maybe. Neither of us had a winner the whole night.'

'Miss him?' Karen asked. 'Your dad?' He'd died, she knew, the year before, cancer.

Ramsden shook his head. 'Don't give it much of a thought.' He looked away.

'He saw all this now, poor bastard'd be turnin' in his grave.'

The street they were looking for ran off to the left, two rows of small terraced houses, flat-fronted, some showing signs of recent renovation, others dwindling towards decay.

The address they'd been given was stranded midway between two extremes, work started and abandoned; a new window in the front downstairs, fresh paint, new curtains; the first-floor window had been removed and not replaced, a sheet of tarpaulin flapping in the wind and failing to keep out the snow that had begun, once more, to fall. Tiles had slipped from the roof and lay like crazy paving across the bare patch of garden. A coat of primer on the front door.

Ramsden rang the bell and, when nothing seemed to be happening, knocked loudly twice.

The woman who came to the door was wearing a black burkha, impossible to guess her age; a child of no more than a few months asleep in a sling across her chest. Seeing Ramsden she took a step back inside; stood impassive in the face of Karen's questions, then called back into the house. The boy who sidled towards them was twelve or thirteen, dark-eyed, hair grown long.

'You speak English?' Ramsden asked.

'Course. So does my mum. She don't like to speak to no strangers, yeah? My dad, he goes crazy.'

His mother had retreated into the hall, a hand cupped round the baby's head.

'You from the council?' the boy asked. 'No. Police. Police, i'n it?'

Karen nodded. 'We're looking for someone who might know a Petru Andronic.'

'Who?'

'Petru Andronic. We were told he lived here.'

The boy was shaking his head, shifting his weight from foot to foot. 'Just me an' my brothers, my sisters, mum an' dad, that's all.'

'And where are you from?' Ramsden asked.

'Tottenham. South Tottenham.'

'Before that?'

'Iraq, i'n it?'

'How long have you been living here? This house?' Karen asked.

'I dunno. Ages. Long time. A year? More'n that. 'Fore my birthday. Yeah, more than a year, got to be.'

'And there's been no one else living here during that time? No one staying with you? A lodger?'

The boy shook his head. Behind him, the baby cried, just once, and was shushed.

'You're sure?'

'Course I'm sure.'

Karen showed him the photograph. 'You ever seen this person before?'

'No.'

'Please look at it carefully.'

'I did.'

'So look again,' Ramsden said.

The boy scowled and murmured something beneath his breath, then, with exaggerated deliberation, did as he was asked.

Nothing.

Karen thanked him for his help.

They tried the other houses in the street. Three people thought they might recognise the face, without being a hundred per cent certain; one man – slow to the door with the aid of a stick, lived there the best part of forty years – deliberated carefully and then said he'd seen him for sure. 'Last year, hangin' round, that house over there. All them plants in the window. That's the one.'

They'd tried there already: no reply. The other end of the street from the address they'd been given, but numbers can become confused, misread, misheard. There were plants clearly visible between slatted wooden blinds, luxuriant, shiny and green. The blinds themselves were white and expensive, the kind Karen had enquired about getting for her flat, then baulked at the cost. There was a small painting visible on the wall – painting, Karen thought, not poster; a standard lamp left softly burning.

'Raising the tone of the neighbourhood single-handed,' Ramsden observed.

They walked back to the main road, sat in a café and ate borek with feta cheese and spinach, shortbread dusted with powdered sugar, drank strong sweet coffee. Fortified, they took the photograph from door to door, shop to shop. Blank faces, suspicious looks: some eager to be helpful, some not. Andronic? Andronic? A lot of shaking heads. You tried Turnpike Lane, maybe? Finally, they went back to the house with the plants.

This time there was a cat on the window ledge, ginger and white, waiting to be let in. When Ramsden reached out a hand to stroke it, it arched its back and hissed.

'Not very friendly, I'm afraid. Still hasn't really settled in.'

He was white, thirties, rimless glasses; neat, short hair. Tan chinos, grey T-shirt, grey sweater in a different shade. The cat slipped past him into the warm interior as, with some care, he looked at their ID.

'Adrian Osborne.' He held out a hand. 'No sense catching your death out here, why don't you come inside?'

He and his partner had bought the place a little over six months ago, summer; kept their flat in Stoke Newington while the bulk of the work was done; downstairs rooms knocked through, new kitchen, shower. Like to put in a big window at the back eventually, more light, but you can't do everything. Not at once. People before, they'd been renting. Not long. Less than a year. Andronic? No, I don't think so. Can't remember exactly what it was, to be honest. But a family. Quite a few of them, I believe. Four or five at least, couple of younger girls, teenage son. Football posters on the walls.

Only met them a couple of times. The father, when we first looked round. Scarcely said a word. After that, it was the estate agent, mainly. Going round with the builder, you know?'

Osborne leaned forward, looked again at the photograph. 'I wish I could be more definite, I really do. I mean, he could have been one of the boys, the boys I saw, but, to be honest, I didn't pay them a lot of attention. It wasn't as if we were introduced or anything.' He slid the photo back along the table. 'I'm sorry.'

'Perhaps you've got a forwarding address?' Karen said.

'Asked for one, several times. Thought they'd leave one when they went, but no.' He shrugged. 'You could try the guy we bought from. He's the one, rented it to them originally. I've got his details, phone number, email. He should have something.'

The cat lifted a paw and looked at Ramsden balefully as they left the room.

The letting agency was just along the Broadway from Shopping City, slush splaying round their feet, splashing up the backs of their legs as they walked. The office was on the second floor, a faint smell of incense mixed with hair oil. The vendor was Asian, Pakistani. Music playing, vaguely classical, guitars. A quick shake of hands, lingering on Karen's just a fraction too long. Manicured nails. Parma violets on his breath. A forwarding address, of course. Mile End, somewhere. A few swift manoeuvres with the mouse, wireless controlled, and there it was on the screen. Mile End, indeed.

'If you're ever looking for property,' the agent said. 'Investment . . .'

Out on the street, Karen breathed in cold air.

'Fancy a drink?' Ramsden said.

'Bit early, isn't it?'

'Early or late. Depends.'

They found a small pub away from the High Road, a few old men wishing their lives away over slow-drawn pints of best. While Ramsden got in the drinks, Karen called in on her mobile, sent a request, the address in Mile End, get through to the local station, send somebody round. They were well into their second round, Ramsden's conversation beginning to veer off into the now familiar fear and loathing, when the call came back: the address as given didn't exist.

Like so many others, Petru Andronic had come into the country, severed all traces, and, until his body had surfaced on that frozen December morning, virtually disappeared.

4

Cordon turned at the edge of the hill, salt from the night air bright on his tongue, and looked back across the bay. Early January and cold as a witch's tit. A forecast of more snow. What kind of a happy new year was that?

Beyond the lights of the far town it was just possible to make out St Michael's Mount, a hump of black against the blackness of the sea. Amongst the huddle of houses to his right, a light flickered and then went out. Collar up, he turned again and continued to climb, cobbled stone beneath his feet, key already in his hand.

He'd bought this place, a converted sail loft in Newlyn, before prices had spiralled out of control. Now all around him were holiday lets and second homes, kids with names like Tristan and Toby and people carriers with customised number plates blocking the winding lanes.

Not that he was quick to judge.

A long room with a kitchen at one end and a bed at the other, lavatory and bathroom partitioned off, it had been somewhere to move into, move on from, part of the plan.

Chief inspector in another five or six years, superintendent by the time he was fifty. One of those nice old Georgian places in Penzance, down near Penlee House, that was where he'd seen himself by then, what he'd fancied. Till some bastard pulled away the ladder and, perforce, he'd stayed put.

His own bloody intransigence hadn't helped.

Passed over, these last few years he'd been stationed in the middle of nowhere cosseting a team of five: two young PCs, wet behind the ears, a sergeant close to his own age, prone to outbursts of gout, and a pair of community support officers who needed all the support they could get. Neighbourhood policing, that's what it was called. Low-level drug use, common-or-garden domestic disputes and routine drunk and disorderlies; inebriated yahoos with public-school accents down from Oxbridge or London for the surf; a little casual breaking and entering. Other things.

In the past twelve months, there'd been several cases of sheep rustling, but more recently even the sheep were getting thinner, barely meat enough on their bones to warrant all that up and down through the heather. The only reason Cordon hadn't jacked it in and walked away before his thirty years were up, he hadn't wanted to give his bosses the satisfaction.

Besides, there wasn't so very long now to go.

So he reported for duty, clocked in, clocked off, kept Home Office directives piled high in a corner until there were enough for a decent bonfire, happy enough to let the powers that be forget he was there.

At home, he sat with his feet up, reading, listening to music, rationing the Scotch. A mishmash, where the music was concerned: Mingus with Eric Dolphy at Cornell; Bach *Partitas* for solo violin; some Ellington; some blues; Britten's String Quartet in C. And the reading? Trollope, his current favourite. *The Way We Live Now.* There was a man who knew a thing or two.

Opposite the one comfortable chair was a television set with its screen turned to the wall. Occasionally, as if to remind himself of the world beyond his own, he would swivel it round and watch the news. Bankers and captains of failed industries slinking wantonly into the shelter of their offshore accounts with their air-brushed mistresses or surgically reconstructed wives; men whose pensions would bring them more in a year than many of the men Cordon knew would earn in a lifetime. Trollope all over again. We never learned.

Hungry, he took the remaining half of pork pie from the fridge. He was just levering the cap from a bottle of Tribute ale, when the mobile sounded from his coat pocket across the room.

The custody sergeant in Penzance. 'Woman here, sir. Bit of a state. Half out of her head on drink and I'd not like to say what else. Not making a lot of sense.'

'My concern?'

'Asking for you, sir, that's all. Thought you'd like to know.'

'She have a name?'

'Carlin.'

Cordon stopped his breath. 'Rose? Rose Carlin?'

'Maxine.'

'You sure it's not Rose? Or Letitia. She could be calling herself that.'

'Maxine, that's what she says. Maxine.'

Cordon looked at his watch. A quick drive eastwards around the bay. Newlyn to Penzance. His car parked at the bottom of the hill. 'I'll be right there.' Pressing the cap firmly back on to the bottle, he took a healthy bite out of the pie and reached for his coat.

The custody sergeant pushed the paper he was reading aside.

'Sorry to call you out, sir. Only way to shut her up.' He nodded in the direction of the cells.

'She's under arrest?'

'There for her own safety. Thought she might sleep it off.'

'Be suing you, next thing you know, false imprisonment.'

The sergeant made a face. 'Human bloody Rights Act, like as not succeed.'

The door to the cell was unlocked, the air inside vinegary with disinfectant. Maxine Carlin lay curled in one corner, face to the wall. She turned only slowly when he spoke her name.

One side of her face was pinched tight, the corner of her mouth aslant; a scab above the right eye had been picked away down to the pink skin beneath. He could smell the drink on her from where he stood.

'You wanted to see me?'

'Took your bastard time!'

'Wanted to talk?'

'Not here.'

She could only walk unsteadily at first, ignoring Cordon's proffered hand. Once they had reached the car, she leaned against the roof until her breathing had become more regular and her head had begun to clear. He drove south past Morrab Gardens and parked along the West Promenade, windows wound down, waiting while, painstakingly, she rolled a cigarette. Faint, under the occasional clamour of gulls, he could hear the rhythmic shushing of pebbles as the tide moved them up and back along the beach.

'It's about Letitia?' Cordon asked.

'That stupid bloody name!'

'Rose, then. What you wanted to see me for, it's about your daughter? About Rose?'

'She's gone missing, i'n't she?'

Missing, Cordon thought: missing from where? He hadn't clapped eyes on her in months, years.

'Her father, he rung me. She was supposed to be going

down to see him, stay for a bit. Hastings, where he's got some excuse for a bloody bookshop. Down from London. Never turned up. Never showed.'

'Changed her mind, perhaps.'

'Called him, didn't she, right before she left. Charing something?'

'Charing Cross?'

'Maybe. I dunno. Meet the train, she told him. Waited half the day. Her mobile switched off each time he tried. Got on to me in the end, see if I knew anything. I didn't know a bloody thing.' She flicked the cigarette away in a shower of sparks. 'Since she moved up there, London, we've not exactly kept in touch. Not like when she was here. Used to be, we was more like sisters. These last few years, never tells me a thing. More secrets'n the Queen of bloody Sheba. Don't even know where's she's living. Not properly. Never been there, never been asked.'

Cordon nodded. 'All this was when? When she was supposed to meet her father?'

'Last week. Beginnin' of last week. Right after New Year.' She rubbed a cracked fingernail against the corner of her eye.

'The two of them, they were close then?'

'When it suited him.'

'But she did see him?'

'Like I say, when it suited him, miserable bastard.'

'And this time, no explanation, she just never arrived?'

'Christ! Didn't I just bloody say so?'

'You've tried contacting her?'

'Much good it did me. Old mobile number, that's all I had. Waste of bleedin' time.'

'And you've not got an address?'

'Just this. Here.' Maxine started scrabbling in her bag. 'Place she used to work. Housekeepin', somethin' like that. Never said too much about it.'

She pushed a piece of paper into his hand. A street name and house number in London, N16.

'And this was when? When she was working here?'

'A year back, got to be. Maybe more. Something though, isn't it? If you're lookin'. Somewhere to start.'

Cordon sighed and folded the paper carefully into his top pocket. She'd been missing, if missing she was, for just a week, not yet quite two. No time, no time at all. The air through the open windows was cold and getting colder, a breeze lifting off the sea.

'You'll do what you can? To find her?'

Cordon turned away. The lights farther around the bay suggested home, a glass of whisky and a warm bed.

'You will?'

'I could make a few inquiries from here. Get somebody to go round, maybe, check that old address. Beyond that, I don't think there's a great deal I can do. Not until we know more. Grown woman, independent. No suggestion of foul play. She's probably fine. Just changed her mind. Last moment. It happens. Went somewhere else instead. Friends.'

'You'll do fuck all.'

Down on the beach a dog was barking excitedly, chasing shadows across the dark.

'I'll do what I can.'

'Fuck all. You'll do fuck all.'

Cordon sighed.

'You're all the fucking same.'

Men, he supposed she meant. Men.

'Don't hear nothin' from her, I'll go up meself. Thought you might bloody help, that's all.' She levered open the door. 'She thought a lot of you, fuck knows why.'

Awkward, she swung her legs round and ducked her head.

'Wait up,' Cordon said. 'I'll give you a lift.'

She chose not to hear. Like someone walking on coals,

she made her way across the street and continued close to the wall. Cordon started after her, but changed his mind. At the edge of the promenade the nubbed paint of the railings was uneven and cold against his hand. *She thought a lot of you.* Out over the sea, the moon showed for a moment from behind a bulwark of cloud, then was gone.

5

The first time he had seen Rose Carlin – Letitia – she had been sitting cross-legged on an unmade bed, the mattress stained with shit smears and rusted blood, eyes winced tight as she injected heroin into the vein at the back of her left knee.

No one had answered when he'd knocked on the door. Himself and four other officers rousting all the houses on the street, a favour passed down from on high. Boarded up most of them, bulldozers on their way, a complex of two- and three-bedroom apartments that would rise up from the detritus of what had once been two-up and two-down family homes. Harbour View. Even the name was a lie.

The only other person in the room, a young male of eighteen or so, sat on the floor, legs outstretched, head angled back against the wall, a leather belt tied off around his upper arm. Cordon knew him from various squats around the town and the toilets near the bus station where he'd jack off unhappy travellers for the price of a half-gram wrap or a pack of cigarettes. Billy Mullins, youngest of five: one in the army, two doing time, another – the black sheep – working eight to five as a council gardener, kids of his own.

'Right.' Cordon kicked his toe against the underside of the youth's worn trainers and hauled him to his feet. 'Now then, Billy, what's it to be?'

Mullins blinked at him once and his head lolled down towards his chest.

Christ, Cordon thought, I don't have time for this. He dragged a straight-backed chair across with his foot and sat Mullins down on it hard.

'Possession, is it? Intent to supply?'

'Fuck off,' Mullins said, but his heart wasn't in it.

Behind them, a sigh slipped from the girl's mouth like air escaping from a balloon, and she slumped sideways on the bed.

'New girlfriend, Billy?'

'What's it to you?'

Her arms were thin, barely flesh on bone, breasts that seemed to belong to a body other than her own. He could have encompassed her thigh, almost, with the span of his hand. There were used condoms, two of them, close by on the floor: Cordon supposed he should be grateful for that at least.

'How old is she?'

'How should I know?'

'Come on, Billy. Fourteen? Fifteen? Younger?'

'Old enough to fuck.'

Cordon kicked the chair from under him and he went sprawling, striking his head against the skirting. Bruise like a blackened egg, Cordon thought, come morning; some smart young duty solicitor waving the Polaroids around like they were Get Out of Jail Free cards.

He helped Mullins to his feet, read him the riot act, watched as he bundled together his few things before skedaddling down the stairs. The girl dressed slowly, as if dazed, as if everything that touched her skin caused her pain. When he reached out a hand to help, she pulled away.

He took her to a café just beyond the street's end, the girl walking half a pace behind. When he asked her what she wanted, she made no reply, so he ordered her a mug of tea and a bacon roll and when she'd wolfed that down he ordered the same again. Dredging up a smile, she bummed a cigarette from someone at the next table. She still hadn't looked Cordon square in the eye.

'Known him long?'

'Who?'

'Billy.'

She wafted smoke away from her face. 'He i'n't so bad. Not so bad as some.'

'He know how old you are?'

'How old am I?'

Cordon shrugged. 'Fourteen?'

'Next birthday.'

Jesus! The word loud inside Cordon's head. 'You living at home?'

'When I can't find nowhere else to go.'

'Family?'

'Mum, sometimes.'

'Social worker?'

'Count 'em, shall I? Bastards every one.' She laughed, showing teeth that were small and sharp. 'This new un, likes to see me down on my knees, praying God to show me the error of my ways.' She laughed again and the laughter turned into a fit of coughing. Cordon went to the counter for a glass of water and when he looked back towards the table she'd gone.

She was outside on the pavement, head down, squatting.

'Thought you were doing a runner,' Cordon said.

'Fat chance. Needed a bit of air.'

When she stood, her head came almost level with his shoulder: tall for her age.

'This social worker, she have a name?'

'Apart from Fuckface, you mean?'

'Apart from that.'

She laid a hand on his arm and let it slide down towards his wrist. 'Look, we could just forget about it, right? No skin off your nose. All the other stuff you must have to do, no sense wastin' time on me.' Her fingers were gently stroking the back of his hand. 'We could go somewhere first if you like.'

Cordon shook her off and stepped away.

The social worker recited the whole sorry tale: Rose's mother, Maxine, was a registered heroin addict with three children by three different fathers; the two youngest, both boys, had been taken into care when they were seven and five. Rose herself had had periods of temporary fostering, but had been allowed back home when her mother had turned a corner at the beginning of the year.

'Which particular corner was that?' Cordon asked.

He nodded towards where Rose sat gouging the dirt from beneath her nails with a paper clip that had fallen from the desk. 'What's going to happen now?'

'I'll take Rose home. Lay down a few ground rules. Make sure they're understood.'

'Ground rules?'

The social worker was getting to her feet. 'We like to keep families together, Detective Inspector, wherever it's humanly possible. If you'd care to come along to Rose's next case conference, I'm sure it can be arranged.'

'Wouldn't miss it for the world.'

Of course, he did. As Rose herself had said, all that other stuff he had to do . . . and one kid among many, what business was it of his? Let Social Services earn their keep as best they could.

If he saw her at all in the next eighteen months, two years, it was a face glimpsed amongst others, a group of girls giggling their way from pub to pub, jousting with some lads down by the harbour where the *Scillonian* came into dock, her voice loud and shrill, giving as good as she got, sharp little features fleshing out. Once, someone who might have been her, touting for business along the Promenade, spangled top and skirt up to her behind; before he could make his way along to check it out, a silver Mondeo had pulled in and, after a brief nego-tiation, whisked her away with a fishtail of wheels.

Then, one summer evening, there she was, arm in arm with a woman dressed just like her, the pair of them parading up Market Jew Street, head to toe in black save the silver rings catching the last of the sun as they walked. Rose's hair was henna red, her companion's bright green.

She didn't just recognise him: she stopped.

'Cordon, right? Detective somethin'-or-other. The bacon-roll man.'

'Detective Inspector. And you're Rose.'

'Yeah. And this is my mum, Maxine.'

'Good to meet you,' he said and held out his hand.

He could see now that she was older, Maxine. Could have passed herself off as an elder sister and on a night out that was probably what she did. Up close, it was the heavy smoker's lines around the mouth that gave her away, that and the residue of a life hard-lived behind the eyes. What was it? Three kids, two in care. She'd be all of thirty-four, thirty-five.

'Still a copper, then?' Rose said.

He nodded.

'Putting people away.'

'A few.'

31

'My mates.'

'Maybe.'

She laughed; he remembered the laugh.

'New leaf, me. Straight an' narrow.' She was mocking him with her voice, her eyes. 'Workin', too. Caff down the arcade. Evenings. Weekends. Thinkin' of goin' to college, right, Mum? Qualifications. NVQs. Veterinary assistant, that's what I fancy. Somethin' like that.'

She said the word veterinary as if she were trying it out, each syllable stepping carefully off the tongue.

'Like animals, then?' Cordon said.

'Better'n people. Most people.'

'Dogs?'

'Yeah, dogs are all right. Why d'you wanna know?'

'I've got this springer spaniel. Never gets enough exercise. If you want to walk her some time . . .'

'How much?'

'Huh?'

'For walkin' her, how much?'

'I don't know. A fiver, maybe?'

'An hour?'

'I was thinking more, each time you took her out.'

'Bog off!' She gripped her mother's arm tighter and started to walk away.

'All right, then, five pounds an hour.'

She turned back, grinning. 'Fifteen minimum.'

Cordon looked at her mother. 'Strikes a hard bargain.'

'Likely had to.'

Cordon nodded. 'Okay, your terms. Agreed. Here . . .' He took a card bearing his police details from his pocket and wrote his home address and number on the back.

'How d'you know I won't turn up with all me mates when you're out, break in, rob you blind?'

'I don't.'

She took the card without another glance and tucked it out of sight. 'Come on, Mum. Stand here talkin' to the likes of him, get ourselves a bad name.'

Cordon watched as, laughing, they headed for the Wetherspoons across the street. College. Qualifications. A proper job. Who was she fooling? Herself? Him? He thought about Rose's leggings and the long sleeves covering her arms, wondering if she and her mum shared needles at home. Still time to follow in her mother's footsteps, an addict and a mother just this side of sixteen: next time he saw her on Market Jew Street, she could be pushing a buggy slowly uphill. Who did he think he was, some kind of benefactor? Guardian angel? Come and walk my dog – what kind of bollocks was that?

6

He didn't see her again for a couple of months. Why did he think he ever would? He was in the middle of scouring out a pan in which he'd been making scrambled eggs – the phone drawing his attention away at the crucial moment and egg adhering to the pan like a second skin – when he glimpsed her face at the small window alongside the door.

'Come for the dog, okay?'

Cordon wasn't certain if she was still in her Goth phase or not: most of the henna had gone from her hair, black waistcoat though, white shirt, black jeans, studs and rings; white lipstick, purple fingernails.

'Fine, as far as I'm concerned. Dog might need some convincing, though. Doesn't take easily to strangers.'

But even as he spoke the springer was energetically wagging her tail and reaching up to lick the girl's hand.

'Yeah,' she said, with a small look of triumph. 'See what you mean.'

'Here,' Cordon said. 'Here's her lead. Take a couple of bin liners for when she does her business. You can let her off past the Tolcarne Inn. That patch of grass by the gallery. Then down on to the beach.'

The girl was crouching down, stroking the dog behind the ears. 'She have a name?'

'Kia.'

'I'll get some treats for her next time. You can pay me for 'em later. Oh, and yeah, know how long it takes, all the way over here from Penzance?'

'Twenty minutes?'

'And the rest. So that's all included, right? My time.'

She slipped on the lead and the dog half-dragged her towards the door. 'Hour or so, maybe, first time. You'll still be here?'

'Sunday. Bar emergencies, my day off.'

'Course. No crime of a Sunday. I forgot.'

When they'd gone Cordon took one more look at the pan, shook his head and dumped it in the bin; next time he went into Lidl he'd buy another.

After that, she stopped by most Sundays, a few summer evenings; it got so the springer could recognise her step before Cordon knew she was even close. From time to time, he'd ask her about home or college, just making conversation, little more: blood out of a stone.

One particular evening, a Tuesday, Cordon not long back from sorting a domestic that resulted, as they often did, in both parties turning on him and telling him to fuck off out, she arrived with a bottle of cheap sparkling wine and wearing what Cordon assumed was one of her mother's cast-offs, either that or a charity shop special, pale purply chenille with a slit skirt and ruched front.

'What's this in aid of?'

'Celebration. My birthday. Sixteen.' She threw herself in the direction of the small settee. 'Means I'm legal.'

'Means you're sixteen.'

'Jesus! Don't you ever lighten up?'

'Rarely.'

'Here . . .' Holding out the bottle. 'Help me get this open.'

He found two glasses and poured the wine, getting only a little on the floor as it fizzed up. It tasted like he remembered cream soda, but cream soda that had turned sour.

'This really your birthday?'

Dipping her finger into the glass, she made a crossing motion, anointing her breasts through the material of the dress. 'Christening, too.'

'How d'you mean?'

'Got a new name, haven't I?'

'Fed up with the old one?'

'Rose, it's not me. Not anyone. Anyone I know.'

'So who are you now?'

'Letitia.'

Cordon did a small double-take.

'You like it?' she asked.

'Different, I'll say that for it.'

'Joy and happiness. What it means. My dad told me.'

Cordon had never heard her mention her father before; hadn't imagined them to be in touch.

'He chose it for you?'

'Sort of.' Head back, she drank some more wine. 'Suits me, don't you think?'

'Maybe.'

'My dad thinks so. Looked right into me, didn't he? Joy and bloody happiness. Saw deep into my soul.'

Cordon waited for the laugh, but it didn't come.

When she left, just a short while later, there was still a good half a bottle remaining. After due deliberation, Cordon poured it down the sink. When she came back to walk the dog a week or so later, Letitia now, neither of them referred to the occasion at all.

She didn't mention her father again, either, only the once,

Cordon getting on his high horse and launching into something of a lecture about the values of doing a little reading, studying – the kind of thing students were supposed to do, though, from his perspective, it seemed few of them did.

'Fuck off!' she said. 'Stop naggin' at me all the bloody time. You're not my bloody father, you know.'

Cordon knew. His own fatherly responsibilities were scattered halfway across the world: a son, Simon, fully grown, who had used his gap year to put ample distance between the pair of them and decided he liked it that way best. The only contact Cordon had – the terse, almost formal requests for funds aside – was the occasional postcard from Santo Domingo, Bogotá or La Paz, just letting him know he was still alive. After Bolivia he'd heard nothing, six months of worry, and then the cards had resumed – Pangai, Lautoka, Auckland, Hobart, Sydney. Pins stuck in a notional map, marking a journey that never seemed to point home.

His ex-wife, Judith, Cordon scarcely spoke to at all: a desultory late-night phone call, usually around Christmas time, pauses longer than words.

You're not my father.

What was he, then? A concerned individual? A friend? Hardly that.

When the other officers, down at the station, got wind of what was happening, there were knowing glances cast in his direction, more than a few lewd remarks. Cordon let them slide.

Then something happened and it all changed.

At four in the morning, on the way home from a night's clubbing and buoyed up by too many pills and too much alcohol, she let herself into his flat and slipped into his bed, and he pushed her angrily back out. Angry at her presumption: angry at himself for being aroused; knowing, somewhere at the back of his mind and in his groin, he'd always regret an opportunity not taken, little enough love in his life, little enough abandon.

She didn't come by again.

The dog padded circles around the room and cast wistful glances at the door. Cordon walked her himself till he could find someone else, a young lad whose father worked at the fish dock down by the quay.

All that was a long time ago, over fourteen years.

Letitia moved away.

If he saw her on one of her visits home, it was a nod of the head, a wave, and nothing more. If he bumped into her mother on her own and sober enough to answer, he'd ask how she was.

Now this.

He made the calls as promised the next day, finding himself passed on from person to person, extension to extension, all to no avail. Nothing about a Letitia or Rose Carlin was known, no accident or serious injury reported, no incident in which she had been named. There was no body of a similar age and size waiting to be identified.

He left it alone. Had half a mind to get in touch with Maxine and see what she'd discovered on her trip to London, always supposing she'd gone, but never followed through.

Other matters intervened. A pub brawl that ended with someone being pushed through a sheet of plate glass. State-of-the-art climbing gear stolen from the car park close by the old Carn Galver mine. A break-in at the post office and general store in St Buryan. At a campsite on Trevedra Common a caravan was set alight, the couple sleeping inside lucky to escape with second-degree burns.

Life, such as it was, went on.

7

Karen still couldn't quite figure Tim Costello out. He'd been in her team for some nine months, detective sergeant down from CID in Leeds, where he'd been part of the Major Crime Unit for three years. Promotion overdue. Before that he'd studied for a degree in Criminology and Forensic Science at the John Moores University in Liverpool, his home city. Not that you could tell that from his accent, with which he could have read the Radio 4 news without causing a flutter. Nicely brought up, Karen thought. His mother probably had him scurrying off to elocution lessons from the age of six or seven.

Costello's mother was Chinese, his father Irish. He'd inherited his father's height and build, all elbows and sharp angles, and his mother's features. His father's father had migrated to Liverpool to work on the docks, back when such work was plentiful and the scratchings in County Galway were poor; his mother's mother had come as a mail-order bride on a ship from Hong Kong. How his parents had met was a story still to be told.

Where Karen was concerned, he was suitably deferential; in his dealings with the other members of the team, including Ramsden, he was inclined to be a little cocky. A little too sure of himself, Ramsden reckoned, a bit too much mouth. Karen wasn't so certain. Give him his chance, she thought, to come to terms, settle down – that happened and he might just blossom, come into his own.

Already had where transport was concerned. Cycled in from home, early hours, on a bike with a carbon-fibre frame and Shimano Deraillieur gears that cost, as Ramsden liked to say, more than his first fucking car. Home for Costello being a flat on the Hackney–Dalston borders he shared with a girl-friend none of them had yet seen.

Lycra padded cycling shorts, black tights and brightly coloured long-sleeved jerseys, headphones clamped to his ears listening to a menagerie of bands like Foals and The Geese, to say that he and Mike Ramsden were several lifestyles apart would be no exaggeration. Karen would like to have consid-ered herself midway between, but she wasn't sure of that either. Sometimes conversations with Costello beyond police work made her feel as if she were taking classes in how another world lives and failing.

Back in the dead days following New Year and their discovery of Petru Andronic's identity, the temperatures low, the skies intent on giving new meanings to the word grey, there'd been a glimmer of a breakthrough in the Walthamstow shooting. The bullets taken from the dead youth's body had been linked to a haul of illegally imported arms and ammunition seized during a raid by officers from the Central Task Force on a warehouse in Deptford. While those officers continued to probe into the identities of those who had both imported the arms and sold them on, Tim Costello was liaising with members of the Met's Forensic Intelligence Team to trace a possible pattern from other shootings in which guns and ammo from the warehouse had been used.

As for the Wood Green stabbing, it was still a case of speculation and blame. The victim, a youth of fifteen, Derroll Palmer, had no known gang connections, but both of the young men previously arrested and then grudgingly released were members of the Bruce Castle Kings, one of the sets of the Tottenham Mandem gang, and were known to Operation Trident; both had records for minor crime, including assault, yet their alibis had been difficult to break down. One youth had admitted under questioning to being present at the scene, an admission almost immediately withdrawn, his solicitor asserting that the statement had been coerced in an atmosphere of fear and intimidation.

Tell that to the kid laying dead, Karen thought, killed for speaking up when another youth had called his girlfriend, whom he was walking home, a skanky whore.

And of Wayne Simon, missing since the Holloway murders, there was still no clear sign. A possible sighting in Gateshead, nothing more. If the reports were right, farther and farther north. Soon, Karen thought, he'd run out of ground.

She was busy finagling her responses to the latest set of quarterly crime figures that had filtered down from on high, when Ramsden knocked on her door and breezed through.

Sod's law, a SIM card been found in the last but one bag of gubbins from the Andronic crime scene to be methodically searched, sorted and labelled; missed on a first, preliminary sortie, it had been buried inside a sodden wedge of shredded newspaper, along with rotting sweet wrappers, flattened cigarette butts, a smear of dog shit and a toddler's missing sock. The original location was noted as the undergrowth to the eastern edge of the pond.

'We know it's his? Andronic's?'

'Not exactly.'

'Meaning?'

'Sent through to Telecommunications Intel. Couple of days back.'

'And?'

'Pay as you go.'

Karen shook her head. The problems with pay as you go from her point of view were legion: little or nothing was straightforward, cash sales and so no bills, to say nothing of the possibility of bogus names, bogus addresses, trails that could easily become meaningless when tracing owners. T. Rex now living in Nirvana. Bollocks like that.

'Any luck,' she asked, 'with the registration?'

Ramdsen grinned. 'Radu Rebeja. Some trumped-up London address.'

'What's so funny?'

'Google him, the guy from Intel said, laughing up his sleeve. Radu Rebeja, the most capped soccer player in Moldovan history. Played most of his career for FC Moscow. Currently Vice President of the Football Association of Moldova. Resident of Chisnau.'

'Probably not his phone, then?'

'No. But Andronic aside, how many other Moldovan soccer fans do we think might have been on Hampstead Heath that night, that exact location?'

'There's a record of calls?'

'Intel still working on it. No promises when, snowed under, the usual. So, you know, don't—'

'Don't hold my breath.'

It could lead somewhere, Karen thought, or it could send them up a zillion blind alleys. Too much information sometimes as defeating as too little. She forced herself to concentrate on her paperwork, one eye on the clock, one ear cocked towards the phone, which failed to ring. By the end of the day, there was nothing further about the SIM card, either way.

It was dark out, had been for the best part of three hours already, the false dark you find in big cities; everything shot through with shop lights, car lights, clouds like a stage set, painted on, the sky an unreal blue, like day for night, the horizon washed in an unreal orange glow.

On a whim she stopped off at Ottolenghi on the way home and picked up a portion of roast chicken with chilli and basil, another of mushrooms with cinnamon, and some pear and cranberry upside-down cake for dessert. Treat yourself, girl, and to hell with the expense.

Back at the flat, she poured herself a generous glass of wine, arranged the food on a tray and settled down to watch one of the Swedish *Wallanders* she'd recorded from BBC4. Angst and murder on the shores of the Baltic. As long as she could divorce it from reality, her reality – and here the subtitles really helped – she could enjoy the somewhat ramshackle way in which the Ystad police were able, week in week out, to wrap up a case within a mere ninety minutes. And her feelings about Wallander himself, or, rather, the actor who played him, Krister Henriksson, had gone from sheer exasperation – as head of a murder squad he could be about as organised as a sack of kittens – to a resigned pleasure in the way he moved from anger and confusion towards a kind of resolution.

Except where his love life was concerned.

There, she knew how he felt.

A night's clubbing, a fit body, a good-looking face in a crowded bar, the slip and slither that moved from the dance floor to the taxi to the final fuck, slow and generous or quick and hard, that was no longer enough. As if, since she'd been in her teens and early twenties, it ever really was.

She pushed away the tray, drank down the last of the glass, switched off the TV. Stood at the window for a few moments, staring out. Saw her own reflection imprinted on a terrace of houses opposite, the darkened tree line that marked the edge of Highbury Fields. Along the street, a quick flicker of light from the interior of a parked car illuminated, for the briefest of moments, the shape of a man hunched behind the wheel.

All day now, all through the evening, the scenes which showed Wallander trying with some desperation to bridge the gulf between himself and his grown-up daughter – trying and failing – she had fought to keep her own father at bay. His birthday – late January – little more than a week away. Seventy-three. Seventy-three he would have been had he lived. The car outside, headlights burning, pulled slowly away from the kerb and passed from sight. He had been running, her father, across the street towards where a group of teenage boys was hassling a single, frightened girl. The boys white, the girl light-skinned, mixed race. Jostling, pushing, grabbing, calling names. The girl, her face besmirched with tears, stumbling to her knees and Karen's father, with a roar of righteous anger, rushing out towards her, towards the surrounding youths, unable, in his haste, to see or hear the van that swung, at that moment, around and into the road, accelerating hard.

Her father's body, as she had never seen it, other than in her imagination, lifted – hurled – into the startled emptiness of the night air, only to fall, broken, torn, by the pavement's edge.

Three days in hospital he lived on, unconscious, sustained by drips and tubes and prayer. Her mother scarcely left his bedside till there was only prayer left and then he died.

Karen came and went, just thirteen and unable to withstand the pain.

Her father dead, her mother had gone back to Jamaica. Unlike her sister, Lynette, who had agreed to go, only to return three years later, Karen had dug in her heels, refused. Not wanting to leave her school, her friends. Already close, her aunt and uncle agreed to take her in. Now, they too, distressed by a city that was no longer, in their eyes, the same place where they had chosen to live most of their adult lives, were back in Spanish Town, retired, resigned.

Karen pulled the curtains closed.

Her father's face flickered like a passing light, then disappeared.

'Cry, Baby, Cry' and then 'Good Night', from Ramsey Lewis's version of the Beatles' *White Album*, piano and strings, accompanied Karen as she removed her make-up and undressed for bed. After just three pages, the book she was reading slipped from her hands and she was asleep.

8

Morning. Cold. Overcast. Upper Street and St Paul's Road at a standstill, cars stacked up in both directions. Karen's mobile rang just as she reached the counter in Caffè Nero. Juggling coins and loyalty card, she flipped open the phone as she gave her order.

'Sorry,' said the voice in her ear, 'no lattes here. Must be a wrong number.' The suggestion of a Midlands accent. Wolverhampton, West Bromwich. She guessed the man from Telecommunications Intel.

'You've got something for me?'

'Sugar? A sprinkling of chocolate?'

'Information?'

'A brand new SIM card, only five calls. Three to a Lesley Tabor, that's Lesley with an E-Y, T-Mobile. Other two to an Orange phone registered to an Ion Milescu – I-O-N, Ion – Milescu, M-I-L-E-S-C-U. All the details in an email. On its way.'

'Thanks. I owe you.'

'Double espresso. Two sugars.'

'Deal.'

*

By the time both addresses had been traced and verified, Mike Ramsden was on his way to Wood Green to check out a possible break in the investigation into the Derroll Palmer murder. A fresh poster campaign and some door-to-door leafleting had jogged the memory of a night cleaner who'd been making her way into work when the stabbing had occurred and she'd contacted her local station. Now it was a question of teasing out the details of what the woman had seen and heard, Ramsden only too aware of the need to proceed with caution. Push too hard and the danger is the witness becomes confused – either that or gives the answers he or she feels are wanted, only to falter later under cross-examination.

Karen picked up the phone. 'Tim, a minute?'

He was wearing a loose-fitting casual jacket over a muddy green V-necked T-shirt, slim-line black trousers and blue-black suede shoes with a rubber sole.

Karen allowed herself a smile. Elvis and the Beatles in one.

'Fancy a break from arms and ammo?'

'Please.'

She brought him up to speed.

'As far as we know, these were the last people he spoke to before he was killed. Just in case they know one another, I want them seen as close to the same time as possible. Less chance of either of them contacting the other. Concocting stories. Okay?'

Costello nodded.

'I thought you could take the girl.'

Which meant Costello heading south across the river to a large comprehensive in Catford. Alien territory though he didn't intend it to show.

Behind a fascia of bare, stunted trees and tall railings, its main buildings a fortress of darkening brutalist concrete, the school, Costello thought, had all the welcoming aura of a Soviet labour camp from the last century. Even the first fractures of grey sky, a timid leavening of blue, didn't do a lot to help.

The youth who met Costello at the gate was chirpy enough, however, if a little disappointed not to find an officer in uniform.

'You sure you're police?'

'Sure.'

'You don't look like no police.'

Costello was quietly pleased.

'So what?' the youth asked. 'You here to nick someone, or is gonna be another of them lectures on drugs and gangs and knives an' keepin' off cheap cider?'

The deputy head, uncertain whether to shake Costello's hand or not, settled for some vague arm flapping and a sideways nod of the head and ushered him along to what looked to have formerly been an office, but was now a depository for some outmoded filing equipment and a convocation of broken chairs.

'You'll be able to talk quietly in here.'

He left the door ajar and reappeared a few minutes later with the sixteen-year-old Lesley Tabor at his side.

'All right, Lesley . . .'

The door closed.

Costello smiled.

'Lesley, I'm Detective Sergeant Costello. Tim.'

No reply. Slouch shouldered, mousy haired, a school uniform of white blouse, navy jumper, navy skirt, grey tights, the girl stared determinedly at the scuffed tops of her shoes.

'Lesley?'

Her face angled up an inch.

'You're not in any trouble, you realise that, don't you? This is not about anything you might have done. Okay?'

Another inch, a first sight of pale eyes.

'I just need to ask a few questions, that's all. A few quick questions, then I'm out of here. Never to be seen again.' He lowered his face, swiftly, towards hers. 'Think you'll miss me? When I'm gone?'

She looked at him then. Miss him? What was he on?

He winked, face creasing into a grin.

'What say we get out of here? Go for a walk in the palatial grounds? Take in some of that winter sun?'

'We can't . . .'

'Come on . . .' Reaching past her for the door. 'What are they going to do? Arrest us?'

There were indeed a few vestiges of sun, just visible above the turrets of a tower block to the east. Sweet papers and food wrappings from break were scattered here and there on the ground around their feet where they slowly walked. Faces, curious, appeared at windows and then were called rapidly away, back to the pleasures of citizenship or ICT, considerations of the opposite angle to the hypotenuse or the importance of the slave trade to the rise of capitalism.

'What are you missing?' Costello asked.

She didn't immediately seem to understand.

'What lesson?'

'Oh, history.'

'I'm sorry.'

'S'all right, it's boring.'

History, how could it be? Wars, alliances, betrayals, dates, the movements of great powers, Costello had loved it.

'What's your favourite then?'

'Um?'

'Subject? Lesson?'

'Dunno. English, maybe.'

She was frowning, squinting up her eyes. Last night's eye shadow not renewed, not properly washed away. They had reached the railings alongside the gate and turned.

'Tell me about Petru,' Costello said.

She stopped. 'Who?'

'Petru. Your boyfriend. Petru Andronic.'

'He's not my boyfriend.' A quick flush of embarrassment or anger.

'You do know what happened to him?'

'Course.'

She looked at the ground, looked away; wanted to be anywhere but where she was.

'I'm sorry,' Costello said. 'For what did happen.'

She was still avoiding his eyes.

'Had you known him for long?'

'I didn't. Not really.' Her voice quiet, quieter. 'Know him, I mean.'

He waited. Knew she'd either talk or walk away.

'Look, he wasn't my boyfriend, right? I only met him, like, a couple of times. It wasn't, wasn't like that, it . . .'

She faltered back into silence.

'What was it like then? Your relationship?'

'There wasn't a relationship.'

'Lesley, we need to know.'

'Why?'

'Because we're trying to find out what happened. Who did that to him. I thought you'd want to help us.'

'I can't.'

'Anything, anything you might tell us, it could help. Even if you don't see how.'

'But I told you . . .'

'He wasn't your boyfriend, yes, I know.'

'So?'

'So what was he?'

'Oh, God . . .' Swinging away.

'Lesley, he phoned you, three times, the night he was killed.'

She started to walk, angling back towards the school, and he walked with her.

'Why did he call so many times?'

'Because he wanted to talk to her, that's why.'

'Her? Who's her?'

She stopped again, faced him. 'I can't tell you.'

'Just let me try to understand. He wanted to talk to somebody else, really wanted to talk to them, it was important – so why not call them, why call you?'

'Because it was how . . .' She bit down on an already jagged nail. 'He wasn't allowed to call her, right? Not any more. Not without . . . He'd call me first and I'd text her and then she'd call him. That was how it worked.'

Why? Costello asked himself and slipped the question to one side.

'That night, then, that's what you did? His girl? Sent a text?'

'Yes.'

'And did she contact him?'

'No. That's why he kept on. Where is she? Where is she? Tell her she's got to ring me.'

'And after the last time? The last time he called?'

'I don't know. I don't think so, no.'

'Do you know why? Had they fallen out? What?'

A ragged breath. 'She was scared, wasn't she?'

'Of him?'

'No, not of him.'

'Then who?'

'Her father, of course. Her sodding father.'

Muffled, inside the main building a bell was ringing; the rising distant sound of voices, people moving.

'Lesley . . .'

'What?'

'Sooner or later, you're going to have to tell me her name. You know that, don't you?'

9

While Tim Costello was making himself familiar with the Borough of Lewisham, Karen's destination was more upmarket: Kensington within spitting distance of Harrods, a small block of purpose-built flats away from the main road. The exterior was outfaced in off-white stone, curved windows with square panes that brought to Karen's mind the deck of a ship, a liner, the kind that cruised people with too much money and time around the world's oceans. Her uncle would talk of watching them come past the long sand spit of the Palisadoes and into Kingston harbour, all those white faces crowded along the rail, eager for the sanitised taste of another culture, the quick whiff of ganja and a frisson of danger.

The name Milescu was clear beside the entryphone.

Karen identified herself and was buzzed through.

Clare Milescu met her as she stepped out of the lift with a firm handshake and a ready, open smile. Close to fifty, Karen thought, and not disguising it, little need: trim, neat, and next to Karen herself, almost petite; short dark hair well cut, laced with grey. She was wearing a dark skirt and pale lavender blouse, black tights, red shoes. Her only accessory, watch aside, a wedding ring.

'Please,' she said. 'Please come in.'

The door to the flat was open behind her.

There were photographs, black-and-white, arranged along both sides of the hall: family portraits, Karen thought, formal, informal, children in their best Sunday clothes, a picnic, an elderly man in a hospital bed.

The room they went into was like something from a magazine Karen might have thumbed through at the hairdresser's. Low settees in muted colours at right angles to one another; blonde wood, glass and chrome; a lamp like an oversized pebble on the parquet floor. More photographs, mounted and framed. The paintwork the palest of violets, barely a colour at all. Someone with money and a certain taste.

A large window led out on to a balcony busy with plants that had survived, somehow, the winter frosts. A wide mirror reflected pale winter light back into the room.

'So, Detective Chief Inspector, is that what I call you?'

'Karen.'

'Then, Clare.' The smile was more genuine this time, less professional. 'Please, sit down. I've made some coffee.'

'I don't want to take too much of your time.'

'Time, for the moment, is the one thing I have plenty of. And besides, Ion isn't here yet.'

'I thought you said . . .'

'He would be here, I know.' A quick glance towards her wrist. 'He stayed with his father last night. But don't worry, he knows you're expecting him.' Another smile. 'For a teenage boy, he's quite reliable.'

Adding that she wouldn't be a moment, she left the room.

Swivelling round, Karen looked towards the photographs on the rear wall. Some, again, in black-and-white, but most in colour. More recent. Young men in T-shirts, some with tattoos, posing; older men in suits, dark haired, stubble, what she thought of as Eastern European faces. A few were staring at the camera, as if on request; others caught unawares, half-turning, as if angry, at the soft click of the camera.

'They're all Ion's,' Clare Milescu said, tray in hand, returning. 'A project he's been working on. *My Country Across Borders.* He's in his first year at the London College of Communication. A degree course in Photography.'

'They're good,' Karen said. 'Accomplished. Not that I'd really know.'

'His father gave him a camera for his twelfth birthday, a really good digital SLR. For the first couple of years after that he almost never let it out of his hands.'

'You and Ion's father . . . ?'

'Ah.' She eased a small cup of espresso in Karen's direction. 'There's milk if you wish.'

'No, this is fine.'

'When you phoned,' businesslike now, 'you said you wanted to talk to Ion about some calls to his mobile.'

'Yes, that's right.'

'They're important, then?'

'An investigation that's ongoing . . .'

'But important?'

'Yes.'

'Otherwise, I mean, a detective chief inspector – I hardly think . . .'

'You know what?' Karen leaned forward, a change of tone, more friendly, taking the other woman into her confidence. 'One thing about rank, being in charge, all the good bits go to somebody else. And all you get, most of the time – excuse the expression – is everyone else's shit.'

Clare Milescu put up a hand and laughed. 'I know exactly what you mean.'

'So, once in a while, instead of detailing a job like this to somebody else, I'll do it myself.' She glanced towards one of the windows. 'Sometimes it pays off. Nice day, what passes for sunshine. Beautiful flat . . .' She held up her cup. 'Good coffee. What could be better?'

Clare Milescu smiled.

'I was wondering,' Karen said. 'Your name. Milescu.'

'My husband's.'

'But you're English?'

'Born and bred.'

'Then how come . . . ?'

'You really want to know?'

'Just interested. Other people's lives.' A small, self-deprecating laugh. 'You always think – you look around, see somewhere like this – you always think, I don't know, how . . .'

The older woman laughed. 'How did they get so lucky?'

'Something like that.'

'And since, for once, you're away from your desk . . .'

'Exactly.'

'Very well. But it was chance, I'm afraid. Nothing worked out in advance, not part of some grand plan.' Clare Milescu stirred a tiny amount of sugar into her cup, so little you could almost count the granules. 'I went out to Moldova with the United Nations Development Programme in '92, not so long after it gained recognition as an independent country. I'd started working for them soon after leaving university. In Moldova we were working with the new government to help improve standards of living – socially, as well as economically. Engage in a dialogue with key government figures, that was our directive. Where my husband, where Paul was concerned I took that perhaps a little too literally.'

Something was alive, a memory, in her eyes.

'He was working for the Ministry of Justice in Chisnau. We began a relationship – it was difficult, he was already married – all the usual – what would you say? – all the usual shit that comes with people's lives. I mean, we weren't that old, but we weren't children.

'Anyway . . .' A sip of espresso. 'We sorted it all out and thank heaven we did because by that time I was pregnant with Ion. We knew enough, both of us – and I feel guilty just saying this – but we felt that, if we were able, we could offer our child a better life here in the UK. So, I got a job at the UN's office in London, my husband had business connections.' She leaned back. 'Here we still are.'

'But not together?'

'No.'

'And you're still with the UN?'

'Unfortunately not. In '03 they relocated their European offices to Brussels. But Ion was already in school, had made friends, so we decided to stay. Besides, my husband's business was doing well. As you can see. For a while I was content to sit around, have long lunches with friends. Play tennis. Go to the gym. But it didn't really suit me at all. Now I'm working with an advice centre for refugees, those from Eastern Europe especially.'

Both heads turned at the sound of a key turning in the front door.

Ion Milescu was slender, almost willowy, his slenderness making him seem taller than he actually was; he had dark hair that fell forward across his forehead, his mother's blue eyes. He was wearing trainers, blue jeans ripped over one knee, a check shirt beneath a jeans jacket which he shucked off as he entered the room and tossed over the back of a chair.

Bending, he kissed his mother's raised cheek and glanced across towards where Karen was sitting.

When his mother made the introductions, he nodded briefly and flopped down on one of the settees. Karen waited to see if he would look again in her direction, instead of staring at the floor, the lace that was working its way loose from his shoe.

'Petru Andronic,' she said eventually. 'I believe you knew him?'

'Who?'

She repeated the name.

'No. Sorry.'

'He's the young man whose body was found on Hampstead Heath just before Christmas. He'd been murdered.'

'Oh, him.' A shuffling of feet. 'Yes, I remember now. But he wasn't anyone I knew.'

'You're sure of that?'

'Yeah.'

'Because it seems he knew you.'

'No, I don't think so.'

'On the night of December 20th, 21st, there were three calls made to your mobile by someone we believe to have been him.'

'Then it must have been a wrong number.'

'Three times?'

'Sure. You put the number into your phone, you put it in wrong, each time you try it comes up the same.'

Until then, he'd scarcely looked her in the eye. Perhaps it was a teenage boy thing, Karen thought, perhaps not.

'The first call was at a quarter to eleven,' she said, 'the second roughly forty minutes later, the last at ten minutes past midnight.'

'If you say so.'

'On the first occasion you accepted the call. Why would you do that if you didn't recognise the number?'

'I don't know. I suppose I didn't pay too much attention. You don't, do you? Not always. You hear the ring tone, you answer.'

'And have a conversation?'

'I've told you, there wasn't any conversation. I can't even remember any of this happening. But if it did, I suppose I just said something about wrong number and that was that. Finish. The end. What does it matter, anyway?'

The merest hint of an accent aside, his English was perfect.

'Three minutes,' Karen said.

'What?'

'The first call, three minutes and seven seconds. A long time to say sorry, wrong number.'

'Look, I've told you . . .' He was on his feet quickly, all signs of his previous lassitude disappeared. 'All I know about Petru Andronic is what I read in the paper and whatever bits of gossip I've heard from friends. Okay? If he called my number like you say, I've no idea how or why, and I've no recollection of talking to him at all. So . . .'

Stepping past his mother's outstretched hand, he stormed out of the room. In the kitchen, the fridge door opened and bottles rattled before it was slammed shut.

Clare Milescu closed her eyes, sighed, looked towards Karen with a rueful smile.

'Karen, I'm sorry. I'm not sure why he's like this. Let me talk to him.'

'Of course.'

The kitchen door opened and closed and after a moment Karen could hear the rise and fall of voices without being able to decipher the words. Then the voices stopped and mother and son returned, Ion with his hands in his jeans pockets, head bowed.

'Ion,' his mother said, measuring her words, 'would like the opportunity to reconsider some of the remarks he's previously made.'

Clare Milescu made more coffee; her son fetched a bottle of Lucozade Sport from the fridge and, at his mother's insistence, grudgingly poured it into a glass. One of the windows out on to the balcony had been opened slightly, allowing a residue of breeze and traffic noise into the room.

The truth was, Ion said, he did know Petru Andronic, but by sight, little more. He'd bumped into him a few times at a café down in Chiswick where some of the Moldovan lads hung out, along with others from Romania and the Ukraine; they'd been involved, all of them, in a handful of scratch soccer games over in Brondesbury Park. He couldn't remember ever having given Andronic his mobile number, but he supposed it was possible. A lot of that went on, mobiles out all the time, the café especially, numbers being exchanged.

'So,' Karen asked, 'when Andronic called just before Christmas, what was all that about?'

He'd been in a bit of a state, excited about something, Ion told her, he'd never really been able to establish what. Something about someone who was supposed to meet him.

'A girlfriend?'

Ion didn't know. Maybe. Yes, probably. But if it was a girl he didn't know her name. Calm down, he'd told him. Give me a call tomorrow. Tomorrow morning.

By tomorrow morning, he was dead.

'Why didn't you come forward with any of this before?' Karen asked. 'When it was all over the news and we were appealing for help? Information?'

A quick glance towards his mother. 'I didn't want to get involved.'

'He was your friend.'

'He was not my fucking friend.'

'Ion!' His mother's reaction was automatic, instantaneous.

'I'm sorry, but how many times do I have to say it? He was not my friend.'

The burr of traffic from outside was more audible than before.

'I really think,' Clare Milescu said, rising, 'Ion has helped you all he can.'

Karen set her cup down evenly in its saucer. 'Thank you. Thank you both.'

Clare Milescu walked her to the door.

'You realise,' Karen said, 'it's possible we may want to speak to your son again.'

'I don't think that should be really necessary, do you?' The smile was there, then gone, the door closing with a firm click. Karen paused, then turned away. Stairs rather than lift.

10

Sasha Martin. Sixteen years and seven months. Sixth form student at the same school as her friend, Lesley Tabor. Only not today.

The house was a stone's throw from Mountsfield Park. More Hither Green than Catford, truth be told. Suburbia, Karen thought, but not quite as we know it. A Range Rover and a customised Mini were parked outside. The hedge had been trimmed to within an inch of its life.

No hawkers, no circulars, no unsolicited mail.

Costello reached past Karen, rang the bell and stepped back.

The woman who came to the door was in her forties, slim, well-toned, fingernails that would have done justice to a bird of prey. Three mornings a week down the gym, Karen reckoned. That, at least. No obvious resort yet to plastic surgery, but it would come.

'Mrs Martin?'

'Yes?'

'Fay Martin?'

'Yes.'

Karen showed her warrant card, Tim Costello likewise.

'We'd like to speak to your daughter, Sasha. They told us at the school she was here at home.'

'You've not come about that, surely?'

'No. No, not at all.'

'Well, then . . .' Her eyes flickered from one to the other, lingering on Costello a fraction longer. 'You'd best come in. Sasha's upstairs in her room.'

Someone, perhaps even Fay Martin herself, had been over-working the Pledge in the hall, shining the occasional table, buffing up the parquet.

'Sasha! Sash! Come on down, there's a love.'

A pause, a door opening, then the usual bored, resentful teenage voice, 'What for now?'

'It's the police, Sash. Just a couple of questions, that's all.'

'What about?'

'Come down and you'll see.'

She raised an eyebrow to signify, kids, you know what they're like, and led them into a living room that was a testament to World of Leather. French windows leading out to a conservatory. A large flat-screen television was tuned to some confessional chat show, sound barely above a whisper – I slept with my girlfriend's sister, my mum's best friend. Faces anxiously searching for the camera as they sought their moment in the mire.

'She'll be down in a minute.' With a flick of the remote she switched off the TV. 'Maybe you'd like to tell me what all this is about?'

'Let's wait for Sasha, shall we?'

Fay Martin looked as if she was about to argue, thought better of it and reached for her cigarettes instead. 'Bad habit, I know . . .' Favouring Costello with a knowing smile. ''Bout the only one I've got left.'

The attractiveness that twenty years before had drawn boys

like flies to the slaughter was holding up well; Karen could sense Tim Costello responding to it alongside her, smiling back.

Sasha finally entered blearily, rubbing her eyes. A voluminous T-shirt fell well past her hips, bare legs, bare feet, fair hair tied back.

'You might have put something else on,' her mother said. 'Made yourself decent.'

'I am decent. I was sleepin', wasn't I?'

Folding her legs beneath her, she plonked herself at one end of the settee, T-shirt pulled down over her knees. A little puppy fat, but her mother's daughter, her mother's features nonetheless.

'Sasha's not been feeling too well, have you, babe? Else she'd be at school.'

'Playing the wag,' Costello suggested.

The girl shot him a look.

'Sasha,' Karen said, 'we need to ask you about your boyfriend.'

'What boyfriend?'

'She hasn't got a boyfriend, have you, Sash?'

'Petru,' Karen said. 'Petru Andronic.'

Some people, when embarrassed, go red, others turn pale. Sasha turned pale.

'He's not her boyfriend,' Fay Martin said. 'Never was, was he, Sash? Not really. Besides, all done and dusted a long time back, eh, babe? What happened to him, though, the boy, reading about it, seeing it, you know, on the news . . . someone you sort of knew, even if it was only just a little . . .'

Face aside, Sasha was suddenly fighting back tears, gulping air.

'Sash, what is it, babe? What's the matter?'

Her mother reached for her hand and the girl pulled away, sobbing, starting to shake.

'Sasha, come on . . .'

'Just leave it! Leave it, okay? You don't understand and you never did.'

'What? Love of your life, was it? That bloody asylum seeker, whatever he was? That waster?'

'What if he was?'

'You stupid little cow! You haven't got the foggiest idea what love is.'

'Don't I? That's all you know.'

'Love I'm talking about. Not getting down on your hands and knees in the back of some bloke's car.'

'Better than fucking your personal trainer three times a night while Dad's out the fucking country.'

'You little shit!'

She slapped the flat of her hand fast across her daughter's face, then swung the hand back, knuckles clenched, against the side of her head.

Sasha cried out.

Karen seized both of Fay Martin's arms and held them fast.

Blood was already starting to trickle from the corner of Sasha's mouth.

Tim Costello fished a tissue from his pocket and pressed it into her hand, then set off for where he imagined he'd find the bathroom and fresh supplies.

Time passed. Tempers cooled. Outside, it was three-quarters dark. Sasha had retreated to her room and re-emerged in a skinny-rib jumper and a pair of old jeans, hair still pulled back from her face. A small scab forming at the edge of her mouth.

Fay Martin had poured herself a gin and tonic, which she'd topped up twice already with straight gin. Tempted though she'd been, Karen had said no to joining her, yes to a mug of coffee – instant, I'm afraid – Tim Costello was on to his second glass of tap water.

Sasha's story slowly emerged.

She had met Petru Andronic early the previous summer, a concert in Victoria Park. Lounging on the grass. Hot Chip. Bombay Bicycle Club. Bands like that. She'd been with her mate Lesley and a few others; Petru had been there with a friend.

'This friend,' Karen asked, 'he had a name?'

'Ion.'

'Ion Milescu?'

Sasha nodded. Karen filed it away.

They got on well, her and Petru, really well, Lesley and Ion too. It was a laugh. As the concert was winding down, the boys asked if they could see them again and after a quick conflab the girls said, why not? After that they saw them quite a bit, at least Sasha did, saw Petru that is. Ion kept texting Lesley, making arrangements to see her, then at the last minute crying off; after a few weeks of that she didn't hear from him at all.

'But you carried on? Seeing Petru?'

'Yes.' A quick glance across at her mum. 'He was nice. Not like . . . not like most other boys. Not grabbing you all the time.'

'Didn't fancy you much, then, did he?' her mother said with a sneer.

'He respected me.'

'Oh, yes?'

'He loved me.'

'Jesus Christ!'

'He was going to marry me.'

'Over my dead body he was.' Fay Martin reached for the gin.

'You didn't know. You didn't care. I wore this ring he give me on a chain round my neck and you didn't even notice.'

'Your father would have skinned the pair of you alive.'

'He wouldn't have had the chance, would he?'

'He warned you to keep away from him, you know he did.'

'We was gonna run away.'

'Run away? Where to? Back to Kosova or wherever he bloody comes from?'

'Moldova. It was Moldova.'

'Should have stayed there, shouldn't he? Then the poor little sod might still be alive.'

Sasha bit her lip and clenched her fists, determined not to cry.

Off in another room, a clock struck six times.

'Sasha,' Karen said, 'I have to ask you. The night that Petru was killed. Your friend Lesley texted you, Petru wanted you to contact him, he was worried, waiting to meet you.'

'Yes.' The word like a slow release of breath.

'But you didn't?'

A shake of the head.

'You didn't text? Call? Anything?'

'No.'

'Why was that?'

'I was frightened.'

'What of?'

She pushed her feet back and forth along the floor. 'My dad.'

Sasha tugged at a thread that had worked its way loose from a rip in her jeans.

'He found out, didn't he? That I was seeing him again. Petru. He'd told me before, he didn't want me seeing him, not talking to him or nothing.'

'Why was that?'

'I dunno. Just never liked him, right from the first.'

'He'd met him, then?'

'Just the once, that's all. I brought him to meet my mum. I thought she'd like him, and my dad he was here. I didn't know. I thought he was, I dunno, off somewhere. Wouldn't've brought him otherwise. Soon as he saw Petru he started in on him – what was he doing here, how was he living, where all his money was coming from? – stuff like that. Not that Petru ever had any money, not really.

'Then when he was leaving, my dad said he didn't want him round here again. Not ever. Didn't want me to have anything to do with him. When Petru started to stand up for himself, for us, talk back, I thought my dad was going to hit him. Petru, he wasn't frightened, but he's a big man, my dad, he'd've hurt him, I know he would. Hurt him bad. That's what he's like.'

She snapped the thread free.

'After he'd gone, he told me I wasn't to have nothing to do with him again. Said he'd stop me using the computer, Facebook an' that, take away my mobile phone.'

'So that's when you started using Lesley as a go-between?'

'Yeah. She didn't mind. Liked it, really.'

'And this particular evening, the one we're talking about, that was how you'd arranged to meet him?'

'Yes.'

'But Hampstead – why Hampstead? Not exactly round the corner.'

'That's why, yeah? No way we're going to bump into anyone we knew. Anyone who knew me and might tell my dad.'

'This would have been late, though. It would have been dark.'

'That was okay. I didn't care.'

'How about getting home?'

A quick glance away. 'I wasn't. I told my mum I was staying at Lesley's. A sleepover.'

'Little liar,' Fay Martin said quietly.

'There was this place, stayed open all night. Burgers and stuff. That's where we'd go, just sit, you know, and talk. What was going to happen, what we were going to do.'

'Do?'

'Once we were married.'

'Holy Jesus!' Fay Martin rolled her eyes up towards the heavens.

'Sasha,' Tim Costello leaned forward, 'you said your dad found out you were going to see Petru that evening – how did that happen?'

'Mum was out and he was here. They'd . . .' She looked towards her mother, then away. 'I think they'd had a row. Mum'd stormed out.'

'I walked,' Fay Martin said, flatly.

'Anyway, he was here and he asked me, you know, where was I going and I said, like, Lesley's, and soon as I said it I could tell he didn't believe me. Made me call her. Didn't stand up to him more'n a couple of minutes, did she? Told him. After that it all come out. Everything. How I'd been going behind his back. Where we was goin' to meet that evening, everything. I thought he was gonna go crazy, but he never. He'd warned me, that's what he said. Warned both of us. Told me to go to my room and locked me in. He'd already took my phone. That's an end to it, he said. Then I heard him leavin'.'

Tears were rolling slowly down Sasha's cheeks.

'You know where he went?'

A shake of the head, shoulders down.

'Sasha?'

'No.'

An ambulance went past along the main road, siren wailing.

'You wouldn't know, I suppose, Mrs Martin, where your husband went to after he'd locked Sasha in her room?'

'Wasn't here when I got back, I know that.'

'And this was when?'

'Eleven, eleven thirty.'

'And you wouldn't have any idea where he might have been?'

'The pub, I dare say. Where he usually went off to when he was in one of his moods. And when he wasn't.'

'Any pub in particular?'

'Four Hands, most likely. Down Lewisham. Landlord has a lock-in most nights.'

'And that's where you think he was?'

'Good a guess as any. Gone three in the morning time he got home, anyway. Hammered didn't come into it.'

'Mr Martin,' Karen said, 'you're expecting him home this evening?'

'Not 'less he's changed his plans.'

'Which are?'

'Over in Tallinn, isn't he?'

'Estonia?'

'Last time I looked.'

'Stag do?' Costello suggested.

'Business.'

'So when are you expecting him?' Karen asked.

'Couple of days, maybe three.'

'Only we'll need to talk to him.'

'What for?'

'Hear his version of Sasha's story. Confirm his whereabouts, the night Petru Andronic died.'

'You don't think he had anything to do with that? Terry? You must be jokin'.'

'Normal procedure, Mrs Martin, that's all.'

'He'll not like it.'

'I'm afraid that's too bad.' Karen placed one of her cards on the table. 'Ask him to contact this number as soon as he returns. We'll need to see you as well, Sasha. Make a statement, what you've just told us.'

'Do I have to?'

'I think so. Best to get it all clear once and for all. Perhaps you could bring her in, Mrs Martin? Tomorrow around ten thirty?'

Fay Martin's glare followed them all the way to the door.

Outside, the air bit cold and Karen shivered. Tim Costello pulled his coat collar up against his neck.

'"He'd've hurt him, I know he would," is that what she said?'

Karen nodded. '"Hurt him bad."'

'And then what was it? Before he went out? "That's an end to it."'

'That's what she said.'

'Out of the mouths . . .'

'I know.' Karen glanced back at the house, silhouette at one of the upstairs windows, Fay Martin looking down. 'You fancy a drink,' she said, 'before we head back?'

'The Four Hands?'

'Why not?'

11

Over the sea the sky loomed unnaturally dark. Midday, near as made no difference. A near complete absence of light. Cordon walked back down the hill, air heavy like a coat about his shoulders. Indoors, he set coffee on the stove to heat, picked a CD from the small pile on the floor and set it in place. Selected track three, early January, 1945: way, way before he was born.

The piece starts off with an easy swing, relaxed, a wash of cymbals behind the horns; and then, without warning, thirty seconds in, the trumpet unleashes itself into a blistering run, a chorus torn from another place, a world moved on. After that – an anti-climax, how could it be anything else? – the trombone and then the saxophone take their own pedestrian time, the sax straining towards the end, wanting more without seemingly knowing how. Only in the closing bars do we hear the trumpet clearly again, skittering irrepressibly around the final statement of the theme – puckish – up and down and in between.

'Good Bait'. Dizzy Gillespie All Stars: New York City, 9 January.

Cordon poured the coffee, added milk.

Set the track to play again.

Concentrated on the sound.

A couple of days now since he had seen the report in the paper? The paragraph in the *Cornishman* concise and to the point.

The body of a woman who was fatally injured after falling under a Tube train at Finsbury Park, north London, four days ago, has been identified as that of Maxine Carlin, aged 46, formerly resident in Penzance. A neighbour, who did not wish to be named, told The Cornishman she thought Mrs Carlin had gone to London to see her daughter.

How many days?

Maxine Carlin, forty-six.

Heroin. Alcohol. Children aborted, almost certainly; children taken into care. Men who spoke with their fists or not at all.

Forty-six.

A wonder she lived as long as she did.

For an instant he saw the train. The speed of it as she fell. The music again, unchanging. Outside, the sky offered no release.

It was none of his business, none. Gone to London to see her daughter. Well, so what if she had? *Gone missing, i'n't she?* Rose. Letitia. *That stupid bloody name!* He saw her face, Letitia's, younger, smiling, the dog lifting her head to lick the back of her hand. Letitia. Rose. *Thought a lot of you, fuck knows why.*

Jack Kiley and himself were of an age. Kiley, ex-professional footballer, albeit briefly; ex-Met. Now eking out a living as a private investigator. Security work a lot of it, private security, small scale: B-list celebrities, sports stars, hangers-on amongst the minor royals. There was a firm of local solicitors for whom he ran checks, chased payments, sat hour on hour in nondescript cafés, staring out through steamed-up windows; hunkered down behind the wheel of a borrowed car, waiting to witness some all-too-human indiscretion, reveal the truth behind the lie: the affair with the best friend's wife or husband; the disability that magically disappeared; a second family on the far side of the city, kids nicely set up in private school; a hopeless addiction to gambling or drugs or being tied up and blindfolded, then hoisted upside down and beaten with a cane.

Kiley still had contacts in the force and used them when he could, favours carried out and called in, information bartered and exchanged; friends in low places he'd collected through the years – Soho, Notting Hill, bits and corners of the East End.

He'd met Cordon three years before, chasing down the wilful teenage daughter of a merchant banker who'd done a bunk from Channing School and gone AWOL with her ageing artist lover in Cornwall. Sixty-four years young, a painter of vivid semi-abstract seascapes, small impasto nudes, his studio in St Ives looked out over the beach at Porthmeor.

After days of intense negotiations, during which many tears were shed and money, a considerable amount of money, was to change hands unseen, the painter joined Kiley in convincing the girl her future happiness lay in the bosom of her family.

He owed, Kiley acknowledged, Cordon a great deal for helping to bring that particular farrago to such a beneficent conclusion.

The two of them enjoyed several evenings in the Tinners' Arms, swapping stories about the job, cases they'd worked, people they'd served under, bastards all; Kiley, a few pints in, going on to embellish tales of his time with Charlton Athletic and Stevenage Borough. Together, they went to the jazz night at the Western Hotel, Mark Nightingale stoking up a local rhythm section, then curry to follow.

'You're ever up in London,' Kiley had said. 'Give us a bell.'

Cordon had leave owing and plenty of it. Brooking no argument, he took what was his due.

'Sure you don't want me to meet you off the train?' Kiley said with a chuckle. 'Trip to the big city. Might get lost.'

'Fuck off.'

Cordon caught the Tube from Paddington, made the change, stepped out from Tufnell Park station into a cold January day, collar raised, duffle bag, army surplus, slung over one shoulder.

Half the shops in the street were shut down, to let, windows fly-posted over. A man of around Cordon's age, no older, sat on the pavement near the cash machine, a sheet of soiled cardboard stretched out beneath him, begging for change.

The charity shop below where Kiley lived was doing brisk business, women mostly, searching through rails of cast-offs to find something for their kids, a new skirt or top for themselves if the money stretched; neat piles of once-read books, videos no longer played, children's games, unwanted presents from aunt this and uncle that, a loving gran.

Kiley's place was on the second floor: bedroom, tiny kitchen, bathroom with a shower and toilet but no bath, a larger room at the front which was office and living space combined. Filing cabinet and metal shelving stood along one wall; a couple of chairs, laptop, printer, answerphone, slimline TV. On the wall opposite hung a painting, pale and undefined, the sea from Porthmeor Beach, part of the deal. If he swivelled round from his desk, Kiley could look down into the ever-busy street.

Cordon dumped his bag, glad to be rid of the weight, and looked around.

'So where is it?'

'Where's what?'

'The couch. You said I could sleep on the couch.'

'Figure of speech.'

Cordon looked at the floor, thin rugs across bare boards.

'It's okay, you can have my bed. Just a couple of nights you said, right?'

'And you?'

Kiley inclined his head. 'Just round the corner. Stay with a friend.'

'She have a name?'

'Jane.'

'Nice. Straightforward.'

'You want coffee?'

'Why not?'

While Kiley was in the kitchen, Cordon looked along the higgledy-piggledy rows of books and CDs. Names he knew; names he failed to recognise. Junot Diaz. K. C. Constantine. Gerry Mulligan. Ronnie Lane.

Mulligan he knew.

He was checking the playlist when Kiley came back in. Track three: 'Good Bait'.

'Don't you ever keep these things in order?'

'What for? Most of them I pick up downstairs. Lets me sort through sometimes if he has to pop out, needs someone in the shop. Good half of them I've never even played.'

'Or read.'

'Or read.'

The coffee was strong and slightly bitter. Good. They sat in facing chairs, angled slightly away. 'So,' Kiley said, 'tell me.'

When he was through listening, he leaned back, legs crossed above the ankles, hands locked behind his head.

'Let me get this right. The younger one, the daughter, she drops from sight, no letter, no phone call, nothing so special about that, happens all the time. But mum gets worried – mums do. Comes up to look for her, ends up under a train.' Kiley shook his head. 'Just about every damn time I go to catch the Northern Line, severe delays due to a person under a train at Finchley Central, a person under a train at High Barnet – somewhere.'

'Finsbury Park.'

'Huh?'

'She went under a train at Finsbury Park.'

'It used to be an incident. That's what they'd say. The announcement over the loudspeaker. An incident at wherever. Of course, you knew, you guessed. Then, a year or so ago, there was a change of policy. Call a spade a spade, suicide a suicide. Maybe they thought it would stiffen a few backs, put people off. Jumpers. Done the opposite, seems to me.'

Cordon nodded. 'I just want to be sure.'

'If she jumped or fell?'

'Yes.'

'Or was she pushed?'

'That, too.'

'You've got reasons for thinking that might be the case? Pushed?'

'Not really. No.'

'Don't tell me. It's a feeling; a feeling in your gut. Won't go away.'

'How did you know?'

'I read it. Read it in the book.'

'Yes?'

'A hundred books. This feeling deep inside, something he just couldn't shake.'

'Doesn't ever happen to you?'

'Course it does. I take Rennies, Milk of Magnesia. It goes away.'

Cordon said nothing, stared.

Kiley leaned forward a little in his chair. 'It happened here just a few weeks back. Someone under the train. Tufnell Park. Police cars coming from every direction. Ambulances. Emergency Response Unit there within minutes. Station sealed off, roads closed. Bloke piloting this hospital helicopter, bright red, brings it down smack in the middle of the crossroads. Major operation, every time. Drilled, rehearsed. Report prepared for the coroner. Detailed investigation. Pushed, jumped or fell, I think they'd know. I think they could tell.'

'I'd like to talk to someone, that's all. Someone involved. Look at the CCTV.'

'Put your mind at rest.'

'Exactly.'

'Then you can go on and find the girl.'

Cordon released a breath. 'Maybe.'

'Regular white knight.'

'Bollocks.'

'You said it.' Kiley sat back and looked at Cordon for a long minute. 'You're doing this why?'

'Does it matter?'

'Not to me.'

Cordon shrugged.

'What's her name again?'

'Letitia.'

Kiley grinned. 'Nothing straightforward there.' Then, 'Might be someone I can speak to, friend of a friend. Open up a few doors.'

'Thanks.'

Kiley wandered off to make more coffee; Cordon went back to the CDs, made his choice, Gerry Mulligan's baritone sax taking 'Good Bait' at a gentle lope.

12

Cordon sat in a room that was squat and square, old copies of British Transport Police press releases on the walls. *Whatever mode of transport Londoners choose, a team of dedicated officers will be there to reassure them and tackle crime: the Chief Operating Officer of London Underground.* Cordon felt reassured. The air in the room was stale. Somewhere on the other side of the door were banks of screens, computers retrieving and storing images from every part of the network.

When he'd woken that morning in the unfamiliar surroundings of Jack Kiley's flat, it had been some moments before he realised where he was, remembered exactly why he was there. Instead of the anguished cry of seagulls, the slow acceleration of buses away from the traffic lights on Fortess Road, JCBs from the nearby Murphy's yard rumbling their way to work.

'Help yourself,' Kiley had said. 'Whatever you can find.' Shown him where he kept the coffee, the tea. If you stood in the centre of the kitchen, you could touch all four walls without having to move your feet.

They'd sat up late the night before, after a meal at the Blue

Moon café along the street. Won ton soup, drunken noodles. Thai beer. Kiley talking about an investigation, tracking down a soldier from the Queen's Royal Lancers who'd gone AWOL rather than rejoin his regiment and return to Iraq. This a few years back, but preying still on his mind.

Kiley had got involved, unwillingly, through someone he'd befriended some time before; spoken to the soldier's mother, distraught, patted her hand, made promises he couldn't hope to keep.

There were children, kiddies, a wife who'd moved them away to another town and filed for divorce. A soldier from the Queen's Royal Lancers with a rifle and ammunition; a man who'd seen things, likely done things most people would blank from their imagination.

He took them, wife and children, the youngest only three. Kiley's face tight, remembering. When they eventually found them, they were camped out in woodland, police helicopter circling overhead. What he'd intended had been unclear, even, Kiley suspected, to himself; his wife frightened he would kill them, the children and herself, anything rather than lose them. Saying it between sobs, over and over.

It was himself he killed in the end, a single bullet to the head. Professional. The children crying, screaming.

'Something like that,' Kiley began, 'you never . . .' then stopped and ordered another beer instead.

Back at the flat, they watched the news. Two more dead from roadside bombs in Afghanistan. More snow forecast for the south-east, temperatures dropping. Senior Scotland Yard officer to come up on trial: conspiracy to pervert the course of justice.

'This woman,' Cordon said. 'Jane. Serious?'

'Schoolteacher. Local primary.'

'Serious, then.'

Kiley poured them both another shot of whisky. Some of

the good stuff, Springbank, cask strength, twelve year old, present from a grateful client. Mose Allison in the background, 'Everybody Cryin' Mercy', one of Kiley's favourites. Cordon had made him play the Mulligan beforehand: a tune he couldn't prise from his mind.

'You ever read those stupid instant interviews in the paper?' Kiley asked. 'Q & A with some celeb. "Ever said 'I Love You' and not meant it?"'

'That's what it's like? With Jane?'

Kiley shrugged. 'Sometimes.'

'Price of a bed,' Cordon said.

The music stopped. Neither man moved. Shrill laughter from the street outside.

'The girl you're looking for . . .'

'Letitia.'

'Yes. You ever . . . ?'

'It's not like that,' Cordon said quickly. A little too quickly.

Kiley shook his head. 'One way or another, it always is.'

Cordon didn't argue.

Tossing back the rest of his glass, Kiley got, with surprising agility, to his feet. 'The morning, then.'

'Yes. Yes, sure.'

Cordon watched him walk across the room, only the slightest limp, the smallest sign of the injury that had ended his footballing career.

The door to the room where Cordon was waiting opened and a man came in, sallow faced, slouch shouldered, the beginnings of a belly, too many hours behind a desk.

'Trevor Cordon?'

'Yes.' Rising.

'Bob Rowe.'

They shook hands.

'Maxine Carlin, you're a relative?'

'Not exactly.'

'Jack said related.'

'Close. You could say we were close.'

Rowe continued to look at him, uncertain.

'Daughter aside,' Cordon said, 'there's really no one else.'

'And the daughter?'

Cordon shrugged. 'Who knows?'

Another moment's hesitation. 'Okay, you'd best come through.'

A bank of screens dominated one wall; individual screens at intervals along long rows, staff intent, heads inclined, some images changing – another camera, another angle – others remaining focused on seemingly empty tunnels, empty walls.

Rowe indicated an empty chair and Cordon slid it across.

'Till we started using this new system,' Rowe said, 'storing all the imagery that comes through just wasn't possible. Fifty, sixty per cent at best. And retrieving what you did have, that wasn't so easy, either. Things would get lost. But now . . .'

He clicked once, twice, a third time and, less than a hundred per cent sharp, an image flicked into place. 'Okay. Finsbury Park station, Piccadilly Line, West Platform, 9.31 in the morning. Tail end of the rush hour. Still busy, as you can see.'

Cordon leaned forward.

'There she is now, your Maxine, just coming on to the platform, looking round.'

Cordon saw a figure that could indeed be her, three-quarter-length coat, scarf; the face, when she turned, darkened by shadow.

'Here now, you see, another camera. She's looking across the track, probably checking her destination. And then she starts to walk away.'

A dozen steps and she was lost to sight, a small surge of passengers moving in behind her, blocking her from view.

'And this,' Rowe said, as the angle changed, 'is where we

pick her up again. More or less on her own for what? Twenty, thirty seconds, before other people come into view, result of an announcement, most likely, asking customers to use the full length of the platform. Several people there now, you see, quite close . . .'

Cordon sees a young couple, both smartly dressed, partly facing: the woman has long, shoulder-length hair that in the picture is bleached almost white; the man bends his head towards her, says something close to her ear that makes her smile. A businessman behind them, middle-aged, striped suit, tie, briefcase, folded newspaper. *Financial Times.* Cliché. Another man, younger, headphones, laptop under one arm. Several others towards the edges of the frame, moving forward as the train approaches, crowding in, virtually impossible to distinguish one from another.

'Let me see her face,' Cordon said.

The image stops, reverses, zooms in, then freezes. The face is pinched, eyes small, dark, uncertain, and Cordon thinks of something trapped, cornered.

'Move it on, just a fraction.'

For a moment, hardly more, Maxine seems to be looking directly into the camera, head raised, mouth opening as if to speak . . . Then, as if in slow motion, she turns away, towards the track, the train; a movement, blurred, down across the frame as she falls and she's gone.

A dark space where she had been standing.

The camera shows a bustle of movement in the wake of her going, the white blur of faces, a mouth opening in a shout or scream, someone pointing. The young woman has buried her face against her partner's chest and he appears to be stroking her long hair.

'That's it?'

'That's it.'

Cordon sat back with a slow release of breath. 'See it again?'

Nothing changed.

In all of three viewings, nothing changed. At the end of each, Maxine Carlin was still dead under the train.

Cordon's shoulders ached.

'I looked at the report before you came,' Rowe said, swivelling in his chair as the screen went blank. 'Read through the witness statements, fifteen of them. People who were on the platform that morning, when the incident occurred. All of those you've just seen. Most, anyway. One or two we couldn't trace. Some of them claim to have noticed her before it happened. Not many, but a few. Standing worryingly close to the platform edge, one said. Nervous, said another, as if she wasn't sure where she was going. If this was her train. One thing they all agreed on, those who were close enough to see: the moment before the train arrived she either jumped or fell.'

'No suggestion that she was pushed?'

'None.'

'Not even accidentally? Passengers eager to get on the train. Find space. End of the rush hour, like you said.'

Rowe shook his head. 'If you're looking for some other explanation, something to hang on to, maybe there's an outside chance. But after what you've just seen, the evidence as it stands . . .' On his feet, he offered a hand. 'I'm sorry.'

Cordon nodded. 'Thanks for your time.'

Rowe led him through towards the outer corridor, the stairs. 'Tell Jack he owes me one, okay?'

13

Not expecting overmuch, Cordon sought out Letitia's last known London address, culled from the scrap of paper Maxine had thrust into his hand. A brief walk from where she had met her death.

Rain fell, almost invisibly, from a sky of palest grey. Paving stones slick and slippery beneath his feet.

The house was midway along a residential street, all of them double fronted, once grand, now shabby, down at heel. Both upper floors of the number he was seeking had been burned out. And not too long since. Woodwork blackened, trails of sooted smoke residue clinging plume-like to the brick. Up close, you could still catch the faint smell of burned wood on the air.

A matter of days, then, he thought. Round about the time of Maxine Carlin's death or just after.

On the raised first floor the windows had been temporarily boarded over; those in the basement partially covered by old sheeting. Bins at the front overflowed with rubbish; several charred mattresses and a broken bed frame leaned precariously against the wall. A sign had been partially removed from the glass above the front door, the faintest outline of letters still advertising some earlier existence: *Bentinct Hotel. Rooms. B & B.*

A while since it had been that, Cordon ventured.

A double line of bell pushes was attached to the side wall, faded name cards alongside, all blank. Cordon set his hand against the front door, prised up the flap to the letter-box and peered through.

'Done a bunk, mate. Scarpered and good fuckin' riddance. Set fire to the place before they left an' all. Someone hadn't nipped in quick with the alarm, whole soddin' street'd've burned down.'

Cordon had spotted the man earlier — ex-boxer, ex-wrestler, scar tissue around the eyes, muscle gone to seed — his dog off the leash ahead of him, in and out of gardens, cocking its leg, rummaging in bins.

'It was serious, then?'

'Serious enough. Half a dozen engines round here, more, middle of the bleedin' night, how serious d'you want?'

'This was when?'

'Last week, just.'

'How about casualties? Anybody trapped inside?'

The man leaned a shade closer. 'That's the thing. Right up till that happens there's people in and out all the time. Blokes, all of 'em. Regular knocking shop, that's what it was.'

'A brothel, you mean?'

'Call it what you like. Never see the same face twice. Then this happens, fire brigade, police all arrive, 'side from cockroaches and the like, the place is empty. Someone after the insurance, either that or clearin' out ahead of gettin' their collars felt. Mind you, don't take many blow jobs to get most coppers lookin' the other way.'

'The people who lived here? Whoever was running the place, you've no idea what happened to them? Where they went?'

'Why's that then? What's it to you?' At the hint of

aggression in the man's voice, the dog growled and snapped and the man cursed it softly and aimed a kick at its ribs.

'Just looking for someone. A friend. Might have worked here a while back. Letitia Carlin. Early thirties, most probably reddish hair. Could've been calling herself Rose.'

'Could've been callin' herself Mary bloody Magdalene for all I know. Kept 'emselves to 'emselves.'

'You don't recall seeing anyone like her then?'

'Wastin' your time, mate, sorry.' With a hunch of the shoulders, he turned away.

Cordon stood back and watched him go. The rain continued to fall in a steady drizzle as he walked, damp seeping steadily into his shoulders and along his back.

'So what now?' Kiley said.

They were sitting in the Tufnell Park flat, the sounds of Mose Allison's piano and Southern-inflected voice barely covering the stop-start of homeward-bound traffic as it made its cautious way towards Muswell Hill, Finchley Central and points north.

Kiley had thrown him a towel on his return, lent a sweater, poured a glass of Scotch and set it down close to Cordon's right hand.

'The father,' Cordon said, 'he's supposed to run a bookshop down in Hastings. At least he did.'

'Thinking of going down?'

'Thinking of it.'

'Hour or so on the train. Victoria, probably. Charing Cross? Come all this way, shame not to check it out.'

Cordon knew he was right. After leaving the house where, according to her mother, Letitia was reputed to have lived and worked, he had stopped off at the local nick and found a uniformed sergeant of around his own age who wasn't averse to talk. There had been reports of the place being used for immoral purposes, but nothing had ever been proved. Not enough to prosecute anyone, at least, take them to court. And, yes, there was some suspicion of the fire being started deliberately, but nothing conclusive in the Fire Officer's preliminary report. Certainly not enough to bring charges, always assuming they'd been able to untangle the maze of paperwork that surrounded the building's actual owners. And no casualties, that was correct. Whole place seemed to have been cleared before the fire took hold.

How much better off, Cordon thought, he would have been pottering around in Newlyn, doing his level best to give community policing a good name.

'Later,' Kiley said, 'there's a pub down Kentish Town, the Oxford. Jazz upstairs some nights. Decent food in the bar. We could give it a try, if you like.'

'Why not?'

The guitarist, over from the Continent somewhere, made noises like a scalded cat. Seated behind a kit that included five cymbals, three tom-toms and a bass drum that looked to have come from a kid's practice set, the drummer bashed and crashed through a polyrhythmic world of his own. Only the pianist, perched high behind an electric keyboard, seemed touchingly aware of old-fashioned words like 'melody' or 'tune'. Eric Dolphy was one thing, Cordon thought, some people's idea of far out, but this was altogether something else.

Downstairs saved it. The premium guest beer was Sussex Old Ale from Harveys in Lewes, rich and dark, and both the steak and the lamb fillet were tasty and tender, nicely pink. An hour or so from closing, Kiley rang Jane and asked if she fancied joining them, which she did. Dark hair; small, neat features; a true and open laugh; hands that were rarely still, emphasising this, demonstrating that. Cordon, enjoying her company, could just see her in front of a class of kids. When she and Kiley headed off together at the end of the evening, leaving him with the key to the flat, he felt a regret he fought hard to understand.

14

It would have been her father's birthday. A picture of him in her mind, another fixed by magnets to the fridge door. A tall black man, open-necked shirt, hair brushed back, the beginnings of a belly, hands — large hands — down by his sides. A street in west London where they had lived. She looked for a smile on his face that was never quite there.

Serious he had been. A serious man.

This country, I don't like the way it's goin'.

Rioting on the streets of Brixton after a black woman was shot during a police raid; more rioting on an estate in Tottenham, in the midst of which a white police officer was hacked — hacked — to death. Earlier that year, the Miners' Strike, police and pickets in pitched battles every night on the television news. And everywhere now, it seemed, her father looked, knots of men, young men, young men black and white, on street corners, unemployed.

At parent–teacher evenings, her father, dressed in his best suit, the one he wore for church, shoes shining for all they were worth — *My girl, how's she doin'?* — pride reflected in his eyes.

Education, my girl, that's the thing. College, university even. Make somethin' of yourself.

A kiss on the forehead after he had read her school report, silver coins pressed down into the palm of her hand.

Make somethin' of yourself, you promise me that. Make a difference if you can.

As if, somehow, he knew he would never live to see her grow.

'You think this is what he would have wanted?' her mother had asked, when Karen told her she was joining the police.

'I don't know,' Karen said. 'But I think so, yes. Yes, I do.'

Her mother had squeezed her hands and said, 'God bless,' uncertainty in her eyes.

Now some days, too many days, if truth be told, it was difficult to bring back, fresh to mind, exactly why she had made the choice she had. Too easy to become mired down in the quotidian, the day-to-day: forms and rotas and outcomes, the minutiae of personnel management and organisation. The lack of apparent progress.

One pace forward, one step back.

What was it that girl used to sing? The one who wished she'd been born black.

Something about little by little? Bit by bit?

Back when Karen had still been a PC – still in uniform, for God's sake – she'd gone out with a hazelnut-complexioned swimming instructor with a predilection for white women who sang the blues. Blues and soul. Dusty Springfield – that was the one. Janis Joplin, Bonnie Bramlett, Lulu, even. All fine up to a point. Making love beneath a blow-up of the Robert Crumb cover for *Cheap Thrills*, with Janis hollering for someone to take a piece of her heart, a piece of something – just about acceptable if it helped the boy get it on.

She still had some of the CDs he'd given her; played them from time to time. *Dusty in Memphis.* Lulu at Muscle Shoals.

Little by little, bit by bit.

Police work to a T.

Once in a while you just had to pinch yourself, remembering why.

The night cleaner who had come forward in the Wood Green stabbing had picked out one of the assailants from a batch of photographs. Hector Prince, street name Mohock, a name derived from the two gangs – the Mohocks and the Hawkubites – who'd terrorised London in the early eighteenth century, beating up women, children and old men after dark. It was something Hector had picked up in a year ten citizenship lesson, one of those rare days he'd bothered showing up at school. A little learning, a dangerous thing.

Only problem was, when Hector had been invited to attend a line-up at the police station, the cleaner had failed to pick him out. And there he was, cocky as a prize-winning bantam when they told him he was free to go, bumping fists with his solicitor outside the station.

A closer look at Terry Martin, following the conversation with his wife, revealed that, in addition to three minor drug busts which went back quite a few years, more recently he had been charged with two serious offences: involvement in a post office robbery in Greenford, and possession of a large amount of high-grade cocaine with intent to supply. The first case had come to court, then fallen apart on the issue of identification; the robbers had worn rubberised Blair and Bush masks throughout and the Crown's other evidence had been less than foolproof from the start. What had stymied the second case, even before the CPS had agreed to prosecute, was the disappearance of the confiscated cocaine from police hands. One of the officers concerned had been warned about his future conduct and transferred to other duties; another had resigned.

In neither instance, then, had Martin been convicted, but even so, the company he was shown to have been keeping was tasty indeed. One of the men charged alongside him for the post office robbery, Graham Arthurs, was currently serving five years for malicious wounding and causing grievous bodily harm; and Arthurs' older brother, Les, had been questioned about his suspected involvement in a payroll snatch at a supermarket in High Wycombe. A second suspect, Kevin Martin, Terry's half-brother, was on police bail, pending an investigation into an incident in Lewisham in which a fifteen-year-old who'd been doing grunt work for one of the local drug dealers had been beaten so badly as to lose the use of an eye.

And there were others in Martin's circle, mostly around the same age, thirty-five to fifty, almost all of them, a couple of Glaswegians aside, from south of the river.

Dougie Freeman. Jason Richards. Aaron Johnson.

Michael John Carter. 'Mad Mike' to his friends.

Ramsden told Karen he'd seen Carter once, during a raid on a club in Peckham where he was employed as bouncer, lift an officer off the ground, two-handed, and hurl him against and almost through the windscreen of the nearest car. After that it had taken half a dozen men to overpower him and hold him down.

And then there was Martin's involvement with the BNP. Several photographs and a short piece of video footage culled from Special Branch files. Martin at full throttle, mouth wide open, shouting racist abuse, singing 'God Save the Queen', the flag of St George fluttering behind him.

All of which was enough, Karen thought, to brace Terry Martin on his return from Tallinn. Taking Tim Costello along would give her a chance to see how well he handled himself, as well as, maybe, offering a little light relief.

15

Terry Martin walked through from airside with the look of an ex-footballer for whom life on Sky Sports News was always going to be a step too far. Close-cropped hair, stubble, pricey suit that he somehow managed to make look cheap. Carry-on held in one large hand.

Costello had written Martin's name in marker on a piece of card and stood amongst a gaggle of minicab drivers and other meeters and greeters, holding it high above his head. His little joke.

Humour him, Karen thought. She was interested in seeing for herself how he handled himself in situations like this. 'You do the talking,' she'd said. 'I'll listen.'

'What's this?' Martin said, his face too close to Costello's for comfort. 'Someone looking to do me a favour?'

'Not exactly.'

The airport had allotted them a small room devoid of decoration save for a CityJet calendar for 2009, open at October, a picture of the Dundee Botanical Gardens in autumn. There was an air vent, a small window that didn't seem to open out on to anything, several stacking chairs and a square metal table.

'Whatever this is about,' Martin said, sitting heavily, 'make it snappy, okay? I ain't got all day.'

'How was Tallinn?' Costello asked chirpily, sounding as if he really cared. 'Successful trip? Business, was it? A little R & R? Bit of both? Sex tourism's the big thing, apparently. Several hundred per cent rise in prostitution. AIDs too, of course. Hand in hand these days, unfortunately.'

'What the fuck is this? Some kind of market fucking research?'

Close up, beneath the stubble, Martin's face was slack and pale. His breath, in Costello's face, was sour. Not enough sleep. Too much airline booze. Burning Tallinn at both ends.

'We'll say business then, shall we?'

'Say what you fuckin' like.'

'What is the nature of your business, Mr Martin?' Karen asked, stepping in, the voice of reason.

'My business?' A burly shrug. 'Textiles, import and export. Tallinn it's mainly sportswear, a little Gore-tex, women's clothing. We bring it in, sell it on.'

'We?'

'My partners and me.'

'Which partners might that be?' Costello asked.

'Never you mind.'

'Dougie Freeman? Mad Mike Carter? Some of your pals from the BNP?'

'You little shit!' Martin slammed a fist down on the table, hard.

Holding his nerve, Costello had scarcely blinked.

'Instead of losing your temper,' Karen said firmly, reckoning Martin was disorientated enough, 'why don't you tell us where you were on the evening of December 21st last.'

'What?'

'December 21st.'

'How'm I supposed to know that?'

'21st December,' Karen said, 'the night you locked your daughter, Sasha, in her room, and left her there till the early hours of next morning.'

'Who says?'

'Sasha. Your wife. They both say.'

'The fuck they do.'

'I could show you the transcript,' Karen offered.

'I'll show you a fucking transcript.' Martin was half out of his chair. 'I'll transcript you into the middle of next fucking week.'

'Sit down,' Karen said. A voice that broached no argument. 'Sit down and answer the question now. Either that or I can have you hauled down to the local nick and let you stew for an hour or so before you answer the same questions there.'

Martin tugged at the front of his shirt, hitched up his trousers and sat back down with a shake of the head.

'Okay, okay. You're just winding me up, I know. But I tell you, dealing with those people, it gets to you. It really does.'

Lowering his head, he pinched the bridge of his nose between finger and thumb, then looked back up.

'Trying to get some factory owner to realise if he doesn't up his output without hiking his prices, he's going to lose every ounce of his work to fucking China before he can turn around. Jesus!' He shook his head, more vigorously this time. 'To think we used to have a textile industry in the country served two-thirds of the fucking world. Now look at us. Having to import every pair of bloody women's knickers from Eastern Europe or the depths of the Third fucking World on account of we can't make jack shit.'

Costello looked impressed; he hadn't been expecting a lesson in world economics. Karen gave it five seconds and repeated her question.

'That evening?' Martin said, Mr Reasonable, 'I went down

the pub, didn't I? What else? Wife'd thrown a wobbly over nothin' and gone stalking off, God knows where. Me daughter's been lying to her back teeth, giving her arse away to some drug-dealing little shite from just about the poorest country on the globe outside fucking Africa. Went down the Four Hands and got stinking. Christmas piss-up on so it weren't a problem. Someone must've poured me into a minicab in the small hours, 'cause I can't remember getting home at all.'

'And you were there all evening?'

'When I arrived to when I left.'

'So there'll be witnesses to that?'

'I suppose so. It was busy, rammed, I don't know.'

'That's not very helpful.'

'The bloke whose shoes I threw up on in the khazi, you could ask him for starters.'

'He have a name?'

'Jimmy. Jimmy something-or-other.'

'I thought it was your local. Regular, anyway.'

'So ask the landlord, why don't you?'

'We already did. Said he remembers you coming in, not leaving.'

'Makes the two of us, then.'

'No memory of seeing you after 'round eleven, eleven thirty.'

'Like I said, it was busy. Wall to wall.'

'Leave there the right side of midnight, cab across London, Hampstead in forty minutes, tops. Half an hour.'

'And why'd I want to do that?'

'You tell me.'

'I don't know, do I?'

'Keep the appointment your daughter had made with Petru Andronic.'

'You're joking. You are joking.'

'Teach him a lesson.'

'No way.'

'You'd already warned him what would happen if he tried to see Sasha again. And there he was, going behind your back. Getting his hands on your daughter. This – what did you call him? – drug-dealing little shite. And by the way, why drug-dealing?'

'Why? Cause it's what they do, isn't it? Not the Poles, the Poles are okay, they know how to do a day's work. Not now, mind you, they've clocked the writing on the wall an' buggered off back to Warsaw an' wherever else it is they come from. No, it's the rest of them. Your Bosnians and Albanians, Moldovans and fucking Romanians. Breed like fucking rats, those Romanian bloody gyppos worst of all, just so's they can send the kids out on the streets, begging. Soon as they're old enough the girls are out whoring and kids like that Andronic are peddling drugs on street corners. All that on top of milking Social fucking Security.'

'The world,' Costello said, 'according to the British National Party.'

'Laugh, you smug bastard,' Martin said. 'Go ahead. One day you'll be laughing on the other side of your cocky little face.'

'Maybe that's what it was,' Karen said, reclaiming the conversation. 'With Andronic. The chance to teach him his place, teach him a lesson. Only it went too far – you'd been drinking after all – got out of hand. Next thing you know . . .'

Martin rocked his chair back then forward. 'No, you had the least bit of evidence put me near where it happened, you'd have had me in cuffs the minute I stepped off that plane. But you've got sod all and you're fishing. That's what this is. Only the line's broke, and, any case, you wanna hook me you best get yourself some better fuckin' bait – so I'm leaving. You want to stop me, arrest me. If not, I'm gone.'

And with neither Karen nor Costello making any attempt to stop him, he walked out the door.

16

'What d'you reckon then?' Ramsden said. 'Martin?'

'Do I fancy him for it?' Karen said.

'Yeah.'

'I'd like to. Like to, but I don't know.'

They were standing at the side door of a pub Ramsden favoured in the bowels of Camden. A fine view of the waste bins and a few parked cars. Ramsden, as he sometimes did, smoking one of his small tightly rolled cigars. Their breath visible on the night air.

It had been an Irish pub when Irish was more in vogue, plastic shamrocks in the window, a greenwood bodhran hanging down above the bar; this last year or so, evenings and weekends, it had been taken over by Goths and heavy metallers; Black Sabbath and Metallica on the jukebox and whip-thin girls with faces powdered white and lipstick the colour of dried blood. Other coppers never set foot there, unless it was a raid. The bitter wasn't bad, either.

'Trouble is,' Karen said, 'there's not a scrap of forensics puts him even close. No murder weapon, no prints, no CCTV. Nothing.'

'Gut feeling?'

'My gut feeling, he could have. He's capable of it, I'm sure. Reason enough in his mind, too, tanked up especially.'

'So what you gonna do? You and sonny boy?'

'Sonny boy's all right. Just needs a little perspective, that's all. Realise he doesn't have to be grandstanding all the time.'

'I'm sure in your guiding hands . . .' A lascivious grin on his face, Ramsden was cheerfully miming masturbation when the door opened sharply and a sandy-haired man took half a step out on to the low porch, stopped, looked from Ramsden to Karen and back again, then winked merrily at Ramsden and withdrew.

'Thinks there's something going on,' Ramsden said. 'You and me. Didn't want to spoil my chances.'

'Yes?' Karen laughed. 'What chance is that?'

Ramsden took a healthy sip from his glass.

'So, Martin, what's your plan?'

'Sonny boy, as you call him, is going back to the landlord at the Four Hands, dredge up some more names, try to get a sharper line on how long that night Martin was in the pub. Then we're checking taxi firms, minicab drivers, anyone who might have had Martin as a fare. And that includes the driver he alleges took him home in the early hours.'

'Could have been a mate, a friend.'

'I know. I can get some of the team talking to his known associates, see if there's anything there.'

Ramsden's look was dubious. 'Lot of manpower, lot of hours.'

'Better suggestion?'

'Bring him in. Make him sweat. Then see what he's got to say. Let me have a word with him.'

Karen smiled. 'Is that the bit where you swipe him round the back of the head with a good old-fashioned telephone directory?'

'Does the trick. Used to.'

'So I've heard.'

Ramsden swallowed down the last of his beer. 'Want another?'

'Maybe. Just the one. But now you've finished that vile little cigar, can we at least go back inside?'

They found a table far enough from the jukebox to make conversation possible. Hector Prince, Ramsden said, was still lording it over the fact that he'd walked away from police custody scot-free, bragging about it, apparently, how there was nothing they could do to touch him.

'Riding for a fall?' Karen wondered.

'Could be.'

'How about that accusation of Martin's?' Ramsden asked. 'The Andronic youth might have been dealing?'

'I don't think so.'

'Gives you another possible motivation. If he'd been siphoning some off, short changing, someone might have been out to teach him a lesson.'

'Some lesson.'

'Sets an example.'

'There's nothing else linking Andronic to drugs. I think that was just Martin blowing off hot air.'

'Even so,' Ramsden winced as a particularly loud riff from Iron Maiden made the room shake and rattled the glasses on the table. 'Could do worse than taking a look at that pal of his again, the one he called that evening. Milescu? Check him out on Facebook, sites like that. Build up a bit more background, can't do any harm.' He winked. 'Wouldn't like to see you cutting off your options too soon, getting tunnel vision.'

'What are you? My manager, all of a sudden?'

Ramsden leaned back, smiling with his eyes. 'Feels that way sometimes.'

Karen smiled back. 'You know what?'

'What?'
'Bollocks!'

Karen was still wearing the vestiges of a smile when she exited the Tube. Whereas working with Tim Costello was interesting, almost fun, watching him showing off a little, seeing how far he could go, with Ramsden everything was easy, like slipping into a familiar pattern, easing on an old pair of worn gloves. What was that song? 'An Old Raincoat Won't Ever Let You Down'. Ramsden was like that. Old and dependable. If distinctly ragged round the edges.

Taking the turning off St Paul's Road into Highbury Grove, wind pulling at her coat and hair, the first inklings of rain, she noticed the car idling ahead of her, ignorant of the traffic. A Volvo, dark blue, shading into black. As she drew close, it pulled away, then slowed. She logged the number in her head, prepared to cross the street, take defensive action, if necessary run.

When she came alongside the vehicle, it slid forward in tandem, the rear window slipping soundlessly down.

'Karen.'

It was Burcher. Detective Chief Superintendent Anthony Burcher. She hadn't known they were on first-name terms.

The rear nearside door opened.

'Get in.'

The car slid off into traffic, commuters on their way back through Seven Sisters, Stroud Green, Stamford Hill, Edmonton. Farther out there were real fields, paddocks, small orchards, golf courses where you could play a full eighteen holes without having to cross a motorway.

It was close in the back of the car, the heater notched up a few degrees too high; the sweetness of peppermints on Burcher's breath.

'Just passing, sir?'

'Something of the kind.'

In front, the driver swallowed a chuckle, remembering he wasn't there. See no evil, speak no evil.

'The Hampstead business, Andronic, something of a breakthrough?'

She told him about the Martins, Terry and Sasha, father and daughter. Her suspicions, unproven.

'And this Milescu boy, he involved? Seriously, I mean?'

No real reason to think so, sir. No more than peripherally. But I suppose it's possible.'

'His father, he was expressing some concern.'

'To you, sir?'

'Friends, shall we say, one or two, high places.'

'I doubt he has reasons to worry.'

'Good to know. Though of course, if there were anything, anything serious, you might just run it by me.'

'Of course.'

Burcher nodded, found something interesting through the opposite window. At the crossroads, without being asked, the driver took a left, then left again.

'Cooperation, resources, you're getting what you need?'

'Yes, sir.'

'Splendid.'

The car came to a halt some sixty metres from her door.

'Walk from here?'

'Thank you, sir.'

The rain was starting to fall more heavily, bouncing off the roof of the Volvo as it moved away. It was beginning to look as if Mike Ramsden was right, a little more digging in Ion Milescu's direction might not go amiss after all.

17

The London College of Communication was a little way south of the river, too close to the monstrous traffic island that is the Elephant and Castle for comfort. For reasons best known to its custodians, much of the frontage was given over to large panels bearing stylishly lit close-ups of a couple passionately kissing. It pays, Karen guessed, to advertise. Amongst a bustle of activity, legions of students were foregathered on the street outside, garbed for the most part like students the world over. She was glad she'd dressed down herself, cotton jacket, sweater, worn jeans, her second-best pair of black Converse. Scuffed leather satchel.

Winter sunshine reflected back off the glass.

Voices raised in greeting. Arms round shoulders. Laughter.

A bus pulling by on its way towards New Cross Gate.

She spotted Ion Milescu walking briskly, winding between small knots of people, rucksack slung over one shoulder.

Karen moved to intercept him and as she did so he stopped to talk to two fellow students, the man seemingly African, the girl Chinese.

'Ion . . .'

At first he didn't recognise her, a face seen out of context.

'I just need a word.'

'I've got a class.'

'A quick coffee, that's all.'

'I don't know.' He seemed flustered, uneasy.

'Look,' the African said, 'if he doesn't want to speak with you . . .'

'No,' Milescu said, 'it's all right.'

'You're sure?'

'Sure.'

The African shrugged – 'Catch you later' – tapped the Chinese girl on the shoulder and they walked away.

'Is there somewhere we can talk?' Karen asked.

What she was hoping for was a little pop-up espresso bar run by a couple of Kiwis working their way round the world; what she got was a tired café between a launderette and a newsagent's, on a small row of premises laid back from the main road; a greasy spoon that had moved some way to catering for its increasing student population, then stalled. Paninis alongside fry-ups; soya milk cappuccinos and mugs of tea you could stand a spoon in.

Karen played safe with an Americano; Ion Milescu a Pepsi.

'A few things,' Karen said, 'have come to light since we talked last. I just wanted to make sure I've got the right end of the stick.'

'What kind of things?' He was looking off in the direction of the counter, the far wall, anywhere but at her.

'You and Petru, for instance, from what you said before, you didn't know him very well at all.'

'That's right.'

'A few kickabouts and stuff like that.'

'Right.'

'Which sort of leaves out Victoria Park.'

104

'What?'

'Victoria Park. Hot Chip. Lesley Tabor. You remember Lesley?'

He mumbled something that might have been slag. She hoped it wasn't.

'You do remember Lesley?'

'Unfortunately.'

'I thought you went out with her, for a while at least.'

'She thought so, you mean.'

'You and Lesley, Petru and Sasha, quite a foursome.'

'It wasn't like that.'

'What was it like?'

'It wasn't like anything. I just went with her a few times because . . .' Ill at ease, he took a quick breath, dipped his head.

'Because?'

''Cause he asked me to.'

'He?'

'Petru. Petru, who clsc?'

'This kid you hardly knew.'

'All right, all right. God!' His voice loud enough to turn heads, the workman on his right glancing up from the *Sun*, a couple of students looking across from the plate of beans on toast they appeared to be sharing.

'All right, we hung out for a while, went to a couple of gigs here and there – he didn't have many friends, I don't know why. After we played soccer a few times, went back to the café . . .'

'The Chiswick café?'

'Yes, after that he sort of latched on to me. For a while anyway. I suppose I felt a bit sorry for him. Living with some uncle over Wood Green somewhere. Least, that's what he said.'

'You didn't believe him?'

'I don't know. It was all a bit — you know — vague. We were going to go over there once, I remember, he sort of built it up, then at the last minute he called it off, something about his uncle being busy, not wanting to be disturbed. Way he said it, just seemed a bit strange that's all.'

'You carried on seeing him?'

'Maybe not as much. I had all this work, you know, college. Different assignments. I was busy, and he — most of the time, he didn't seem to be doing anything. Just hanging out. And then there was all that stuff with Lesley. Her friend, the one Petru was going with, Sasha, every time I'd see her it'd be, oh, why don't you get in touch with Lesley, send her a text, she's dying to see you, blah, blah, blah. I got sort of sick of it.'

Karen took a mouthful of coffee. No better nor worse than she'd expected.

'Petru, you say he spent a lot of time just hanging out?'

'Yes.'

'He didn't have a job, then? Wasn't studying, anything like that?'

'He'd applied. Some college, to do I'm not sure what. Computer stuff, maybe. IT. I don't even know if he got in or not. If he did get a place, he never took it up.'

'And a job? Presumably if you were going out places, he had cash in his pocket from somewhere?'

'I don't know. He helped out his uncle sometimes, that's all he ever said.'

'Doing what, d'you know?'

'No.' A quick shake of the head.

'There's a suggestion that he might have been dealing drugs.'

'Petru?'

'Yes.'

'No way.'

'You seem pretty positive.'

'Yes.'

'How can you be so sure?'

'He wouldn't even . . .' He hesitated.' If ever, you know, there was something going round, a smoke, a few pills, he'd always pass. Always.'

'That doesn't mean . . .'

'I know. But, no, Petru getting mixed up in something like that, I just can't see it. Really.'

He looked at his watch.

'I should be going.'

'Okay. Fine.' She pushed her half-full cup away. 'This uncle — Petru didn't mention a name? An address?'

'Afraid not. He never said anything much about himself at all. Except something once about missing his family, his mother especially. So I guess he wasn't living with them at least. I got the impression she was still back in Moldova.'

Karen nodded. So far any attempts to contact Petru Andronic's next of kin via the Moldovan Embassy in Dolphin Square had foundered amidst red tape and inertia. She would get one of the team to make a fresh attempt, diplomatically kick a few backsides.

Out on the street, Milescu following, she took two paces, then stopped. 'Apparently your father's been talking to my boss, my boss's boss. Whatever you've got yourself involved in, he seems a bit concerned about.'

'You serious?'

'Uh-huh.'

'He's crazy. I'm not involved in anything.'

I hope not, Karen thought. She slipped one of her cards into his hand. 'Anything you want to talk about, any time, just give me a call.'

18

The rest of the day passed, for Karen, in some sort of middle-management haze. Questions that were at best half-answered, leads that petered out into blind alleys, areas of inquiry that became abruptly stalled; the distant but familiar sound of heads being banged, relentlessly, against brick walls.

She stopped off at the supermarket on the way home and picked up a couple of ready-cooked meals and some discounted wine. Showered, she was just slipping the lamb kofta and rice into the microwave, a bottle of Shiraz already opened, when Ramsden called, his voice harsher than usual, more abrasive. The sound of a fist being rasped along raw brick.

Karen swore to herself as she listened; switched off the microwave.

'Be there, Mike, soon as I can.'

Hector Prince's body had been found jammed into the lift of a high-rise off Tottenham High Road, his left foot and ankle sticking out and preventing the door from closing, the lift marooned on the fourteenth floor. There were numerous stab wounds to his left side and down the backs of both legs, the cuts deep into the muscle of the thigh; his right shoulder blade had been shattered by a heavy blow from something like a baseball bat; something like the baseball bat that had crushed his cheekbone and splintered the cranial bone above the left eye.

He was still alive when the paramedics got to him, breathing but only just, his blood matted against the material of his cuffed fleece trackies and sticking against the already sticky lift floor.

One of the long-term tenants on the floor above, hearing the sounds of the assault, had dialled 999, and, watching from his balcony, seen the attackers flee. Now the lift and stairs were cordoned off, some officers already down on their knees searching for evidence, others beginning the thankless task of knocking on doors.

Karen stood in the courtyard, hands wrapped around a takeout coffee from a fast food place on the High Road, the coffee still retaining the smell of grease and burning fat.

Mike Ramsden ducked under the tape and made his way towards her.

'Half a dozen of them by the sound of it,' he said. 'Fronted Prince while he was in line waiting to get his bucket of chicken wings, chased him in here, caught up with him on the stairs. Whether he got into the lift himself, trying to get away, or they pushed him in there isn't clear. They did a runner when someone raised the alarm.'

'Witnesses?'

'One so far. Saw them legging it from way up. Black, or so he thinks. Hoodies. No surprises there.'

'Payback, then. For Derroll Palmer. That's what we're thinking?'

'Looks like. Once we'd brought Prince and he'd walked away, bragging about it, as far as Palmer's cohorts were concerned he was marked meat.'

109

'You think he knew that?'

'Kids like Prince — what did he call himself on the street? Mohock? — they take their life in their hands each time they step out the front door. Part of the charge, the buzz, that risk. Never knowing when you might get capped.'

'I thought Palmer wasn't gang related?'

'He was killed on gang turf, that's enough.'

'Wood Green, MOB gang, then? First port of call?'

'I'd reckon. Talk to someone at Trident tomorrow, see if I can't get them to throw us some names.'

Karen turned aside as a shiver ran through her. Not just the cold. The whole senseless, bloody business. Revenge, respect, tit for tat. Standing up to be counted. What was it just the other day? One youth stabbing another to death for calling him a pussy on Facebook.

Most times it didn't get to her, not like this, but now, suddenly, it did.

The waste.

Ramsden read it in her eyes. 'Go home,' he said.

'What?'

'You're here. You've showed. No call for you to stay.'

'Mike . . .'

Not roughly, he rested a hand on her arm. 'You look wasted, go home.'

'I can't.'

'One of the privileges of high rank. Delegation. Go on, get some sleep, I'll close up here. See you in the office first thing.'

She still didn't go, not for the best part of another hour, but then, when there really was nothing more she could do, she decided to take Ramsden at his word.

The kofta was cold; she took one bite and dumped the rest into the bin. The red wine tasted sour. She made herself a cup of weak tea instead, two sugars, and drank it while she got ready for bed. The book she'd been reading was on the floor, a scrap of paper marking her place; she picked it up and began to read.

Black Water Rising: Attica Locke.

Houston, Texas in the late sixties. Revolution in the air. Aretha Franklin singing Sam Cooke's 'A Change is Gonna Come'. Stokely Carmichael, about to throw in his lot with the Black Panthers, speaking at a student rally on the subject of Black Liberation, speaking to those few Negroes, armed with their passports – their university degrees – who had escaped into middle-class America. Integration was not the way. Integration meant accepting that your own culture, your own way of life was worth nothing, not worth hanging on to.

Karen could remember, as a young woman, dancing to that slice of seminal James Brown in a way that would have made her poor aunt feel shamed, shaking her hips, hands in the air, singing it loud, how she was black and proud.

Those young people, young men from Tottenham and Wood Green; those like Hector Prince who were ganged up, others like Derroll Palmer, caught between – no danger of them joining the white middle class, getting university degrees. Their choice, she wondered, or somebody else's? And if so, whose?

Kids like that, Ramsden had said, they take their lives in their hands each time they step out the front door.

And here she was, a black woman who, as one of her sisters had informed her when she was still out patrolling the streets, was wearing the white man's uniform, enforcing his laws. No answer from Karen, other than to move on, the sister had spat in her face.

Some days, years later, she still reached up a hand to wipe it away.

Only when she could feel her eyes failing did she set the book aside and switch out the light.

19

Carla James had been in Karen's year at secondary school, a bit of a star even then; the lead in the school production of *The Wiz*, her picture all over the local paper, Acton's own Diana Ross. In the sixth form she had hung out with the guys who were forever putting together some band or other, rumours of recording contracts that never quite came off, Carla laying down vocals that somehow got lost in the final mix. Her boyfriend then was an athlete on the fringes of the national team, a sprinter; thigh muscles, Carla told them all proudly, like you wouldn't believe.

Karen would go with her sometimes, evenings, down to the track to watch him train: stretches, drills, strides; sweat dripping off him beneath the lights, making his body shine.

Honey to the bee.

A levels over, Carla applied to drama school and failed to get in; she got a job in a bar instead, sang back-up for a band that did Motown covers in places like Basingstoke and Stevenage, and took classes, part-time, at the Poor School near King's Cross – movement and voice, dialect, singing, stage fighting, Shakespeare and contemporary text. At the end of the year, she reapplied and was accepted. All of that more years ago than she cared to remember.

There were still periods when she signed on or worked in bars; in between there was the odd show in Manchester or Liverpool; twelve weeks understudying an all-black production of *Cat on a Hot Tin Roof* in the West End; bits and pieces of telly — *Wire in the Blood*, *Silent Witness*, *The Bill* — usually, as she put it, standing around on street corners with my skirt up my arse looking for business, waiting for someone to smack me upside the head with a hammer.

Right now she was at the National, Jacobean tragedy, twenty-three performances at the Cottesloe, then out on tour. Carla playing five different roles and loving it.

They met at a place near the theatre, loud music, Mexican food and cocktails, Carla's voice rising above everything: 'Karen! Girlfriend! Over here.' Carla with brightly beaded hair extensions, cleavage to die for, colours that clashed as deliriously as something in a Matisse painting.

After a hug and a kiss and a perfunctory, 'So, how's it all going?', Carla set off, as Karen knew and hoped she would, on a rousing and ribald account of the previous few months of her life that drew applause and laughter from listeners at the surrounding tables.

After a day of no progress whatsoever, other than Hector Prince's mother, between convulsions of grief and angry tears, identifying her son in the sterile cold of the morgue, Karen hadn't wanted to spend the evening alone.

'Don't turn round now,' she said, as the waiter delivered a fresh pair of mojitos, 'but that guy over by the back wall, is he looking at us?'

Carla leaned over and fiddled with the strap of her shoe. 'Black turtleneck, short hair, that the one?'

Karen nodded.

'I should hope so.'

'No, really. I'm serious.'

'What? You fancy him? Doesn't look like your type.'

'No, it's not . . .'

''Cause I can go over, make an introduction . . .'

'No.' She grabbed hold of Carla's arm. 'No, it's fine. Just jumpy, that's all.'

'Okay, okay.'

The next time Karen looked, the man had gone.

'Bad day, huh?'

'Bad couple of days.'

'Want to talk about it?'

Karen shook her head.

They went to a club across the river, just a nightcap, vodka tonics. When someone stumbled over his feet asking her to dance, Carla just laughed. 'I ought to be heading home,' she said, glancing at her watch. 'Matinee tomorrow.'

They stood on the Embankment, looking out over the river, the slow trail of lights down towards St Paul's.

Carla lit a cigarette.

'Let me have one.'

'I thought you'd given up.'

'I did.'

Something caught Karen's eye up on the bridge. The flash of a camera. Tourists capturing the city, the Thames at night.

'If it was ever really getting to you,' Carla said, 'you know, really doing your head in, you'd chuck it all in, right? Step away.'

'Yeah. Yeah, of course.'

Even as she said it, she wondered if it were true. It was her life, after all. What else could she do? And besides – *Make somethin' of yourself*, her father had said. *Make a difference if you can.* She owed it to him to keep trying.

*

Five minutes later, she and Carla were in the Underground, different destinations, separate trains. A five-minute walk for Karen from Highbury and Islington, five or six, soft echo of her footsteps along the pavement. Someone, somewhere playing Al Green's 'Belle', a song she'd always loved; an upstairs window left open, volume just high enough to tempt her into singing along. The living-room light was on as she'd left it, muted through closed curtains. Key in her hand, she looked up and down the empty street.

Inside, she slipped the bolt and turned the key. Switched on the TV and listened to the canned laughter from some rerun comedy as she moved around the flat, taking off her clothes. The man in the Mexican place earlier, standing up against the wall, bottle of Dos Equis in his hand; she knew him, someone like him. The way he had looked at her. As if he were in the job. God! What was this? Burcher on her tail from nowhere, checking up on her, asking questions. Ion Milescu's father expressing concern, friends in high places, and now she was getting paranoid.

Ridiculous.

She clicked off the light.

The man in the restaurant: off duty or on?

The bedroom struck cold. Curling into position on her side, knees drawn up, one hand close to her face, she was asleep before realising she'd closed her eyes. Flat out.

And still she dreamed.

20

Come all this way, Kiley had said, with reference to the bookshop Letitia's father ran in Hastings, shame not to check it out. Besides, it was too long, Cordon thought, though little time enough, since he had seen the sea. The smell, catching the air from as far back as the railway station, drawing him down.

He made his way past the chippies and the pizza parlours and the petty amusement arcades, on past the signs advertising Smugglers Adventure and Underwater World to where the fishing boats, bright reds and blues and greens, sat propped on a slope of pebbles beneath the East Cliff; net houses, narrow and all-over black, stood tall, shielding them from the road.

Cordon walked between the boats, sniffing the air, listening to the squawk and call of gulls, relishing the roll of small stones beneath his feet. Letitia might even like it here, he thought, the south coast, remind her of some of the things – few enough – she missed about home. A touch closer to Penzance than Finsbury Park.

He sat.

Letitia's face came clear to his mind. Not that last time, the last time so far, herself and Maxine dolled up to the nines, a night out on what passed for the town. This was Letitia at sixteen, just old enough, as she had put it, to be legal; Letitia the night she had let herself into the flat with the key she used when she came to walk the dog; let herself into the flat and into his bed, and Cordon, caught between fantasy and dream and recognising, just in time, the warmth and reality of bones and flesh, had pushed her out, and, stumbling to the bathroom, hand across his all-too-humanly tumescent cock, had splashed cold water in his face, and when he looked up, had seen Letitia's face behind him in the mirror, half-mocking, half-exposed from the pain of being rejected, cast aside.

After that, between Letitia and himself, it had never been the same. And still there were times, when, unbidden, the memory returned, caught him off guard, riven between desire and shame.

He lifted a stone and weighed it in his hand before skimming it out to sea. One bounce, two, and he had turned away before it had sunk from sight.

Back beside the main road, he crossed against the traffic and headed for the centre of the old town.

The shop was tucked away between a web of narrow streets, the sign over the door in faded purple paint, *Clifford Carlin, Bookseller. Antiquarian and Second-Hand.* A couple of boxes stood partly blocking the entrance – *Any Book 10p.* Inside, books rose, floor to ceiling, up every wall; tall shelves of paperbacks, arranged by type, jutted out, maze-like, across the floor.

Taking his bearings, Cordon paused before a large selection of Westerns: *Jubal Cade, Herne the Hunter, Apache, Edge.* Who was that writer his father had liked to read? Louis L'Amour? They were here in their dozens. And there was somebody else, he was sure. Oakley someone, was that possible? Oakley Hall?

In the far corner, near the window, there was a children's

section with a little plastic table and chairs, crayons in old coffee tins, scraps of paper on which to draw, copies of old *Beano* annuals fanned out, one above the other. A pair of Goths was looking at the section labelled Alternative Medicine & Psychotherapy; an earnest young man, head angled awkwardly sideways, was browsing through Science Fiction & Fantasy.

Music played from a battered beat box perched precariously atop a tower of encyclopedias. Twangy guitar, slapped bass, flailing vocals – rockabilly? Is that what this was? Cordon glanced at the red cover of the CD as he stepped past. Charlie Feathers. He was none the wiser.

Carlin – he presumed it was Carlin – was talking to a customer weighed down with plastic bags that seemed to contain all his worldly goods. Long hair pulled back off his face and tied in a pony tail, goatee beard, Carlin was wearing a faded T-shirt from the Rolling Stones tour of '76. Late fifties he'd be, Cordon hazarded, early sixties. Ten years, or thereabouts, older than he was himself.

The customer demanding all of the proprietor's attention, Cordon looked again at the Western shelves, and there was Oakley Hall, but out of sequence. Not *Warlock* – he remembered the title now – that was the one his father had read, not once but several times; there had even, Cordon thought, been a movie. This was a tall paperback, close on three hundred pages: *Separations*. A painting on the cover of a deep canyon, sheer cliffs leading to slate blue water.

He turned to the beginning and read the first sentence.

When Mary Temple read in the Alta California *that a white woman had been reported seen in an Indian village in Arizona Territory, she knew it was her sister.*

So many stories, Cordon thought, fact or fiction, began with someone looking for someone else. Searching. He closed the book and carried it with him to the desk, the man with the carrier bags just leaving.

'Two-fifty?' Cordon queried.

'If that's what it says.'

'Most of the others are less.'

'That's 'cause most of the others aren't so good.' Something sparkled, some fragment of gold, inside Carlin's mouth when he smiled.

Cordon passed across a five-pound note and kept his hand out for the change.

'Your daughter,' he said.

'What?'

'Your daughter.'

'Who says I have a daughter?'

'Rose. Letitia.'

Coins spilled through Carlin's fingers. 'You're what? Police?'

'More a friend.'

'Of Letitia's?'

Cordon nodded. 'Down to you, that. The name. Or so she said.'

'Suited her. Back then especially.'

'Joy and happiness.'

'That's what it means.' He shook his head. 'Never liked Rose. Her mum's choice, not mine.'

He broke off long enough to sell one of the Goths a book on Ancient and Medieval Necromancy.

'You heard about her mother?' Cordon asked. 'About Maxine?'

Carlin nodded.

'The reason she was in London,' Cordon said, 'as far as I can make out, she was looking for Letitia.'

'Meant to come here, wasn't she? Right after New Year. Called to say she was getting on the train. Last I heard of her. Till a couple of days back. Got a postcard. Here – I've got it somewhere.' He started to rummage through one of the desk drawers. 'Lake District somewhere. Here you are. Keswick.'

Cordon looked at a picture of artificially coloured lakes and mountains; spidery writing, kisses, a name.

'Working in a hotel, that's what she says.'

'Why there?'

'Why not? Law to herself, Letitia. Don't seek to reason.'

'You're not worried then?'

'No. I mean, I was, a bit anyway. But now I've heard . . .' He gestured with his hands. 'With her, that's the way it is. Since she was knee high to a grasshopper it's been the same. Mind of her own. Wouldn't bend. Break, maybe, but not bend. And since she got of an age, no stopping her. Here today, gone tomorrow.' A hasty smile. 'Mostly the latter.'

He looked at the book in Cordon's hand.

'You want a bag for that or . . .'

'No, thanks, you're fine.'

'Down for the day, is it?'

'Something like that.'

'Letitia phones – not as that's likely – but if she does, who shall I say it was asking?'

Cordon fished out one of his cards and placed it on the desk.

'Police, then. I was right.'

Cordon shrugged.

'Police and a long way from home.'

Maybe too long, Cordon thought.

'Enjoy the book,' Carlin said.

'Do my best.'

Charlie Feathers was still doing his thing as Cordon walked to the door, just hitting the closing chorus of 'We're Getting Closer to Being Apart'.

21

In the short space of time Cordon had been in the bookshop, the weather had changed: a cold wind buffeting along the narrow street, the first thrusts of rain. There was a pub a short way down on the opposite side, an exterior of blackened wood and brick. Cordon bought a pint of Timothy Taylor's Landlord and took it across to a corner table, prepared to wait it out, the bookshop entrance just visible through a smear of glass. Two sups and he cracked open his book, the search for the sister, the missing girl. He was at chapter six, 'Eureka' – a journey downriver, shooting the rapids – when Carlin emerged and carried the boxes of sale books back inside; then, duffle bag on his shoulder, drab green waterproof still unzipped, he padlocked the door and turned away towards the interior of the town. Cordon swallowed the last mouthful of his lingering pint, used a beer mat to mark his place, and, book in hand, set out after him.

As the street broadened into a T-junction, he quickened his pace, crossing into a narrow ginnel between housebacks, then climbing a tall flight of stone steps that changed direction midway, following the line of the cliff.

Below, he could see the patchwork of boats stretched out across the stones below, the beach where he had sat earlier, staring at the sea. The rain less insistent now, little more than mist.

Gulls wheeling above his head, riding the wind – for a moment he could have been back in Newlyn – he continued to climb until the top of the steps was reached and the land levelled out, a crown of bushes ahead and a well-worn track posted to Hastings Country Park and the Saxon Shore Way. For a moment he thought Carlin had slipped from sight, but there he was, hood up, following a grass path away to the left; less hurried now, slowed perhaps by the climb, the realisation he was nearly home.

The path dropped down towards the rear gardens of some thirties houses, conservatories stuck to their backsides like carbuncles; a narrow ginnel leading out on to a quiet street, a crescent, the fading toll of an ice-cream van the only clear sound.

Cordon waited to see where Carlin was headed; watched as, at the gate to number seventeen, he fumbled out his keys. Dark curtains were partly drawn across the windows of the downstairs bay. In the garden, a gnome, three foot high, wore a black beret at a rakish angle on its head, dark glasses covering half its face, a Ban the Bomb symbol painted in psychedelic colours on its chest. A few desultory snowdrops gathered in a cluster beside the gravelled path.

Cordon waited until the front door had opened and closed.

The gate squeaked a little at his touch.

No bell, he knocked.

Carlin opened up with a flourish, prepared to repel some unwanted vendor of overpriced homeware or charity beggar lobbying on behalf of a home for blind donkeys.

The sight of Cordon knocked him back, but not for long.

'Decided to catch a later train?'

'Something like that.'

'It's not about the book? Changed your mind? Because if it is, we open again tomorrow at ten. Fifty per cent of the cover price if you return it within six days. Twenty-five thereafter.'

'It's not the book.'

Carlin nodded, gave a little tug at his wisp of beard. 'She's not here, you know.'

'So you say.'

Carlin held his gaze, then stepped back inside, leaving the door wide open. Cordon followed him, clicking it closed at his back.

There were posters from various rock concerts framed on the walls; photographs of singers and musicians Cordon mostly failed to recognise. In a gilt frame above the empty fireplace was a self-portrait of Peter Blake holding a copy of *Elvis Monthly*. Not the original.

Books were everywhere: in piles on the floor, haphazard on the table, wedged along the window ledges, seated on chairs. A collection of poems by Frank O'Hara, the cover a mass of sharply angled reds and blues; *Beats, Bohemians and Intellectuals* by Jim Burns. A ginger cat with a large head and a bushy tail sniffed at Cordon disinterestedly and padded away.

'Tea or coffee?'

'Either. Whichever's easiest.'

It turned out to be tea. Wagon Wheels in the kind of wooden biscuit barrel he remembered from his gran's sideboard.

'Didn't know you could get these any more,' Cordon said, helping himself.

'Relaunched in 2002. Any smaller, mind, they'd bloody disappear.'

It was true: two bites and gone.

'You can search the place if you like,' Carlin said. 'For Letitia. If you don't believe me.'

Cordon said nothing; waited. Drank some tea.

'After her mum and I split up,' Carlin said eventually, 'I didn't really see her for years. Oh, at first I tried, you know, going back down – I was in Bristol then, working in this music shop, guitars mostly. But Maxine was out of her head half the time and there were always other blokes around. We were still married, officially anyway, not that it mattered to her, not one bloody scrap. Then, when she had the first of the boys, and moved in with his dad, some druggy living in a squat in Penzance, things turned nasty and I kept away. Wasn't as if Rose – that's what she was then, Rose – wasn't as if she paid much heed if I was around or not. Least, that was how it seemed.'

He looked at Cordon for some sign of understanding. Men together, something of the kind.

'Didn't see her for years after that. Not from when she was four or five up till she was near thirteen. I was in Brighton, then. My first little shop. Down the Lanes.'

He lifted his cup, but didn't drink.

'Run away from home, hadn't she? Got my address from some card or other, birthday, something of the sort. Stayed for a couple of days till I put her on the bus back home. Turned up regular after that – not often, but regular. Every eighteen month or so, couple of years. Whenever things got too rough at home, out of hand. Whenever she reckoned as how she couldn't cope. Letitia, by now. Using God knows what. Track marks on her arms. Did what I could to talk her out of it, but it weren't no good. Small miracle she saw twenty-one, but she did.'

He drank his tea then; sat back and crossed his legs at the ankles, searching Cordon's face. 'What kind of a friend exactly? You never said.'

'We crossed paths a few times.'

What was he going to say? She used to walk my dog?

'Line of duty?'

124

'Sometimes.'

'This, though, not official?'

'Not official.'

'Personal, then?'

'Her mum . . .'

'Maxine.'

'Maxine asked me, see if I could find her. After she never showed here. She was worried.'

'About Letitia?'

'Yes.'

'Not before time.'

Cordon spread his hands, palms up.

'And now that you've not found her?'

'The card. The Lakes. Seems as if she's probably okay.'

'I didn't fake it, you know.'

'The old postcard trick.'

'Here, I'll show you. Take a look at the postmark.'

'I did.'

'Still you came round here.'

'Mistrustful bastards, police. Case of having to be. Goes with the job.'

Carlin gestured towards the door. 'Sure you don't want to look around? In case I've got her stashed away upstairs after all?'

'It's okay.' Cordon set down his cup, got to his feet. 'Curiosity satisfied. But if you do hear from her, you will let me know? Ask her to call me, at least.'

'Okay, no problem.'

'Maybe I'll see you at the funeral?'

'Maxine's?'

'There'll be an inquest, of course. Bound to be. But the way everything's pointing, accidental death, straightforward enough. Shouldn't be long before the body's released for burial.'

'I'm not sure,' Carlin said. 'Maxine and I, we said our goodbyes a long time back.'

'Fair enough.' Cordon moved towards the door. 'Thanks for the tea.'

On the walk back into town he ran over what Carlin had told him, what he'd learned. The date Wagon Wheels were reintroduced aside, maybe not a great deal. He'd pass on the details of Maxine's funeral to Carlin just in case, time and place. They might even find their way on to Letitia, now they were sort of back in touch.

The next London train was due in thirty minutes and he bought a newspaper to while away the time. More troops promised for Afghanistan. Failing bank to pay New Year bonuses in excess of fifteen million after all. Four-year study shows that children of families with only one parent living at home are less likely to go on to university. How many hours, how many thousands, Cordon wondered, did it take for them to come up with that?

He found a window seat on the train without difficulty, leaned back and opened his book but failed to read more than a few lines. No fault of the author's. Letitia happily working at a hotel in the Lake District, welcoming guests, supervising, perhaps, the change of bedlinen, the servicing of rooms, arranging taxis to the station, excursions to Beatrix Potter's house or William Wordsworth's grave – what was wrong with that picture?

22

Paul. Paul Milescu. Were it not for Google, Karen would never have known that Paul was the fourth most popular male name in all of Moldova. How had Clare Milescu put it, harking back to the time she spent in the country working for the UN? A directive urging them to engage with members of the government, one she'd taken all too literally. Paul Milescu had been something important in the Ministry of Justice and, despite being married, he had become popular with her, too.

Now they were separated, going their different ways. Clare still fighting the good fight, following her conscience, working with refugees, while Paul, once in London, had used the connections he'd built up and gone into business. Nothing wrong with that. Except now it seemed he'd tried using those connections to bring pressure to bear on Karen's investigation; pressure enough to get a detective chief superintendent out trawling the streets of north London at night like something out of Len Deighton or John le Carré.

Explicable enough, in a way; commendable, even – a father's natural instincts, offering protection to his son, wanting to keep him from trouble. Or was it more? A pre-emptive move to keep the police at arm's length from himself, his family, his business?

What was his business?

Here Google didn't really help. Import/export, that and not a great deal more. Importing and exporting what? No details, certainly. Maybe, like Terry Martin, it was sportswear, women's clothing. And possibly Martin was right, Karen thought, it was all we did in this country any more, import stuff made cheaply elsewhere now that we made hardly anything ourselves – and what we did seemed to be owned by someone else. The Americans, despite their fading economy, had controlling shares in everything from chocolate to Liverpool Football Club; the Russians had a football club of their own and half the expensive properties in London, while just about everything else was being snapped up by the Chinese.

She looked again at the paucity of information on the screen.

A PO box address, phone number, fax, email. Perhaps she should simply pick up the phone, dial the number, ask him outright?

Hey, Paul . . .

Then again, perhaps not.

She had a friend, Tom Brewer, in the Intelligence Unit of Economic and Specialist Crime – sort of a friend, they'd met on a Home Office course a few years before, shared a few drinks, he'd asked her out, she'd said yes and then said no – she'd give him a bell. No favours to call in, just a hint of what might have been. Brewer newly married she'd heard, two stepsons and a semi-detached in Child's Hill.

She left a message, didn't have to wait too long for him to respond.

'Karen, long time no see.'

'A small favour, Tom, that's all.'

He rang back in a couple of hours. 'Milescu, everything

pretty much above board as far as I can see. Connections with a couple of firms exporting bauxite and aluminium; partners in Russia and Romania. Some export trade seems to be tied up somehow with Italy; exactly how isn't too clear. Then there's a quite profitable import business in chemicals linked to the Ukraine.'

'Nothing chancy?'

'Not that you could lay a finger on. Ever since the country joined the World Bank in '92, trade has blossomed – from a very low base admittedly – and Milescu's just ridden the wave along with it. The fact that he's clearly got connections close to the heart of government probably hasn't done him any harm. Contracts put out to tender, he's going to be near the head of the queue more often than not.'

'But nothing illegal?'

Brewer laughed. 'Down to your definition of illegal. But in a way that might be of interest to us, officially, I'd say no, pass.'

'Thanks, Tom.'

'Maybe we could meet up for a drink some time? It's been a while.'

'Sure, I'd like that. You could bring your wedding photos for me to have a look at.'

He laughed and called her something not very nice.

The next time her mobile went it was Carla, who'd texted her twice already: Ronny Jordan at the Jazz Café, she had to be there.

'Carla, I can't.'

'Come on, girl. That guitar. "After Hours". That sound. Sex on six strings.'

'You know what? I'd love to, but—'

'But nothing. No excuses, come on, I'll see you there. Ten thirty, eleven, that's when it kicks off. Okay?'

'I don't know, Carla, I'll see. Maybe. But no promises, right?'

Ten thirty, eleven: by then, most nights Karen reckoned to be tucked up in bed with a glass of red and a good book.

She glanced at her own reflection in the darkening window. She didn't believe she'd just told herself that, but she had. Girl, as Carla would say, you're getting old. Old before your time. She should make the effort to get down there after all: race home, get changed into something suitably funky and cab it to Camden.

Ronny Jordan: 'The Jackal'; 'A Brighter Day'.

Tempting as it was, she knew she'd do no such thing.

Carla was standing in line, the crowd thickening around her; stop-start of traffic at the lights, exhaust fumes dispersing pale grey into the night air. If the temperature dropped much more it would be freezing hard by the time they emerged the far side of midnight.

She hunched up the collar of her padded coat and shuffled a few short paces forward, even though they were not really moving, the queue simply becoming more compressed. Someone's elbow poked into her back and she turned, the man's face an apologetic leer.

'Sorry, darlin'.'

Sorry, darlin', who spoke like that any more? Outside of *EastEnders*, that is? The East End itself, mostly Bangladeshi now as far as she could tell, other than a few smart young Metropolitans busily rebranding it with artists' studios and architect-designed apartments.

'Seen him before, have you? Ronny? Fuckin' brilliant.'

His nose pushed, like a chisel, down from the centre of his face, his teeth, when he smiled, were large and yellow – horse's teeth.

With a quick, dismissive shake of the head, Carla edged forward. This guy was actually hitting on her. Unbelievable!

Unable to move farther, she squeezed herself towards the wall.

130

As well she did.

In retrospect, she heard the car approaching fast, faster than was safe; the sudden braking, shouts and screams from those positioned near the kerb, and then the shot. A single gunshot. Loud. Close. No backfire. Little doubt what it was.

Someone cannoned against her from behind and, as she turned, stumbling, something splashed, warm, stickily wet, across her face, and the man with the chisel face was suddenly in her arms. Close up, hissing through yellow teeth, before, heavy, he fell away, and Carla, stooping, aware – amidst the shouting, the panic – of three more shots, one echoing into another and then the squeal of brakes, a car door slamming, the engine accelerating fast away.

There was a long moment in which nobody seemed to speak or move, and the dead man – she supposed he was dead – lay at her feet, one arm stretched out, fingers bent back by the wall, as if trying to tunnel to safety.

The side of his head no longer seemed to be there.

Carla shook. Shuddered. Jumped when a hand gently touched her arm.

'You're hurt,' the young woman said, pointing. 'Your face. It's bleeding.'

Carla blinked the blood away from her eyes and brought her fingers gingerly to her cheek. She could hear the sirens, police and ambulance, drawing closer. Knew she should use her mobile, contact Karen: as soon as she stopped shaking, she would.

23

By the time Karen arrived the street was cordoned off from below the crossroads north to the junction with Arlington Road. Uniformed officers, yellow tape, police vehicles in abundance.

The lights over the Jazz Café still stood out brightly, but the blue shades had been pulled down low across the windows and the interior was dark. People stood around in twos and threes outside the immediate cordon, stunned, too stunned to go home; talking in an abstracted, desultory way, some of them, to officers with notebooks at the ready. Ronny Jordan had departed long since, the short journey from dressing room to limo, from limo to his hotel.

Karen knew the senior officer on the scene, a detective inspector from Albany Street who'd been pulling a late shift when he'd taken the call. Blue-black raincoat, thinning hair, heavily lidded eyes; hands in pockets, his voice gravelly from too many cigarettes, too little rest.

'It's a bastard,' the DI said.

Two dead, one at the scene, a single bullet to the head; the other, gunned down as he ran, had been shot three times, twice in the chest, once in the neck. He had bled out in the ambulance on the way to the hospital. DOA.

'A real bastard.'

Karen agreed.

She found Carla sitting in a huddle of clothes in the entrance to the Odeon cinema opposite, leaning back against the wall. One of the attendants had fetched her a cup of sweet tea and tissues to wipe the blood from her face. It still clung here and there to her skin, tendrils of her hair.

The moment Karen approached, she burst into tears.

Karen squeezed her shoulders, gripped both hands hard.

'I told you, didn't I?' Carla said, forcing out a smile. 'I told you you'd be missing something.'

Karen squatted down beside her. 'You okay?'

'What's it look like?'

'You weren't hit?'

'Just frightened out my fucking wits.'

'And you didn't see . . . ?'

'I didn't see anything. Just this guy, the one, you know . . .'

Carla clenched her eyes closed and he was still falling towards her, only slowly now, slowly as if through water, and she was reaching out to catch him, because, automatically, it's what you do, and, just for a moment, he was there in her arms, safe, then gone.

'Just the guy who got shot,' she said, recovering. 'Nothing else. Not the . . . the shooter. Is that what you call him? The shooter? Too many of those cop shows, you learn the language, the lingo.'

'The gunman, maybe,' Karen said. 'It doesn't matter.'

'Either way, I didn't see him. Not really. Just someone ducking away, back towards the car.'

Karen nodded. Knew she didn't need to ask Carla about the car itself, there'd be descriptions of that by the dozen, too many, too many of them conflicting. The gunman, the same. The man behind the wheel. Too many witnesses as against too few.

'I'll organise a driver,' Karen said. 'Get you home. Sometime tomorrow, you'll need to come in, make a statement.'

'No. Let me wait here for you. I don't think I can face going home on my own.'

'Here, then.' Karen reached into her bag and took out her keys. 'Take these. Go back to my place, wait for me there. I'll have someone run you over. Get out of those clothes, shower, get some sleep. I'll get back as soon as I can.'

'You're sure?'

'Sure. There's a spare set of keys at the office, I'll pick them up on the way.'

Karen bent quickly and kissed the top of her head.

'See you later.'

It was close to four in the morning by the time Karen finally got back to her flat, later than she'd intended. Carla was curled up in her bed, wearing an old pair of borrowed pyjamas and snoring lightly. Karen tiptoed back out of the bedroom and into the kitchen. Hot chocolate. Toast and jam. The initial work at the scene complete, the local DI had been only too pleased to pass the investigation along to Karen and her team – Homicide, that's you, after all. More aggravation than he needed. On the settee, Karen made the mistake of closing her eyes and was asleep within moments.

She woke less than an hour later; threw the uneaten toast into the bin, poured cold chocolate down the sink and swilled out the mug; swallowed down two Ibuprofen with water; swiftly showered; changed. She thought twice about waking Carla, who was still sleeping, out to the world, and finally decided against it. Left her a note instead. Later in the day, she'd seize a minute, phone or text, arrange for her to come in and make a statement, make sure she was okay.

Less than an hour later, she and Mike Ramsden were in her office, going over what they knew, what they needed to know, what needed to be done.

The vehicle used, most witnesses seemed to agree, was a black BMW X5, the registration less certain, save an agreement on the numbers 233. CCTV was being monitored, a selection of possible registrations had been sent to DVLA in Swansea; high-end hire-car firms were already being checked.

The individual responsible for the deaths of both men – the gunman, the shooter – had been variously described as shortish, tall, of medium height, slim and stockily built. Dark haired, save for one witness who had him wearing a beret and another who swore blind he was bald, and dark skinned. You mean black? No, not black. Asian. Not Asian? Middle Eastern, then? No, not that either. Swarthy, that was the word. Dark skinned, like I said before. White, but dark skinned. European.

The man shot dead on the pavement alongside Carla had been identified from the contents of his wallet as Aaron Johnson. The second victim had no ID on him whatsoever: no credit cards or driving licence, no mobile phone – all of that suspicious in itself.

Aaron Johnson, forty-three years old, an address in Lewisham: one of the half-dozen or so names Tim Costello had come up with when he was checking out Terry Martin's associates.

Killed with a single shot to the head.

A gang hit, had to be.

Yet, according to his record, Johnson had served only a couple of brief spells inside, neither more than eighteen months, petty thieving, robbery; one charge of unlawful wounding had been shunted aside before it came to court, another of aggravated burglary was dropped when both witnesses suffered a convenient amnesia. Nothing that suggested heavy gang involvement, the kind of retribution that had been meted out here.

Perhaps, Karen thought, he was stepping up. Out of his league.

She called Gerry Stine, the Intelligence Support officer who'd proved so useful in helping identify Petru Andronic's body at the beginning of the year. After listening for several minutes, Stine cut across what Karen was saying. 'Afraid you're priming the wrong man. Little off my field of expertise. But if you want a better suggestion, I can field a few names.'

The one Karen lighted on first was Warren Cormack, a DCI within the Project Team of Serious and Organised Crime Command, SCD7, which dealt, according to the rubric, with multi-dimensional crime groups, ethnically composed gangs and proactive contracts to kill. She'd heard one or two good things about him in the past; now was the time to see if they were true.

His office phone directed her to his mobile, which instructed her to leave a message, the voice just this side of brusque. Give him a couple of hours, Karen thought, then move down to the next name on the list.

Less than an hour later, Cormack called her back. He'd heard about the Camden shooting; thinking it almost certainly gang related he had started making a few preliminary inquiries himself.

'Still no ID on the second hit?' he asked.

'Not so far.'

'Description?'

'Caucasian male, aged between thirty and thirty-five, medium height, dark hair, blue-grey eyes. That's about all.'

'No identifying marks? Scars? Tattoos?'

'Not a one.'

'Dental records?'

'Nothing so far.'

'Innocent bystander.'

'Could be.'

'Lived a clear and blameless life.'

'Why run?'

'Wouldn't you?'

She could hear faint traffic sounds, as if Cormack were standing near an open window. Run? Yes, she'd run. Run, duck, hide. But would the gunman risk identification and possible capture if his prime target was already down?

'Tell you what,' Cormack said, 'send across some pictures, head and shoulders, full face, profile, you know the kind of thing. I'll get them fed into the system, see what emerges.'

'How long?'

'Check that through? Might strike lucky. This time tomorrow? Don't come up with anything by then, I'm probably not going to be able to help.'

'Thanks, anyway,' Karen said. But he'd already rung off.

24

Twenty-four hours. Warren Cormack was as good as his word. They met, at his suggestion, in Victoria Tower Gardens, just beyond the Houses of Parliament and overlooking the Thames. Tide out, gulls scavenged along a narrow strand of muddy bank strewn with discarded rubbish. New Scotland Yard was no more than a brisk stroll away, pleasant enough beneath a wash of wispy cloud, a patina of palish blue.

Cormack proved to be younger than he'd sounded on the phone, younger than she'd anticipated, less abrupt. Slim features, neatly suited, off-white shirt, pearl grey tie, still the right side of thirty-five.

'This okay by you?' He gestured towards a bench facing out towards the river, Lambeth Palace and St Thomas' Hospital on the opposite bank.

'Fine.'

'Not usually too many people around.'

'Bolt-hole, then?'

'Something like that.'

Sitting, he loosened his tie just a little; one arm, crooked, along the back of the bench. Making her wait. One of a brace of ragged crows hopped hopefully close, then hopped away.

'Jamie Parsons,' Cormack said, finally. 'The pictures you sent over. A definite match.'

'He's known?'

'Only tangentially. That's why he wouldn't have shown up on your radar. Bottom-feeder stuff, really. Does a lot of footwork for a guy called Gordon Dooley, who we certainly do have an interest in.'

'Dooley?'

'A dealer, fairly big-time, contacts all along the south coast, Margate, Brighton, Portsmouth, Southampton. Main source of supply was through the Netherlands, Rotterdam, but since Border Agency and Customs seem to have succeeded in stemming that particular flow, for now at least, he's been having to look elsewhere.

'There's no definite proof, but we think he's behind a spate of raids on cannabis farms across the south-east. Most recent was in Essex, the outbuildings of a disused farm close to Manningtree; before that, a deconsecrated chapel just outside Great Yarmouth. Just those two raids, upwards of two thousand plants stolen, that's going to yield around fifty metric tons of cannabis for illegal sale.'

'And these farms, who's behind them?'

'Difficult to say. Precisely. The workers at both premises were mainly Chinese, illegally trafficked into the country, very little English. They'd been badly beaten, some of them, during the raids, tied up with baling wire. Terrified out of their wits. They're not going to give us a great deal, even if they wanted to. But most of that trade – what isn't still in the hands of Dooley and his ilk – it's the province of organised gangs originating in Eastern Europe. Turkey. Albania.'

A pleasure boat went past them downriver, heading towards

Tower Bridge and beyond that to the Thames Barrier, hardy souls on deck wrapped in scarves and fleeces, the voice of the tour guide torn by the breeze.

'Dooley,' Karen said, 'if he is involved, presumably he's not going to be carrying out these raids single-handed.'

Cormack shook his head. 'South London, that's his stamping ground. Home patch. Recruiting, that's where he'd look. No shortage of possibles, keen for a ruck. Especially if there's a good chunk of cash at the end of it. A couple of known associates with more than a propensity for violence. A few hangers-on.'

'Parsons being one.'

'Parsons being one.'

'And Aaron Johnson another.'

'Maybe. A reasonable assumption. But we don't know for sure. As it stands, nothing to say they knew one another before Camden. Not much to link them together aside from a liking for Ronny Jordan.'

'How about Terry Martin?'

'You looking for a connection?'

'Maybe.'

'Any special reason?'

She told him about Petru Andronic's murder, her suspicions that Martin might have been involved.

'Well, it's a name we know, more through the company he keeps than anything else.'

'Company?'

Cormack smiled, shifted his position on the bench. 'How about this? One of Dooley's hard men got out of the Scrubs just a month before the raid in Manningtree. Went inside for going after some guy Dooley reckoned had been holding back on his payments; left him with a ruptured spleen and more broken ribs than you could easily count.'

'Let me guess, Carter.'

140

'Mad Mike himself.'

'The link, you think, between Martin and Dooley?'

'One of them, I'd say.'

'So how involved in all of Dooley's dirty work do you think Martin might be?'

'Difficult to say. Anywhere between not at all and very. As muscle, maybe. More than that . . . ?' He shrugged his shoulders, dipped his head.

'He's not dealing himself, I suppose?'

'Not as far as we know. There was a suggestion a while back that he might have been smuggling in drugs along with his shipments from the Baltic. Couple of containers were opened and searched – nothing but plastic wraps of cheap clothing on their way to small-scale shops and market stalls up and down the country.'

Karen sat back, starting to run the possibilities, the variables, through her mind. 'How do you want to play this?' she asked.

'You run with your investigation, let your team know as much as you think they need. We'll keep up our surveillance on Dooley, maybe widen it to take in a couple of the others. Anything important starts to show, I'll put you in the frame.'

'Likewise.'

'Okay, good.' He got to his feet and Karen followed. A scattering of scruffy pigeons made as if to take flight but their hearts weren't in it.

Karen thanked him, meaning every word, shook hands, and set off towards Westminster Tube station. The protesters she understood to have been moved on from Parliament Square still seemed to be present in quite large numbers. No tents any more, no one sleeping rough, but banners a-plenty. *Capitalism STILL isn't Working. Stop the War in Afghanistan. Bring Our Troops Home Now.* And alongside that last, writ large, the ever-increasing numbers of fatalities from what some general or politician, without irony, had named

Operation Enduring Freedom, the total growing, growing, growing, year on year.

Compared to that, she thought, crossing against the slowly moving traffic, what she had to deal with, serious in its way, was small beer indeed.

25

The cemetery was just south of the road that separated Heamor from Penzance proper, an expanse of land protected by trees and closely studded with markers in marble and stone. Late afternoon, the winds that had earlier scoured the day had all but died and the light was fading in the sky. Cordon's own father was here, had been here for some little time; his grave, as he would have wanted, plain and largely unadorned. Three lines from Robert Louis Stevenson, cleanly carved . . .

> *Under the wide and starry sky,*
> *Dig the grave and let me lie.*
> *Glad did I live and gladly die.*

Cordon had found them in a book of verse that had lain beside his father's hospice bed, uneasily underlined.

Three plots away lay the grave of an unknown French merchant seaman, a victim of the First World War, who for some reason had washed up on this part of the coast. There were other sailors buried there, too, Cordon knew; they had learned about it at school. Seventeen of the crew of the trawler *Wallasea*, killed in an attack by German surface craft down in Mounts Bay in January 1944. In his primary class they had made drawings, heavy the lurching blue of the heaving sea, the sky above erupting with the scarlet crash of exploding shells. The teacher had taken them to the causeway that leads, at low tide, across the edge of the bay towards St Michael's Mount and had them stand there, silent, staring out, thinking the unthinkable. His fingers had been cold, Cordon remembered, the first inklings of returning water pooling around the thin soles of his plimsolls.

Only the smaller of the two chapels was in use today, Maxine's friends a staunch but motley crew: some who'd known her from the streets, the squats and sleeping rough, those who'd survived; others she'd known from the Churches Breakfast Project or Addaction Community Support; a few neighbours from the street where latterly she'd lived, one of whom had invited mourners back to her house after the ceremony for sandwiches and tea.

Of Maxine's immediate family, there was no sign.

No Clifford Carlin.

No fostered children.

No Letitia: no Rose.

Seated on hard wood, knees pressed against the pew in front, Cordon struggled to concentrate on the clergyman's words, the benign platitudes, the elisions that skated over a misplaced life. An irregular death.

Behind him, an elderly man's suit exuded an almost over-powering smell of mothballs. Heads bowed, tears here and there were sniffed or coughed away.

When the organist wheezed out the introduction to the 23rd Psalm, 'The Lord is My Shepherd', Cordon turned smartly and pushed his way outside.

She was standing immediately opposite the double doors, pale raincoat unbuttoned over a black dress, her mouth a dark red gash across her bloodless face.

Startled, Cordon stopped in his tracks.

'Not a ghost,' Letitia said. 'See.' She plucked at the skin tight on her cheek. 'It's real.'

The lines, the gauntness made her somehow more attractive, Cordon thought, not less. Then banished the thought as quickly as it came.

'Been a while,' she said.

'Yes.'

'How long?'

'I don't know. Years.'

'Too long, that's what you're meant to say.' Mocking him with her eyes. 'You don't look any different – that too.'

'It's true.'

'Is it, bollocks.'

'We all get a bit older.'

'Not you. You were always fucking old.' She reached into her bag for a cigarette.

'Now you're running some hotel in the Lake District.'

'Anything wrong with that?'

'Bit slow for the likes of you, I'd've thought.'

'Gets too quiet we go down the Pencil Museum for a bit of a laugh.'

'We?'

'Me an' anyone else who's around.' She glanced towards the doors. 'Let's shift before we get knocked down by the crowd.'

They stood by a section of stone wall, yew trees to either side. Car headlights hollowed yellow and amber along the road at their backs. Fifty metres away, the upturned earth of a freshly dug grave.

'She came to see you,' Cordon said, 'in London. Maxine.'

'Silly cow.'

'She was worried.'

'Because I didn't want to spend time listening to my dad's

old records while he tells me what I could've done with my life?' She flicked ash towards the ground. 'I changed my mind, didn't I? No fuckin' crime.'

'But you did see her? In London?'

'Jesus, what's with all the questions?'

'Did you see her?'

'No, I never saw her. Didn't know she was there, did I?'

'She had an address, Finsbury Park.'

'So?'

'She would have gone looking for you there.'

'And not found me.' Letitia turned towards the doors. 'They're coming out now, we better move. See her – what is it? – committed to the earth.'

Cordon fell in step beside her, rested his hand on the crook of her arm. 'Maxine. The train. You really think she fell?'

She knocked him angrily away. 'She's dead, right? Inside that soddin' box. A closed bloody coffin 'cause of what the train . . .'

She ran an arm across her face, her eyes.

'You want to play the fucking policeman, don't do it with me. We understood?'

Fragments of earth showered against the coffin lid, small stones bounced once and slid off to the sides. The trowel passed from hand to hand. Ignoring it, Letitia reached down and scooped up raw dirt from the ground, then, leaning out over the graveside, let it fall between her fingers till there was nothing but air.

There should have been rooks cawing at the sky, Cordon thought, but instead there was silence, a moment of almost true silence, and then the awkward shuffling of feet, a few mourners already, hands in pockets, moving away. He had been thinking of his father, the meticulous way he would plan each step, each journey, each and every trip they made to this or that bird sanctuary or wildlife refuge; the small notebooks in which he would record everything they had seen. A meticulousness that had driven the young Cordon close to distraction.

If a thing's worth doing . . .

He did hear a bird then, rook, crow or jackdaw – his father would have known in an instant – but when he raised his eyes to look the bird was not there but in the past.

Shoulders brushed by him as he stood unmoving, remembering the last time he had bent to kiss his father's cheek, the roughness of the older man's unshaven face, the smell of something slowly rotting on his breath. Leaving, he had stepped out into a failing light much like this.

Gradually, he realised someone was standing beside him.

'Are you all right, love?' A woman, round faced, bundled in black. He didn't know who she was.

'Yes, thanks. I'm fine.'

'Sometimes it takes a while.' She squeezed his hand. 'You'll come back to the house? No sense letting all that good food go to waste.'

When he looked for her, Letitia had already gone. Taken one of the taxis, doubtless, that hung, like carrion, around the cemetery gates. From there to the station. The early evening train. Plymouth, then Bristol. Where then? East to London, north to the Lakes?

Back home, Cordon slapped some music on the stereo, splashed whisky into a glass. *You want to play the fucking policeman, don't do it with me. We understood?* And, underneath that, his father's patient tones: *If a thing's worth doing . . .*

He jacked up the volume, stared out across rooftops to the bay.

Eric Dolphy in Champaign, Illinois, March 1953. 'Something Sweet, Something Tender'.

Who did he think he was trying to kid?

147

26

One of these mornings, Karen thought, she'd step outside and not feel the bite of frost on her face and know winter was finally over. But not yet. She tightened the scarf at her neck and fastened the last button on her coat. Her breath curled like pale smoke on the air.

Carla had returned to her own flat and would be back at the National that evening, treading the boards. 'The show,' as she'd said, 'had best go bloody on. And I do mean bloody. More bodies per minute with these Jacobeans than Camden can come up with in a year.'

Karen had expressed her concern.

'Best thing for me,' Carla had assured her. 'After this week there's a break and then we're off on tour. Milton Keynes, Woking and points west. Bringing Middleton to the masses.'

But when Karen had clasped her arms round her in a farewell hug, she had felt Carla's body shake and read the residue of fear in her eyes. She wished there was more she could do for her, more to help, but didn't know what it was. Maybe, in time, the impact of what had happened would lessen, though she would never fully forget. Maybe, Karen thought, Carla would find a way to use it in her work.

She was crossing the street when her mobile rang. Tim Costello. Reports of a drug-related shooting in Camberwell had come in, a seventeen-year-old youth with known drug connections found in the early hours of the morning with gunshot wounds to his legs and back.

'Some link with Walthamstow, that's what you're thinking?'

'It's possible.'

'On your bike, then, sunshine.' Karen felt herself grinning. She'd been wanting to say that for ages. 'Get yourself down there. And don't let anyone bully you around.'

She snapped the connection closed.

Mike Ramsden was waiting in her office, cigarette smoke acrid on his breath, skin loose and baggy around his eyes. Karen found herself wondering, not for the first time, where he'd slept, his bed or someone else's, a couch, the floor.

'You okay?'

'Been better.'

'Want to talk about it?'

'What? You're my mother now?'

'Suit yourself.' She slid into the chair behind her desk. 'Terry Martin, how'd it go?'

'Difficult to find a more innocent man. Shocked at what had happened over at Camden, what he'd seen on the news. Specially when he saw one of the blokes killed was someone he knew. Used to, anyway. Aaron Johnson. Hadn't seen him in a twelvemonth, maybe more. Not as much as clapped eyes on him. Bit of a falling-out. No idea what he was into these days. Something a bit iffy, he'd not be too surprised, but he'd no idea what.'

'And Parsons? He knew Jamie Parsons?'

'Just a name, he reckons. Heard it a few times, bandied around. Wouldn't know him if he bumped into him on the street. Not that he'll be doing that any time soon.'

'You believed him?'

'Like I believe water flows uphill, yes, I believed him. Not the same as having proof.'

'And we still haven't been able to shake his alibi for the Andronic murder?'

'Not so far.'

Karen sighed; shuffled some papers across her desk. 'The car. Camden. Better news there?'

'Some. Stolen from outside a house in Totteridge twenty-four hours earlier. Right off the drive.'

'Reported?'

Ramsden nodded. 'Some bigwig with a firm of financial consultants in the City. Bonafides checked down to the colour of his socks.'

'Not turned up since?'

'No, but it will. Dumped somewhere. Likely torched.' Ramsden shook his head. 'Bloody waste. Nice motor like that. Next to brand new.'

'And Tottenham? Hector Prince?'

'Still waiting on Trident.'

Karen held a breath; released it slowly. 'Okay, press on. We'll talk again later.'

'I don't doubt.'

Karen switched on her computer. Time for a quick rattle through her emails before checking her in-tray, getting some shape into the day.

Tim Costello was back by mid-afternoon. First signs were the weapon used was a 9mm pistol, most likely a Glock. Pretty much the weapon of choice. Forensics would be checking the ammo against that used in Walthamstow and the chance it might have come from the same batch that had originated in Deptford, the pistol also.

'Okay, Tim,' Karen said. 'Let me know how things develop.'

She'd seen the victim's naked body in the morgue, the Walthamstow murder, skinny arms popped with needle marks, lesions on his skin. His face, parchment white, the face of a boy, a young man never growing old. Another victim, she thought, of the same lack of opportunity and education as Hector Prince. A different colour, but the same skewed culture.

For a moment, she closed her eyes, as if in prayer.

But praying, as she knew, no longer got it done.

Perhaps it never had.

The phone rang and she answered it. Listened, making brief notes as she did so. Dialled another number, internal, passed the information on, setting another line of inquiry in motion. It was what you did. Kept going through the procedures, fingers crossed, hoping sooner or later something would fall into your lap.

Much on your plate right now? All under control?

Karen shook her head. You did what was possible. Conscientiously. Avoiding error. And at the end of the day you went home. Never leaving it all quite behind.

As if you could.

27

Cape Cornwall was where Cordon sometimes went when he wanted to be alone and think; also to remember. And marvel. The extremity of the ocean that tipped out at that point against the rock. He zipped up his heavy jacket and started to climb; stood, finally, at the summit, facing out, oblivious to the wind, the cold.

He had come here first with his father, racing him to the top and then, breathless, pointing out beyond the lighthouse to the waves, the possibility of seals, pods of dolphins, basking sharks. His father focusing the binoculars, patient, waiting. The young Cordon anxious, eager to be up and moving, scrambling down the monument then round, faster and faster each time.

'For God's sake, sit still for a moment. Go on, it won't hurt you, sit.'

And then from his father's rucksack, the brown bread sandwiches, carefully cut; the Thermos flask. The book of birds; of grasses; of wild flowers: neatly annotated, ticked.

Cordon watched now as a little egret — see, he remembered — tugged something from between the pebbles back of the water's edge and flew away. Were there moménts, he wondered, when his son, off in Australia, looked up suddenly from whatever he was doing, startled by a memory of something they had done together, father and son, something they had shared?

He shook his head.

Argued, they'd done that. Little else.

Families, it was what they did. Fought, argued, walked out, walked away, tried to keep in touch and failed. Maxine Carlin had gone up to London to see her daughter, prompted by some unnecessary fear, and, not finding her, on her way home, unused to the busy thrust of the London Underground in the rush hour, had fallen under a train and been killed.

Clear as that.

The inquest, the inquiry had found nothing suspicious: accidental death. Her daughter had thrown black earth on to her coffin and walked away. *You want to play the fucking policeman, don't do it with me. We understood?* We were understood.

People wanted help or they didn't.

Friendship the same.

Love, even.

He kicked the toe of his shoe against the hardness of the rock, and, rising, set his back to the sea and took the slower, more winding path back down towards the old chapel that had long been converted to a cattle byre and now sat in partial disrepair. Away to the left, descending, he could see the tall chimney of the Kenidjack arsenic works, which in Victorian times had provided a compound that, when mixed with chalk and vinegar, women, anxious to lighten their complexion, had not only rubbed into their arms and faces but eaten.

He'd learned that from his father, of course, that and the fact that before antibiotics, another compound of arsenic had been used for curing syphilis. When it wasn't being used as poison.

A bit of good and bad in everything.

What his father had believed.

He had just made it to where his car was parked when his mobile rang. Not a number he recognised.

'Look, I'm not sure if I should be phoning you . . .' Clifford Carlin's voice was troubled, shaky. 'I didn't know what else to do.'

'What's happened?'

'Letitia — she came here after the funeral . . .'

'Tell me what's happened.'

'Nothing. Nothing, just . . . ever since she got here . . . she's been, I don't know, worried. Frightened, even.'

'What of?'

'That's it, she won't say. Not clearly, not exactly. But there have been these calls to the house. And people, she says, driving past, hanging round.'

'You've seen them? These people?'

'No, no, not really. But she's not making it up, I'm certain. She's scared. And if you know Letitia, you know she doesn't scare easily.'

'What about the police? If she's in some kind of danger.'

'She won't. She said no. No police.'

'You phoned me.'

'Like I said, I didn't know what else to do.'

A Land Rover backed into the space alongside him and Cordon moved away, down towards the stone wall that marked the car park off from the land that tumbled down towards the sea.

'Are you still there?' Carlin asked.

'Yes, I'm here.'

'The thing is, Letitia, I don't even think it's herself she's most frightened for. It's the boy.'

The line went dead, leaving Cordon staring out across limitless water.

What boy? he asked himself. What boy?

154

28

He was three years old. Rising four. He stood close to his mother, face fast against her hip, one hand clinging to the strands that were unravelling from the borrowed jumper she was wearing. Her father's jumper. The boy's grandfather. A lick of dark hair hung loose across his forehead; his brown eyes wide with uncertainty and fear.

'What the fuck are you doing here?' Letitia's greeting.

The child flinched at the anger in his mother's voice and clung tighter, closer to tears.

Cordon said nothing.

Off to one side, Clifford Carlin shuffled his feet.

'It's you, isn't it?' she said. 'You stupid interfering bastard.' Pushing the boy away, she lunged at her father and raked her nails across his cheek.

'Christ, Letitia!'

'Stupid, stupid, stupid!' As he turned from her, she pummelled his back with her fists.

'Mum! No, Mum, no. Don't. Don't.'

The boy tried to pull her away and she flung out a hand

and caught him in the face and for an instant he stopped dead, as if in shock, then screamed.

'Oh, Jesus! Now see – see what you've done? The pair of you?'

There was blood at the corner of her son's mouth, starting to trickle down his chin and on to his neck.

'See what you've made me fucking do?'

'Letitia, listen . . .'

'Here, sweetheart, here. It's all right.' Pulling a tissue from her pocket, she dabbed it at the boy's face. 'It's nothing, really. Just a little cut. There, look. It's already stopped.' Crouching, she hugged him to her. 'I'm sorry. Mummy's sorry.'

The two men looked at one another and Clifford Carlin shook his head. A few moments later, without saying anything more, he left the room.

The boy was sobbing now, but quietly, face pressed against his mother's chest.

'Letitia . . .'

'I told him . . .' She spoke to Cordon without yet turning to look at him. 'I told him, this stuff that's happening, don't say anything, not to anyone. It'll sort itself out. Leave it be. Say anything to anyone, anyone at all, it'll only make things worse.'

'He was worried.'

'Of course he was fucking worried. I'm worried. Worried sick. A sight more now you're here.'

'Maybe I can help.'

'Yeah?'

'Yes, why not? Try, anyway.'

'Try?' She laughed. 'Fuckin' try?'

She stood to face him.

'Sir Lancelot, now, is it? Knights of the Round fucking Table?' She shook her head. 'Okay, here we are, me and the kid, in need of rescue maybe and what do we get?' She laughed, ragged and deep. 'That bloke with a broken lance on some old nag. I saw a film about him once. That's you, Cordon, about as much use as a tit in a trance.'

Cordon drew a slow breath and continued to stand where he was, the boy peeking out at him from behind his mother's arm, only looking away when Cordon smiled.

Later.

They were sitting side by side on the stairs, the middle landing. It had seemed as good a place as anywhere. Clifford Carlin had gone in to open up his shop and left them to it.

Cordon sat with a mostly empty can of Carlsberg wedged between his feet; Letitia was drinking vodka and Coke, not the first.

She was still wearing one of her father's old sweaters, faded jeans, feet bare, chipped polish on the toes. She'd pulled her hair away from her face and wiped most of the tiredness from around her eyes. The child was in one of the rooms above them, sleeping, thumb in his mouth, making occasional sucking sounds, a plastic stegosaurus tight in his other hand.

She'd cuddled him close earlier, the pair of them loving, silent; something inside Cordon's gut had twisted like fish caught on a hook.

'Your son,' Cordon said quietly. 'I don't even know his name.'

'Danya.'

'Danya?'

'Ukrainian. Means gift of God. Some fucking joke.'

'And that's what you call him?'

'What his father calls him. I call him Danny. Dan.'

'His father?'

'Anton.'

'Also from Ukraine?'

'Oh, yes. From Odessa. Yellow and blue blood in his veins.'

She brought the glass to her mouth, a swallow rather than a sip. 'Anton Oleksander Kosach. Oldest of five brothers. Anton, Taras, Bogdah, Parlo, Symon. Parlo and Symon are twins. Bogdah, the third eldest, he's still in the Ukraine.'

'The rest are here?'

'Most of the time, yes. Anton's here legally. Taras, too, maybe. The others, I'm not so sure.'

'And he wants you to come home. Anton. The pair of you. That's what all this is about? The phone calls, whatever. That's what he wants?'

'Danny, that's what he wants. Me, I doubt if he could give a flying fuck. Not any more.'

'But he wants you to go back, right? To wherever. You and Danny?'

'His son, he goes on and on about his son. As if I've stolen him away. As if I've no intention of ever going back.'

'And have you?'

A pause. Letitia fiddling with her hair. 'I don't know.'

'So he's right?'

'No, he's not fucking right.'

'But if you've left him . . .'

'I told you, I just don't know. I don't know, okay?'

'So what is this?'

'This?'

'You and Danny, here?'

'The funeral, my mum's funeral – Danny, I was going to take him – but then I thought, no, no, time enough for all that. So I brought him here, to my dad, just a few days, right? While I was down in Penzance.'

'He knew this? Anton, he knew?'

'Sort of, yeah.'

'And that was okay?'

'Okay? Okay with Anton is he's got you practically under lock an' key, knows where you are every minute of the fuckin' day. Him or his bloody brothers. Only wanted two of 'em to come down all the way to fuckin' Cornwall with me, didn't he? Parlo and Symon. I told him, I don't want no Ukrainian bloody gangsters hangin' round my mum's funeral.'

'Is that what they are then? Gangsters? Some kind of Soviet Mafia?'

She shot him a look, then turned her face away.

Anton, Letitia had told him earlier, had called her mobile when she and the boy hadn't arrived back as expected, called and texted; threatened her, threatened her father, issued ultimatums. Forty-eight hours more. Then he would send someone to bring them back. She had already seen cars passing slowly along the street outside; glimpsed a face she thought she recognised.

Not enough to be sure.

Cordon straightened, stretched his arms. The edge of the step above was sticking uncomfortably into the small of his back.

'We have to keep sitting on the stairs?'

'No one's forcing you to sit anywhere.'

'For God's sake . . .'

'What?'

'Why does everything with you have to be so bloody difficult?'

'Because it is.'

He shook his head. There was a cry from above them, muffled, Danny caught in a dream.

While she was settling him, Cordon went downstairs. Tipping what remained of his lager down the sink, he set the kettle to boil and started opening cupboards. There was a jar of instant coffee, untroubled for some time, the granules set in a stiff rind that resisted the first taps with a spoon.

'Decent stuff he keeps in the fridge,' Letitia said from the doorway. 'And there's one of those filter things somewhere. Try the sink.'

Cordon switched on the radio as he waited for the coffee to drip slowly through. The middle of a news broadcast. The economy. Ethnic clashes in Uzbekistan. Afghanistan. Still Afghanistan. When had it all started, the first Anglo-Afghan war? Eighteen thirty-fucking-nine! Wars without fucking end. It made him angry in a way he didn't quite understand. It all seemed so far away, another world. But then, even his own life in Cornwall seemed distant now, something seen through bottled glass, a blur. And this – threats of violence, Ukrainian gangsters, recrimination – perhaps the world, the real world, was coming to him?

He found Letitia at the back of the house, smoking a cigarette. The sky above was muddy grey. Beyond the garden end the land rose up towards the cliff top and, on the far side, the sea. Dragging over two plastic chairs, he set the mugs of coffee down on uneven ground.

Letitia was staring off into the middle distance, shapeless in those shapeless clothes, scarcely any make-up on her face, no longer young. Despite everything, Cordon thought, she had some desperate kind of beauty. Beyond looking. Some steeliness; resilience, despite everything.

He wondered if this Anton saw the same.

The mother of his child.

His son.

I doubt if he could give a flying fuck.

Cordon wondered if that were really true.

Letitia dropped the butt of her cigarette on to the drying earth and pressed down on it with the sole of her shoe. Taking the chair next to Cordon, she picked up her mug of coffee and gave it a sniff.

'Sugar?'

'Two. Two and a bit extra.'

She smiled. 'What's that, then? Long memory or just plain luck?'

'Copper's instincts. Training. Every little detail.' He tapped the side of his head. 'Never know when it's all going to come in handy.'

'Gonna help us here, are they? Your instincts?'

'Depends.'

'Oh, yeah?'

'Last time you spoke to him, Anton, what did he say?'

'You mean, aside from sweetheart and darling and how he loves me more than life itself?'

'Aside from that.'

'If he doesn't see my ugly whore's face within twenty-four hours, me and Danny, he's going to send someone to come and get us.'

'He won't come himself?'

'Too much like begging. Losing face. He'll send someone. Possibly the twins.' She grimaced. 'Give those two bastards an excuse and they'll slit your throat and laugh about it. Whole world's a bloody video game where they're concerned.'

'You said you'd seen someone already. A car.'

'Maybe. I'm not sure. Could have been nothing. Imagination. I don't know. Then again, it could be someone local, someone Anton knows, repaying a favour. Brighton, maybe. He's got contacts down there. I know. Could be that. Making sure I was still here, hadn't done a runner, me and the kid. Letting him know.'

He looked at her, the set of her mouth. 'You're not going back, are you? You've made up your mind.'

'No.' Smoke drifted upwards as she lit another cigarette. 'No, I don't think so. Not to that.'

'Whoever it is he sends, you think they're going to take that laying down?'

'About the only way they will.'

'They'll use force?'

'What else?'

'Then we should tell the police, local. They'll have a patrol car drive by, maybe station someone outside.'

She shook her head. 'How long for? And even if they did, the minute Anton thinks I've done some kind of deal with the police, that's it. He'll get to me, no matter what.'

She lit another cigarette. 'I've been around him too long, know too much. He wouldn't want to take that kind of a risk.'

Know what? Cordon wondered. Too much of what?

'What could he do?' he said.

'Kill me. Have me killed. Take Danny. And you wouldn't be able to stop him. Even if you tried.'

Cordon started to speak, but she laid a finger across his lips.

'Listen, it was good of you to come. Daft, but . . .' She shook her head. 'You're not a bad bloke, for a copper, specially. But this . . . this isn't dealing with druggies in the bus station down by the harbour; out looking for someone lost on the moors or hauling bodies back out of the surf. This is something else, Cordon. Another world. Let it go.'

29

Afternoon turned evening. The temperature dropped, reminding them it was winter still. Clifford Carlin went into town for fish and chips and brought them back wrapped in pages from the local paper.

St Leonards man narrowly escapes being first in Britain to die of snake bite since 1975.
Petula Clark president of Hastings Music Festival.

Carlin hadn't known she was still alive.

He decanted the food on to plates, offered salt, vinegar, tomato sauce. Buttered bread. Poured mugs of tea. Even lukewarm, the chips retained some bite, the cod flakey inside its batter and pearly white. Danny ate with his fingers, despite his mother's attempts to get him to use a fork.

Before they'd finished eating, Carlin went over to the record player and slipped a nearby album from its sleeve. Jazzy piano, smooth voice, banks of strings.

'Christ,' Letitia said, 'can't we get through just one meal without you making us listen to that old junk?'

'Charlie Rich,' Carlin said, unrepentant. 'The original Silver Fox.'

'You don't fuckin' say.'

'Mum,' Danny piped up, 'you said a naughty word.'

'Just shut it and eat your chips.'

Cordon excused himself, went out into the garden to make his call. Kiley's voice, when he answered, was slightly breathless, as if he'd been hurrying up several flights of stairs.

'Jack,' Cordon said, 'I need a favour.'

'Not going to turf me out of my bed again, are you?'

'No, not that.'

'Where are you now, anyway? Back down in Cornwall?'

'Hastings.'

'I thought that was over.'

'Yes, well . . .'

'Okay, out with it. What do you want?'

'These famous connections of yours. You don't know anyone in – I'm not sure what it'd be – Serious and Organised Crime, maybe? Someone involved in keeping tabs on criminals from Eastern Europe operating over here.'

Kiley gave it a moment's thought. 'I might have, why?'

'I need someone to check a name for me.'

'That's all?'

'For now.'

'Let's have it, then.'

'Kosach. Anton Oleksander Kosach.'

'Say it again slowly.'

Cordon did. Kiley wrote it down.

'Russian?' Kiley asked.

'Ukrainian.'

'Okay, leave it with me. I'll get back to you soon as I can.'

'I owe you one, Jack.'

'A pint or two when I see you.'

'Done.'

Cordon heard the click of a lighter and saw Letitia in the doorway, watching.

'Girlfriend?'

'Work.'

'This time of night?'

'Just checking in. Making sure the neighbourhood's being properly policed in my absence.'

'And is it?'

'Even the seagulls behaving themselves.'

Letitia nodded and went back inside.

Cordon decided on a walk around the block, a couple of blocks; before he knew it, almost, he was down at the sea road, the shore. Fishermen here and there on the shingle: standing, some of them, feet firmly planted, legs splayed; others seated on small canvas chairs, two or three lines each. One of them whistling quietly to himself. The wink and blur of cigarettes.

He tugged the collar of his jacket up against the wind, felt the round hardness of pebbles beneath his feet. Anton and Letitia. Letitia and Anton. He'd known couples where the woman had left and taken the children with her; just threatening to leave, sometimes that was enough. Some men threw up their arms and said good riddance, some cried; some, a few, arranged to meet on neutral territory, talked it all through, who and how to share, who to pay. And then there were others. Men for whom leaving was a direct assault, a challenge to their power, what they saw as their rights, their self-esteem.

Leave me, they said, and I'll take the kids, strap them in the car and drive us all off the cliff edge into the sea. Leave me and I'll kill myself, I swear it. Let you live with that on your conscience the rest of your lousy life.

One man he knew, a trawler owner out of Newlyn, when his wife left him, painted her name in letters a metre high on walls up and down the town, the name and the word WHORE in brightest red alongside. And when she came back six months later, penitent, ashamed, begging forgiveness, he beat her within an inch of her life and threw her out again.

He'll kill me, Letitia had said. Have me killed.

Cordon could see the lights from the amusement arcades along the front, the distorted sounds of Chicory Tip from the early seventies. 'Son of My Father'.

Time to be heading back.

Danny was long in bed, fast off; Carlin had disappeared up to his room. Letitia was sitting, curled up, at one end of the settee, a bottle of wine on the small table close by, a glass in her hand. The television was switched on, the sound low, some programme about old England by the look of things, church spires, market halls, baptismal fonts, an earnest young man gesturing enthusiastically as he mugged for the camera.

'Thought you'd sodded off,' Letitia said. 'Done a runner.'

'Sorry to disappoint.'

'Here,' she slid the bottle towards him. 'Get yourself a glass, have a drink.'

He did as he was told.

She tucked her feet up tighter beneath her. 'Have a seat.'

'You watching this?' Cordon asked, pointing at the set.

'Not so's you'd notice.'

Cordon switched it off with the remote; sat at the opposite end of the settee, legs crossed at the ankle. Letitia had replaced her father's old sweater with something of her own, softer, closer fitting, a skirt instead of blue jeans. Let down her hair.

'You've not heard anything?' Cordon asked. 'Anton, no calls?'

A shake of the head.

'Maybe he's calmed down, seen sense.'

'Yeah. An' pigs can fly.'

The curtains had been pulled most of the way across, leaving space enough for the lights of the odd passing car to shimmer through. Quiet enough to hear the occasional cat cry, the footsteps of someone out walking their dog. Cordon thought he could hear, lifted on the wind, distant and indistinct, the occasional taint of music from the town, but he was never sure.

He reached down and refreshed Letitia's glass and then his own.

'Anton,' he said. 'You want to tell me about him?'

'Like what?'

'I don't know. Anything. You and him, for instance.'

'What? Our romance? How true love found Letitia at last? Rich Ukrainian sweeps her off her feet like Cinder-fucking-rella.'

'If you like.'

'Fuck off, Cordon.'

Cordon shrugged, took another drink.

'You want to know the truth?' she said.

He shrugged. 'Up to you.'

'The truth is this, this story, I'm the Ugly Sister, right? Running some knocking shop in Streatham. Nursemaid and matron to scabby little whores from every godforsaken bit of Eastern Europe, selling their skinny arses to send money back home an' pay off what they owe. Forever bitching and bloody complaining. Not that I blame them.

'Anyway, one night there's this big party. Anton's there, guest of honour, fifty-pound notes spilling out of his pockets like bloody Kleenex, everyone kowtowing to him like he's something special. Coke. Champagne. Enough pills to start a fucking Salsa band. The girls putting on some kind of lezzy sex show. Anton, he's got the pick of the crop, and fuck if he don't choose me. "What I want's a real woman," he says. "Not some kid, doesn't know what it's all about." Crap like that. As if I've got any choice. So, anyway, I show him, don't I? Not a lot to lose. Wants to see what a real woman can do, why not?'

She grinned, remembering, enjoying the discomfort on Cordon's face.

'Only sent for me again after that, didn't he? Couple of nights later. Bloody great limousine. Roses in his hotel room. Coke laid out on the pillow like them little chocolates the maid leaves, hoping for a tip. More fucking champagne. Wants me to blow him in front of the mirror while he pretends to slap me around. No pain, no gain, right?'

A quick glance at Cordon to see how he'd take that, make sure he was paying close enough attention.

'After all that palaver, instead of chucking me out he says he wants me to go and work for him. Reckons he can trust me. This place in Feltham, out near the airport, that's where it was first. Hostel. Sort of. Finsbury Park came after. Asylum seekers, that's what it was, mostly. Little more than kids, some of them. A lot of them. They'd stay there a few weeks, month maybe, then move on.'

'Move on where?'

'I don't know.'

Cordon looked at her until she looked away.

'Move on where?'

'I don't know. Wherever he wanted them. Could be anything. Anywhere. Anything he had a hand in. Him and his brothers, the guys they used to hang around with. Pizza parlours, that's where a lot of 'em went, this chain of pizza parlours, all across the fuckin' Midlands. Working twelve-hour fuckin' shifts. Some, they went off to cannabis factories, worked there, least that's what I heard. Never knew for sure.'

'And brothels? Massage parlours? How about those? Like the one in Streatham.'

'Maybe.'

'And that was okay?'

'Okay? How d'you mean?'

'Helping pimp these people – kids, isn't that what you said? Little more than kids. Pimping them into prostitution.'

'Christ, Cordon! Listen to yourself, will you? When did you take holy fucking orders?' She brought her glass down hard against wood and the wine splashed up over her hand. 'Let me tell you about those girls, yeah? Over here from Bela-bloody-Rus or somewhere, illegal, broke, barely speak half a dozen words of the fucking language, it's either lay back and spread your legs or get sent home and freeze your arse off on some autobahn, looking to suck off lorry drivers for the price of a salami and a loaf of bread.'

Cordon was slowly shaking his head. 'Social Services, then, that's what it was? What you were doing? Picking up the slack from the local council. Part of what's his face's Big Society?'

'Sod off, Cordon, you sarcastic bastard.'

'Yes, right, fine.'

He got as far as the window, lifting back the curtain to look out. The street lamp nearest to the house was no longer working. Lights were still showing faintly, here and there along the street; the darkened silhouettes of parked cars. Then, deep in the shadows, a movement. Cordon tensed, uncertain. Someone local, she'd said, a possibility, someone he'd used before.

He looked again: there was nothing.

His imagination.

The boy whimpered in his sleep and as Cordon turned, Letitia got to her feet.

No further sound, she sat back down.

'Danny,' Cordon said, with a glance towards the stairs. 'You and Anton, having a child together, that seems like something serious.'

Letitia reached for her cigarettes.

'Once I was there, working, Feltham, things running

smoothly, I didn't see him for weeks at a time. One of his brothers, sometimes; Parlo usually. Checking up. Then, when he did come by, Anton, sometimes he'd ignore me, part of the furniture, sometimes not.'

Smoke lingered at the corners of her mouth.

'One of those times, I got careless.' She smiled a rueful smile. 'Got myself knocked up. Okay, I thought, stupid cow. Termination. Not the first time, likely not the last. Made the mistake of saying something and it got back to him. And, course, when he learns it's a boy, he's bloody beside himself. Next thing you know he's waving flowers, making promises, threatening what he'll do if I abort his child. Sets me up in a flat he's got in Pimlico and insists on this gynaecologist with umpteen letters after his name and fingers like spiders. Soon as Danny's born and we're out of hospital, he takes us into this place of his outside London. Down in Surrey. Like a bloody mansion, i'n it? Swimming pool, jacuzzis, the whole bit. Woods all around.'

She set down her cigarette, sipped some wine.

'So there we are, we're living together, right? Two, three months it's like fucking paradise. Then he starts getting bored, you can tell. Bored with me, bored with the kid. Half the time now he's not there, and when he does come home, four in the fucking morning, I can smell these other women all over him. First I tell myself I don't care, but then I realise all I am's a fucking nursemaid and housekeeper, so I try and have it out with him and he loses it, each time I try and talk to him about it, he loses it . . .'

'He hits you.'

'He loses it and wants to throw me out, but there's Danny, and by this time he's crawling around, bumping into things, breaking things. In the end he suggests I go and look after this place in Finsbury Park, take Danny with me till he can go to nursery. For a time, this is fine. Finsbury Park's a dump, the house is filthy, falling apart. But at least it's calmer. Anton's – well, Anton's being really nice again. Charming.

'Then things start to go wrong. I don't know the ins and outs, so don't ask, never did. Some kind of dispute, that's all I know. Business. Anton and me, we have this furious row. So bad, I'm frightened – for the first time, truly frightened. I lost it, totally lost it and did a runner, an' he sent some of his people after me. Dragged me back.'

She looked away.

'What happened then weren't pretty. And then, a few days later, it's all calmed down again. But tense. Something's changed. Happened. Not with us. Outside. I don't know what. But it's like he's expecting trouble. Take Danny and keep him safe, he tells me, out of the way. His brother, Taras, he's bought this hotel in the Lakes, some kind of investment. Go up there for a bit, he says, help Taras, lay low till this trouble gets sorted.' A lazy shrug of the shoulders. 'You know the rest.'

When the phone went, they both jumped.

Letitia picked it up.

No trace of an accent, the voice was English, harsh and clear.

'Off the road that goes north out of the town through St Helen's. There's a caravan site on your right, this side of the railway tunnel. Just past the edge of the woods. Tomorrow morning, be there, ten sharp. You and the boy.'

30

A few of the caravans looked as if they might be lived in year round, though signs of occupancy were few. Most stood empty, waiting for summer residents, short-term rentals, six hundred a week for a twin berth and counting. Along one side, a phalanx of empty concrete stands, weeds starting to push through, cracks appearing. Before the season there'd be a lick of paint, a few flowering shrubs, a stiff broom; the kiosk that now stood empty, partly boarded over, would be back in business, selling milk and bread, Calor gas, cereals, cheap DVDs and morning papers.

Off to one side, someone had been dismantling an old trailer, wheels and planks of splintered wood, the chassis bare and rusted over. Metal glinted for a moment in a sudden shaft of sun, bright through lowering skies.

Jack Kiley had called back first thing.

Anton Kosach was currently under investigation for his possible participation in money laundering. He was also suspected of involvement in people trafficking, prostitution and the illegal import and sale of arms. The works.

He had been targeted, questioned, never charged.

'Nice guy,' Kiley had remarked.

Cordon looked at his watch. Fifteen minutes shy of ten. The local east–west train disappeared into the tunnel on its way towards Warrior Square. Behind him, the trees at the wood's edge leaned in together, tall and mostly bare. Dust kicked up as he walked and left a grey film across his shoes.

Crouching down towards the dismembered trailer, he selected a length of rusted iron and backed away towards the space between two empty caravans.

Minutes later, a car slowed and, without indicating, turned into the yard. A silver Merc with alloy wheels. No subtlety here.

Engine switched off, the driver sat for several moments before swinging his legs round and climbing out, the click of the car door behind him soft and precise. Broad shouldered, not tall, he was wearing a blue Nike zip-up jacket with loose-fitting black trousers, leather shoes. Late thirties, Cordon guessed, early forties, just starting to go to seed.

As he watched, the man double-checked his watch, lowered the zip on his jacket midway down.

Iron held down flat against his thigh, Cordon stepped into sight.

'Who the fuck are you?'

'Never mind.'

'Where's the woman? The boy?'

'They're not coming.'

'They better fuckin' be. S'posed to be here now.'

His face was flushed, cheeks swelling out.

Cordon walked towards him, taking his time. 'You're not listening,' he said.

'Don't give me fuckin' listening. You call 'em, get 'em here, or fuckin' else.'

Cordon shook his head, the brittle edges of the iron biting into his hand.

Angling his head to one side, the man hawked phlegm and spat at the ground, then, as if making a decision, he arched suddenly forward, reaching round to the back of his jacket as if he might be going for a gun.

The one chance, likely the only one he was going to get, Cordon hit him with a fast swing, smack against the underside of the elbow with a crack that made him scream.

'You bastard! You broke my fuckin' arm.'

In for a penny, Cordon hit him again, the knee this time, and the man went down in a sprawling heap. Cordon pressed his foot down hard against the damaged leg and pulled the pistol from where it had been resting against the small of the man's back. One click and he pocketed the magazine. The gun he hurled away as far as he could.

'You'll live to fuckin' regret this.'

'I hope you're right.'

Cordon rested the rusted end of iron against the man's sweated forehead, oblivious to the pain in his eyes.

'A message for Anton . . .'

'I don't know no fucking Anton.'

'Then whoever sent you on his behalf. Steer clear. The woman and the boy. Well clear. This isn't the way.'

Stepping quickly round him, Cordon freed the keys from where they'd been left in the Merc and launched them in a high, steepling arc, deep into the woods.

'Bastard!' the man shouted. 'You're gonna fuckin' pay for this. Fuckin' pay.'

Cordon thought, one way or another, he was probably right. Walking away, breath raw, his heart hammered inside his chest. This time he'd managed it without a scratch.

31

Late afternoon. Karen was on the M1, heading north. A pool car, unmarked, no more than a couple of years old, clutch tight as an old man's chest. The traffic travelling out of the city was already beginning to bunch and stall. When they played their second Neil Diamond track within the hour, she switched off Magic FM and, slipping an Aretha CD into place, notched up the volume just a tad.

The call had come through that morning, high-pitched, hesitant, a definite accent — South Yorkshire, somewhere close? — a young woman sounding early twenties at best. Jayne Andrew. No s. Jayne with a y. An address in Mansfield. Wayne Simon, he'd been hanging round the Four Seasons shopping centre where she worked. Where she lived, too. No doubt, no doubt at all. Used to go out with him, didn't she? Years back. Two or three, at least, must be. She'd been into the local police station and they'd said they'd have a word with security in the centre, drive by the house where she lived, but, far as she could tell, they never had. Told her to call the police in London, so that's what she'd done. She hoped that was okay?

'Fine,' Karen had assured her. 'You did the right thing.'

Ramsden, Costello, the rest of her team were out of the office, busy; she could have sent someone junior, but somehow she fancied it herself. As long as what the woman was claiming panned out and it wasn't just another lonely fantasist, desperate for some attention, this was the best lead they'd had. And there was the weather – earlier there'd been scarcely a cloud worth its name overhead, the sky a pale but definite blue, all the promise of a lovely, late winter day. A still-distant harbinger of spring. Just right for a drive, an hour or more alone in the car with just the stereo for company. A change is gonna come, sang Aretha, and who was to say she was wrong?

Jayne Andrew was whey faced and small boned – petite, the word – four or five months' pregnant and just beginning to show. Hair that had once been dyed blonde hung lank past her face; grey eyes, dark lashes, surprisingly long. She was wearing a loose top, stretch pants, slippers on her feet. She squinted at the identification Karen showed her without really seeing it and invited her inside.

The block of flats where she lived looked to have been built in the seventies: flat-fronted, flat-roofed, a rectangular box of identical units with a straggle of grass out front and cream-coloured exterior walls in sore need of several fresh coats of paint. Jayne Andrew's flat was on the upper floor, neat and small, the furniture a mixture of what Karen assumed were hand-me-downs and newer stuff from Ikea.

'Not working today?'

She shrugged. 'Keep cutting back, don't they? Three days a week at the moment, that's all there is.' She touched the curve of her belly. 'Not as that'll matter much pretty soon.'

'When's the baby due?'

'June. June 15th.'

'And is this the dad?' Karen pointed at the photograph framed above the television, a young man in military uniform, staring out.

'That's Ryan, yes. He's with the Royal Engineers. A corporal.'

'Nice-looking man. Handsome.'

Pride reflected in the younger woman's eyes. 'He's in Afghanistan. Helmand.' She pulled at a stray length of hair. 'He's always telling me, don't worry, don't worry, I'll be fine. An' I know he will. He's careful, Ryan. Not like some of them – things he's told me. But even so – you see these things on the news, you know, his family has been informed, and all them people linin' the streets . . .'

She turned away to hide the prick of tears.

Karen rested a hand on her shoulder and she flinched.

'I don't know about you,' Karen said, stepping back, 'but I wouldn't mind a cup of tea.'

'Yes, of course. Sorry, I didn't think . . .'

'Why don't you let me . . . ?'

'No, no, You sit down. Please.'

Karen stood by the window instead. A short, bow-legged dog, some kind of bulldog cross, was waddling its way across the patchy grass below. A young woman in a puffa jacket, no more than late teens, surely, went past along the other side of the street, one child strapped into a buggy, another lagging behind. Over the crowded hotchpotch of rooftops, the sky was beginning to darken, the evening soon setting in.

The tea came in bright mugs, placed carefully on coasters. 'I didn't know if you wanted sugar . . .'

'No, thanks. This is fine.'

They sat for a moment, awkwardly, one leaning forward, the other back. Jayne Andrew avoiding Karen's gaze. The tea, as Karen's grandmother might have said, looked as if it lacked the strength to stand.

'Wayne Simon, how did you know him?'

'Before, you mean?'

'Yes, before.'

'That were ages back. Before I met Ryan. I was out wi' me mates. Sat'day night, you know. Wayne was there on his own, this pub we were all in. Up here working. Construction, what he did. Started chattin' to us, just, you know, friendly like. I thought he were nice. Not loud or rough or anything.' She looked directly at Karen for the first time. 'When I heard what he's supposed to have done. His wife and kiddie. I couldn't believe it. Just couldn't.'

'Back then, though, you went out with him?'

'For a while, yes. A few months, maybe, six at most. That were all.'

'It was serious, though?'

'He thought it were.'

'And you didn't know there was somebody else? Down in London?'

'Course not.'

Karen swallowed down a mouthful of weak tea. 'So what happened?'

'Nothing. Nothing really. No row or anything. Not then. Wayne went back down to London when the job he was working was over. Like all of a sudden it didn't matter.'

'And you were upset?'

'Not really. Like I said, it were always more serious for him'n for me.' She pushed her hands up across her face. 'Only set eyes on him the once after that till now. Just the once. Fetched up here, didn't he? Out of the blue. Bangin' on the door. Shoutin' all kinds of things. Filthy things, some of them. Been drinking, mind you, but all the same. I was with Ryan by then and thank God he were out, cause Ryan'd've killed him. Still would, if he found out what was happening.'

178

'And now, he's been what? Making a commotion? More of the same?'

'No. That's it. He just stands there, right up against the shop window. One minute he's there and when I look again he's gone. As if I'm making it up, but I'm not. Most times I'm on the till, see, close by the door and there's only the glass between us.' She shivered. 'The manager, he's complained to security but that don't seem to make any difference 'cause the next time you look he's back again.'

'And he doesn't say anything?'

'Just the once. I hadn't even seen him, not that day, didn't know he was there. An' all of a sudden he comes up behind me. "How come," he says, "you filthy slut, you whore, you're carryin' another man's baby?" Whispers it, right in my ear. I started crying, couldn't help it. Then when I dared look round he'd gone.'

She reached out for Karen's hand.

'I'm frightened. Frightened he'll do something. Hurt me. Hurt my baby.'

Karen squeezed her hand. 'It's okay. I had a word with the local police on the way up. Maybe they weren't taking this as seriously as they should. I'll go and see them in person before I leave. Suggest a panic button. The minute you see Wayne again, if he approaches you, you activate that, it'll go right through to the station. I'll ask for a drive-by outside here every hour through the night. And see if we can't get someone in plain clothes in the shopping centre to help out security.' She squeezed the small hand again. 'Nothing will happen. He's not going to hurt you, I promise.'

'But if he—'

'I promise. You've got my word.'

Another saying of her grandmother's started jinking round inside her head as she stepped back out on to the street, something about promises being like pie crusts, crumbling, she thought, at the merest touch.

179

She was back on the motorway, heading south, headlights spindling about her, when her mobile rang and she pulled over on to the hard shoulder.

Ramsden's voice, off-pitch, urgent. 'On your way back down? Might want to make a detour. Stansted. Something you ought to see.'

32

She had read it somewhere: the smell of a slaughterhouse, blood and piss and shit and fear. The sweet bite of vomit at the back of the throat.

For a moment, she swayed, eyes glazed.

She had seen death before, too many times, but not like this.

She had to force herself to look again, to see.

Kebab shop, she thought. That's what it reminded her of. A kebab shop, late at night: walking home, two, three in the morning, head furred and thick from too much vodka, too many cigarettes, the overlapping stink of sweet chilli sauce and slowly turning meat; the man behind the counter, bored, tired, wiping his fingers down the front of his filthy apron before slicing the meat into veinous, bloodied strips. Except that these slabs of scored meat, hanging from the aluminium struts of the roof, had arms and legs and heads; the latter barely recognisable, burned, gouged, torn.

Bile caught in her mouth and she held it there while her body juddered before swallowing it back down.

Her head swam.

The belly of the nearest man hung down in folds, half covering his shrivelled cock and balls.

'Outside,' Ramsden said quietly, close behind. 'Talk outside.'

He touched her arm at the elbow; started, gently, firmly, to steer her towards the doors.

As Karen stepped through into the air, Scene of Crime officers turned aside.

The light bit at her eyes.

The parking area, surrounded on three sides by multi-level storage units, was busy with police vehicles, ambulances, unmarked cars.

Karen counted, slowly, one to ten inside her head.

'What do we know?' she asked.

'Found by a delivery team from the airport. Come to collect a container, evening flight to Ankara. Poor bastards, got more than they bargained for.'

'The bodies. Any idea how long they'd been there?'

'Best guess so far, early hours.'

'This morning?'

'Be a sight worse, else.'

He gave it a moment, watching her eyes. 'Security comes round every couple of hours. Two men usually, sometimes one.'

'This morning?'

'Just the one.'

'Handy.'

'Nothing noted in the log. Call out now for him to come back in.'

Karen looked up at the CCTV cameras attached to several of the buildings; another, mounted on a high stand, slowly revolving, centrally placed.

'Funny thing,' Ramsden said, following her gaze. 'System went down, two thirty, thereabouts. This whole area. Malfunction. Didn't get up and running till close on four.'

'Coincidence?'

'What's that? An explanation waiting to happen? Don't you soddin' believe it.'

'What then?'

'Bloke in charge went off conveniently sick. A while before they could get someone else in to cover. Couple of uniforms, local, went round to his address. Nobody home. We're still looking.'

'Whoever worked them over,' Karen said. 'All that was done somewhere else. That's what we're assuming?'

Not really a question that demanded answering. Anything else, there would have been far more blood than there was: ceiling, walls, floor. And even there, that close to the airport, too great a risk of noise. Slow screams of a dying man. Three dying men. She realised she didn't know exactly how they had died.

'Two of them,' Ramsden said when asked, 'a bullet to the back of the head. Small calibre by the look of it, close range. After they'd been worked on, my guess, not before. Biggest of the three, apart from what's been done to his face and hands, no obvious cause.' He shrugged. 'Maybe his heart just gave out.'

'No way yet of knowing who they are?'

'Not as yet. Once the computer guys get to work on the faces we'll have a better idea what they looked like before all this. Run 'em through the system after that. See what pops.'

Nodding acknowledgement, Karen stepped away, slowly turned and looked up into the sky. A late plane, taking off, its lights curving gradually upwards into the night sky. Wherever it was heading, she wished she were on board, bound for wherever. Anywhere. Anywhere but here.

33

'Croissant?'

'What?' Letitia's voice was harsh, bruised by sleep.

'Croissant? It's a sort of curved doughy thing, a bit like—'

'I know what a fucking croissant is.'

'Good. Here. Have one.' Cordon sat on the side of the bed, paper bag in his lap.

Letitia shook her head and, shuffling into a sitting position, pulled the pillows up against the headboard and leaned back. The sheet slipped as she twisted round, leaving one breast exposed. Outside, rain was falling lightly; you could hear it faintly against the shutters.

'Where've you been anyway?' she asked.

He held up the bag. 'To get these.'

'I didn't hear the car.'

'I walked.'

'In this?'

He shrugged. 'Live in Cornwall, remember? You get used to it.'

His hair had been darkened by the rain; shoes and

waterproof jacket he'd taken off and left just inside the door. His idea had been to give himself time to think, think — what was the expression? outside the box? — but all he could see was the same set of imponderables, the same set of walls.

They'd taken the ferry from Portsmouth to St. Malo. Letitia's father had driven them to the port and then continued on his way towards Bristol, old friends he hadn't seen in far too long a time. The bookshop was locked up. A sign: *Closed Till Further Notice.* After what had happened, there would be people coming round, he didn't doubt; more friends of Anton's, asking questions, none too fussy about how they got their answers. One more consequence of Cordon's actions.

'Who in God's name d'you think you are?' Clifford Carlin had asked. 'Shane? Sorting out the bad guys? Setting things to rights?' Jack Schaefer. Alan Ladd in buckskins. One of Carlin's favourites. Cordon's, too.

'Something like that,' Cordon had answered. He was taller than Ladd, he knew that for a fact.

'Great!' Letitia had said when he told her what had happened at the caravan site. 'You're going to get us all fucking killed, you know that, don't you?'

It was a risk, a possibility. Simply, he hadn't seen what else he could do. He'd said as much to Jack Kiley when he called him later, explaining the situation, asking if there were any ways in which Kiley thought he could help.

'What?' Kiley had replied. 'A couple of nights' bed and board and suddenly I'm your guardian angel? Picking up the pieces?'

'Sorry, Jack. Bit out of my depth.'

Kiley gave it some thought. 'Letitia and the kid, they've got passports?'

'I think so.'

Uncertain where they might go after the funeral, what they might do, Letitia had taken that precaution, at least.

'What you've got to do,' Kiley said. 'Buy a little time.'

After arriving in France, they'd taken a bus into Dinard, as Kiley had instructed, just a little way west along the coast. A fading old seaside town, mostly closed down for the winter. Grand hotels on the seafront boarded up, shuttered across. Only the one café open on the promenade, where Letitia sat and smoked and read whatever paperbacks she'd bought on the ferry, while Cordon and young Dan played desultory games of football on the beach.

'Be patient,' Kiley had told them. 'Sit tight. I'll get back to you soon as I can.'

For some reason, there was a statue of Alfred Hitchcock peering out across the water, surrounded by stone birds. A casino under redecoration. They found a little place across from the art gallery that sold good pizzas and sat there for hours, sheltering from the wind, listening to the same music playing over and over.

Kiley phoned again on the third day. One of Jane's friends at the school had a holiday place in Brittany, a village just a couple of hours' drive from where they were. Not even a village, a hamlet. Four dwellings and only one of them occupied year round, an old man and his dog. They could stay there, till Easter if necessary. Sort out what they were going to do.

'Might need your help there, too, Jack,' Cordon said.

'Tell me something I don't know.'

Cordon hired a car and drove it as far as Lamballe where he changed it for another. If anyone was going to be on their trail, he wanted to make it as difficult for them as possible. At the Carrefour in Guingamp they loaded up with supplies; the nearest village, some three or four miles from where they would be staying, had a *boulangerie* and nothing else.

*

'For Christ's sake!' Letitia exclaimed.

'What?'

'That bloody croissant. You're getting crumbs all over the bed.'

'Didn't realise you were so fussy.'

'Yeah, well . . .'

They heard the toilet flush and then Danny's voice telling them it was raining. A moment later he appeared in the doorway, tousle haired, sleepy eyed, dinosaur pyjamas.

'I'll get the coffee on,' Cordon said.

'You do that.'

She lifted the covers and the boy slid in beside her, Letitia turning to slide an arm comfortably around him, kiss him on the forehead – 'Why don't you just snuggle down?'

Feeling a stranger, Cordon left the room.

It was a converted farmhouse, low and long, a *longère*, thick stone walls that had stood for more than a century. Brown shutters, red paint around the window frames starting to blister and fade. A garden front and back, gravel, lawn and shrubs. A few stunted apple trees. Other trees, taller, shielded the house from the road. Scots pine? Cordon wondered. Breton pine, perhaps? Was there such a thing? His father would have . . . he stopped the thought on hold.

Inside there were three bedrooms, a bathroom, a living room, a wide kitchen with a refectory table and a tap that permanently dripped. You could have fitted Cordon's old Newlyn sail loft in twice with space to spare. No need for them to get under one another's feet.

Letitia seemed to be in denial: whenever Cordon tried to get her to talk about what they were going to do, consider their options, 'There are no fucking options,' was the best he could get.

Letitia stayed in bed late, drank supermarket wine and

cooked a few unwilling meals. Listened in a half-hearted fashion to the Madeleine Peyroux CD that had been left in the portable stereo. Without too much of an argument, she let Danny talk her into helping him do one of the several jigsaw puzzles he'd found in one of the cupboards, played hide-and-seek with him until that too palled and she ran her hand through his hair, kissed his cheek and begged for a rest. Time to do a little reading instead.

When she'd finished the Martina Cole she'd bought on board, she tried some of the books the owners had left around – Ian McEwan, Rose Tremain, Julian Barnes – but with limited success. Sometimes she just sat, collar hunched up, on a folding chair close to the front door of the house, smoking cigarette after cigarette and staring at the empty lane beyond the gate.

As far as Danny was concerned the whole thing was just a holiday, a place to run around; the owners clearly had kids of their own and there were toys in boxes, DVDs of *Toy Story*, *Chicken Run*, *Tintin*, *Planet Earth*. There was even a child's bike with a slow puncture in the rear tyre forever in need of pumping up, and Cordon taught Danny, after a fashion, to ride. Wobbly circles that ended less and less in tears and bumps and grazed knees.

'Don't make him too fond of you,' Letitia said one afternoon, her voice edged like a rusted blade. 'He's already got one father to get over. He doesn't need a fuckin' second.'

Cordon drove to the town and bought lamb chops and a bottle of good Scotch, Johnny Walker Black Label. Scoured the bins of cheap CDs and found an old recording from the Paris Jazz Festival in 1949, remastered: the Tadd Dameron Quintet with Miles Davis.

He'd called the headquarters of the Devon and Cornwall Police in Exeter when they'd arrived and spoken in the vaguest terms of the need to take an extended break, leave without pay; let them try turfing him out a few years short of his pension if they cared to, if they dared. Serve them right for putting him out to grass for having a mind of his own, playing the awkward bugger one too many times.

Even so, they couldn't stay there for ever.

A fantasy family.

Lives in hiding.

Recipients of someone else's good nature.

Funny thing, Jack Kiley had told him, but a few days after he got one of his contacts to run a check on Anton Kosach, as Cordon had asked, he'd had a caller himself.

'SOCA,' Kiley said, 'Serious and Organised Crime Agency. Bloke looked like a bloody tax inspector. Wanted to know about my interest in Kosach. Gave the impression I might have crossed some line. I spun him a bunch of lies and half-truths, how the name had come up as part of something I'd been helping out on, steered well clear of mentioning names. Not sure how much he bought of it, if any. Asked him why he was so interested, of course, but he wasn't giving anything away. Mr Kosach is one of a number of people who are currently under investigation, that was the sum of it. Hands off, in other words. Steer well clear. Thought you should know.'

'Thanks, Jack,' Cordon had said.

He hadn't mentioned it to Letitia.

Then one day when he got back to the farmhouse after taking a stroll around the narrow lanes, the door hung wide open.

There was no one there.

His chest tightened; skin dimpled cold along the backs of his legs and arms. The book Letitia had been reading was on the ground beside her chair; Dan's borrowed bike lay on the grass. Inside there were no signs of anything amiss.

He walked to the end of the lane where it met the road, then a short way in both directions, seeing no one. The earlier chill had disappeared and the sun was filtering weakly through the clouds. Their names when he called them echoed back to him along the still air.

Going inside, something caught his eye. Something white, a scrap of paper on the floor. A note Letitia had scribbled that had blown from the table, the wind through the open door. *Gone for a walk. Thought we might catch you.* Cordon broke the seal on the Black Label, poured a small measure into a glass, his hand shaking only slightly as he raised it to his mouth. For God's sake, he told himself, get a grip.

For some minutes he stood in the doorway, listening for sounds of them returning, looking into the space beyond the trees. They wouldn't have gone far.

Back inside, he set the newly acquired CD to play: track two, another version of 'Good Bait'. You could never have too many. He smiled as the trumpet rose above the crackle of sound. Miles not yet cool, only twenty-three, still trying to sound like someone else, like Dizzy, not yet his own man.

That was how it happened, Cordon thought, you started by copying, learned through doing. Experience. Some did. Some never learned.

'All right,' Letitia said, the words out of her mouth almost before she was through the door. 'Sit. Listen. I've been thinking.'

Her skin had taken on some vestige of colour, no longer the putty-like grey it had been more or less since they'd arrived. She looked five years younger; there was, if not a sparkle, liveliness in her eyes.

'We can't just stick here and bloody fester, right?'

'Right.'

Dan was tugging at Cordon's sleeve, anxious to show him the shells he'd collected from the garden earlier, tiny shells that lay mixed with the gravel, each one no bigger than a fingernail.

'Danny,' his mother said, 'just go and play outside, okay?'

Disappointment flooded the boy's face.

'Ten minutes,' she said, ruffling his hair. 'That's all. We're playing catch later, remember? Why don't you go and get some practice.'

He pouted. 'I can't on my own.'

'Throw it up against the wall. Just mind the windows, that's all.'

'You won't be long?'

'I promise. Now off you go, go on.'

The boy grudgingly outside, Cordon pulled out one of the chairs from the table and sat down. 'So, what's the brilliant idea?'

'No need to be bloody sarky.'

'I'm sorry. Go on.'

'Taras?'

'Who?'

'Taras. Anton's brother.'

'The one with the hotel . . .'

'In the Lakes, exactly.'

'What about him?'

'Well, for one thing he liked me . . .'

Cordon raised an eyebrow.

'Liked me, not fancied me. Well, maybe . . . but we always got along, that's the thing. He liked Danny, too. And he was reasonable. Not like Anton. You could talk to him and he'd listen.'

'And you think that's what we should do? Talk to him?'

'What someone should do, yes. Get him to talk to Anton, make him listen to reason.'

'You think that's possible?'

She shrugged. 'It's got to be, hasn't it? For Danny's sake as much as anyone's.'

Cordon glanced towards the door. 'You think he misses his father?'

'I don't know.'

'I've never heard him mention him. Not once.'

'That doesn't mean he's not thinking about him.'

Cordon nodded, thought that was probably right. Children did, young children. Seemed to need to. Until they grew up, grew away . . .

'Besides, Danny or no Danny, we can't just stay here for ever. It's not real. We've got to go back to England sooner or later and when we do I don't want to be looking over my shoulder all the time in case Anton's crazy twin brothers are going to be there, waving guns in our faces.'

Cordon angled his chair round away from the table and looked at her carefully. 'What do you want? Longer term, I mean.'

Letitia took a breath. 'I just want to go back and be getting on with my life. Our lives. Danny and me. I don't know where. Not yet. But one thing's certain, Anton, no way am I going back to live with him, that's over. And he's got to accept it. If he wants to see Danny on some kind of regular basis, that's fine. If he wants to take him places, weekends, holidays, that's fine, too. But Danny's living with me.'

As if on cue, her son's voice came from the garden, 'Mum!'

'A normal life,' Letitia said. 'Is that too much to ask?'

Cordon shook his head. It shouldn't be, but maybe, in this instance, it was. And for Letitia, what was normal anyway?

'No,' he said. 'No, I don't think so.'

'Your friend Kiley,' she said, 'you think he'd do that? Talk to Taras? Some kind of go-between?'

'I don't know. We've asked a lot of him already.'

'But he might.'

Cordon nodded. 'He might.'

Letitia's face broke into a rare smile, a grin almost, carried away on her own idea. 'Good-looking, is he? Fit?' She winked. 'I'd make it worth his while.'

'Mum!'

'Coming!'

She reached out towards Cordon's shoulder as she passed, her fingers brushing the bare skin of his neck; just a touch, but it sent a shock through him as if he'd been grazed by electric wire.

34

Not so long ago, it would have been a smoke-filled room. Silk Cut, Benson's King Size, the occasional small cigar. The air acrid and blue. Not a black face, not a woman in sight. Now it was pristine, anonymous, the lingering scent of air freshener and cheap polish. The faint hum of central heating. A table, centrally placed, and seven chairs, three occupied. Burcher stood by the window, looking out through the double glazing.

They were on the eleventh floor, a view south and west across London, far beyond the Imperial War Museum and the Elephant, out towards the old Battersea Power Station and the television mast at Crystal Palace, topping out at over two hundred metres.

Karen they kept waiting outside, a small room across the corridor, coffee, bland and undrinkable, in a plastic cup. A week-old copy of the *Standard* to read. She had chosen black, a black trouser suit neatly cut, straight-legged, angled lapels; a cream shirt, buttoned to the neck. Boots with a low heel. Little make-up, save around the eyes; no ornamentation, no rings. Hair pushed up and back and held in place.

'Want me to come and hold your hand?' Ramsden had asked.

'As if.'

So far, only one of the three men whose bodies had been found at Stansted had been positively identified. Valentyn Horak, a Ukrainian last arrested eighteen months previously, accused of involvement in drug smuggling and prostitution; several weeks before the trial, all charges had been dropped when the CPS judged there was insufficient evidence to secure a conviction.

Though neither of the other two victims yet had names, all the evidence – tattoos, dental work, physical appearance – suggested that they too were from the Ukraine or somewhere similar, in the country illegally.

Karen had been unable, as yet, to erase the memory; scrub the lingering smell from her skin.

A civilian with a slight stammer invited her to join the Detective Chief Superintendent and the others, held the door open, then disappeared whence she had come – all of this without once looking Karen in the eye.

Three heads turned towards her as she entered; Burcher's did not.

Warren Cormack, of course, she knew. Same suit, different tie. A suggestion of a smile as she entered, he stood and offered his hand.

Seated directly across from him was a man she didn't recognise. Mid-forties? A little older? Hair neatly trimmed, almost an old-fashioned straight back and sides. His suit jacket, a thin pinstripe, he'd removed and hung carefully from the back of the chair alongside, shirtsleeves rolled neatly back at the cuff. There was a small cut above his top lip as if he'd been uncautious shaving. Cardboard cut-out eyes.

Then there was Alex Williams. Alexandria. Tailored jacket. Square hands. A face that was handsome rather than pretty.

Hair cut short, like a boy's. Had she not known her to be happily married and living with a husband – who was something in the media – and their three children in a large terraced house in Herne Hill, Karen might have mistaken her as gay.

When they'd first met, Alex had been seconded to Homicide and Serious Crime; no bullshit, no backing down, a fast learner – Karen had liked her. Admired her, even. Now, two promotions, four years later, she was back in the Specialist Intelligence Service, SIS, and the darling of the Met's PR department – equal opportunity works, motherhood and a career both attainable, here was the living proof. It helped that her husband worked, most of the time, from home; that they could afford a succession of nannies and au pairs.

'Karen, good to see you again.' Her handshake was swift and firm.

Leaving his post at the window, Burcher moved to the chair at the table's head.

'Getting to be something of a habit, Detective Chief Inspector, turning up bodies like that.'

'Homicide, sir. Goes with the territory.'

Alex Williams stifled a laugh.

Burcher tensed but let it pass.

'Purpose of this meeting, bring you up to speed. Alex, you know. Warren, too, I believe. And this . . .' a quick nod of the head, 'is Charles Frost from SOCA.'

'Charlie,' Frost said, helpfully.

'Charlie's keeping something of a watching brief.'

Like buggery, Karen thought. She'd had dealings with SOCA before. Double-dealings. It still rankled badly. With barely a nod in Frost's direction, she took a seat alongside Cormack, across from the others. Mixed doubles.

'Warren,' said Burcher from the umpire's chair. 'Valentyn Horak, for Karen's sake, why don't you give us a little background?'

Cormack opened the folder in front of him, a quick glance as if to refresh his memory, then let it fall closed. 'All right. Some of this, Karen, you'll be familiar with, in principle anyway, the incursion of various crime organisations from the other side of what used to be the Iron Curtain. One good sniff at the joys of the free market and they take to it like ducks to water. Drugs, at first. That's the big thing, still is, in a way. But with the fall in value of cocaine, for example, there's been a move towards consolidation. Groups from the Ukraine, Albania, lesser players such as Moldova. Coming together for the common good. Theirs not ours. And with a certain sharing of resources, they've begun to diversify. People trafficking, that's where a lot of the money is now. Migrant labour. Prostitution.

'This last couple of years they've specialised more and more in the trafficking of young people. Fourteen to seventeen. Technically, children. Some of them get pushed out on to the streets selling cigarettes, counterfeit DVDs and the like; some work fifteen, sixteen hours a day in dodgy pizza parlours; others are forced into brothels. Brothels, massage parlours, whatever you call them. That's where the serious money's made.'

He leaned forward, hitting his stride.

'One underage girl – or boy – can earn two fifty, three hundred pounds a day. Minimum. Just do the maths. You could be talking six, seven thousand a month, easy. From just one kid. Close on eighty thousand a year. Two, three years till they're used up, over the hill. Kick them out on to the streets and start again.

'This last eighteen months I've been leading a Project Team looking into the London end of this, liaising with SOCA at a national level. And with SIS, through Alex here. Getting hold of evidence, solid evidence, finding people willing to go on record, stand up in court, it's not easy. You know, I think, what happened with Horak previously. We thought we had him and then we didn't. We get so far and then the ground tends to slide out from under us. These last few months, though, have been interesting.'

He paused for water.

'Up until recently, most of our long-term home-grown dealers have been happy enough to take their supplies from the Albanians, the Bulgarians, whoever. Business being business. But for some of them, it stuck in their craw. And just lately they've been kicking back. Taking out some of the lower level guys, frightening them off, clawing their way back up the chain. Intercepting shipments that have been coming in by way of the Channel Tunnel, or, in one or two cases, offloaded off the coast. And then hitting where it hurts. Karen, we've talked a little about this. Raids on cannabis farms right across East Anglia and the South-East.'

'For which,' Karen said, 'you think Gordon Dooley is responsible.'

'Our information suggests Dooley is behind it, yes. The extent to which he plays an active part, we're still not sure. As you know, he's currently under surveillance. And, though we've no definite proof, nothing quite yet to get us knocking down doors, there's good reason for supposing a South London gang centring round known villains like Mike Carter and possibly, just possibly, Terry Martin, is providing the muscle.'

'The same gang,' Burcher said, intervening, 'of which Parsons and Johnson, our two bodies from Camden, were charter members.'

'The same.'

'So, Camden was an organised hit by Horak or someone close to him – East European, anyway, that's what we're thinking – a warning. The response to which was that bloody business out at Stansted.'

'It points that way,' Cormack said.

'Tit for tat.'

'Yes.'

'Anything you can do, I can do better.'

For one bizarre moment, Karen thought the Detective Chief Inspector might be about to burst into song.

'The earlier murder,' Burcher said, 'Andronic, the kid in the pond, you see, Karen, any connection?'

She took a moment to consider her answer.

'I'm not sure, sir. We do have some information that he might have been involved in some occasional low-level dealing, but I can't see him being visible enough to attract the attention of someone like Martin or Dooley. Although . . .' She hesitated.

'Go on.'

'Terry Martin's daughter had been seeing Andronic very much against his wishes.'

'And for that,' Alex Williams said, speaking for the first time, 'he would have killed him?'

'I think it's possible, yes.'

'Possible,' Burcher said, 'though I believe, despite the best efforts of you and your team, unproven.'

'So far. Sir.'

Burcher let it pass.

'These murders,' Karen said, 'Stansted, Camden, I'm assuming from what we've heard – the point of this meeting, really – you'll be wanting my team to step away.'

Burcher cleared his throat. 'Not necessarily so.'

'But everything Warren's just said, the nature of what's happened, what lays behind it, this has to be a Project Team operation, surely? They've got the resources, the background. All we'll do, muddy the waters. Get in the way to no good cause.' She leaned back in her chair. 'We've plenty enough on our plates as it is.'

199

No one spoke. A slight scuffing of feet beneath the table. Uneasy glances.

'As I say, not necessarily the way we see it,' Burcher said. 'Not at all. Everyone else here – Warren, Alex, Charles—'

'Charlie.'

'Right, Charlie. They're all intent on the bigger picture, you're correct about that, of course. Whereas you, your team, specific aims, objectives – homicide investigation, your field of expertise.'

Not what you said last time, you bastard, Karen thought; not what you implied.

'So, we'd like you to push ahead on the Camden killing, Milescu, too, concentrate your energies there. . . .'

'And these last two murders, Stansted . . .'

'As and how they're linked, yes. Liaising with Warren, of course.'

'That's a big stretch, without help. . . .'

'Any request for extra bodies, extra hours – sympathetically met.' Burcher lifted the papers in front of him and tapped the ends into place.

'Alex, anything you want to add?'

'Not at this stage, thank you.'

'Charles?'

'Charlie. Yes, just one thing. For some little time now, we've been taking an interest in the activities of a certain Anton Kosach. Businessman from the Ukraine. No links with Horak as far as we've been able to establish. Bit more establishment, more upmarket. Oil money to begin with. More recently mineral products, high-end motors, transportation. Owns a number of properties, a place in Surrey worth upwards of fifteen million amongst them. Numbers amongst his friends one or two with possible connections to people trafficking. As far as we've made out so far, these connections are purely social, but that's by no means definite. And Kosach's various enterprises put him in a good position to facilitate money laundering on quite a large scale. Again, nothing definite, nothing proved. But we're watching. SIS also.'

A glance towards Alex Williams, who nodded agreement.

'So,' Frost concluded, 'should Kosach's name show up on anyone's radar, I'd appreciate a heads-up forthwith. Alex, also.'

Burcher thanked him, thanked everyone, brought the meeting to a close. General movement, a scraping of chairs.

'It's been a while,' Alex Williams said, falling into step beside Karen in the corridor outside.

'Yes, I know.'

'I'll give you a call. Come over. Bit of a catch-up.'

'Okay, fine. I'd like that,' Karen said, without quite believing it would happen. Busy people, busy lives. Alex Williams, busier than most.

At the foot of the stairs they exchanged smiles and went their separate ways, Karen fast-dialling Mike Ramsden as she did so, setting up a meeting of their own, how to proceed from here.

35

Not quite able to settle, alert for sounds of an approaching car, strange voices, a vehicle turning into the lane, they had fallen, nevertheless, into something approaching a routine. Letitia was the more listless, the more likely to lapse into moods of depression, alleviated by her son's almost omnipresent good humour.

Kiley had made contact with Anton's brother, Taras, as requested; driven up from London and met him at an Ibis hotel, off the M6 north of Preston. Phoned Cordon to report.

Anton was under a lot of pressure, Taras had told him, seeking to explain his brother's behaviour. Business, it does not always run well. He chose not to elaborate. And on top of that, this thing with Letitia and his son . . . much as he liked Letitia, Taras said, she was in the wrong. Taking a man's son away from him, his flesh and blood.

Taras had gripped Kiley's arm. 'In our country, in Ukraine, it is most important bond. Family. Father and son. Holy, you understand? Here, in England, perhaps is different. But for us, for Anton . . . And what did she think, Letitia? She could run, hide forever? And you, you know where she is. Her and the boy.'

Kiley had shaken his head.

'You must.'

'Not exactly.'

'This man with her . . .'

'A man with her?'

'This man, he is her lover?'

'No.'

'You are sure of this?'

Kiley nodded.

'Then why?'

'A friend.'

'A fool.'

'Perhaps.'

'You know where they are,' Taras said again.

'She wants to be certain nothing will happen to her,' Kiley said. 'If she returns. Her or the boy. She wants to know that Anton will sit down with her and talk, talk reasonably.'

'Of course.'

'A lawyer should be involved.'

'No lawyers. He does not like lawyers.'

'An accommodation needs to be reached. Equal access to the child.'

'Equal, no. He will never agree. Danya is his son.'

'Equal access and a financial arrangement of some kind, to look after the boy. The exact details can be sorted later.'

Over and over, Taras was shaking his head.

'I was told you were a reasonable man,' Kiley said. 'A good man. Someone who could be trusted to do the right thing.'

Taras flexed the fingers of both hands, the knuckles cracking, one after another. 'I will speak with him. My brother. Do what I can. I will let you know.'

'Thank you.'

'But no promise.'

'I understand.'

'What d'you think?' Cordon had asked Kiley, once the conversation had been relayed.

'My best guess?'

'Of course.'

'My guess would be, sooner or later Anton will come round. Pretend to, at least. Agree to terms, and then, when he's got them in his sights, renege on the whole thing. Till then, I'd keep a weather eye.'

'You're a pal, Jack.'

'Just wait till you get my bill.'

Cordon took it as a joke; hoped against hope that it was. All too aware that Kiley had already gone the extra mile and beyond. Loyalties stretched close to breaking point, he shouldn't wonder.

'As soon as Taras gets back to me,' Kiley said, 'I'll let you know.'

They were still waiting.

In the kitchen, next to Letitia, Cordon was Heston Blumenthal and Nigel Slater rolled into one. 'Cordon Bleu again, eh?' Letitia had joked, on her way from bathroom to bedroom through the kitchen. The towel she was holding wrapped around her slipped just a little as she turned away.

Cordon used a fork to turn the sausages in the pan, where they were cooking with onions, a couple of bay leaves and a scattering of fennel. The potatoes were simmering, ready to be mashed with milk and butter. He poured a splash of red wine in with the sausages, another into the gravy that was thickening in a small saucepan to one side.

'You'd make someone a lovely husband,' Letitia said, coming back into the room. 'Anyone ever tell you that?'

'Not recently.'

She picked up his glass and sampled the wine. Made an approving face and poured some generously into a glass of her own.

'You could tell Danny dinner's nearly ready,' Cordon said. 'Drag him away from the TV.'

Some forty-five minutes later, plates that had been full were close to empty; even Danny had made short work of two fat sausages and a good dollop of mash soaked in gravy. Only the onions had been pushed to the side of his plate and left.

'Now tell me there's apple pie,' Letitia said.

'Afraid not.'

'Anything?'

'Pears. Cheese.'

'What kind of cheese?'

'Goat's.'

She put two fingers in her mouth and mimed throwing up and, laughing at this, Danny had a coughing fit that reduced him to tears.

Cordon did the washing-up and Letitia, having run a bath for Danny, dried.

Cordon opened a second bottle of wine.

Letitia washed her son's hair, rinsed it, and rubbed it dry. Kissed him and tucked him up in bed. Read him story after story until his eyelids fluttered closed. Kissed him again, gently, sat watching him a while longer, then tiptoed away, angling the door quietly closed.

She was not going to lose him, no matter what.

There was a sliver of moon in the sky; faint clusters of stars. Close against the open doorway, Letitia shivered and lit a cigarette. Cordon was standing midway between the house and the barn, staring up into the sky. His father had taught him the names of all the constellations and now, though he could trace their patterns with his eyes, Orion aside, he could not have named a single one.

It didn't matter, he told himself, why should it? But in some way he couldn't quite explain, not knowing was letting his father down; dishonoured him; what he stood for, what he was.

'Don't you have a son somewhere?' Letitia had said to him the other day. 'South Africa, somewhere? Australia?'

He hadn't answered.

Her cigarette sparked now in the darkness.

'Danny sleeping?' he asked, turning in her direction.

'I think so.'

She thought he was going to stop beside her as he drew level, but instead he carried on into the house.

36

Ramsden had been right about the car used in the Camden shootings, the BMW; it had been found on the upper level of a supermarket car park out at St Albans, burned to a blackened shell. The lab techs had done what they could – cyanoacrylate fuming, VMD – but to no avail. If there was a link back to Valentyn Horak, always assuming Horak and his associates had been responsible, this wasn't it.

So far, they had had no success in discovering whatever vehicle had ferried the bodies to Stansted, nor where Horak and the others had been tortured prior to being killed. Gordon Dooley, suspected of being behind the crimes, avenging the gunning down of two of his own, was still under careful surveillance and was placing not a foot out of line. The only regular visits he made were to his ageing mother in a care home in Haywards Heath and to the chiropractor dealing with his back, spatial realignment of the spine. The only phone calls to one of his ex-wives, urging a reconsideration of the amount he was currently paying in child support, and to his bookmaker ahead of meetings at Kempton, Haydock and Southwell.

The CCTV operator who'd conveniently phoned in sick on the evening the three bodies were placed inside the airport storage unit, was still adamant that his migraine had been real, no one had got to him, no pressures exerted, no payment made. His bank account showed no unexplained sums as income; a search of the flat where he lived in Harlow had discovered no suitcases crammed with used banknotes on top of the wardrobe or under the bed. Taking up the floorboards yielded only dry rot and a small family of mice.

'Bastard's lying through his back teeth,' Ramsden said and Karen thought he was right. But proving it, like so much else . . .

The security officer supposedly on patrol that evening had proved an easier nut to crack. Up to a certain point. Sick about it, wasn't he? Sick to his stomach about what had happened. Never would have imagined it, never in a million years. These two fellers had approached him, he told Ramsden, just a couple of nights before. All we need you to do, they said, turn a blind eye. To what? He didn't know to what, didn't ask. Bit of jiggery pokery with one of the containers, he imagined. Something smuggled in. Stuff being knocked off, stripped from the manifest. If he'd thought for a moment it was going to be anything like it was . . .

'How much?' Ramsden had asked. The room a sweat box, despite the outside temperature; low ceilings, space just enough for a metal table and chairs, the only window locked fast, heating turned up deliberately high.

'How much?' Ramsden said again.

'How much what?'

'How much they drop you?'

'I told you, nothing.'

'Listen, you miserable little scrote, don't fuck me around. How fuckin' much?'

'Couple of hundred, that's all.'

'And the rest.'

'No, no, straight up.'

'Yeah?'

'Yes.'

'Come cheap, then, don't you? 'Less you knew them, of course. Make more sense that. Old mates pulling a favour. That how it was?'

'No. No, I swear.' Sweat pouring off him like rain.

'You did know them, though.'

'No.'

'No?'

'Never seen 'em before. Not till that night. I told you. Never.'

'You're lying.'

'No.'

'We'll see.'

'I told you, my oath.'

'Your what?'

'My oath. My word.'

Ramsden grated out a laugh. 'Your fucking word! Not worth a fiddler's fart and any self-respecting silk who gets you on the stand'll have the lies stripped off you so fast you'll be up there shivering with one hand hanging on to your scrawny balls and the other covering your arse.' He laughed again, pushed back his chair. 'You're going down, you miserable little dipshit, down for a long time, unless you give me something I can use. You understand? We understood?'

'Yes. I mean, no. I dunno. I dunno if I can.'

'Pentonville. Brixton. The Scrubs. Aiding and abetting, that'd be the least of it. Accessory to murder, I'd say. Depends. 'Less, of course, you recognise the shit you're in. Give us a reason for putting in a word. Show us how good you are, remembering faces, naming names.'

Head bowed, the security officer closed his eyes. Sweat

dripped from the end of his nose. His voice was a whisper, little more. 'I'll do what I can.'

'Say again?'

'I'll do what I can.'

Ramsden allowed himself a smile. It wasn't to last for long.

Four sessions: faces on the computer, folders of well-handled 6 x 4s, try as he might the man failed to pick out a single face, a single name. He was lying, of course, just as the CCTV operator was lying, but what could they do? The threatened possibility of a jail sentence against the embedded certainty that if he grassed sooner or later someone would use a blade on him, likely even cut his throat, in the nick or out.

In her office later, Karen read the anger, the frustration on Ramsden's face.

'Bastard!' he said, slamming a fist down on to her desk. 'Chickenshit bastard!'

'It'll come. You know it will. Sooner or later, it'll come.'

Not soon enough for Burcher. True to his word, he had made more officers available, civilian support staff, too, but for that he expected results. Homicide, he had said, holding back just a little on the irony, your field of expertise. There'd been an urgent message just that morning: the Detective Chief Superintendent would appreciate a progress report ASAP. So far she hadn't returned the call.

When the phone rang, she thought it was possibly Burcher himself, snotty and impatient, demanding action, answers.

Counting towards ten, she picked up on six.

'We were going to have a catch-up?' Alex Williams' voice, pleasant, even.

'Yes.'

'How about this evening? Short notice, I know, but if we keep leaving it . . .'

'No, this evening's fine.'

'You remember how to get here?'

'I think so.'

'Around seven, then? Seven thirty? See you then.'

'A date?' Ramsden said, eyebrow raised, having heard just one side of the conversation. 'All right for some.'

37

It was dark by the time she arrived, had been dark for a good couple of hours. The house was quintessential South London suburban: generous bay windows, white paint, red brick; an attic room with a steeply angled roof. Shrubs in pots in the small front garden; a bare bed with the earth set hard from where it had last been turned. A child's scooter resting against the green recycling bin. *Please! No Junk Mail!* stickered to the letter flap in the front door.

Karen rang the bell.

The door opened to a small child wearing Miffy pyjamas; startled eyes, curly hair: Alex stood behind her, denim shirt hanging loose over blue jeans, bare feet, glass of wine in her hand.

This is what I've been missing, Karen thought. For that brief moment, it mattered.

'You found us again then. No trouble?'

'No trouble.'

'This is Amy. Say hello, Amy.'

Amy did no such thing.

'Hello, Amy,' Karen said, leaning towards her, and Amy wriggled away.

Alex laughed. 'Come on in.'

What had been two good-sized rooms had been knocked through to make a large space that was filled, nevertheless, with soft-cushioned settees, easy chairs, a dining table of scrubbed pine, more chairs, magazines, comics, a flat-screen television, children's toys. Paintings vied with bookshelves for space on the walls; one section crowded with children's drawings, brightly coloured, starting to curl.

Amy had retreated behind one of the settees and was clutching a one-eyed bear. Another girl, older, sat cross-legged on the floor, reading a book. A boy of eight or nine lay on his tummy, watching a programme about seals on TV, the sound turned down to a whisper.

'I think they were all in bed, last time you were here,' Alex said. 'So, that's Ben, that's Beth, and Amy you've already met.'

Self-conscious, Karen said, 'Hi,' and was predictably ignored.

'And I'm Roger.' Alex's husband was wearing a long butcher's apron, flour on his hands, flip-flops on his feet. 'We did meet before, though I don't expect you to remember. And I won't shake hands or you'll get this all over you. Dumplings. For the casserole. Lamb, I hope that's okay.'

A smile and a nod of the head and he disappeared back to the kitchen.

'Just sling some of that stuff off there and have a seat,' Alex said. 'Let me get you some wine. The kids will be in bed any time soon and we can eat. After that we'll talk. White or red?'

It was past nine. Between them they'd cleared the table and loaded the dishwasher, then Roger had excused himself to go upstairs and wade through his emails. Alex had stuck some Chopin on the stereo and opened another bottle of red.

'Stansted,' Alex said, 'all the crap that goes with it. They're hanging you out to dry on this, you realise?'

'Pretty much.'

'They'll let you and your team keep ferreting around, kicking up as much dust and trouble as you can. Hoping you'll shake something down into the net. Anything useful that looks as if it might bear fruit, they'll have it for their own, work it whichever way they can. Whatever's deemed expedient. And if you come up short, fail to get a result, well, nobody else but you to blame.'

'What else could I do? Tell Burcher to take a hike?'

'Not exactly.'

'And besides – Warren, Charlie and Alex, wasn't that what he said? Intent on the bigger picture. All three of you. Or isn't that true?'

Alex shifted position, folding one leg beneath her. 'No, it's true. As far as it goes. But, you know, SIS, we can be pro-active in the gathering of intelligence, but basically we're there to support. What's the rubric? Something about helping prevent harm and enforcing legislation against organised criminal networks at National Intelligence Model levels 2 and 3.'

Smiling, she drank some wine.

'They use us, sweetie, like we're all using you. I just wanted to be sure you knew.'

Karen sighed and settled back into the comfort of her chair; she'd eaten too much – too much casserole, too much crumble. Her bed was the other side of London and she had an early start next day. Nonetheless, when Alex reached the bottle in her direction, she nodded and held out her glass.

'Let me ask you something,' Karen said.

'Go ahead.'

'Valentyn Horak, one of the victims at Stansted, he was subject to a surveillance operation before, yes?'

Alex nodded.

'Placed under arrest, charged – presumably with the go-ahead of the CPS.'

Alex nodded again.

'Everything's fine almost up to the trial and then, out of the blue, someone at the CPS decides, after looking through the evidence again, oh, no, sorry, this isn't going to stick, and recommends no further action be taken.'

'Yes. At least, that's what I understand.'

'And you don't think that's a bit funny?'

'Funny, no. Lazy, maybe. Slipshod, possibly. And whether that's down to the officers involved in the arrest, or the CPS barrister, I don't know. Most likely a combination of the two. But, Karen, you know, it happens. More often than we'd like. More often than it should.' She sipped some more wine. 'Water under the proverbial bridge.'

'You don't think it might have been a matter of money changing hands?'

Alex looked at her appraisingly. 'Whose hand did you have in mind?'

'Take your pick.'

'It's possible, I suppose, but . . .' She shook her head a trifle wearily. 'Corruption, it's there, certainly. Fact of life. Just turn on the news.'

'But in this case?'

'If there's anything more than the usual vague suspicions, I haven't heard.' Alex pushed herself to her feet. 'Let's go into the garden. I need a cigarette.'

Who was it who said in London you could never see stars? There they were, peppering the purple darkness above their heads; the night clear and cold, intimations of a frost.

Alex's lighter flared.

'Sure you won't join me?'

'Sure.'

'I always thought you smoked.'

'I did.'

'When did you give up?'

'Which time?'

Alex laughed. The tip of her cigarette bobbed like a firefly in the dark.

'It's nice out here.'

'Yes.'

'Quiet.'

'Yes.'

They stood there, silent, absorbing the small sounds around them. Other people's lives. Lights were showing, muted, at the rear of several other houses, but not many. Alex's husband and children were inside sleeping. The other side of the city seemed far away.

Karen shuddered involuntarily, as if someone had stepped over her grave.

'You okay?'

'Yes. Yes, fine. Just thinking.'

'What about?'

'Whatever it is I'm missing.'

'Are you missing something?'

Karen looked into Alex's face before answering. A long moment, wondering. 'Probably. Yes, maybe.' A small laugh, shake of the head. 'I don't know.'

Alex touched the back of her hand to the smooth skin, slightly chilled, of Karen's arm. 'Best go back inside.'

Dropping her cigarette, she ground it out on the path.

In the kitchen, Alex made coffee while they waited for a cab and Karen asked about Roger's job — she could never remember exactly what it was — the kids, how the two eldest were getting on at school. In less than the promised fifteen minutes, the driver was at the door.

'Anton Kosach,' Alex said, as they stepped into the hall.

'The guy Charlie Frost was interested in. You've not turned up anything that involves him, I suppose?'

Karen stopped. 'Kosach, no. Why d'you ask?'

'Oh, no special reason. Just thought you might have run across the name, at least, that's all.'

Karen shook her head. 'If I had, I'd've reported back. You'd've heard.'

'Yes, of course.'

The cab was in the middle of the road, indicators clicking on and off.

Alex squeezed her hand, brushed her cheek. 'Keep in touch.'

Karen gave the driver her address and settled back. Her head had started to swim and it wasn't just the wine.

38

Karen woke to the low thrum of music from the flat above; rolled over slowly, groaned, raised herself gingerly up on to one elbow, reached out and illuminated the small bedside clock. 6.03. What the hell was going on? For weeks on end it was as if no one was there, not even the faintest of footsteps criss-crossing above her head, and now, suddenly, it was whatever sad DJ had pulled the early breakfast show on Kiss or Choice, kicking things off with a chunk of dubstep reggae her neighbours seemed to be playing at full volume.

When she sat up something akin to a squash ball caromed, side to side and front to back, inside her head. Wincing, she closed her eyes and levered her legs slowly round, and as her feet touched the floor, the music stopped.

Thank you very much.

Gingerly, she made her way to the bathroom, peed, splashed water in her face, pressed two paracetamol out of their foil and swallowed them down. The last time she'd had a hangover to equal this had been Carla's birthday the previous September, the night Carla had insisted on treating them to her

impression of Christina Aguilera at full shriek and she herself
had come close to copping off with a startlingly beautiful black
man who claimed to have played for Leyton Orient.

Now, as then, she should never have had that last glass of
wine. Although, at Alex's, she hadn't realised she was drinking
much at all.

Pulling back the curtains, she gazed out into the empty
street, the convoy of parked cars. A cyclist in reflective gear,
front light pulsing, swished past and out of sight.

Karen leaned slowly forward and rested her forehead against
the welcoming glass.

She was in the kitchen, making coffee, trying to decide
whether or not she wanted toast, when her mobile trilled to
life.

That bloody phone!

Tim Costello's voice. A shooting outside the twenty-four-hour
Tesco at Woodford. Close on four in the morning. Sixteen-
year-old using the ATM. Bullet wounds to the side, shoulder,
backs of the legs. Taken to Whipps Cross. Still touch and go.

'The ATM, a robbery?'

'Either that or drug related. Local Drug Squad've had half
an eye on him. Lot of manoeuvring going on, apparently.
Usual squabble over territory.'

'Could be a hit, then.'

'Possibility.'

'Witnesses that early?'

'Not so far. But CCTV. Still checking.'

'Let me know, Tim, anything shows.'

'Will do.'

She was barely out of the door when the phone rang again.
The switchboard with a call from a Detective Sergeant Barry
Morgan, a hostage negotiator in the Notts Police.

'Got a situation here. Mansfield. Armed male holding a
pregnant woman hostage. Both known to you, I believe.'

Karen drew breath. 'Jayne Andrew?'

'You got it.'

'Wayne Simon.'

'Wanted in connection with the murder of his partner and their child, back end of last year, is that right?'

'Yes.'

'Any history? Anything useful you can tell us?'

'Useful? He's been stalking her for a while. Work and home. I made the point when I was up there not so long ago. Strongly, I thought. The likelihood of something like this happening. Obviously not strongly enough.'

Morgan said nothing.

'What's the likely outcome here?' Karen said. 'Which way you leaning?'

'Hard to say. Blokes like Simon, not exactly rational. Spoke to him a couple of times on the phone. Her mobile. Lot of anger, not a lot of sense. Since then no one's picking up. Case of waiting it out, I'd reckon.'

Karen heard her own voice, low and persuasive: *He's not going to hurt you, I promise.*

'I'm on my way,' she said.

'Likely no need.'

'Anything happens, get me on this number.'

Karen broke the call and, taking care not to move her head too sharply, bent low and reached for her shoes.

It was a grey kind of day. Clouds the colour of pale slate that presaged snow. Karen drove too fast, using both her siren and magnetic beacon to clear a way through the traffic that clustered along the motorway between Leicester and Nottingham.

A command post had been set up some seventy-five metres from the front of the block in which Jayne Andrew lived, rutted tarmac and muddied grass in between. Residents of the neighbouring flats had been evacuated as a precaution, the immediate area cordoned off.

Barry Morgan met Karen with a quick handshake and ushered her inside. Made the introductions, senior firearms officer, incident commander. More handshakes and down to business. A plan of the flat's interior had been stuck up alongside the windscreen. Living room and kitchen with windows to the front, door leading out on to a narrow balcony, bedroom and bathroom with windows to the rear. Armed officers were already in position.

'Last sighting,' Morgan said, 'best part of half an hour since. Living-room window. Lass standing there with Simon close behind her, knife to the side of her neck here.' He rested two fingers just behind the jawline, immediately below the ear. 'Cowardly bastard.'

'Maybe should have taken him out then,' the firearms officer said. 'Clear head shot for a full five seconds.'

'No need,' Morgan said. 'Not while there's a risk of hitting the woman. Not while there's time.'

'Is there?' Karen asked. 'Time?'

'Happen.'

'When did you speak to him last?'

'An hour back. Same barely coherent ranting as before. What a crock of shit the world is. Everyone conspiring against him. Doing him down. Women especially. Whores, the lot of them.'

'He's not made any demands?'

'Just threats. If we come near the flat, attempt any kind of rescue, he'll cut her throat.'

'And if we don't?'

'Cut her throat anyway. Later rather than sooner.'

The firearms officer lifted clear the binoculars through which he'd been watching. Spoke to Karen. 'Killed this young woman, didn't he? Hammered the life out of her. Cut her about for good measure. And the kiddie, killed her too. Next time my lads get an unobstructed view of the target, let me give the order. One in the brain pan. All the consideration he deserves.' He hawked up phlegm from the back of his throat and, nowhere to spit it, swallowed it back down. 'Eugenics, where people like Simon are concerned, not such a bad idea after all.'

For some moments, no one looked at anyone else.

Then the sound of a police helicopter circling overhead.

'You've spoken with her,' Morgan said to Karen, 'must have got some impression. How d'you think she'd stand up to this?'

Karen was remembering the pale-faced young woman who'd made her tea, talked about her boyfriend out in Afghanistan, talked about the coming baby. About Wayne Simon.

I'm frightened. Frightened he'll do something. Hurt me. Hurt my baby.

'Not too well. She's not strong, physically strong. Low self-esteem. And she'd be scared, scared for the baby.'

'Any idea why he's latched on to her the way he has?'

'Men like Simon, they're drawn to women they see as weak. Easier to bully, knock into shape. Then, when those women start thinking for themselves, trying to break away, the Simons of this world react the only way they know how. Lash out.'

'End of lecture,' the firearms officer said, as much to himself as anyone, loud enough to be sure Karen had heard.

No one had seen hide nor hair of Jayne Andrew for a full thirty minutes, just glimpses, shadowy, of Simon moving around the flat without apparent direction, this way and that.

Karen remembering again her vain promise she would come to no harm.

Morgan dialled the number for Jayne Andrew's mobile, the one on which he'd spoken to Wayne Simon before. While it was still ringing there was a sudden movement behind the living-room curtain, the window opened and two mobile phones were hurled down on to the grass. His and hers.

'Fuck,' Morgan said softly and lowered his head.

'Stage two,' the incident commander said, not without a certain satisfaction.

Morgan was already fastening his bulletproof vest. Moments later, he was stepping out of the van, loudhailer in his hand. 'Wayne, listen to me. There's a way out of this. For everyone. For you. Nobody has to get hurt, no one has to come to any harm. You hear me? You understand?'

No movement. No response. No reply.

'Just let me see Jayne, let her come to the window on her own. I just want to see that she's okay. Then you can let her go. Let her leave.'

Snow was starting to flutter slowly down, catching in Morgan's hair as he moved steadily forward, one careful pace at a time.

'No one's hurt here. Nothing's happened. Nothing that we can't talk about reasonably, between ourselves. You and me. But you have to let Jayne go first. Then we can talk. All right, Wayne? We can sort this all out.'

While he was still talking the door opened and Jayne Andrew stumbled out, one hand thrust out in front of her, the other clutching her belly; her face, her front, dark with blood.

Morgan dropped the loudhailer and started to run.

'Go, go!' the firearms officer shouted, and immediately armed officers began to advance from either end of the balcony, weapons raised.

Karen was running herself, stumbling a little on the uneven ground.

Jayne Andrew tumbled into the arms of the first officer to arrive and, taking her weight on his free arm, he turned her away from the balcony edge and towards the wall and lowered her slowly down. Which is where she was when Karen reached her, still crouching, holding herself and sobbing inarticulate sounds through trails of snot and tears. That close, the blood startlingly bright on her face and hands.

Not hers.

Karen carefully raised Jayne Andrew's head and wiped her face, took hold of her then by the arms and lifted her to her feet; put one arm round her and held her tightly as she walked her towards the stairs, the waiting paramedics, the ambulance, a warm bath and caring hands, the first of many nightmares, flashbacks, some kind of a future.

At least she was alive.

Wayne Simon had slashed his throat across while holding her close, the blade puncturing the carotid artery behind the jawline, below the ear.

He lay on his back, legs akimbo, arms outstretched, head to one side, a beached fish on dry land, the severed flesh open like a second mouth.

Flowers of blood stippled across the floor, along the wall.

'Look!' Wayne Simon had said, the moment before he cut his throat. 'Look what you made me do.'

Karen drove back more slowly; urgency, expectation drained. The promised snow flaked across the windscreen, sticking here and there beyond the wipers' range. She thought of Carla, wondered how she was, living in provincial digs and stepping night after night into the spotlight to enact *The Revenger's Tragedy*, more familiar now with the quickness, the arc of blood. She thought of Alex, the enviable assuredness with which she worked and lived, the quick touch of her hand upon her arm.

At the service station, she drank coffee, black, and checked the messages on her mobile phone. CCTV at Woodford had shown two men running from the scene of the shooting, one of them Liam Jarvis, previously arrested and then released in connection with a similar shooting in Walthamstow. A fresh warrant had been issued and a search carried out at his last known address, as yet no sign.

39

Cordon had tried bringing up the subject of what had happened to Maxine, Letitia's mother, a number of times, but on each occasion got little response other than an impatient sigh and shake of the head, clear signs that as a topic it was closed. On other occasions, the reply was more emphatic. 'How many more times, she fell under the fucking train!'

It wasn't until they were sitting outside, one evening, dusk closing around them, Danny in bed early, exhausted by the day, that Letitia raised it herself.

'Parlo, he was there at the house when she come round. Question after bloody question. Wouldn't take no for an answer. Threatened to clip her one and she laughed in his face, told him if he did that she'd be back with the police.'

'How d'you know this?'

'He rung Anton, didn't he? On account of she'd mentioned my name, said who she was, who she claimed to be. Anton told him to frighten her off, make sure she never come back.'

Letitia stopped and poured herself more wine.

'That's what he did. Followed her to the station.'

'Pushed her under the train?'

'Not according to him. Lost sight of her on the platform. Only saw her again at the last minute, just as the train was coming in. Tried to elbow his way through the crowd towards her, but with everyone else pushing and shoving, fighting to get on, somehow, he says, she went under. He hadn't been able to get near her. Nothing he could do. Walked away.'

'You believe that?'

'That he walked away? Got out of there as soon as he could? Sure, of course.'

'That he didn't have anything to do with what happened?'

She shrugged and reached for her cigarettes. 'What's it matter? Pushed, fell, either way? Not going to bring her back, soft cow.'

Cordon bit back his words. Her mother, not his. Her life to live.

Neither of them mentioned it again.

Jack Kiley had been in touch that morning. According to Taras, his brother was gradually coming round; just give him a little longer and he thought Anton could be persuaded to agree to some kind of reasonable arrangement, shared access to his son in exchange for financial support. Just give him a little more time.

Time they still had.

Venturing out into the surrounding area, they found, less than fifteen minutes' drive away, a family theme park with bouncy castles and trampolines and pedalos; a small paddling pool, where Danny screamed with delight at the sudden shock of cold; a petting zoo with sheep and goats and a pair of long-eared donkeys, shaggy in their winter coats.

Emboldened, they drove north to the Pink Granite Coast and followed the path as it wound between vast, impossible formations of rocks shaped by the sea and the wind; parked

227

above the empty swathes of sand at Beg Léguer, where Cordon and Danny combed rock pools for shrimps and tiny crabs, while Letitia sheltered out of the wind and smoked and read for the second time a Maggie O'Farrell she'd found stashed behind all those dry and clever men on the bookshelves where they were staying.

On a shopping expedition to the Carrefour in Guingamp, Danny picked up a flier advertising the Haras National de Lamballe, the national stud. Guided tours at three p.m., Tuesdays to Sundays. The illustration showed a stallion rearing irresistibly up into the sky, its mane catching the rays of the sun.

'Please!' Danny cried. 'Please!'

Smiling at his anticipation of such pleasure, Letitia agreed.

Lamballe was where they had switched cars, no more than an hour and a half away; Cordon could call in at the office while they were there, extend the period of loan. Give the boy his wish.

The sun shone, still weakly, but without a breeze they could delude themselves of its warmth. The tour of the stables was more interesting than either Cordon or Letitia had expected – some of the huge Breton horses weighing up to a ton – and Danny, in his element, ran from stall to stall, glowing with excitement; when the tour guide pointed to some hay and asked if he wouldn't like to help feed one of the horses, it must have felt like heaven.

Afterwards, they sat outside a patisserie in the town square, Cordon and Letitia drinking coffee and sharing some kind of almond pastry, while Danny sipped hot chocolate through a straw and bit down into a coffee éclair so hard the cream splurged out from the far end, all over his face and hands.

Letitia caught Cordon's look and instead of giving him a warning glance, she allowed herself a smile.

'Good day?' he asked, as they settled back into the car.

'Not bad.'

Leaning across, she kissed him on the cheek, and from the back seat, Danny issued a little squeal of delight.

It couldn't last.

40

Hugo French lay there, blocking out the sound, for as long as he could. Turning over, turning back. Moving the pillow beneath his head. Covers tugged this way and that. Kids. No, not kids. Older. Young men by the sound of them, their loud, overlapping voices rising up to the second-floor bedroom where he slept. Young blokes, not so very long out of the pub, standing around outside the house, arguing the toss. About what, Hugo didn't know. Couldn't tell. Just the odd word clearly audible, the pattern of phrases repeated over and over, the slightly dodgy double glazing unable to keep them out. 'No, wait. Wait, wait, wait. Listen. Just fucking listen!' Every second or third word, the swearing. Like some kind of punctuation, like breathing.

Time was, it would have been Mary awake before him, pushing back the duvet and padding to the window, thinking nothing of throwing it open and sticking her head out, complaining.

People sleeping . . .

Haven't you got a home to go to . . .

Call the police if you're not careful . . .

Not any more. The space beside him cold and uncomprehending. He rolled over on to his side and as he did so, the noises seemed to falter and fade. Thank Christ! They were moving away.

But then again . . .

'Listen, you bastard! Listen, will ya! Fuckin' listen!'

Over and over and over . . .

Hugo levered himself into a sitting position, feet seeking out his slippers; tightening, as he stood, the cord of his pyjamas; reaching his old dressing gown down from behind the door. For heaven's sake let me buy you a new one for Christmas. That old thing's a disgrace.

Carefully, he shuffled to the window. Stood there for several moments, nervously, before easing a small space between the curtains and squinting down through the gap.

Yes, he was right. Four young men, standing in a tight little group, facing one another, hands every now and then gesturing, heads lifting with the rise and fall of voices. On their way back from some party, he supposed, an extension at the pub on the corner. Nothing wrong with his eyesight, he didn't recognise any of them. Not from this street, he was certain. Not from round here. Why they'd chosen this street, he'd no idea. Unless that was their car, parked right by where they were standing. He hadn't seen that before, either. Nothing flash, nothing racy. Could be theirs, no saying.

One of them turned abruptly and started to walk away, and Hugo thought, okay, this is it, at last they're going. But right off he seemed to change his mind and turn back again and now . . . now what were they doing? One of the others leaning over the roof of the car, something being tipped out onto a piece of . . . foil, was it? . . . yes, a piece of foil . . . and one of the others dipping his finger and then putting it inside his mouth, rubbing it across his gums. Hugo didn't believe what he was seeing. This perfectly ordinary, quiet street, not yet two in the morning, four blokes, illuminated by the nearest street light, not giving a bugger about who saw or heard them, messing around with drugs – cocaine, he supposed that's what it was, cocaine – he'd read about it enough times, seen it on TV. Maybe that's what they'd been arguing about all along, buying or selling, he didn't know, the price, who was to pay, how much.

It angered him; knotted inside him.

And the blank windows opposite, blinds down, curtains closed, none of the neighbours, not that he really knew most of them, not now, not any more, no one interested, sleeping through it all, not caring.

Below, one man pushed another and laughed, then went back to what they were doing.

The telephone was on the bedside table.

The community support officer when he'd called round – some kind of scheme they had, crime prevention – had left a card with the number of the local station. You keep it there, where it's handy. Any strange noises, anything untoward, don't be afraid to use it. What we're there for. Your taxes.

Not my taxes, Hugo remembered thinking, not now it was just a few bits and pieces and the pension.

He dialled the number.

Dawn Pritchard was parked up outside the twenty-four-hour convenience store near the junction when the call came through; her partner, Richie Stevenson, inside buying God knows what. Snickers, Peppermint Aero, KitKat, Bounty. Likely a can of Coke or Red Bull. Whatever it took to get him through the rest of the shift without dropping off. The wonder was, all the sugar and stuff he gorged on, he still looked like a stick insect, so thin when he turned side-on it was just possible to miss him altogether. Whereas Dawn, as she knew to her cost, only had to look at a bar of chocolate or even a Diet Pepsi and she was having to loosen the buttons at the front of her uniform jacket.

'Richie!' Passenger door open, she shouted across the pavement at the figure standing chatting at the counter. 'Come on, let's shift it.'

The call from the dispatch room had been graded S for soonish, as opposed to I for immediate, which Dawn knew gave them an hour's window in which to respond, as against a maximum of eight to twelve minutes, but so far the night had been quiet as the proverbial, and anything was better than nothing.

'What is it?' Stevenson asked, peeling back the wrapping from a KitKat, snapping it in half and offering her two fingers.

She shook her head. 'Group of men causing some kind of disturbance. Possible drug involvement. That part's uncertain.'

'Lady Margaret, you said?'

'Lady Somerset.'

Big houses, semi-detached for the most part; a few still family homes, but not many; the majority divided into flats, two, three or even four to a building. The address she'd been given, another hundred metres along on the left side, before the road curved downhill.

'Where they supposed to be, these blokes?'

'I don't know, just standing around.'

'Well, no bugger here now, they've scarpered.'

'No, wait up. There, over there.'

'Where?'

'There.'

They were sitting inside a silver Saab, silver-grey, four men; the interior light on and then, as the police car approached, swiftly switched off.

'What do you think?' Stevenson said.

233

Dawn pulled up just sufficiently ahead of the Saab to block any attempt to drive away.

Both officers got out of the car.

While Stevenson went around the rear of the Saab and on to the pavement, Dawn knocked on the driver's window and motioned for him to wind it down.

Stevenson shone his torch from the other side: four faces, young and white, blinking away from the light, heads down, avoiding his eyes.

'Now I need you,' Dawn was telling the driver, 'to step out of the car.'

No movement.

'That would be now.'

He swore not quite beneath his breath, loud enough for her to hear, and, with all the disdain he could muster, did as he was told. Early twenties, Dawn thought, if that. Dark hair, curling up against the collar of his leather jacket, perhaps unfashionably long. Not bad-looking, she could see that; a fit-looking bloke and no mistake, but too young. Too young for her, at any rate.

'Driving licence,' she said. 'Any other identification.'

'What for?'

'Licence, don't argue.'

'We weren't doin' nothin', just talkin'.'

'Just do as I say.'

His eyes caught hers, decision made. Flung out an arm, catching her high across the face, as he turned and started to run.

Dawn thrust out a leg, tripping him so that he fell, half-fell against the bonnet of the car, rolling awkwardly away, one hand pushing up from the ground till she brought her baton down hard against the bone, the elbow, the crack clear and loud and lost in his scream as she struck him again, a full swing down against the top of his shoulder, the reverberation jarring her own arm, making her fingers tingle.

The moment the driver had tried to make off, all three passengers had bolted from the car, the near-side door slamming against Richie Stevenson's legs and sending him stumbling back against the privet hedge; Stevenson recovering quickly enough to give chase and bring down the slowest of the runaways with a rugby tackle that wouldn't have looked out of place at Twickenham or Murrayfield, even if it did tear his trouser leg against the edge of the kerb and badly graze both knees.

'Okay, you little shit. You're nicked.' Just like *Life on Mars*.

Hugo French stood in the doorway, still with his dressing gown over his pyjamas, soft slippers on his feet. He'd never imagined the police would respond as speedily as they had, half-prepared to be fobbed off with some excuse or other when he'd phoned, but pleased now that he'd gone ahead and everything had panned out the way it seemingly had. A little excitement no bad thing, he supposed, straightening his back automatically as the female officer made her way towards him, the young oaf that she'd dealt with so competently now handcuffed in the back of the police car and, from the sound of it, reinforcements on the way.

Memory not what it was, he'd taken the precaution of jotting down a few things on a scrap of paper, what he'd heard and seen. You never know, he might even be called on to give evidence somewhere down the line. Now wouldn't that be something, name in the local paper he'd not be surprised. Mary would have liked that, in her quiet way been proud. Not that she'd have said.

'Mr French?'

He held out his hand.

41

There were more beggars on the street now, Karen thought, as she made her way to work, several sitting crouched up against the walls outside the Tube. Earlier in the year it had been two, then four, then five; this morning, between the edge of Highbury Fields and the station, she'd passed half a dozen. Two women, one of them little more, seemingly, than a girl; four men. Three of the men with mangy dogs beside them, bristle-mouthed, whippet thin, all sheltering, as best they could, from the rain.

Inside the forecourt, two more men, collecting for charity, stood shaking buckets at the incoming travellers: flood disasters here, AIDS sufferers there, poor and disabled everywhere.

Karen fished into her purse for stray coins, slapped her Oyster card down on the reader and joined the throng. The train was crowded, people standing cheek by jowl, but by some good fortune she managed to squeeze into a seat. A few minutes along, they slowed to a halt. Due to a signal failure at King's Cross, they were being held in a queue. Mutual groans, shaking of heads. The last time this had happened, it had been a good thirty minutes before they moved. No signal that far underground, there was no sense in trying to phone ahead, warning she'd be late. With a scowl, she reached her book from her bag.

Tim Costello was waiting at her office door when she arrived, sporting a new jacket in industrial denim from somewhere like G-Star – a couple of hundred at least, Karen guessed, plus change. Someone with money enough to spare.

'Want my opinion?' Karen said, treating him to a quick up-and-down. 'A little short, maybe, in the sleeves.'

Costello, bless him, essayed a faint blush. 'This guy,' he said, 'Brendan Cullen, brought in a couple of nights back, Kentish Town. Doing smack off the roof of his car right under a bloody street light, if you can believe that.'

'I can believe anything. But what's it got to do with us?'

'When they searched the car they found a 9mm Glock and ammo in the boot, hidden beneath the spare. Intel reckon it's the one used at Woodford. Double-checking now.'

Karen's eyes brightened. 'He's been charged?'

'Possession of a firearm and ammunition in a public place.'

'That's all?'

'So far.'

'What's he saying about the gun?'

'Not his.'

'Surprise, surprise.'

'Thought maybe I should get myself down there, Kentish Town, ask a few questions.'

'Okay, but don't go stepping on any toes.'

Costello grinned. 'Fairy footsteps, I promise.'

Costello stood looking at Cullen through one-way glass as he stonewalled question after question, smirk like a razor cut across his face.

Brendan Cullen. Bren.

One leg was hooked nonchalantly across the other, tapered jeans, white T-shirt under a grey hoodie, one studded ear, a neat blue tattoo along his neck. Twenty-two? Twenty-three? He'd been practising for this since the local beat copper had first dragged him in, kicking and blaspheming, eight years old. Dad and granddad both doing time. Brother, one of them, in care. Another, the oldest, in the army, overseas; matter of time, Cullen thought, sad bastard, before he came home in a box.

So far, he'd admitted little or nothing. Possession of a small amount of a Class A drug for personal use only. Taking and driving away.

And the handgun found in the boot of his car?

Not his.

Not your gun?

Not my car.

Ba-boom!

Stolen, like he'd said, from the free parking area close to the Forum a couple of nights before. As for the unlicensed weapon tucked under the spare, together with a box of shells, no idea they were there. Nicking a motor, you didn't exactly hang around to search the boot now, did you? A grin, switched off as easily as it had been switched on. Just shows, can't trust nobody nowadays.

Cullen leaned back even farther; peered at Costello through lowered lids as he came into the room and one of the other officers left. Costello identifying himself for the tape.

'The pistol, you say you'd no idea it was in the car?'

Cullen looked up in the direction of the camera and yawned. 'We got to go through all this again?'

'Before you went off and met your mates, you didn't tuck it away under the spare yourself?'

'No.'

238

'You're sure?'

'Jesus, how many more times—'

'Then how come one of your prints is on the gun . . . ?'

'What?'

'Up against the trigger housing, underside of the barrel.'

'Bollocks!'

'Okay, it's a partial, but enough there to bring it up on the database. Ridges, bifurcations, whorls – amazing what they can do with AFIS nowadays. But you're a bright boy, you probably know all that kind of stuff, right?' Not over-egging it, just enough to spread a little confusion, plant a sliver of doubt in Cullen's mind.

Cullen staring at him and Costello holding that gaze and, without too much hostility, passing it back, beginnings of a smile around the eyes, willing him to believe the lie.

'Of course,' Costello said, 'your brief will tell you a partial print on its own may not be enough to convince a jury, might not even stand up in court, but if I had as much as a partial print of mine on a weapon that had been used in at least one near-fatal shooting, I wouldn't like to take that risk. Would you?'

'What shooting?'

'Woodford, not so many nights back. Unlawful wounding, grievous bodily harm, could be attempted murder, depends which way the CPS want to go. Kid doesn't pull through, likely turn out to be the real thing. Go down for that and by the time you get out you'll be lining up for your Freedom Pass and your old age pension both.'

'Bollocks,' Cullen said again, but without conviction.

He reached for the plastic glass of water that had sat, up to then, untouched on the table getting warm, and as he did so, Costello reached out also and, for the briefest of moments, covered Cullen's hand with his own.

'Your gun, Brendan, fair enough, face the consequences. Not your gun, my advice, say now before you're in too deep.'

As Costello moved his hand away, Cullen lifted the glass. The water in his mouth was brackish, stale.

'Liam's,' he said quietly.

'Sorry?'

'It was Liam's, the gun. Liam Jarvis. A favour, like.' He looked away.

Costello did his best not to smile. 'Why don't you tell me how that favour worked?'

Karen listened carefully, tapping the tabletop lightly with the end of her pen. Cullen's story: Jarvis had told him to get rid of the gun, instead of which, Cullen had clung on to it, thinking to lie about it being clean and sell it on – that the reason he'd had it with him that evening, but the prospective buyer had cried off. After which the smack took over and his sense of purpose became a little vague.

'Last time we went looking for Jarvis,' Karen said, 'he proved hard to find.'

'So eager to get into our good books,' Costello said, 'Cullen might've given us a hand there, too. Reckons there's little Jarvis likes better than a few frames of snooker of an afternoon.'

'Anywhere special?'

'Snooker hall, Old Kent Road. Not far from the Thomas à Becket.'

Her aunt used to love watching it on TV, Karen remembered, snooker; hour after hour from the Crucible, the movement of the colours, deep green of the baize.

'You'll need back-up,' she said. 'No point in taking risks. And best take Mike Ramsden with you. Just in case.'

42

When they arrived, Jarvis was coming towards the end of what would surely have been a winning break, two reds left on the table and the colours all lined up, nice and potable. He swung a cue in Costello's direction, but his movement was too slow, his aim adrift, maybe he wouldn't have sunk the black after all. Costello ducked easily beneath the swing and delivered a sharp kick immediately below the knee. Before Jarvis could hit the floor, three officers had seized hold of him and flung him on to the table, arms and legs akimbo, balls everywhere.

His opponent took the game by default.

Once Jarvis had been hauled away, Costello foolishly took up Ramsden's challenge and lost the best of five frames in next to no time, Ramsden clearing the table on two occasions without Costello pocketing a single red.

'One of those games,' Ramsden said, as he relieved the younger man of much of the contents of his wallet, 'where luck has bugger all to do with it. Craft, son. Practice. That . . .' winking, 'and a good eye.'

*

In the interview suite, Jarvis had done his level best to suborn Brendan Cullen as a congenital liar. Why in God's name would he be giving Cullen a gun? To throw away? Dispose of? What kind of idiot would do that? Cullen, of all people. But images of himself, clear as if in HD, making off after the shooting in Woodford, added to some careful reminders of the factors behind his original arrest – witnesses who had placed himself and Rory Bevan in Walthamstow at the approximate time of the shooting – brought about a change of tack.

Yes, all right, maybe he'd passed along the pistol to Cullen. Maybe. But that night in Woodford, it'd just been about making a few threats, right, showing face. Warn the kid, back off, that was all. Stick the gun in his face and watch him shit himself. But, of course, for Rory fuckin' Bevan, that wasn't enough. Mad bastard that he was. Rory, who squeezed the bloody trigger, that was who.

'You mean, like the time in Walthamstow?' Costello had asked, mild as you please.

'Yeah, like that,' Jarvis said. 'Just like that.'

Since when, Rory Bevan had been brought in and charged and now the pair of them, Bevan and Jarvis, were busy putting one another in it, passing the blame, talking themselves into the best part of sixteen years and change.

Well, Karen thought, they'd needed a break, deserved one, and, at length, it had come. She eased back the curtains to reveal pavements that were dark and slick from early morning rain. The first strands of light were stretched almost to breaking point across the sky.

She set the kettle to boil, showered, dressed, switched on the radio – more bad news of the economy – and almost immediately switched it off again, opting for music from the stereo instead. Humming along, she made toast and coffee, fixed her make-up, checked her phone. Three messages and half a dozen texts, one from Carla, two from her sister, one from her mum in Jamaica, all of them wanting, deserving, a little of her time.

She made a promise to phone her mother, at least; rinsed cup and plate in the sink and left them to dry, then reached for her coat. Her boots could have done with a lick and a polish, but what the hell. . . .

A good hour later she was at her desk, checking rotas, signing forms, wondering where her next cup of coffee was coming from, and there was Mike Ramsden, looking for all the world as if he'd spent the night on a park bench, but balancing two cups of coffee, one above the other, a smile crinkling up his face regardlessless.

'The lottery?'

'Not exactly.'

'Do tell.'

'CCTV on the approach roads to Stansted – nothing at the storage units themselves, as we know, so that's been our best bet. Poor bastards going swivel eyed, hour after hour of sodding tape. Concentrating on vans, seemed the most likely, and you can imagine how many of those there are shuttling in and out. Need checking, each and every one, but it looks like in the end it might've paid off. Clocked a Ford van coming off the slip road from the M11 just after four in the morning, heading for the airport, Volvo saloon following, S60 by the look of it, dark green. An hour, give or take, later, the same journey in reverse. Van's a Transit 360, registration clear as a bell at one point, leased six weeks before from a garage in Milton Keynes.'

'Leased to? False name, don't tell me.'

'Thought at first it was, but no, I don't think so. D & J Foods. Office in Milton Keynes. Dennis Broderick, director. His name on the letterhead.'

'Good work. And Cormack, he's up to speed on all this?'

'Thought you'd like to do the honours.'

243

Smiling her thanks, Karen punched in Warren Cormack's number.

A little over twenty-four hours later, prompt as before, Cormack got back to her with positive news. As well as Broderick's office in Milton Keynes, there was another in Luton, plus storage facilities in a small industrial park off the A1 close to Bedford and, until six months previously, on a disused airfield at Wing, close to the Bucks–Beds border.

'Bit of help from the local force, we've been checking those out. Nothing at Bedford, not so far, but a patrol car from County Division went out to the airfield first thing. Not immediately clear which of the buildings Broderick might've rented, so they looked around. Found, maybe, more than they bargained for. One of the older buildings, disused for quite a while by the look of it. Blood all over the place inside. A lot of blood. Not new but no doubting what it was. Burned clothing. And more. Hooks and chains where somebody might have been tied.'

Karen could feel the adrenalin beginning to race. 'They've got the place secured?'

'Tight as a nut. Their words.'

'And where is it exactly? Wing, you said?'

'M1 north. A5, then west. An hour's drive, give or take. I'll meet you there.'

The airfield had been the home of No. 26 Operational Training Unit for RAF Bomber Command during the Second World War, and then was used as a gateway for large numbers of returning servicemen during the late spring and early summer of '45. After the war it squandered into disuse, weeds growing up through the cracks that spidered across its two runways; Nissen huts and hangars falling into disrepair. Now, partly reclaimed as farmland, it was also the home to a small number of light industrial units along the edge closest to the road, though a few of the old buildings still remained.

It was in one of these that the local officers had made their find.

Cormack was waiting when Karen arrived, smart in a blue-black overcoat, unbuttoned, grey cashmere scarf. And not alone. Scene of Crime officers in attendance, others from the project team Cormack was heading.

'It's this way,' he said, and Karen fell into step beside him, others following.

When they reached the outbuilding, Cormack pushed open the high-arched wooden door and stepped back, letting Karen enter first. She took three paces and then stopped, allowing her eyes to become accustomed to the levels of light.

Chains slowly sharpened into focus, hanging from hooks attached to beams above, and switching her, in her mind's eye, back to the container shed at Stansted, the butchered bodies, the smell of butchered flesh. Chains that would have held men fast while others did their work. Slow, careful work essayed with relish and not a little skill.

Karen fancied she could scent the blood rising still from where it had congealed, near black, impasto like, close to where she stood. Something rustled amongst the mouldering debris in the farthest corner and scuttled away.

'Seen enough?' Cormack said, moving quietly alongside her.

'Yes.' She could taste it in her throat, like bile, thick enough to choke.

'We ought to move back. Let Forensics get started.'

They stood outside under an opaque sky, not speaking, not yet. Cormack kicking gently at a tuft of grass that had squeezed up between the slabs of concrete, small concentrated prods with the end of his toe. Karen brought her hand to her mouth and shivered, little to do with the wind that scythed across from the perimeter, the eastern edge of the field.

Cormack reached into his pocket for his cigarettes, offered one to Karen, who shook her head, then accepted.

'I've given up,' Karen said, as Cormack, cupping a hand round his lighter, flicked it to life.

'Me, too.'

The soft grey of their smoke dissipated upwards and was lost.

'Until Forensics have got a match from the blood,' Cormack said, 'there's no way to be sure. It could be animal blood even, not human.'

'A little black-market butchery on the sly?'

'Not impossible.'

'This was the place Broderick used for storage till recently?'

'This and one of the newer buildings, down by the road.' Cormack swivelled slowly round. 'Quiet, the immediate area pretty deserted. At night, especially. Not what you'd call a busy road.'

'And Stansted – that's how far?'

'Seventy-eight point four-two miles. Estimated time of journey, one hour, twenty-seven minutes.' Cormack grinned. 'The wonders of modern technology.'

'You've spoken to him? Broderick?'

'Not yet. But he's got a house just outside Cublington, just a few miles west of here. Why don't we go and see if he's home?'

43

The house was just beyond the village, set amongst mostly arable land, a low wall winding towards a five-bar gate and then a line of trees, bare branched, and curving away. The original farmhouse had been translated into something L-shaped, contemporary; a new wing, mostly steel and glass, extending at right angles to the refaced brick of the main building.

Of the two barns, one was in use as a garage: a Land Rover and an empty space. The second seemed to contain nothing but old farm equipment, rusting over, a haphazard collection of ancient tools, spades, long-handled rakes and scythes. Perhaps someone was considering starting a farm museum? How we used to live.

In a smaller shed, wood had been neatly stacked after sawing; enough to last out what was left of the winter. The sun little more than a suggestion overhead.

There was another vehicle on the drive in front of the house, sporty, red, expensive – the distinctive Alfa Romeo crest. Karen thought she had seen Uma Thurman behind the wheel of one, courtesy of Pearl & Dean, at her local cinema.

No bell in sight, Cormack used the knocker, brass on brass. Once, twice, once again.

The woman who opened the door was above average height, shoulder-length hair nicely, expensively cut; a cashmere sweater, grey skirt snug at the hips, red shoes with a low heel. A figure that suggested the right number of hours spent in the gym, the pool. A little work around the face, Karen thought, but not too much. Careful make-up. Green eyes. Mid- to late forties? Fifty at a pinch.

'Mrs Broderick?'

'Who wants to know?'

Cormack showed identification, rank and name.

She nodded, smiled. A flicker, then it was gone. 'For another seven days, five hours and so many minutes, guilty as charged. After that . . .' She reached out both hands, fingers spread wide. 'Divorce, it's a wonderful thing. Either that or kill the bastard. What does Shakespeare say? Lug the guts into the other room? Leave him for the cleaner to trip over next morning.'

For an instant, the smile returned. 'Probably not the bit about the cleaner.'

'Is he here?' Cormack asked, persevering. 'Your husband?'

'Thankfully, no.'

'Not behind the arras somewhere?'

An eyebrow arched in mock surprise. 'A policeman who knows his *Hamlet*, I am surprised.'

'Advantages of a good comprehensive school education.'

'Is there such a thing? How heartening.'

Enough of the chit-chat, Karen thought. 'Mrs Broderick, if your husband's not here, do you have any idea where he is?'

'Off traipsing after a golf cart somewhere; either that or slutting over some poor escort-agency tart paying off her student loan.'

'Any idea when he might be back?'

'Other than hopefully after I've gone, I'm afraid not.'

'You won't mind if we take a look inside?' Cormack said.

'You've a warrant, of course?'

'Not at this moment. But, I assure you . . .'

'Oh, what the hell? Come in, help yourself. Liberty Hall.'

She stepped aside. Cormack went on through, leaving the two women facing one another, close enough for Karen to be able to smell the alcohol on the other's breath.

'Cathy. Cathy Broderick.'

'For now.'

'Yes, for now.'

'Karen. Karen Shields.'

'And it's your job to soften me up. Gain my confidence. Woman to woman. While the man does the searching.'

'Something like that.'

'So let's have a drink.'

Karen followed her beyond where the oak flooring changed to matt black tiles and into a long room with glass at both sides, partly shielded now by blinds, and exposed steel beams. Black leather chairs on tubular frames.

'Dennis met this architect somewhere, the golf club I expect. Convinced him that modernism was the way to go. Hates it, of course, now that it's done. His quarter-of-a-million-pound fucking folly, as he calls it. Never comes in here at all.'

The far end was dominated by a large painting, a repeated pattern of crimson whorls on a white background, each overlapping the other. An ice bucket sat on a Perspex table, wine bottle protruding, a small tray of glasses, one used.

'Please, sit. These are actually more comfortable than they look.'

Not difficult, Karen thought.

'I suppose it's no use offering you a glass of wine?'

'Afraid not.'

'Chablis. *Grand cru.*' Cathy Broderick helped herself. 'No sense leaving it for Dennis. He'd as soon Carlsberg out of a can.'

'You've been married how long?'

'The subtext to that question, if my opinion of him is so low, why stick around so long?'

'Maybe.'

'When you've been milking the cash cow – or, in this case, cash bull – as long as I have, it's difficult to put all that aside.'

'Give back the Alfa Romeo, for instance.'

'Significant birthday present. Attempt to get me to change my mind.'

'About the divorce?'

'About my lawyer screwing him for every penny we can get.'

'He's not short of them, though? Pennies?'

'The original self-made man. Market stall to millionaire in thirty short years. Started on fruit and veg, moved on to processed meats, from there to a company providing ready-cooked meals to schools, hospitals and nursing homes across five counties.' She raised her glass. 'Here's to hard work, graft and the necessary greasing of palms.'

Warren Cormack had appeared in the doorway. 'Access to the cellar? It's padlocked across.'

'There's a key behind the clock in the kitchen. High-tech security.'

Cormack nodded and turned away.

'Gordon Dooley,' Karen said, 'your husband knows him well?'

'Gordon?' She hesitated just a little too long over her answer. 'They used to have, I don't know, some business arrangement together. I don't think he's seen him in quite a while.'

'What kind of business would that be?'

'I really don't know.'

'Processed meats? School meals?'

Cathy Broderick smiled. 'I shouldn't think so. Gordon was asking him for some help, that's all I know. Money advice. Some cockamamie project or other, I dare say.'

'He does know him pretty well, then?'

A snort of laughter. 'Since they were kids on some poxy estate in South London. You should hear Dennis tell it, in his cups. How they nicked stuff from Woolworths and sold it on street corners to raise enough for their first market stall. Peckham, Saturday mornings. The thing is, Dennis he moved on, legit. Gordon, I've never been so sure. And now I've said too much.'

She splashed some more wine into her glass.

Cormack had been listening at the door for a little while. Of Dennis Broderick there was no sign.

'Would it surprise you to know,' Cormack said, 'Gordon Dooley's last known trade was in illegal drugs? Import and supply. Heroin. Marijuana. Cocaine.'

'Surprised? No, not really. Never really liked him, Gordon. Too brash, loud. Too full of himself. Full on. Dennis should have dumped him years ago, but there was always something, made him hang on.' She drank some more of the wine. 'Take the boy out of South London, but you can't . . . You know how it goes.'

'He wouldn't be involved? Some kind of partner?'

A laugh, genuine, open. 'Dennis? Drugs? He'd run a mile. All I can do to get him to take a couple of aspirin for a hangover. No, not a chance.'

'And you've no idea,' Cormack said, 'where he is now? When he might be home?'

'Like I said, none at all.' Not a whit unsteady, she was on her feet. 'Only conversation we have nowadays, through our lawyers.'

He nodded. 'Thanks for your time.'

'Yes, thank you,' Karen said.

'Helping out the forces of law and order. A pleasure, always.' She walked them to the door.

'The old aerodrome,' Cormack said, 'out at Wing. Your husband has some property there, doesn't he? Somewhere he uses for storage?'

'He used to. Not for a good while now, not as far as I know. Why d'you ask?'

'Oh, nothing important. Thanks, again.'

'One thing,' Karen said, glancing at the Alfa. 'You're not thinking of driving? The next little while? Automatic disqualification and a possible six months in prison, that's without the fine. I should stay put. Either that, or send for a cab. And if you are thinking of ringing your husband, dispute or no dispute, do tell him to get in touch. Nothing he should be unduly concerned about, just a few small matters need clearing up.'

'What do you reckon?' Cormack asked, once they were back at the car. 'She on the outs with her husband as much as she says, or do you think a lot of that was for our sake?'

'You mean that could all have been a big act? I'm not so sure. But it's not impossible. She could be phoning him right now, warning him to stay clear.'

'We'll have someone keep an eye on the house. Soon as he turns up, we'll know. Nothing by this time tomorrow, we'll go looking for him.'

'And Forensics, how soon d'you think it'll be before we get something definite from them?'

'Lean hard enough, maybe a couple of days. Meantime, I'll suggest SIS take a closer look at Broderick's business dealings. Check his phone records and so on. And hope we turn up something on the Volvo. Link that to Dooley and we're really getting somewhere. At last.'

'Amen to that!'

Karen drove back down to London with Aretha at full volume all the way. *Lady Soul*, *Spirit in the Dark*, *Aretha Live at Fillmore West*. Those old albums: singing in a way that made you believe.

44

More often than not, the mornings began in a slow drift of rain that laced across Cordon's face as he strode the lane to the boulangerie and back, rucksack slung over one shoulder, protecting the croissants on his return. It suited him well, this small routine, the chance to stretch out, the time to himself. Birds, lively at that hour, singing their presence, darted between the trees to either side; Charolais cattle heaving themselves from the ground in the adjacent fields, coats creamy white in the haze of lingering mist.

By the time he arrived back at the house, Letitia would, with any luck, have stepped out from the shower and set the coffee on the stove; Danny would either be sitting up in bed, rereading for the umpteenth time one of his books, or be stretched out full length in front of the television watching cartoons.

Don't get too fond of him, Letitia had warned, but in the circumstances it was hard not to. Considering all that had happened to him, being wrenched without proper explanation from one home, one country to another, Danny was

254

surprisingly equable, ever eager to play, to please. His ready laugh and quick response brought a smile to Cordon's face and, however sentimental, a touch of gladness to his heart.

All right, he knew what it was about. Understood that what he was doing, at least in part, was reconstructing the relationship with his own son that had so desperately failed. Even at Danny's age there had been tensions with Simon he was aware of only in retrospect: tensions that came in part from the hostility that had been building up inexorably between his wife, Judith, and himself; partly from the way Cordon had pushed the boy too hard in a vain attempt to keep him in line. *Do this and do it now. Don't bloody question me, just do it! Do it, you understand?* Until, by his early teens, the boy had turned quite against him.

You're not a father, you're a fucking policeman!

Cordon had slapped him hard, unthinking, and the boy had punched him back.

Punched and run.

Neither the first time, nor the last.

One life, one chance: when they were young, small, dependent for the most part, though they learned fast, accumulating more skills and knowledge than they ever would again, those early months and years seemed to move slowly, grinding on and on — then suddenly they were twelve, thirteen, and everything went past in a rush of hormones and angry words.

It came to Cordon in slack moments when his mind had stalled: in dreams.

The things he should have said and done.

Now passed and gone.

Don't get too fond of him, Letitia had said of Danny. *He's already got one father to get over. He doesn't need a fuckin' second.*

Quite right, Cordon thought. Buggering up one young life enough, never mind a second.

Kiley had phoned two days before: Taras had set up a meeting between himself and Anton which had been cancelled at the last moment; since then, nothing. No response to Kiley's calls. The Ukrainian's mobile permanently switched off, texts denied, messages ignored.

'Stick with it, Jack, okay?' Cordon had asked. 'Can you? We can't stay here forever.'

The reply had been a hesitant, 'Okay.' Followed swiftly by, 'But I've got other things on the go, you realise. For some of which I even get paid.'

'I'll pay you, if that's what you want.'

'Forget it. I'll do what I can.'

Since then, nothing. And Cordon was aware how far he was pushing the limits of friendship, the repayment of a small debt that had, in reality, already been paid off many times over. All he could hope was, that beyond his basic decency, Kiley was in it for the mystery, the need to see things through to their conclusion, find out how they'd been put together, how they ticked. Wasn't that one of the reasons people became detectives?

The old man's dog ran towards him from the nearby house, yapping, and when it got too close, turned tail. Letitia was just in the act of lifting the coffee pot from the stove.

'Warm milk or cold?'

'Cold is fine.'

Cordon swung the rucksack round and shook the croissants from their paper bag down on to the waiting plates.

'Jam?' Letitia asked.

'Jam.'

Passing, she kissed him on the cheek.

'What's that for?'

'Tip for the delivery boy. What else?'

*

The rain failed to clear until mid-morning, later than usual, and when it did they drove out to the nearby park and watched Danny tire himself out on the bouncy castle and the trampoline; afterwards, they stopped off at the crêperie at the edge of the village for a late lunch.

Back at the house, the afternoon slipped harmlessly away. They had a supper of pâté and cornichons, toasted bread, cured meat and cheese. Pears with a thick, marled skin that were delicious once it was removed.

Wine. Always wine.

Danny fell asleep where he was and had to be carried to bed.

Letitia put a cardigan around her shoulders and stood in the open doorway smoking a cigarette, while Cordon collected up the dishes and cleared the remnants of food into the fridge.

'When did they say we have to leave?' Letitia asked, turning back into the room.

'Here? Easter at the latest.'

'You think we could stay that long?'

'I don't know. Maybe.' Leaving or staying, he didn't know which held the most danger.

He went and stood behind her, close enough to smell the scent of whatever it was she used to wash her hair through the night air, the smoke from her cigarette. Save for a scattering of stars and a faint sliver of moon, the sky was an almost solid black.

When Letitia leaned back, accidentally or not, he could feel the warmth of her body against his chest, the bare flesh of her arm sliding across his, the curl of her hair brushing soft against his neck.

'Remember that time you kicked me out of your bed?'

'No.'

She laughed. 'Regret it now, don't you?'

'No.'

'Lying bastard.'

She laughed again and, swivelling, raised her head and kissed him on the mouth, the taste of wine and tobacco clear and strong on her tongue, and just as he began to kiss her back, his arms closing tight around her, she pulled away.

'It's getting cold, let's go inside.'

Once there she kept her distance, refilled her glass and took it into the other room; switched on the TV and sat, half-watching, chatting inconsequentially as if nothing had happened. When, an hour or so later, she said goodnight, her fingers brushed his neck as they had once before and left him wondering what, if anything, that meant.

Listening, through the lowered television sound, he heard her enter the bathroom, then leave, and then the closing of her bedroom door. Minutes later, he switched off the TV, went back into the kitchen and saw to the dishes, made sure the doors were locked and secure.

A half-inch of light showed under the door of Letitia's room.

In the near-darkness, Cordon held his breath, then turned away, crossing to his own room, his own bed. And lay there, still listening, half-expecting her to come to him.

Three nights later, without hint or warning, she did. Her first touch breaking him from sleep.

'What . . . ?'

There was light enough through the shutters to see the smile forming on her face, the outline of her breasts beneath the T-shirt that she wore, the dark patch between her legs.

'Letitia, you . . .'

'Yes?'

'You can't . . .'

'Oh, Cordon, why don't you just shut up?'

Leaning down she kissed him hard, her hand reaching for him through the sheet.

He gasped at her touch and, as he arched his back, she

258

dipped her head and took one nipple, then the other, in her mouth, licking, teasing them tight, taking them between her teeth and biting gently, then enough to hurt.

Slowly, she ran her tongue along his chest and up into the hollows of his neck, the corners of his mouth, his eyes, his mouth again, and then, suddenly, hutching up her legs, she slid down, taking him inside her, deep inside, deep – 'Oh, Christ!' – Cordon shouting out, head back, mouth wide, eyes screwed tight as she pressed down on him again until her hips ground against his and he thrust back, shouting, shouting her name, her voice rising against his – 'Come on, Cordon, for fuck's sake! Fuck me! Fuck me! Fuck!' – Cordon grasping her hair, wet and slippery now with sweat, and then, with a wrench, rolling her over until he was above her, bearing down, wanting to bury himself inside her, hard, hard as he could, wanting to hurt her, yes, hurt her, hear her scream. 'You fucker! You fucker! You fuck!'

Later he would think that beneath everything he heard the door, the sudden forward step, sensed the sweep of an arm and began to turn, but it was all lost inside Letitia's scream, whether of orgasm or what she'd just seen over his shoulder he'd never know, and then something metallic slammed hard against his head, then again full in the face, not once, but twice, and all he knew was a lance of searing pain, then nothing at all.

45

They arrested Dennis Broderick at Heathrow: Broderick intent on catching a few rays at Sharm El Sheikh, ten days booked at the five-star Savoy Hotel on White Knight Beach, garden-view room at a special bargain price, all meals included. He was helping himself to an extra portion of hors d'oeuvres in the business-class lounge when Karen approached him, Ramsden at her shoulder, other officers at the doors — Warren Cormack back at headquarters, happy to leave the fieldwork to others and concentrate on the search for the missing Volvo.

When Karen put a hand on his forearm Broderick jerked back, spilling sour cherry sauce down the front of his lightweight linen suit, worn in anticipation of the Egyptian sun.

'Dennis, whatever is it?'

Emphatically not Mrs Broderick, his companion was some-where in her early thirties, peddling twenty-five. All those hours on the sunbed and a painful full Brazilian bikini wax about to go to waste.

The downward turn to her mouth was severe.

Ramsden cupped a hand beneath her elbow and ushered her to where a female officer was waiting.

Broderick did his best to stare Karen down, then, when that failed, began blustering: mistaken identity, false arrest. Only at the mention of his being marched out of there in handcuffs did he fall quiet.

'I'm not saying another word,' he said, 'till I've contacted my lawyer.'

'Good idea,' Karen replied pleasantly and stood aside while two of the officers led him away.

Forensics had found quite copious traces of blood belonging to both Valentyn Horak and one of his henchmen in the building on Wing aerodrome. Checking out the Ford Transit, which was found, stripped of its number plates, at the rear of the D & J Foods storage area off the A1, proved more difficult. The assumption was that heavy plastic had been used as an inner liner, covering walls and floor, and set carefully in place before the bodies were transported; after which the interior was carefully washed out after the load was delivered. Not just washed, scrubbed within an inch of its life.

No prints, nary a one.

Painstaking work with Luminol did, however, finally reveal several minute traces of blood between the flange and panelling on the rear door. Sufficient to obtain a match: proof positive Horak's body had been in the van.

It was agreed that Karen would begin questioning Broderick, Ramsden in attendance; Cormack would be watching via a video link in an adjoining room and able to speak to Karen through a small attachment, newsreader style, behind her ear.

Broderick's lawyer was sandy haired, spectacled, off-the-peg suit, leather briefcase stuffed to the gills; the mints on his breath not quite strong enough to disguise the garlic in whatever he'd recently been eating.

The air in the room stale, yesterday's air, the temperature a notch or two too high.

Broderick fidgeted with the lapels at the front of his suit jacket; stopped; started again. A quick look towards Karen, then down at the table. Scratches, pencil marks, daubs of Biro, veins of sweat that had sunk into the grain.

'Tell us,' Karen said, 'about the van.'

'Van?'

'Ford Transit 350, diamond white, manual transmission. Registered, June 2007. Mileage, 51,302. Leased from Webster Garage and Autohire in Milton Keynes on behalf of D & J Foods. That van. Paperwork in your name. See?'

She swivelled a photocopy of the agreement round on the desk, counted a slow three, swivelled it back.

'Your signature, agreed?'

'Seems to be, yes.'

'Seems?'

'All right, yes. So what?'

'You personally leased this van?'

'Yes.'

'For what purpose?'

For a moment, he blanked.

'Simple question, why, when you did, did you lease the van?'

'My client,' the solicitor said, intervening, 'runs a successful and expanding business which trades across the South-East of the country and up into East Anglia. As such, additions to the delivery fleet are a quite normal part of its operations.'

'Absolutely,' Karen said. 'Very nicely put. But our interest is in one particular vehicle. The uses to which it might have been put.'

'Uses?' Broderick said. 'Uses? You've just been told. Meeting orders, making deliveries, what do you think? You want to see the manifests, I can show you. Two hundred and fifty pre-cooked meals to a primary school in Spalding. More of the same to a group of nursing homes in Saffron Walden. Vacuum-packed sausages and salamis to Londis stores right across Essex, from Chelmsford to the Thames fucking Estuary.'

Patches of bright colour stood out on his cheeks.

'And these?' Karen said, sliding the photographs from their folder. 'You delivered these?'

Broderick looked, caught his breath, looked again.

'Oh, Christ!' he said softly, and angled his head away.

The solicitor leaned forward, then forward again, as if he couldn't quite believe what he was seeing in four glossy 10 x 8s.

'The bodies of three men,' Karen said. 'Systematically tortured, mutilated, finally killed. Murdered. Then transported in that van, your van, to a storage unit at Stansted airport. That's the delivery we're interested in.'

All trace of colour had gone from Broderick's face.

'I'd like a break.'

'Later.'

'Now. Please.'

'My client,' the solicitor said, 'has just undergone a considerable shock—'

'I'm sorry, we need to continue.'

'Then I insist that my protest be documented—'

'Five minutes,' Cormack said in Karen's ear. 'Five minutes, ten. No harm.'

'Very well,' Karen said. 'A short break, agreed.'

She didn't like it, but she knew Cormack was right: the last thing they wanted, whatever Broderick might say rendered inadmissible by accusations of shock tactics, statements obtained under duress.

When Broderick sat across from her again, some ten minutes later, he seemed calmer, a degree more composed.

'Have you any idea,' Karen asked, 'how your van——?'

'Not my van.'

'Your firm's van, could have been used in the way I've described?'

'If it was.'

'It was.'

He looked as if he were about to argue the point, but, after a quick head shake from his solicitor, changed his mind. 'None at all.'

'After it was leased, the van was kept where?'

'The Bedford depot.'

'Off the A1?'

'The A1, right.'

'Not at Wing?'

'No.'

'You do have a storage unit there?'

'Not any more.'

'So the van . . .'

'The van would have been based at Bedford, as I said.'

'And how many people would have had access to it there? Yourself aside.'

'Four? Five? Possibly more.'

'How many more?'

'I don't know. I can't say for sure.'

'Run a tight ship,' Ramsden observed.

'The keys to all the vans are kept in the office,' Broderick said. 'Other than at night, they're not locked away.'

'So anyone could come along, just borrow one of your vehicles?'

'In theory, yes.'

'In practice?'

'In practice there's a daily schedule, someone there in the office, logging them in and out.'

'Twenty-four hours?'

'Um?'

'Logging them out, twenty-four hours a day?'

'Obviously not.'

'You don't keep a check on mileage?'

'If one of the vehicles was getting a lot of extra use it would be noticed, yes, but otherwise, no.'

'And do they get used?' Ramsden asked. 'Your employees, personal use. Outside normal hours. That happens? Running the kids to the football, stuff like that?'

'Sometimes, yes.'

'Use them sometimes yourself?'

'Once in a while.'

'Recently?'

'Not recently.'

'You sound very certain.'

'I am.'

'How can you be so sure?'

'I know, because apart from shifting it round the yard a couple of times, since we took delivery of that van, I doubt I've been behind the wheel.'

'Well, somebody was.'

'Yes, well. That's sort of your problem then, isn't it? Not mine. So if there's nothing else . . .'

He glanced at his solicitor, who gave a small nod.

'I do think,' the solicitor said, 'my client has helped you all he can.'

Broderick started to rise, push back his chair.

'Ask him about Gordon Dooley,' Cormack said in Karen's ear.

'Gordon Dooley,' Karen said. 'He's a friend of yours?'

'Gordon?' Broderick hesitated, sat back down. 'Yes, why?'

'A good friend?'

'Ye-es.'

'Close.'

'Not exactly, no.'

'But you've known him a long time?' Karen asked.

'Since we were kids.'

'At school together.'

'That's right.'

'Since when you've kept in touch.'

'Pretty much.'

'And this friendship, how would you define it?'

'I'm not sure what you mean.'

'Social or what?' Ramsden asked. 'Drink down the pub, dinner a few times a year with the wives. Birthdays, stuff like that?'

'Yes. Yes, that's right.'

'And business?'

'What business?'

'That's what we're asking you.'

'No, not really.'

'Joint ventures?'

Broderick shook his head.

'Not what we've heard.'

'Heard? Who from?'

'Your wife, for one.'

'That bitch! All she knows is the price of Botox and which delivery boy's worth a quick fuck.'

'That's as maybe.' Karen said. 'But according to her, you and Gordon Dooley had a business relationship in the past. Probably not the kind could be traced back through Companies House.'

'Fuck off,' Broderick said, but without conviction.

'You know, of course, what your friend Dooley's business is these days?'

Broderick affected to give it some thought. 'Some kind of buying and selling? Scrap, he was into that for a while, I know. Stripping out old houses and flogging the proceeds.' He shrugged. 'That kind of thing, I suppose.'

'Drugs,' Karen said.

'Do what?'

'Cannabis, amphetamines, heroin, cocaine. Take your pick. About as many outlets across the country as you've got for your whatever it is, chorizo and corned beef.'

'I wouldn't know. Didn't know.'

'You disapprove?'

'His business is his business.'

'No matter what?'

'Look,' Broderick aimed a finger, 'Gordon's breaking the law, and I'm not saying he is, your affair, not mine.'

'We're in danger of losing it,' Cormack said. 'Get back to the van.'

'Why you?' Karen said.

'What?'

'Surely you've got people working for you who can do jobs like that? Why did you personally go and lease the van?'

'God! Who knows? Most probably I was there, in the area, I don't know.'

'And you needed another van why?'

'I don't remember.'

'Try.'

Broderick gave a theatrical sigh, assumed the face of the sorely put-upon. 'Far as I recall, we had one van in for long-term repairs, another had broken down somewhere the day before. Hitchin, Hertford, Hatfield, one of those.'

'And that's why you leased the van?'

'Yes.'

'Not because Gordon Dooley asked you?'

'Dooley? What the hell's Dooley got to do with this?'

'You tell me.'

'Nothing. Absolutely nothing.'

'You sure that's not why he phoned you three days running, up to and including the day the van was hired?'

'I doubt Gordon's phoned me three days running his whole life.'

'Our records show otherwise.'

'I trust,' the solicitor said, 'you haven't been accessing my client's phone records without a warrant?'

Karen smiled.

'Or hacking into his mobile phone?'

'Who d'you think we are?' Ramsden grinned. '*News of the World?*'

'What I suggest,' Karen said, 'Dooley phoned you three days before you went out to Milton Keynes, wanting you to get hold of a van in such a way there would be no clear link back to himself. Could be you needed a little persuading.'

'Bullshit,' Broderick said. 'Never happened. Absolute bloody fantasy.'

'Conjecture,' said his solicitor. 'Fishing expedition, pure and simple. Only this time, no bait.' He tapped Broderick on the shoulder. 'We're leaving.'

'I'd like to put on record,' Karen said, 'our thanks to Mr Broderick for so wholeheartedly helping us with our inquiries.'

She managed to hold her smile till he'd left the room.

46

The Centre Hospitalier de Guingamp was on the rue de l'Armor, one of the principal roads winding north from the town centre. Kiley had spent enough time in hospitals to recognise the antiseptic smell, the mixture of frayed hope and resignation on patients' faces, the hushed purposiveness of staff as they busied this way and that. He could remember the forced cheerfulness of the surgeon after the second, failed, operation on his leg. *Find a more sedentary game after this, perhaps? Less in the way of physical contact. Ping-pong? Chess? Soccer for you henceforth, Jack, will be* Match of the Day, *I'm afraid, Saturday nights. You and Gary Lineker.* It twinged now, the leg, at the memory.

Cordon was in a side room at the end of the ward, a window looking out on to a phalanx of tall firs, their branches bright from the recent rain.

A drip had recently been detached, the stand still close alongside the bed. Bandages around the head, traversing the corner of one swollen eye, stitches threading their way across bruised skin.

The rest of his face was bloodless, pale.

In the way that people in hospital frequently did, he looked to have aged ten years at least.

'Took your fucking time,' Cordon said.

'Few things to arrange. Came when I could.'

'Good of you to bother.'

'Call I got, made out you were at death's door. 'Stead of a few bumps and bruises. Couple of cracked ribs. Might not've hurried if I'd known.'

'Bastards must've put the boot in when I was out.'

'Lucky it was nothing worse.'

Cordon knew it to be true: he could have lost an eye; he could have been dead.

'Want to tell me what happened?' Kiley moved a book, sat on the side of the bed.

'What's to tell? Whoever it was got somehow into the house, a window at the back somewhere, I don't know. Suckered me. Left me unconscious. When I came round, Letitia and Danny had gone. Car disabled, something with the carburetter, I don't know, tyres fucked. After God knows how long I managed to crawl as far as the lane, rouse the old man. Must have passed out again after that. Woke up here. Tubes sticking out of me like some bloody porcupine. Someone from the local gendarmerie waiting at the end of the bed.'

'How much d'you get away with telling them?'

'Between my French and his English, not a great deal. Attempted burglary, that's what I said. Woke and caught them in the act, got this for my troubles. Too dark, too quick to be able to give a description. Left it at that.'

'You didn't mention Letitia? The boy?'

Cordon shook his head.

'How about Kosach? Anton?'

He shook his head again. Not a good idea. Winced at the pain.

'Down to him though, you reckon?'

'Difficult to see what else.'

'And you think that's where they are now? With him?'

'Good bet, I'd say.'

'He can't just keep them prisoner.'

'He can try.'

A nurse stepped into the space, hovered, went away. The low hum from the central heating continued, unabated. Outside, the rain had started up again, buffeting the windows.

'When this happened,' Kiley said, 'there was no warning?'

'No.'

'I'm surprised they got the drop on you, all the same.'

'Preoccupied,' Cordon said. 'A little preoccupied.'

Kiley read the look in Cordon's good eye. Made the universal sign. 'Thought it wasn't like that between you?'

'It's not.'

'What was this then? A one-off? Pair of you got carried away? Or just a little something to alleviate the boredom?'

'Does it matter?'

'Not to me. But it might make it tougher for her with Anton, if he knows she's been screwing around.'

'I wouldn't exactly call it that. Besides, he knows she's no angel. And Danny's what he wants, not Letitia.'

'In that case, why not just take the boy?'

'Would have been difficult, bringing him out of France, back into the country on his own. All that much easier if Letitia agrees to play along.'

'She'd do that?'

'Pragmatic, that's Letitia. Besides, I can't see she'd've had a lot of choice.'

Kiley walked across to the window and looked out. The

sky, shadings of deep purple and the occasional yellowish streak, was a similar colour to the skin round Cordon's left eye.

'You know,' Kiley said, 'I came to Brittany once when I was a kid. First time ever in France. Cycling holiday with the school. Some kind of exchange. First night a bunch of us shook off the teachers, went into town. First one café, then the next. One after another, pointing at the bottles behind the bar. Spending what little bit of money we had fast as we could. Sick, sick, sick as a dog. After that there was a curfew. Local police on duty to keep the stupid *Anglais* from causing any more commotion, getting drunk. Couldn't have been much more than sixteen stupid years old.'

He smiled. 'Met my first girlfriend on that trip, too. Pen pal more or less till I left school.'

'Thinking of looking her up?' Cordon asked caustically.

'I did once. What? Dozen years ago? On holiday with a couple of friends. She was still living in the same place, little village outside Vannes, out near the Atlantic coast. Mistake. Five kids, moustache, wide as a house.'

'What did you expect?'

'I don't know. Things like that, they nag at you.'

'What kind of things?'

'Oh, missed chances. Roads not taken. Relationships allowed to drift. Always that nagging question, what if, what if?'

'French air, is it?' Cordon asked. 'Bringing out all this philosophy?'

'I dare say.'

''Cause if it is, sooner you get back across the Channel the better it'll be.'

'Had a word with the doctor on the way in. Four or five days it'll be before you're discharged. That, at least.'

'Nothing to say I can't discharge myself,' Cordon said. But,

272

as he moved, some unspecified pain speared through him and he gasped loudly, hands gripping the sheets.

'When I come back later,' Kiley said, 'I'll bring grapes. A deck of cards. See if I can't win some money off you while you're disabled.'

47

The Volvo had been found in a scrap dealer's yard outside Erith, close to the Thames Estuary at Crayford Ness. The same Volvo that had been stolen from the Westfield Shopping Centre in Shepherd's Bush – 4,500 parking spaces, valet parking available, a lot of cars from which to choose – and then shown up on CCTV, tailing the leased Transit en route to Stansted and back; now with its engine removed, doors and side panels disassembled, chassis ready to be winched away. Bits and pieces for the fingerprint boys to play with. Girls, too. The result: one right index finger on the steering column, with a partial alongside; another partial, left little finger, on the fascia. Palm print on the inside of the offside door.

Where would we be, Karen thought, without computers, AFIS, DNA?

Answer: even farther behind.

The prints taken from the body of the Volvo confirmed what the dealer had already told them: the identity of the individual who'd brought it in – Stuart Dyer, just twenty-one years old and recently arrested for possession of a Class A drug with intent to supply, but then released. Two previous charges of possession of a controlled substance, one dismissed, the other for which he'd served a little juvenile time. His co-defendant in both cases was his cousin, Jamie Parsons. Parsons, who did scut work for Gordon Dooley and, because of that association, was gunned down outside the Jazz Café in Camden, presumed victim of an attack for which the torture and eventual murder of Valentyn Horak and his henchmen was a reprisal.

Give it time and, eventually, gradually, it all tied together.

When Ramsden, with some serious back-up, called round at the tower-block flat in Foots Cray where he lived, Dyer was sitting with his mum watching daytime TV, an ad for stairlifts screening when Ramsden came into the room. Dyer with a can of Kestrel in his hand, his mum favouring cider, both of them smoking, some kind of bull-headed mastiff growling through its slobber at their feet.

Dyer made as if to bolt, but then, reading the glint in Ramsden's eye, thought better of it.

'What the fuck're you after now?' Mrs Dyer asked. 'Why'n't you leave the boy alone?'

Jeremy Kyle appeared on screen to loud applause, doubtless about to reveal some poignant personal dilemma to the audience. Lifting the remote from the corner of the settee, Ramsden muted the volume.

'Hey! I was fuckin' watching that!'

The dog growled lazily, then lowered its head.

'Sorry, Mrs Dyer. Just wanted a word with young Stuart here.'

'Yeah, well, s'posin' he don't want a word with you?'

'What's it to be, Stuart?' Ramsden said. 'You want to talk here or down the station?'

'I got a choice?'

Ramsden grinned, showing crooked teeth.

'Just wait, yeah,' Dyer said, 'while I get me fuckin' coat.'

'Take it easy on him, yeah?' his mum said, once he was out of the room. 'Lot of mouth, but he's not very bright. Easy led, know what I mean?'

Taking back the remote, she raised the volume loud.

Dyer sat uneasily, rocking the chair back on its metal legs. Grey drawstring hoodie with A & FITCH in white lettering down the sleeve. Tangle of dark hair. Something of a pretty-boy face, save for a cluster of whiteheads sprouting around his mouth. Half-hidden beneath his lashes, grey-green eyes.

Ramsden had asked one of the officers to fetch a Dr Pepper from the vending machine and Dyer drummed on it haphazardly with his fingers, nails bitten down.

Feigned nonchalance.

If he wasn't already squirming inside, he was really as stupid as his mum had made out.

'The Volvo,' Ramsden said, 'let's start there.'

Nothing.

'Come on, Stuart, don't piss me about. The one you dumped in Erith. Snagged it from Westfield, remember? Volvo, S60, dark green. Asked for it special, did he, Arthurs? Dougie Freeman, maybe. Whoever it was, brought you in as driver. Get us a nice motor, Stuey, something with a bit of speed, comfortable. Volvo'd be handsome.'

'Dunno what you're talkin' about.'

'Come on, Stuart. Your prints are all fucking over it and, if that weren't enough, we've got you barellin' down the road to Stansted on CCTV.'

'Bullshit!'

'You think so?'

Dyer took a swallow from the Dr Pepper, bought a little time. Cleared his throat.

'Just say. Just say, mind – and I'm not admitting anythin',

right, but, like I say, just s'posin' I took the motor, right, like you said, all that'd be, takin' and drivin' away. No one's gonna send me down for that. Lose my licence, maybe, six months, a year. Small fine, time to pay. Pro-fuckin'-bation.'

'Stuart, Stuart, you're not listening. The minute you got behind that wheel, that journey out to Stansted, you were getting into something a lot more serious. More serious than you believe. Accessory, Stuart, that's you. Accessory to torture. Better than that, murder.' Ramsden shook his head. 'You done it this time, boy, and no mistake.'

The colour had blanched from Dyer's cheeks and there was a pronounced twitch in one of his grey-green eyes.

'You want to take a look, Stuart? Take a look at these?'

With exaggerated care, Ramsden fanned out half a dozen photographs taken inside the storage unit, three bodies, like so much casual slaughter, hanging down.

'Pretty, don't you think?'

Dyer bit into his lower lip hard enough to draw blood.

'Of course,' Ramsden said, a change of voice, change of tone, 'I can understand why you'd have wanted to be involved. Jamie Parsons, him as was gunned down in Camden, he was your cousin, yeah?'

Dyer nodded.

'Any kind of payback, only right you'd want to be involved. Family, yeah? Your mum'd have told you, I'm sure. Got to stand up, Stu. Be counted on this. But I bet she never, you never, thought it would come to this . . .' Tapping the photographs. 'Am I right, Stuart? Am I right? You never . . .'

There was panic now, bright and darting, in his eyes. The kind you see in rats, Ramsden thought, trapped up against the wire.

Slowly, he leaned in, not enough to frighten, just enough to reassure. 'What we need to talk about, Stuart, is how you got yourself mixed up in all this. See if there isn't something we can do. Some way round this, don't leave you in the dock along with everyone else. Culpable homicide, Stuart, three times over. Life inside. You don't want that.' Reaching across, Ramsden patted his hand. 'Okay, Stuart? Okay? Let's see what we can do.'

'This is all on tape?' Karen said. 'Transcribed?'

Ramsden grinned his crooked grin. 'Even as we speak.'

They were in her office, evening, late, but no one was going home. Sandwiches, half-eaten; coffees, growing cold. Through the blur of half-glass, other officers moved around as if underwater, sat hunched over their desks, computers, accessed this list and that, pressed keys, made calls.

'He's named everyone?'

'Everyone in the car, the van. Everyone involved.'

'Jesus.'

'Les Arthurs, Kevin Martin, Jason Richards riding with Dyer in the Volvo, Dougie Freeman and Mike Carter up ahead in the van.'

'Just Kevin Martin?'

'Yes.'

'Not Terry?'

Ramsden shook his head.

'Shame,' Karen said.

'Yes. No Dooley, either. Too careful to get his hands dirty, this kind of business. Just a name, where Dyer's concerned. Barely that.'

'Who was it, then, set him up?'

'Arthurs, apparently. Told him there was going to be some serious payback for what had happened to his cousin, Jamie. Give them a good working over, that's what Dyer reckoned. What went on out at Wing, he didn't know about. Not till after.'

'Even though he was there?'

'Sent him off for pizza, didn't they? His story. Twenty-mile round trip in search of fifteen-inch pepperoni pizzas. Maybe when this is over he'll get a job with Domino's.'

'You believe all that? Believe him or d'you think he's just stringing us along?'

Ramsden shrugged. 'I'd say, bit of both. But right now, it suits us to take what he's saying as gospel. Long as it keeps him talking. And, besides, what he's given us so far, Carter and Arthurs doing most of the heavy stuff, fits in pretty well with what we might have guessed. Nasty bastards, both of them. Sooner they're off the streets the better.'

Karen nodded. 'I've had one conversation with Burcher already. Due another one tomorrow.'

'No plans for lifting Arthurs and the others till then?'

Karen shook her head. 'Watching brief only. Till we're told otherwise. My guess, they'll want to wait till they're sure everything's in place, make one fell swoop.'

'Just so long as they don't hold off too long, let 'em slip away. And make sure they remember who got 'em this far. Don't let the bastards grab all the glory.'

A rueful smile came to Karen's face. 'Trust me on that one, Mike. Trust me.'

48

This time the meeting was in a hotel close to the Westway, a conference room on the eleventh floor. Corporate anonymity. Silent through triple-glazed windows, three lanes of slow-moving traffic eased their way, ghost like, towards the city centre; drivers, whey faced, bored, listening absently to the radio, smoking, illegally using their mobile phones. On the table, jugs of water, glasses, a selection of sweet biscuits, notepads and pens bearing the hotel's crest and name. At intervals the air conditioner cut in above the radiators' low hum.

Sterile enough, Karen thought, should it be necessary, to perform an operation.

Burcher.

Cormack.

Alex Williams.

Charlie Frost.

Karen had made her report first, bringing them up to speed on her team's progress: the links between Dennis Broderick and Gordon Dooley; the evidence that placed Valentyn Horak and two others on their way to Stansted inside the van Broderick had leased at Dooley's request; Stuart Dyer at the wheel of the second vehicle – Dyer who placed five of Dooley's known associates at the place where Horak and two others were tortured and probably killed.

'No chance he's going to recant?' Cormack asked. 'This witness?'

'Always a chance,' Karen said. 'What I'd be more concerned about is someone getting to him. Persuading him to change his mind or shutting him up for good.'

'We can cotton-wool him, surely,' Alex Williams said. 'Protective custody.'

'Not something we've been conspicuously good at recently,' Cormack chipped in.

'We won't lose him,' Burcher said. 'Lessons learned.'

'The sooner, then, maybe,' Karen said, 'we pick up Arthurs and the rest, the better.'

'Let's not lose sight, though, of the bigger picture,' Burcher said. 'What we still don't have, as far as I can see, is anything watertight that ties Dooley in to all this – Broderick's assertion, aside, that it was Dooley talked him into leasing the van in the first place.'

'Must count for something,' Karen said.

'Not a bloody lot.'

She flashed him a look.

'There has been one other development,' Cormack put in swiftly, 'might prove useful. By dint of promising to revise his immigration status, we've persuaded one of the Chinese workers picked up at one of the raided cannabis farms to start cooperating, remembering a few faces. So far we've come up with Mike Carter, wielding a machete. And Carter's links back to Gordon Dooley are, I think, pretty well documented.'

'It's something,' Burcher said. 'Still not enough.'

'I don't know,' Alex Williams said. 'Maybe Karen's right.

281

Lift Arthurs, Carter and the others now. If they think there's mileage to be gained from shopping Dooley, that might just give us what we need. It could even panic Dooley himself into some kind of false move. Leave himself open.'

'From our point of view there's one big risk in going in too soon,' Charlie Frost said, speaking for the first time. 'SOCA's main interest here, as you know, is at the money-laundering end of things. And as you also, I think, know, one of our principal targets, Anton Kosach, has — or, rather, had — links with Valentyn Horak which were starting to become more clearly defined at the time of Horak's unfortunate demise. Quite large amounts which were being paid into one of Kosach's subsidiaries, from where it would be moved around offshore, washed through a couple of shell companies and thence . . .'

A smile came to Karen's face: she liked the thence.

'. . . and thence to a numbered but otherwise anonymous account in the Caymans—'

'Or Jersey,' Alex Williams suggested.

'Or Jersey. Either way, there's some clear evidence that Dooley, after successfully moving in on Horak's operations, has been in contact through intermediaries with Kosach, in order to move the extra money he's been accumulating out of the country.'

Capitalism, Karen thought, such a wonderful thing.

'Some evidence,' Frost concluded, 'but not quite enough.'

'How much longer do you need?' Burcher asked.

'How much can I have?'

'I don't know.' Burcher threw up his hands. 'Warren? What do you think?'

'Well, everything we know suggests Kosach's a major player. And not just money laundering. His hands are dirtier than that. People trafficking. Prostitution. It would be great to bring him down. But I can see there's a risk. Delay too long and we could lose everything. The whole shooting match.'

Burcher massaged his scalp. Thought. Waited. Thought some more.

'All right, the way I suggest we proceed is this. Karen, your team, with some assistance, keep Dooley's thugs under surveillance. Warren, you look to Dooley himself. This to give Charlie as reasonable a time to get the evidence as he needs – and no use SOCA being timid about this, Charlie, we're talking days not fucking weeks – and the minute it seems as if Dooley or anyone else we've got tabs on shows signs of panic and starts to run, wc bring the whole lot in at a gallop. No exceptions.'

He looked round the table.

'All agreed?'

They were agreed.

Karen was hoping to catch Alex Williams on the way out, but Burcher made his own claim. 'Alex, a few minutes of your time?'

The door closed behind them and Karen walked on to where Cormack and Charlie Frost were waiting, midway along the corridor, for the lift.

49

Cordon's left eye still looked as if he'd walked into a door just a few days before; either that or said the wrong thing to the wrong man in the wrong bar. More than enough of those around, as the previous night's drinking with Kiley had proved. That great barn of a place on the corner where they showed the Gaelic football amongst them. Cordon had lost his footing at one point, his balance still not being what it was, banged his sore ribs against the end of the bar and let out a shout louder than the one that had gone up when Mayo scored the winning goal in the last minutes against Sligo at Quigabar.

Jane had been with them early on, but, in deference to what was to come, had made her excuses and left them to it. A shame, Cordon had thought. A nice girl, though she'd not have thanked him for calling her that; a pleasant woman, attractive, intelligent, both feet firmly on the ground.

What was it, he wondered, that had stopped him getting hooked up with someone like that, instead of the flotsam that, since the implosion of his marriage, had formed the basis of what he might have jokingly called his love life. Primary schoolteachers of the West Country, where had they all been when he needed them? Busy, Cordon assumed, filling in assessment forms, looking the other way.

Of course, the job hadn't helped. By and large – and there were exceptions – it was a certain cast of woman who was attracted to the idea of going out with a policeman. And, from his experience, your average primary schoolteacher was not amongst them.

He wondered how Kiley did it. Downplaying, somehow, both his past years in the Met and his present role as a private eye in favour of what? A few old footballing scars and tales of his glory days with Stevenage Borough and Charlton Athletic?

Face it, he was jealous.

The nearest he'd got to what might be termed a relationship with a normal woman lacking criminal tendencies or connections had been his marriage to Judith and look what had happened there. A year or so of low-level lust and largely unfulfilled expectations, then the slow disintegration into brittle silences, betrayal and mutual recrimination. Result: a cold divorce, years of winnowing distance, and a son who, as far as he could tell, held them both in more or less complete contempt for the way they'd fucked up their lives and done their level best to do the same to his.

All with or without Philip Larkin's blessing.

And if his future lay with the Letitias of this world, God help him.

And them.

Letitia, he wondered where she was now. What had happened? If, as he assumed, those who had taken her had returned her whence she had fled, what forgiveness, if any, might she have found in Anton Kosach's arms? What forms of retribution might have been taken?

And Danny? Danya?

The bright smile on the boy's hopeful face snagged for a moment on his memory and, best as he could, he brushed it away.

Don't make him too fond . . .

Yes, well, like a lot of things, easier said than done.

He checked his watch. Already twenty past one. Back by twelve, Kiley had said, twelve thirty latest. A meeting with the local solicitor he sometimes did investigative work for which must have gone on longer than intended. Been parlayed into lunch, perhaps.

A flurry of voices drew Cordon to the window. Kids from the local comprehensive pushing and shoving, blocking the pavement, oblivious to anyone other than themselves. Small knots of them, standing smoking, eating from fast-food containers. One couple pressed up against the window of Sainsbury's Local, kissing, tonguing, his hand inside her top and no one caring.

Fifteen, sixteen – in Cordon's life, a long time ago. More than the sum of years.

He crossed to the stereo, pressed play and jacked up the volume. Amongst the last batch of CDs Kiley had filched from the charity shop below was a Nina Simone. 'You'll want to take a look at this,' Kiley had said. 'Collecting versions of "Good Bait", aren't you?' At first, he'd thought he was having a laugh, taking the piss, but there it was, 'Good Bait', just Simone's piano, one hand at first, slowly fingering out the tune, as if uncertain, then, after a while, the left hand coming in, and no vocal, no vocal at all. Bit of a sacrilege, probably, Cordon reckoned, but on the whole that was how he preferred her.

After close on a couple of minutes, bass and drums swing in and from there things become more emphatic, more outgoing. The last couple of chords were ringing out as Kiley came through the door, takeout coffees from the corner café balanced neatly in one hand.

'Just time to drink these down, then we're out of here. Message from Kosach's brother on my mobile. He's agreed to meet.'

'You or me?'

'Both. Here in London. Some Ukrainian restaurant on the Cali.'

'Where?'

'Caledonian Road. Between King's Cross and the arse end of Holloway.'

The place they were looking for was on a strip of betting shops and second-hand furniture stores, launderettes and dodgy cafés. There was a *Closed* sign on the door, but not for them. The interior was dark, just a single light showing. Whatever lunchtime rush there'd been had long since disappeared. Taras Kosach sat at a table by the side wall, a glass of wine in front of him, smoking. No one was about to tell him how many by-laws he was breaking.

As Kiley and Cordon approached, he stubbed out the cigarette and, half-rising, offered Kiley his hand. Cordon he glanced at, nothing more.

'Sit,' he said.

They sat.

'You want wine?'

'Sure,' Kiley said, 'why not?'

Without any apparent signal, a waiter appeared with a bottle and two fresh glasses. The wine was dark and thick, like plum brandy.

Taras was somewhere in his forties, Cordon thought, a darkish complexion, darkened further by several days' stubble, dark eyes; nicotine stains on his fingers, but the nails smoothed into even ovals, manicured. Some kind of balm or cologne that cut through the lingering smell of food from the kitchen.

He was looking at the markings round Cordon's eye, the residue of swelling.

'I think, perhaps, you are lucky guy.'

'You'll understand,' Cordon said, 'if I don't see it in quite the same way.'

Taras shrugged. 'What you did, it was very foolish.'

'Story of my life,' Cordon said, amiably.

'Story?'

'You wanted to see us,' Kiley said.

Taras lit another cigarette. When he tilted back his head to release the smoke, there was a scar line, thin like a razor cut, across his neck.

'A message from my brother. For you, especially.' His eyes on Cordon. 'What's done, is done. He holds no . . .' he searched for the word, 'no malice. You understand?'

Cordon said nothing.

'You understand?' Taras said again. 'Is finished.'

He drank some wine.

'And Letitia?' Cordon said.

'What of her?'

'Exactly.'

'She is with her family. None of your concern.'

'You say.'

'Yes, I say.'

'I think,' Kiley said, 'we would like to be sure of that, that Letitia is okay.'

'And the boy,' Cordon put in.

Taras waved a well-groomed hand. 'Is no longer your business.'

Kiley started to say something, but Cordon cut him off. 'You listen.' He jabbed two fingers towards Taras' chest. 'I'm the one decides what's my business. Not you or your brother or anyone else. Understood?'

A small nod from Taras, a retreat.

'Last I knew of Letitia and Danny,' Cordon said, 'they were being taken by men who were dangerous and almost certainly armed, and I doubt would have any scruples about using as much force as they thought was necessary or they could get away with.'

Taras opened his mouth as if about to protest, but Cordon paid no heed.

'You tell me Letitia's back in the bosom of her family, well, I want proof. Proof that she and the boy are okay and not being held against their will. Then you can say it's no longer my business. And not until.'

He eased away, hands gripping the table edge.

Steadying himself, Taras drew deeply on his cigarette and set it carefully down; picked up his lighter and rolled it across his fingers.

'And if this does not happen as you wish?'

Cordon leaned forward again, his voice lowered to little more than a hiss. 'Then I'll move heaven and earth to make your brother's life an absolute misery. Pull in every police contact, every favour I can. Dig into every nasty little corner I can find. By the time I've finished he'll wish he'd never clapped eyes on Letitia, never heard my name.'

Taras lifted his glass and swirled the contents around the sides before he drank. 'You are in no position, I think, to make threats.'

'Try me.' Cordon held his gaze.

Something inside Taras' head switched gear. As if he had been prepared for this. Plan B.

'I will talk to my brother. Tell him your concerns. I'm sure there will be a way to do as you wish. Put your mind at rest.'

A smile leaked from his face.

Pushing back his chair, Kiley stood, Cordon following suit. Behind them, a waiter hovered near the door.

'Forty-eight hours,' Taras said. 'No more.' Then looked away, as if dismissing them from his mind.

Back on the street, Kiley nodded left. 'Let's walk.'

A short way along, they crossed against the traffic and cut away from the main road into a street of tall, Victorian houses, plane trees, skips, aspirations.

'All that guff about moving heaven and earth,' Kiley said. 'Where'd that come from?'

'God knows.'

'I thought for one minute you were going to deck him.'

'I was.'

'What happened?'

'My good nature got the better of me. That and my natural discretion.'

Kiley laughed. 'Natural bollocks!' he said.

'That, too.'

50

The sky seemed to lower itself, shroud like, over Karen as she walked. The car she'd squeezed into a space in the parking area alongside East Heath Road and from there she'd made her way down towards South End Green, the forbidding grey of the Royal Free hospital rising directly ahead. She bought coffee in a takeout cup and crossed back on to the Heath, taking the path that led towards the mixed bathing pond, where, at the tail end of the previous year, she had seen Petru Andronic's young face staring blankly back at her through the ice.

Today, there was no ice, though the wind that sliced across the surface was keen enough to make Karen shiver and pull her scarf closer round her neck, the temperature no more than four or five degrees above freezing.

Behind her, a dog barked loudly, suddenly, and a small child cried in its buggy as its mother, or, more likely, the au pair, hurried it on past.

Karen tore a hole in the lid of the cup and held it in both hands as she drank.

The wind sent the water scurrying towards her in iron-grey waves, splashing up close to where she stood. Soon, the surrounding bushes and trees would be in bud and despite the ripples that had flowed out following his death, they were not much closer to solving Andronic's murder than they had been in those first few days.

Whether it was somehow linked to the mayhem that had followed, or a consequence of his relationship with Terry Martin's daughter, Sasha, was still not clear. Only Karen's instincts leaned her this way rather than that, and still without a shred of proof.

Follow your gut, Mike Ramsden would tell her. Follow your gut.

Much good had it done.

Her reflection gazed back at her, dark and uncertain at the water's edge. What had happened here was still as slippery, as opaque as it had ever been, and other things were only slowly falling into place. A watching brief over the Stansted murders meant a watching brief. SOCA were still following leads, back-tracking accounts over borders and across continents; careful work undertaken with the aid of the Internet, the computer, the cautious and less than legal hacking of mobile phones.

Frustrated by the lack of apparent action, she had called Cormack that morning and been able to raise nothing but his voicemail; left messages for Charlie Frost that went unanswered. She had considered calling Burcher direct, then thought better of it. Called Alex Williams instead.

'Alex, any idea what's going on?'

'In general, or in particular?'

'Particular.'

'For once, no one's telling me anything. I had a meeting with Warren scheduled for yesterday and he cancelled. Charlie's busy ferreting around, doing whatever it is Charlie does.' She laughed, a warm sound down the line. 'If I didn't know any better, I'd say it was the boys playing with boys' toys, keeping all the fun to themselves.'

'Surely not.'

Alex laughed again. 'First thing I do hear, I'll let you know.'

That was that.

Stooping, Karen scooped up water in her hand, and, ice cold, it ran back between her fingers, torn a little, sideways, by the wind.

Time to move on.

As she straightened, something snagged her attention: amongst those busily walking either way along the path, a young woman standing quite still on the rise beyond the pond's end. As if watching, looking on. Hooded jacket zipped close about her face.

Just a moment more and then she turned and, merging with the others, began to walk away.

Karen started after her, stopped.

Her mobile claiming her attention.

Again.

Ramsden.

Again.

Officers from Operation Trident, with whom he'd been liaising, were poised to make arrests the following day in connection with Hector Prince's murder.

'You're going along?' Karen asked.

'Just for the ride.'

Little, Karen knew, he liked better than the pre-dawn raid, the battering ram, the chase upstairs, the outflung boot, the fist of steel. The stuff that small boys' and middle-aged detectives' dreams are made of.

'Mike,' she said. 'Keep your head down, okay?'

He called her a rude name in reply.

Karen bunched her empty coffee cup in her hand and, dropping it in the nearest bin, made her way back towards the car.

51

After Weybridge, the car in which Cordon was travelling turned off into the first of a series of narrowing minor roads — not Cornish narrow, he thought, lacking the sharpness of angle, the high stone walls — and they were deep in the Surrey countryside. Every so often, the glimpse of a square church tower, a sign leading to a farm largely unseen, small bands of cattle arranged in a painterly manner along a burgeoning hill. The true heart of England, Kiley had told him, where the money grows. Merchant bankers and rock stars, nice people. It had been made clear that Kiley's part in the affair was over, the arrangements made, this was for Cordon alone.

The driver, bull-necked, sullen, had snapped shut the sliding glass separating him from the interior, leaving Cordon to the stale smell of air freshener and his own thoughts.

'He will see you,' Taras Kosach had said, 'my brother. It is agreed.'

'And Letitia?'

'He will meet with you, Anton. Talk. Set your mind to rest.'

Somehow, Cordon didn't think that would necessarily be the case.

The car slowed and turned left along a lane overhung with trees that were still short of bud, filtering out the grey of the sky. A quarter of a mile along and then a private road. Woodland to either side. Warning signs, recently repainted: *No Access. Private Land.* Wire fencing, recently renewed.

A little farther and then a gate of wrought iron set between columns. CCTV cameras focusing down. The driver punched numbers into a metal panel, spoke briefly into the small microphone alongside.

Something nudged at Cordon's stomach.

Anticipation?

Fear?

After the set-up, the house, to Cordon at least, was something of a disappointment. A mock-Tudor sprawl, all pitched roofs and sharp angles, dark timbering squared across white plaster, mullioned windows. Tiny cameras that swivelled towards him as he stepped from the car.

Three shallow stone steps to the doorway.

Two men approaching, neither of them Anton Kosach. Mid-twenties, unsmiling, the obligatory leather jackets over black turtlenecks, dark trousers worn a size too tight at the crotch.

One of them gestured for him to remove his coat, then raise his arms.

What were they expecting? A wire? Some kind of weapon?

They ran their hands around his waistband, across his back and chest, high along his thighs, between his legs. Threw back his coat.

'You wait.'

Cordon took several steps back across the gravelled drive and looked up at the main section of the house. No signs of life. No sound, other than a brief chattering of birds across acres of lawn.

Was Letitia actually here?

And Danny?

He looked in vain for any sign of a scooter, an abandoned bicycle, a rubber ball, a toy.

The door opened again and a man came out: Anton Kosach, certainly. Taller than his brother, Taras, but similar features, the same dark eyes. His dark suit was well cut, the jacket unbuttoned, palest of pale blue shirts, no tie, soft, expensive shoes.

'Mr Cordon . . .' Kosach began. 'Or should it be Inspector?'

'Mister is fine.'

'Not police business, what brings you here?'

A shake of the head.

'Good. Welcome, then.' He held out his hand.

The accent was only slight, the handshake firm and smooth.

Kosach studied Cordon's face, then stepped back and offered him a cigarette and, when Cordon refused, lit one for himself. For a moment, soft smoke hung on the air.

'Please, let us walk.'

The path led away from the house, between groomed shrubs with crocuses and a few late snowdrops lingering in the shade. 'My brother says you are concerned about Letitia and I am not sure why this should be.'

'Most times, when a woman has to be dragged back by force after being threatened and frightened half out of her wits, I'd say there's some cause for concern.'

'Threatened? Frightened? I don't think so. And no one was dragged.'

'Your thugs broke into the house in the middle of the night and beat the shit out of me before hauling Danny and Letitia back to where they didn't want to be.'

'Mr Cordon, those thugs, as you call them, are men I trust.

And they assured me they used as little force as was necessary to release my wife and son.'

'Your wife?'

Kosach halted. 'Of course, what did you think?'

Cordon could only stare back at him, nonplussed.

'And as for – what did you say? – being where they do not want to be . . .' He gestured back towards the house with a sweep of his hand. 'Why would they not want to be here? Where they belong.'

'I know what she told me,' Cordon said.

'You heard, my friend, what you wanted to hear.'

When the path divided, they went towards a small stand of silver birch, a robin puffing out its chest on one of the branches until they came closer and it flew away.

'It is true,' Kosach said. 'Letitia and I, there was an argument, a . . . misunderstanding, I think you would say. She is headstrong. If you know her at all, you will know this. Things were said.' He shook his head. 'All that is forgotten. You have, I think, this saying, forget and forgive.'

'I want to see her,' Cordon said.

'I am afraid that is not possible.'

'Hear her say in her own words this is where she really wants to be.'

Kosach looked at him through narrowed eyes and laughed. 'Of course. All this time I thought you were some kind of father to her, you look after her, protect, you are policeman, after all, but no, you are in love with her yourself—'

'The hell I am!'

'You are in love with her and that is why you think she cannot be happy with someone else.' He smiled. 'Believe me, my friend, I understand.'

'Yeah? Well, understand this, no way am I your fucking friend.'

'And now you are angry and upset.'

More than anything else, Cordon wanted to punch him in the mouth, shut out the supercilious, patronising crap, the accent that came and went. With an effort, he kept his hands to his sides.

The path circled back towards the house.

Neither man spoke again until they had arrived back at the main door.

'I want to see her,' Cordon said again.

'And I have told you—'

'She's here?'

A pause. 'Yes, she is here.'

'Then let me speak to her. If she says the same as you, without duress, then that's an end to it.'

'An end?'

'Yes.'

Kosach studied him again, staring at his face. 'You are a man of your word?'

'As much as any man.'

'Very well. Wait here.'

Kosach went briskly inside and the two men who had searched Cordon reappeared and stood, arms folded, on the steps to either side of the door. The help living up to the stereotype, at least.

Five minutes shaded into ten.

Cordon shifted his balance from one foot to the other, flexing the muscles in his calves. A small jet of pain nagging, intermittently, at the base of his left leg, the foot. Achilles heel?

Kosach reappeared at the door.

'Please. Come inside.'

Letitia stood in the curve of a stairway that swept up from an expanse of tiled floor. Pale, little make-up, some shadowing around the eyes, a bruising of colour across her mouth. Her hair had been dyed a darkish brown and held her face in a tight frame. No smile; no more than a hint of recognition in her eyes. Cordon wondered if she were ill, or merely very, very tired. The clothes she wore, drab shades of grey.

'Letitia?'

Barely a movement at the sound of her name, his voice.

'Your friend, Letitia, he has a question to ask. He wants to know if you're happy here. Are you happy, Letitia?'

'Of course.'

'And is anyone keeping you here against your will?'

She looked puzzled, as if the question made little sense.

'Do you want to stay here?' Cordon asked.

A flicker of the eyes.

'Because if you don't . . .' moving towards her, towards the foot of the stairs, 'if you don't you could leave with me, now. You understand what I'm saying? You could go, you and Danny, now.'

As if at the sound of his name, the boy appeared on the landing above, and, seeing Cordon, called his name and started to run towards him, two, three steps at a time, until his father's warning shout of 'Danya!' stopped him, teetering, in his tracks.

'Letitia?' Cordon said again, but her head was turned towards Kosach, not to him, the look that passed between them then impossible to read.

'Danya,' Kosach said, 'go to your mother. Now.'

Cautiously, the boy retreated up the stairs and clung hold of his mother's skirt, one of her arms around his shoulders, tight, the other gripping the balustrade, wedding ring in plain sight.

'If it's what you want, Letitia,' Kosach said, stepping quickly to the door, throwing it open, 'you can go.'

Other than tightening her grasp of Danny's shoulders, she didn't move.

Still at the door, Kosach shifted his gaze towards Cordon. 'An end to it, I think that's what you said.'

The anger that still simmered inside Cordon was cauterised by disillusion, disappointment, lack of understanding.

His shoulders sagged.

'The driver will take you back,' Kosach said. 'I do not expect to see you again.'

52

Karen had promised to meet Carla, early evening, nothing fancy, just the two of them, a small celebration.

'Celebrating what?' Karen had wanted to know.

'Wait and see.'

Carla had suggested the American Bar at the newly refurbished Savoy Hotel, but when they arrived, just shy of eight o'clock, there was already a queue for seats and fighting your way to the bar was, Carla suggested, about as easy as getting to one of the lifeboats on the *Titanic*.

They made their way along the Strand to the lobby bar at One Aldwych, where, although busy, they not only found two recently vacated high-backed armchairs within minutes of arriving, but had a delightfully camp waiter at their side as soon as they were comfortably seated.

Carla ordered champagne cocktails – at £12 a pop, a small saving on the Savoy – and to go with them, a little something, as she put it, yummy to nibble on.

'So,' Karen said, leaning forward so as to be heard, 'what's the big news? Don't tell me at last Hollywood's come calling?

You and Brad Pitt? Leonardo? George Clooney, even. Old, maybe, but not too old.'

'Better than that, darling.'

'What's better?'

Carla was laughing. 'Me in uniform.'

'What?'

'Uniform. Like the one you used to wear. Till, like, I get promoted.'

Karen was looking at her gone out. 'Just let me get this straight. You're going to be . . .'

'Playing you. Yes, that's right. I mean, not really you. But someone like you. This black policewoman who starts out walking the beat, but then after she helps solve this specially grisly murder she gets made up to detective. Oh, and I get to sing. Just karaoke, but, you know, real songs.'

Karen accepted her cocktail from the waiter, drank most of it down in a single swallow and ordered two more.

'It's ITV, their new series. *Black and White*. At least, that's what it's called for now. Might change. Something a bit more sexy.'

'And this is all — what? — definite? Definitely happening or . . .'

'No, it's definite. This company making it, the real deal, yeah? *Shameless*, you know? *Skins*. That's them. Tons of stuff. BAFTAs and Lord knows what all over the walls.'

'And how did you . . . ?'

'Why me, you mean?'

'Yeah, I suppose so.'

'This guy, one of the producers, saw me at the National, didn't he? That Jacobean thing I've been touring. Got in touch with my agent. Would I be interested in coming along for a chat sometime. Chat, my black arse! Lunch at the Groucho, thank you very much. Ended up more or less offering me the part before he'd signed for the bill.'

'More or less.'

'That was then. Now it's a done deal. Well . . .' She laughed. 'More or less.'

'And this part, this role. This black policewoman. How big is it?'

Carla chuckled. 'Girlfriend, it's the lead!'

'Say again? A police series with a black woman in the lead?'

'Why not?'

'Come on, Carla, in the States, maybe. What is it? HBO? But here. ITV?'

'Well, there is this other guy. The whatever, Detective Chief Inspector. He's white.'

'And he's in charge.'

'Yes. But only in name. And I mean, not really. What they're going for, you see, is something like the couple in that show that was on the Beeb. *Ashes to Ashes*? That what it was called?'

'*Ashes to Ashes*, great. And you're what? Keeley Hawes?'

'I suppose.'

'But in black face.'

'Hey! Hey!'

'Hey what?'

'Why are you giving me such a hard time?'

Karen shook her head and sighed. 'I don't know. I'm sorry, I—'

'I thought you'd be pleased.'

'Well, I am . . .'

'Pleased for me and well, I guess, pleased 'cause of what it is. You know, someone – well, someone like you . . . Oh, you know what I mean.'

'A positive role model?'

'Yes.'

'If that's what it turns out to be.'

'At least, give it a chance.'

'I know. I'm sorry. It's just . . .'

'Just what?'

Karen shrugged.

'Not a great time, you think, for being a role model for women of colour. Out in the real world, that is.'

'Something like that, yes.'

The operation to arrest the suspects identified in the killing of Hector Prince had been carried out that morning. Five addresses in the Wood Green area raided, one hundred and fifty front-line officers involved, thirty of them armed, with three teams of firearms officers in reserve. As things had played out, there was considerable local resistance, in the course of which seven officers were injured, one seriously, when a length of stone coping was thrown from the ninth-floor balcony of a block of flats. When the ambulance arrived to provide assistance, it was attacked with bricks and bottles and, in one instance, a home-made firebomb.

Media comparisons were made to the killing of PC Keith Blacklock on the Broadwater Farm Estate back in '85. The *Sun*, *Mirror*, *Sky News*, all had a field day.

In a different situation, the spectacle of Mike Ramsden, blood running like a dark zigzag down his face from where a chunk of brick had torn his forehead, seizing the microphone from some hapless young reporter and telling her to stick it up her scrawny arse, might have been one to cherish. As it was, for Ramsden a sore head and a serious reprimand were in order, with Karen, as his senior officer, not exempt from the latter.

And what proliferated were accusations of black mob rule.

No, not a great time.

'I'm sorry,' Karen said, 'and it's great, you're right.' Leaning across, she gave Carla a hug. 'And I am really pleased for you, okay?'

'You better be. 'Cause once this show gets rolling, it's you I'll be relying on for on-the-spot research. You realise that? In fact, why don't I see about getting you taken on as some kind of special adviser? You'd be perfect.'

'Thanks, Carla.' Karen held up both hands. 'Thanks, but no thanks.'

'We'll see.'

Leaning back, Carla sampled one from a nicely overpriced dish of salted anchovies. Karen looked around for the waiter, refills needed.

'Tell me,' she said, 'if you're the black in this, who's the white?'

'The guy?'

'Yeah, the guy.'

'They're not sure. A lot of names, but nothing yet nailed down.'

'Names, like who?'

'Oh, Damian Lewis, that was one. And that guy from *The Wire*, the cop, you know?'

'McNulty?'

'Yeah, him.'

'The Irish one?'

'Yes, but he's not Irish. Well, his mother was, I think. But he's English. Went to Eton. How much more English can you get?'

'You'd never know it.'

Carla smiled. 'Nothing's what it seems, girlfriend. You should know that by now.'

Karen thought she was probably right. After one more round, the sound around them rising up to the high ceilings and reverberating back down, they decided to call it a night. Go their separate ways.

Her head less than clear and nursing the beginnings of what might be a hangover, halfway towards Holborn station Karen hailed a cab. When she alighted outside her flat some fifteen minutes later, there was a car she didn't recognise parked a little way down, someone in shadow behind the wheel.

Karen hesitated, thought for a moment about going over, banging on the car window, showing her warrant card, but why bother? Just someone sleeping it off.

Fishing her keys from her bag, she went, without hurrying, up the steps towards the front door. As the key turned in the lock she heard the sound of a car door closing, steps approaching.

'Thought you were never coming home. Thought I'd be stuck there all night.'

Alex. Alex Williams. Holding what looked suspiciously like a bottle of single malt.

53

'Auchentoshan.'

'What?'

'How you say it, apparently. Aw-ken-tosh-an. At least, that's what the guy in Oddbins told me.'

'And he'd know.'

'Doubt if he's been north of Luton in his life.'

Karen had fetched two glasses; tumblers, but heavy bottomed enough to be close to the real thing.

There was a standard lamp with a shade in an odd colour of lime green in one corner; a small anglepoise on one of the shelves near the stereo. The curtains were drawn across, shutting out the London night.

With a choice of the one easy chair or a two-seater settee which abutted it at right angles, Alex had taken the chair. A low table sat between, cluttered with several unopened brown envelopes, the previous week's *Highbury and Islington Gazette*, a book of short stories by someone with the unlikely name of Maile Meloy, and a letter from Karen's mother in Jamaica.

Karen dumped them all on the floor and set the glasses down in their place.

Alex swivelled the stopper from the bottle, leaned forward and began to pour.

'I shouldn't, you know,' Karen said.

'On the wagon?'

'Just the opposite.'

'Heavy night?'

'Champagne cocktails at One Aldwych, if you please.'

'Date? Celebration?'

'Not a date. My friend, Carla.'

'That's the actress, right? I met her once. Some party?'

'God, that was years ago. How on earth d'you remember?'

Alex smiled. 'Collect information, store it away, it's what I do.' She tapped a finger against her temple, pushed a hand up through her short crop of hair. 'All here, in the hard drive.'

Karen sat back, glass in hand. 'You're lucky. All I've got in there is mush.'

'You say.'

The whisky was bright, not peaty, slightly sweet and went down a dream.

'So what do you think?' Alex asked.

'About what?'

'This.' Alex held up her glass.

'It's good. Very good.' She lifted the bottle. 'Not heard of it before. More of a vodka drinker, I suppose.'

'It was Roger introduced me to this. Couple of Christmases back.'

'How is he? Roger?'

'Fine. Off to Whitby with the kids. Bit of a half-term ritual. Stiff sea breezes and walks along the pier. Thinks it's character forming.'

Karen laughed. Carla aside, it was with Alex, she supposed, that she felt most relaxed. Alex herself certainly looked relaxed enough, feet tucked up beneath her, wearing what seemed to be her usual off-duty outfit of blue jeans and a denim shirt, worn out and unbuttoned over a pale lavender vest. Her coat she'd shucked off the minute she came through the door.

In comparison, Karen, still in her glad rags, felt overdressed.

'I guess,' Alex said, leaning forward again to top up their glasses, 'I should have brought something to go with this. Something for ballast. Fancy crisps, at least.'

'Oh, wait. Wait.' Karen jumped up, heading for the kitchen, then wished she hadn't moved quite so fast. 'I've got crisps out here. Sea salt and something or other. Two for one in Tesco. And there's salami in the fridge. At least, I think there is. And cheese.'

She scurried round, unwrapping, finding plates, ferreting out a jar of olives from where it had got trapped behind the Tabasco and the soy sauce. When she turned, Alex was there, standing in the doorway. Just leaning, leaning sideways against the frame, one foot crossed over the other, hands by her sides.

'Need some help?'

The light from overhead was catching the red in her hair.

'No, thanks. It's okay, I'm fine.'

From nowhere, Karen wanted to touch her hair.

Alex smiled: stayed where she was.

Pearl of her skin.

Karen fumbled a fork and it clattered to the floor.

'It's okay,' Alex said, taking half a pace forward. 'Leave it where it is.'

Karen caught her breath. And then she was touching her, touching her hair, the crown of her head, the ends where they tapered softly down towards her neck. The corner of her mouth. Then kissing her.

Oh, Christ!

Alex's hand on her breast.

When Karen woke it was past four. A line of sweat zigzagged, dry and crystalline, from her navel to the hollow of her neck. Beside her, one arm raised up towards her face, Alex slept. Mouth slightly open, a faint whistle of breath.

Karen needed to pee.

As she swung her legs round from the bed, Alex stirred.

'It's early,' Karen said. 'Go back to sleep.'

But when she returned, Alex was sitting up, pillows propped at her back, smiling sleepily.

'Get you something?' Karen asked. 'Juice? Tea?'

'Juice would be great. Thanks. And then tea.'

'Peppermint? Builder's?'

'Peppermint.'

Karen brought it all to the bed on a tray and climbed back in.

'Thank you.' Dipping her head, Alex kissed her on the shoulder.

'What for?'

A grin on Alex's face. 'The tea, of course. What did you think?'

It felt strange, the two of them, sitting there like that after what had gone before. Strange, Karen thought, but somehow natural. Natural yet strange.

'You make a habit of this?' Karen asked.

'With you? I'd have remembered.'

'That wasn't what I meant.'

'I know. And, no, not exactly.'

'But you knew, when you came round. Waited.'

'What I wanted, yes. At least, I thought I did.' She stroked Karen's arm. 'I wasn't at all sure about you.'

Karen covered her face with her hands.

'Regrets?' Alex said.

'No. Yes. Yes, a million of them, probably. But no. Not really. Not at all.'

'Come out together after breakfast then, shall we? You know, an announcement. Facebook. Twitter.'

Karen had to look at her carefully to be sure she was joking.

'Can you imagine . . . ?'

'All too easily.'

It was still dark outside and would be for a good couple of hours.

'Roger,' Karen said. 'What if . . .'

'Roger's in Whitby, remember?'

'Yes, but does he . . . ?'

'Know sometimes I swing the other way?'

'Yes, I suppose so.'

Alex smiled. 'What he doesn't know, can't hurt him.'

'You believe that?'

'Maybe I have to.' She lifted her tea. 'When I've finished this, I'll go. Maybe a quick shower.'

'Breakfast? There'd be time.'

'No, it's fine.'

'Toast? There's toast. Could be.'

'Okay, toast it is.'

Toast with marmalade; with the last few scrapings of Marmite; with raspberry jam. Uncertain in the kitchen, doing her best to ignore the alcohol ache in her head, Karen made coffee as she listened to the throw of water in the shower.

Alex emerged looking fresh, still towelling her hair. Karen pulled back the curtain and they sat at the table in the shallow bay, looking out across the empty street.

'Burcher,' Alex said suddenly. 'Has he ever said anything to you about a Paul Milescu?'

'You mean Ion's father? Ion, the friend of the Andronic boy?'

'Yes.'

'Why d'you ask?'

'That last meeting. You remember Burcher asked me to stay behind? A private word.'

Karen nodded.

'It's Milescu he was asking about. Were we investigating him? If so, at what level? What reason? Did we think there was any link with Kosach? Anton Kosach. Anyone else we'd been discussing?'

'He give a reason?'

'Not really. Name had cropped up, something vague like that.'

'That's interesting,' Karen said, leaning forward. 'Quite early on in all this, way back before Camden or Stansted, when it was just an investigation into the Andronic murder, I'd been out to talk to Ion Milescu and Burcher came looking for me − no two ways about it − stopped me on the way home. Quizzed me about the boy's involvement. Claimed his father had been making waves, calling in favours. Friends in high places, that's what he said. After that, I did a little checking, spoke to Tom Brewer in Economic and Specialist Crime. Worst he could come up with, Milescu had maybe sailed close to the wind a few times, but no more no less than anyone else.'

Alex took a quick glance at her watch. 'Well, Burcher, Milescu, something's going on somewhere.' She took a last swig of coffee and got to her feet.

'That morning in December. When you were called out to the ponds, early. How long did it take Burcher to arrive?'

Karen thought, shrugged. 'No time at all. In the area that night, he said, staying with friends.'

'Paul Milescu's address,' Alex said. 'New End Square, Hampstead. Might be nothing to it, but maybe the friends in high places include Burcher himself.'

54

Cordon's first instinct after seeing Letitia had been to retreat back down to Cornwall and put as much distance between them as he could. Finito. An end to it, as he'd said. Case closed. Except there had never been a case, not in any orthodox sense of the word. And who was he to investigate it if there were?

A woman whose life had ended beneath a train – by accident or design he still didn't know and likely never would. Another who had disappeared. Except not really, other than by her own choice. Put herself in harm's way. And here he had come, clumsy, slow witted, shielding his eyes when they should have been open. Floundering without jurisdiction; without direction. Whatever he had allowed himself – driven himself – to be drawn into involving Letitia was something he had never properly understood. Some private battle between herself and her husband, if that's what he truly was, in which he'd been little more than a pawn.

What, after all, had he done? Achieved? Beyond rescuing someone who, in the end, only wanted to be found?

Still he didn't go.

Sat morosely around Jack Kiley's flat, talking very little or not at all. Spent a few long, slow afternoons in sad boozers in the back streets of Kentish Town, awash with self-pity and bad beer.

'Come on,' Kiley said, one early evening as the light was fading. 'I've got just the thing.'

They took the overground from Gospel Oak to Leyton Midland Road and joined the crowd on its way along the high street to the floodlights of Brisbane Road. Orient versus Dagenham and Redbridge, a local derby of a kind. Raucous shouts and laughter. Stalls selling burgers, sausage and bacon rolls: the sweet scent of frying onions rising up into the evening mist.

They took their seats high in the main stand just as the teams were announced, prior to running out on to the pitch. Years since Kiley had stood in the tunnel waiting, nights like this, his stomach still knotted with the anticipation, sweat, cold, seeping into the palms of his hands.

Then, there they were, the crowd on its feet, both sets of supporters chanting, applauding; the players jumping, stretching, easing tight muscles, moving into position, eager for the whistle that would break the tension.

At least, Kiley could watch now without kicking every ball, feeling every tackle, rising up to meet every cross with his head. Alongside him, Cordon was being drawn more and more into the action, putting in his share of oohing and aahing as the play moved swiftly from end to end, shots missed, shots saved, the referee coming in for the usual amount of stick, offsides wrongly signalled, penalties not given.

At half-time it was one apiece, the home team shading it but not by much. Still level then, and not through want of trying, less than quarter of an hour to go.

'They'll do it,' Kiley said, 'you see if they don't.'

On the eighty-seventh minute, Charlie Daniels ran on to a punt upfield, turned the defender and raced towards the line; swung his foot and sent the ball hard and low across the face of goal and the striker, diving forward, headed it past the sprawling goalie into the net.

Pandemonium.

Game over.

They were waiting for them when they returned. Two men parked back along the road, between the burned-out supermarket and the school. The man from SOCA in his insurance-agent threads who'd quizzed Kiley before, together with a second, burly in leather jacket and jeans, his minder perhaps, in case things got out of hand.

'Not a coincidence,' Kiley said, 'meeting again like this.'

'Afraid not.'

'And I suppose you'll want to talk inside?'

'If that's acceptable to you.'

Acceptable, Kiley thought, would be if they went their merry way; if he had never let Cordon talk him into getting involved.

He could sense the big man watching Cordon on the stairs, as if he might be about to make a break for it, take to his heels.

'Charlie Frost,' the man from SOCA said, once they were in the room. His companion remained unnamed.

There were enough chairs, just, for them all to sit. Kiley's hospitality began and ended there.

'When we spoke before about your interest in Anton Kosach,' Frost said, addressing Kiley, 'what you told me, not to put too fine a point on it, was a pack of lies.'

'I wouldn't exactly say lies.'

'A name you'd come up with while looking into something else, I think you said? No more than that.'

'Things moved on.'

315

'So it appears.'

Bending, Frost reached into the briefcase he'd been carrying; perhaps, Kiley thought, he was about to sell them insurance after all. What he took out was an iPad, which he switched on, opened a file, and swivelled in their direction.

'There. You might take a look at these.'

The first image was of Taras Kosach, entering the Ukrainian restaurant on the Caledonian Road; then Kiley and Cordon arriving, leaving, Cordon with an upward glance towards a camera he had no idea was there.

Next, Taras with another man, later that same day – date and time at the foot of the screen – the pair of them standing outside, smoking. Taras and his brother, Anton.

Then a piece of video: an empty lane, restrained sunlight. Several seconds without movement till a dark saloon comes into view, travelling towards the camera, going past, a face at the rear passenger window in dark outline.

Freeze-frame.

Zoom in.

Cordon staring out.

'You recognise,' Frost said, 'where you are? The occasion?'

Cordon nodded, said nothing.

A number of images then, taken with a telescopic lens in fairly quick succession. Cordon moving between the car and the house; Kosach's minions in their black turtlenecks, waiting to greet him. Search him. The front door opening. Anton Kosach, the pale blue of his shirt bleached almost white. Then nothing.

'It's been difficult,' Frost said, 'for us to gain as much access as we might have liked. Without alerting the target, propelling him, possibly, into flight.' A discreet cough into the back of the hand. 'But, to be crystal clear, that is you, Mr Cordon, paying Mr Kosach a visit? There's no room for doubt?'

'Evidently not.'

'Then in what capacity, may I ask?'

No reply.

'I ask, because, as far as I am aware, the remit of the Devon and Cornwall constabulary does not stretch quite this far.'

Supercilious bastard, Kiley thought.

What Cordon was thinking didn't show, not even in his eyes.

'Mr Cordon . . . ?'

'I was visiting a friend.' Cordon's voice flat and ungiving.

'Anton Kosach, he's a friend? Is that what you're saying? Anton . . .'

He told them. With the dull precision of someone making a report to a superior, which, in a way, was what this was. Letitia. Her mother. Danya. The apparent break she'd made with Kosach and his efforts to get her to return. He said nothing of the work Letitia had carried out on Kosach's behalf, in his employ – the brothel, the halfway house – other things he might only have guessed at.

Frost listened with interest, rarely taking his eyes from Cordon's face. His companion was more distracted, bored even, as if none of this really mattered; wanting to be away.

Kiley stood, stretched; made an offer of tea or coffee, a little late in the day.

'The investigation into Kosach's affairs,' Frost said, 'it's near to reaching tipping point, I suppose that's fair to say, and any new contacts we've been monitoring closely.' A nod towards the iPad. 'As you can see. And we were a little intrigued at the nature of whatever relationship it was you had. But after the usual checks . . .' He smiled. 'No conspicuous spending, no unexplained large payments into either of your accounts . . .'

Cordon blinked; Kiley bristled, but held his tongue.

'. . . the explanation you've given doesn't diverge too far from what we know. Indeed, adds a little grace note here

317

and there, and I thank you, Mr Cordon, for that. But one thing I would urge you both, where Anton Kosach is concerned, you don't go near, don't try to communicate with him in any way.'

He was on his feet, minder at his side. 'Apple cart. Upset. You know how it goes.' He turned back at the door. 'The game tonight, who won?'

'Orient,' Kiley said. 'The odd goal.'

Frost nodded. 'Always been something of a Spurs fan myself.'

Figures, Kiley thought.

From the window he watched them get into their car and drive away.

'I'm sorry, Jack,' Cordon said. 'Dragging you into all this.'

Bit late for that, Kiley thought. He fetched two beers from the fridge. 'Leaving it alone, walking away, you going to be all right with that?'

Cordon popped the can. 'Case of having to, wouldn't you say?'

He saw Letitia, holding her son tight on the stairs; face betraying little or no emotion, giving nothing away.

55

The warrants were issued: Michael John Carter and Leslie Arthurs for the murder of Valentyn Horak and two others, identities as yet unknown; Carter also on three counts of inflicting grievous bodily harm with intent and for conspiracy to supply cocaine and cannabis; Kevin Martin, Douglas Freeman and Jason Richards for conspiracy to murder and inflicting grievous bodily harm. Gordon Dooley for the importation, repackaging and distribution of cocaine and cannabis and for conspiracy to inflict grievous bodily harm. Anton Kosach for money laundering, conspiracy to traffic human beings into the UK for the purposes of forced labour and conspiracy to traffic women for the purposes of sexual exploitation.

Officers from Serious and Organised Crime Command, Homicide and Serious Crime Command and SOCA were involved, along with others from SO19, Armed Response, and Operation Support. Close on four hundred, all told.

An hour before sunrise.

Synchronised raids.

Two Metropolitan Police helicopters were on standby, their

initial use denied by the noise involved, the necessity of surprise.

At the briefing, in a primary school just south of the river, Burcher had emphasised the importance of coordination, keeping all phone traffic and radio contact to a minimum, nothing that might constitute a warning.

'And if I see some scumball reporter from the *Sun* or *Sky News* within spitting distance of any part of this before we're through, I'll track back the leak and when I find who was responsible, personally hang them by the balls off the middle of Westminster Bridge, am I clear?'

He was clear.

Warren Cormack went over the details a final time: timing, location. Six addresses in South London, two within a couple of streets of one another, which raised potential difficulties due to the number of officers necessarily present in a relatively small area. The most recent information had all targets *in situ*. Thanks to Google Earth, every targeted address had been theirs in glorious full colour; every side passage, back entry, dormer window, every crack in the masonry.

Charlie Frost put in a few words about SOCA's involvement and made a case for Kosach being the most important single target, with Gordon Dooley a close second. Karen stood a little to one side, not called upon to address the troops and not minding; her place at the top table clear and reserved, her team crucially involved.

'Not wetting your feet on this one?' Ramsden said to her with a grin, the briefing over, personnel moving away.

'Too senior. Leave the heroics to others. Sit back and garner praise.'

There was a brightness in Ramsden's eyes, the expectation, the testosterone dripping off him like sweat. All geed up to go over the top, in with the milk, what he was born for or so it seemed.

Karen looked around the now almost empty hall. In what? An hour, two at most, they would know how successful they had been.

Les Arthurs was tucked up in bed, sleeping like a baby.

Dougie Freeman, alerted by sounds below, bolted up the stairs to the attic, thence through a narrow window and out on to the roof, bollock naked, his efforts loudly applauded by the officers who had taken up positions on the rooftops to either side.

Kevin Martin, reactions dulled by a considerable amount of wine and spirits the night before, to say nothing of some quite energetic sex with his half-brother's wife, had barely time to swing his feet round towards the floor before two pairs of hands seized hold of him and pushed him the rest of the way, face squashed sideways against the carpet. Fay Martin, leaning back against the headboard as she reached for her cigarettes, seemed as much concerned that she had snagged one of her nails as anything else.

Jason Richards had been on his way back from the bathroom, woken as usual by the need to pee, when the first police vehicles arrived; minicab for the woman who lived opposite, he thought, early shift at the hospital, but then when he glanced out through the blinds he knew it was something else.

Trousers, shirt, jacket, shoes: Walther PPK from the wardrobe shelf.

'Here,' he said, tossing his mobile to the startled Italian waiter with whom he'd spent the night. 'Gordon Dooley, the number's in there. Dooley. Tell him to scarper.'

And he was gone.

Out through the side door of the kitchen into the adjoining garage, out again from there into the rear garden, two shapes ahead of him crouching, waiting; one foot up on the dustbin and he was over the side wall and running; only a weak trellis between the next pair of gardens and he crashed through it, vaulting a low brick wall to the rear and then past a garden shed and a greenhouse into a narrow passage between the backs of two houses and out on to the adjacent street.

Empty.

Cars parked close at either side.

There was a children's playground at the far end and beyond that a high-rise that was a warren of stairwells and walkways, a good quarter of the places squatted or empty.

He was running, keeping low, close alongside one of the lines of parked cars, when the first officer appeared suddenly ahead of him, just three car lengths away, arms spread, blocking his path.

No time to change direction, Richards decided to go through him, straight-arming him in the chest, following up with his shoulder, the officer – young, Asian – grabbing hold of Richards by the back of his jacket, the momentum sending them both sprawling across the pavement, stumbling up by way of some garden railings, a privet hedge, the officer with his arm now around Richards' neck and squeezing hard, Richards choking, reaching into his pocket for the Walther and swinging it round into the policeman's face – once, twice – hard enough to open the skin above the cheek, below the eye, the grip loosening but not failing; one more blow with the pistol against the side of the head behind the ear and the officer's legs gave beneath him, his fingers closing nonetheless on Richards' collar and dragging him down, the pair of them on their knees – all of this happening in moments, seconds, sounds of pursuit ever closer, gaining – 'Leggo, you stupid fuck!' – no let-up in the officer's grip, Richards pressed the muzzle of the gun against his shoulder and fired.

Shock lancing across the policeman's eyes.

Richards scrambling to his feet and running.

Ahead, a police vehicle swerved broadside across the road,

cannoned against two parked cars and swung to a halt, doors opening, armed officers in helmets, full protective clothing, jumping out, the wheels still spinning.

The first of them dropped into a firing position at the pavement's edge, shouted a warning.

Headlong towards him, Richards raised his weapon, pointing.

The marksman called a second warning, then dropped him with a single shot to the chest that seemed – surely an illusion? – to lift him off the ground, legs bicycling in the air, before he dropped down, seconds from dying if not already dead, blood beginning to trickle slowly from beneath the body, filigreeing its way along the cracks between the paving stones and down towards the gutter.

It was to Mike Ramsden's great disappointment that his own involvement was less dramatic. Having pulled strings in order to nab his target, Mad Mike Carter, he was disappointed to find Carter in shorts and singlet, sitting cross-legged on the mat in the basement he'd adapted into a home gymnasium, sweaty and smiling after the first half-hour of his regular early-morning workout.

'Didn't have to come through the front door like a fuckin' train, you know? Could've rung the fuckin' bell.' Rising, he threw the towel from round his neck towards Ramsden. 'Here. Put in a bit of time, why don't you? Looks like you could fuckin' use it.'

He was still laughing as, arms pulled sharply back, the cuffs were snapped shut behind him.

Alerted by the phone call, Gordon Dooley made his getaway minutes before the police arrived; avoiding a roadblock by driving across two suburban gardens, scattering shrubs and rose bushes like some profligate guerrilla gardener, before accelerating over the centre of a roundabout and away, leaving two pursuing vehicles in his wake. One of the police helicopters picked him out, fifteen minutes later, his distinctive Porsche Cayenne SUV heading east along the M26 at upwards of one hundred miles an hour.

Time, just, to close the motorway at exit 4 and channel him south along the A228 towards Leybourne and West Malling, where, this time, the roadblock was more comprehensive, helicopter hovering low now overhead.

No fool, Dooley slowed, stopped, stepped carefully from the car, hands raised, and began to walk towards a phalanx of armed officers. Following instructions, he lay face down in the centre of the road, arms stretched wide, legs apart.

Almost a full sweep.

Almost.

When the SOCA officers, supported by others from SO19 and the Major Crime Investigation team of the local Surrey force, arrived at Anton Kosach's residence, the bird, as the saying goes, had flown.

All that awaited Charlie Frost and his team, alone in that sprawl of a house and grounds, were Letitia and her son; Danya still in his bed, surrounded by stuffed animals and posters of animated superheroes, Letitia in a white towelling dressing gown, sitting at the breakfast bar in the kitchen with a cup of lemon and ginger tea.

When asked about her husband's whereabouts, she shrugged. 'How the fuck should I know? Maybe he went out for a pint of milk.'

It was all Frost, normally the most self-contained of men, could do to stop himself slapping her round the face.

56

The operation, as a whole, was deemed a success. Was paraded as such to the press, the media generally.

Five arrested in dawn raids across London and the South-East. Charges ranging from drug dealing to murder.

Criminal gangs behind a vast drug and money laundering network with illegal profits estimated at £100 million smashed in a series of carefully coordinated raids.

£100 million, it had a nice ring to it.

People remembered.

Burcher, the public face of policing on this occasion, stood before the cameras and talked of assiduously accumulated intelligence, meticulous planning, acts of individual bravery.

'This operation has laid bare, once and for all, the link between drugs and violence which lies at the very heart of the Class A drug industry in this country.'

Drugs and violence. Reminders were provided of what had happened in Camden, at Stansted. Photographs, video. Viewers may find some of these images disturbing.

'The unfortunate shooting by a police marksman of an armed member of the gang, who had previously shot and wounded a police officer and was seeking to evade arrest, has been referred, as a matter of course, to the Police Complaints Authority. The wounded officer is happily expected to make a full recovery.'

Karen left the official piss-up early, found Ramsden in the adjacent car park, leaning against somebody's Toyota Land Cruiser, kids' car seats in the back, enjoying a cigarette.

'Not yours, I assume?'

'Joking, right? Know what these fuckers cost?'

'Fifty thousand?'

'And the rest.'

A smile crossed Karen's face.

'What?'

'Oh, nothing.' She had been remembering, back when she was seven or eight, Bible class. Thou shalt not covet thy neighbour's goods.

'So,' Ramsden said, 'celebrations over?'

'Just getting started.'

'Not inclined to join in?'

'No. You?'

Ramsden scowled. 'Chance to get bevvied up, shag someone else's wife. Quick poke up against the wall. Who needs it?'

Not me, Karen thought.

'Getting old, Mike,' she said.

'Too bloody right. Pension, five years off. Can't bloody wait.'

'Go on. They'll have to drag you out, kicking and screaming.'

'Don't you believe it.'

He lit a fresh cigarette from the butt end of the other. Offered the pack to Karen, who shook her head. There was a silver flask in his inside pocket. Brandy. They passed it between them, ignoring the occasional bursts of music and laughter that sallied out from the main building.

It used to be that officers like Ramsden did their thirty years and, much like the soccer players of yesteryear, took over a newsagent's or managed a pub. Now it was security, parading around an Arndale Centre somewhere, taking grief from kids for stopping them skateboarding up and down the aisles, and keeping a weather eye out for professional shop-lifters who routinely got away with several thousands' worth of goods a day. Either that or wearing a peaked cap and ersatz uniform behind some gated community stockade.

Poor Mike!

She looked at him with care as she passed the flask for the last time. The lines etched into his face were real, the shadows around his eyes.

'Got to go,' Karen said, stepping away. 'Someone tomorrow needs a clear head. Early start.'

'Drop you anywhere?'

'No, it's fine.'

Fine for some. Right now, Karen was all but wiped out. As early a night as was still possible and then bed.

Sod's law, her mobile. Not a number she recognised.

Charlie Frost.

'A few minutes of your time?'

Back at the celebration, Charlie Frost had looked hangdog, even in a life-changing Jackson Pollock tie. Forewarned, his principal target, Anton Kosach, had evaded capture, leaving the country via a private airfield close to the Sussex coast. He was believed to have joined his twin brothers, Parlo and Symon, in Sofia. Or another brother, Bogdah, in the Ukraine. Taras, the only one left in England, was helping with inquiries, as was his wife: both were expected to be released eventually without charge.

On the plus side, SOCA had taken away evidence enough from Kosach's house – computers, portable hard drives, bank statements, address books, diaries – to see him behind bars for thirty years if he were ever foolish enough to set foot in the country again, or try and settle anywhere with whom the UK had a valid treaty of extradition. One way and another, Kosach, Frost had calculated, had been responsible for laundering as much as £1 million sterling a day.

The interior of Charlie Frost's car smelt faintly of polish, a distant waft of pine. There was plastic still covering the rear seats. Not a crumpled crisp packet, a discarded tissue anywhere.

'You remember I raised the possibility before,' Frost said, 'some connection between Kosach and Paul Milescu?'

Karen nodded.

'Nothing yet I'd care to swear to, nothing I'd want repeated beyond the confines of this car, but we may have found a link. Money being filtered through one of Milescu's companies, fetching up first in Luxembourg, then the United Arab Emirates, then Singapore. From there, as of now, we're not too sure, but if it's not into a numbered account, the details of which are tattooed somewhere safe inside Anton Kosach's brain, I'd be surprised.'

He treated Karen to a rare, thin-lipped smile.

'The thing is this. Details have come to me of a possible relationship between Paul Milescu and Detective Chief Superintendent Burcher. Now were this the case – and I am treading very carefully here, you realise, nothing has been proven – but were that so, then one would want to ask whether any information passed from Superintendent Burcher to Milescu about the operation recently undertaken could have found its way to Kosach in time for him to flee the country. And whether, in exchange for such information, any, em, favours were returned.'

Jesus, Karen thought. She wasn't sure what was expected of her, what she was meant to say.

'I believe there was an instance,' Frost said, 'in which the

Superintendent attempted to intervene in an investigation you were running on behalf of Milescu's son?'

Karen was stopped in her tracks again. 'Alex Williams, she told you this?'

'All I'm asking is for you to accept or deny.'

'That the Superintendent intervened?'

'Yes.'

'That's not the word I'd use.'

'What then?'

'He asked that if anything serious came out of the inquiries we were making about Ion Milescu, we let him know.'

'And did you?'

Karen shook her head. 'There was nothing. Nothing crucial. Nothing to say.'

'But you inferred from this, this off-the-record – it was off-the-record . . . ?'

Karen nodded.

'. . . from this off-the-record conversation, that Super-intendent Burcher and Paul Milescu were close in some way? Friends?'

'Not necessarily, no.'

'But, surely, approaching you in that way, unorthodox at the very least?'

'Yes, I suppose so.'

'Yes?'

'All right, yes.'

Karen took a breath. How she had got herself in the position of seeming to defend Burcher, she didn't understand.

'Am I to take it, then,' she asked, 'that the Detective Chief Superintendent is under investigation?'

Frost smiled. A second time in almost as many minutes, something of a record. 'It's more than possible a few more questions may be asked; unofficially, I imagine, at first. Some perusal of bank statements, financial affairs, something of that accord. A little later, if necessary, the Regulation of Investigatory Powers Act could be invoked. But all this, in the future if at all.'

Karen knew her place in this. Were she to say anything to Burcher – to warn him, but why should she? – if she were to say anything to anyone it would eventually be known. Her card marked. Accomplice at worst. Untrustworthy, certainly. Any further promotion denied.

'Is that it, then?' she asked.

'Certainly,' Frost replied. 'For now. And thank you, Detective Chief Inspector, for your time.'

57

'Good Bait'. Dexter Gordon on tenor saxophone, stooping and slurping through the tune like a man sidestepping mud; the piano, distant behind him, sounding the notes like someone in a school hall more used to accompanying morning assembly, the morning hymn.

Cordon drank coffee as he listened, polished his shoes.

After two more days in London, when Jack Kiley's hospitality was stretched almost to breaking point, he felt, by his lugubrious presence, Cordon had returned to Cornwall and the confines of his sail loft, the expanse of views across the bay. Returned to his post, his job, the small team of neighbourhood officers greeting him as if he'd barely been away.

'Nice trip?'

'Safari, was it? See the world?'

Cordon had seen the world, all right. Part of it, blinkers removed.

After a week of doing precious little but check back through the files, reading over what he'd missed, he was summoned first to Penzance, then to the Cornwall and Isles of Scilly Commander in Truro. Polished buttons, gold braid. The Commander, not Cordon.

'Bit of a cowboy, all of a sudden, that's what I hear.'

Cordon said nothing, read the commendations framed behind the Commander's desk.

'Letter here from someone called Frost, Serious Organised Crime Agency, gist of it seems to be you've been planting your size twelves where they're not wanted, messing around with the big boys, organised crime. Suggests some kind of review, tighten the reins, a watching eye.'

'Yes, sir.'

What else was he supposed to say?

'What was it then, going off like that? Some kind of midlife crisis? Most people go out and buy a flash car they can't afford, have an affair, a bit over the side. That what it was? A woman? Some woman involved?'

A slow shake of the head, knowing, resigned.

'Christ, Cordon, I always had you down as someone, push came to bloody shove, could be relied upon. Bit of a barrack-room lawyer once in a while, but basically sensible. Know your own limitations.'

'Yes, sir.'

'You realise I could have your guts for garters over this. Disciplined and suspended and, most likely, cashiered out without as much as a farewell note?'

'Yes, sir.'

'Any good reason I shouldn't?'

'No, sir. Not really.'

'You stupid bastard!'

'Yes, sir.'

The Commander gave Frost's letter a second, cursory, glance. 'How many years have you got in now?'

'Twenty-five, sir.'

'Pension in five more.'

'Yes, sir.'

'Want to throw that all away?'

'No, sir.'

'Good. Out of your system then, is it? Back down to earth?'

'Yes, sir.'

'Take one more liberty, make one more false move, and I'll have you hanging off the fucking yardarm, understood?'

It was understood.

Ten minutes more, a few niceties, a final final warning, and he was back out on the street. Tregolls Road. Time enough, before heading back, to nip down to Lemon Quay and look through the jazz section at HMV.

A woman. That what it was? Some woman involved.

The Commander hadn't needed to tell him, he'd been a bloody fool about that too.

Three days later, a card came from his son. Australia. A picture of what was it? A koala? He could at least have managed a landmark somewhere, a view of the Harbour Bridge, was that too much to ask?

Dad, just a quick card. All settled here now. An effort, but worth it. You should come out some time, visit. Before it's too late.
Yrs, Simon.

Too late? Too late for whom? Or what?

And all – who was the all? And settled? Settled where? His son's life remained largely a mystery, one he gave little or no sign of wishing Cordon to solve.

Cordon scrutinised the postmark, blurred by the rain and disappearing off the edge. Melbourne, is that what it said? He hadn't known there was a plan to move. A new job, is that what it was? And how should he have known? Another card, perhaps? Some letter that had not been received.

Cordon propped the card up against one of the speakers.

Tried to imagine himself hunkered down on a flight more than halfway across the world and failed.

Work to be done, meanwhile. The theft of a camera from a Japanese tourist at Land's End. A sighting, near St Just, of a thirty-eight-year-old man wanted in connection with a recall to prison. Theft of lobster pots at Portheras Cove.

He was only half listening that evening, a brief summary of the news. A police operation in London and the South-East involving the Serious and Organised Crime Agency and units from the Metropolitan Police. Angling the television screen round from the wall, he found Channel 4, Jon Snow. Some library footage of officers in full gear, flashing lights, speeding vans. A sudden edit, change of scene. 'And here,' Snow's voice, 'is the private airfield within sight of the Channel, from which this man, Anton Kosach, wanted for questioning in relation to charges of money laundering on a vast scale, is said to have, literally, taken flight and disappeared.'

The image of Kosach on the screen was clear, unmistakable.

Cordon's first instinct, phone Letitia.

What for? Why? What would he say?

The only number he had, an old mobile. Out of commission when he tried it. No longer operational.

Kosach gone, so what? Done a bunk, leaving, presumably, Letitia and the boy. Nothing on the news to say otherwise. After fully fifteen minutes of telling himself there was little point, he rang Kiley.

'Jack, I don't suppose you've been watching the news?'

Kiley met him off the Paddington train.

'Thought I'd bloody seen the last of you.'

Cordon gave a helpless shrug.

'Never mind pissing off the few good contacts in the force I've got left, wheedling out answers to your bloody questions.'

'Okay, Jack. I'm sorry, okay?'

Kiley shook his head.

'So,' Cordon said, 'what do we know?'

'Best I can tell, she was taken in for questioning. Kept overnight. What did she know about Kosach? Possible whereabouts, contacts, numbers, anything that might help trace where he'd gone. Disclaimed all knowledge, apparently, same with questions about his business, how he made his money. Didn't know a thing. Spending the stuff, that was all she'd been interested in. That and bringing up his son.'

'She's not been arrested?'

'Not up to yet. Volunteered what information she could.'

'In a pig's eye.'

'And the rest.'

They were sitting high up above the station concourse, looking down on the apparently directionless maze of people below.

'You'll go and see her?' Kiley said.

'I will?'

'You've not come all this bloody way to talk to me.'

The train went from Waterloo. Taxi from there cost an arm and a leg. 'Right bloody commotion out here the other night,' the driver said. 'You'd've thought it the beginning of World War Three.'

Danny ran across the lawn to meet him and this time no one called him back.

Cordon tousled his hair, lifted him up and swung him round, set him back easily down when he screamed with delight.

'Well,' Letitia said, from the doorway, 'after the Lord Mayor's Show and no fucking mistake.'

He followed her indoors, Danny alongside him, chattering nineteen to the dozen: the police raid on the house, the most exciting thing in his young life.

They sat, slightly awkwardly, across from one another, Danny

335

still talking, tugging at Cordon's arm until his mother told him to run along, just for a couple of minutes, give them some peace.

'So, to what do we owe the honour?'

He hesitated, just for a moment, lost for words.

'I was worried about you.'

It sounded pathetic. It was.

'No need. Not now. Look . . .' She gestured around the oversized room, the fading, expensive furnishings. 'Sitting pretty.'

'You can't stay here.'

'Why not?'

'I don't know. I just thought . . .'

'Thought what?'

'Now he's not here, you could go. Leave. You and Danny, there's nothing stopping you. Go anywhere.'

She was laughing. 'Anywhere? Down to Cornwall with you, start a new life? That what you're thinking?'

'Maybe. If that's what you wanted.'

'Back down to where I've spent half my life trying to get away from.'

'All right, then. You said it, anyway, not me.'

'But it's what you were thinking.'

'Not really.'

'Liar. Bloody liar.'

Lighting a cigarette, she arched back her head and let the smoke slide upwards from the corners of her mouth.

Already, Cordon was wishing he'd never come.

'What will you do, then?' he said.

'Like I say, stay here long as I can.'

'You can afford to do that?'

She sat forward. 'When the police were here, searching, taking stuff away by the truckload, anything to do with Anton's business, one or two little things they missed. Place this size, have to take it to pieces, bit by bit, to find everything.' Her face creased in a smile. 'Leather holdall, good leather, too. Behind the panelling in one of the bathrooms, the one Danny uses most often. Five-hundred-euro notes, packed to the brim. Got to twenty thousand and stopped counting. When that's all gone, I'll find something else.'

She fixed him with a look, narrowed her eyes. 'You know me, Cordon. Resourceful, i'n't that the word?' A laugh, throaty. 'Maybe not the one you're thinking.'

She was on her feet.

'That cab you came in, I don't suppose you told him to wait?'

He shook his head.

'No, well, I'll call one. Trains every half-hour from the station.' She caught hold of his arm. 'Christ, Cordon, don't look so glum. It's all turned out okay. For now, anyway. Bugger the future, that's what I say. Look after what's happening now.'

Reaching up, she kissed him on the cheek.

'You're a soft bastard, Cordon, you know that, don't you? Always was.'

He didn't need telling.

'Why don't you go find Danny? See him before you go. Tell him he might come down some time, see you in Cornwall. He'll like that. I can always put him on the train.'

58

It had kept circling around in Karen's brain, hovering over everything else, never settling. On the rare instances she came into contact with Burcher in the ensuing weeks, he seemed much the same as before; no signs of being under particular stress, under fear of investigation. When she bumped into Alex Williams – a brief conversation on their way back from separate meetings – she came close to asking her about passing on something told in confidence, but the moment wasn't right. If there were rumours of the Chief Superintendent being involved in some criminal conspiracy, she didn't hear them, not directly. Just that same insistent, distant, buzzing. Work to do, she ignored it as best she could.

A party to several interrogations herself, a close witness to others, it became clear that the various members of Dooley's gang responsible for the Stansted killings were intent upon shifting blame from one to another. Talking themselves, as Mike Ramsden put it, into life inside with less chance of parole than I've got of pulling off an accumulator at fucking Ascot.

More tenuous, but promising, the earlier set of arrests officers from Operation Trident had made in connection with the murder of Hector Prince had been followed by another, four young men currently being held for questioning, the magistrate's court having agreed to an additional time in custody.

Only the death that had, in a way, begun it all, remained unsolved. Petru Andronic, his dead eyes staring blankly up at her through the ice. Terry Martin, their prime – their only – real suspect untouched by the recent spate of arrests, his alibis still unbroken.

'How long is it, girlfriend,' Carla asked over a late-night vodka tonic, 'since you gave yourself any kind of a break? Had a proper holiday?'

They went to Fuerteventura: five nights in a four-star hotel on the edge of Jandia, just six hundred metres from the beach. Some days they didn't even get that far. The hotel had three swimming pools, sauna, jacuzzi and spa. Karen rested, allowed herself to be pampered, read trashy novels, tried to erase the buzzing from her head.

On their final night, Carla talked her into joining her on stage towards the end of the karaoke. 'Respect', 'Single Ladies', 'Sisters Are Doin' It For Themselves'.

As an encore, 'It's Raining Men'.

It wasn't.

They slept, each, alone. Flew back into Gatwick the next day feeling, if not cleansed, then, at the very least, refreshed. Even the sun was shining. The visibility as they approached over southern England was clear and good; the winds, a low five miles per hour from the south-west. They laughed and joked aboard the Gatwick Express, said how they must do that again and before too long. Autumn. An autumn break before the cold of winter. Snow and ice.

At Victoria, Carla gave Karen a big hug and they went their separate ways.

Karen saw the news placard on her way down into the Tube.

House fire in North London. Arson suspected. Seven dead.

Seizing a copy, her eyes raced down the page.

Address in Wood Green . . . seven killed, five others being treated for severe burns . . . leg broken, jumping from upstairs window . . . firefighters beaten back by the intensity of the flames . . . unconfirmed rumours that three of the dead had recently been questioned in connection with the murder of Hector Prince . . . asked to comment on the possibility of revenge as a motive, there was no response from . . .

She punched in Ramsden's number.

'Been trying to raise you,' he said, 'since early this morning.'

Karen had deliberately switched off her mobile.

He gave her the address. One of a row of terraced houses, cramped together east of Wood Green High Road. When she saw Ramsden, he looked as desolate as the scene before him. Brickwork blackened, windows shattered and shorn of glass; front door badly charred and hanging from a single hinge. The last wisps of soot, restless on the air. Inside, a glimpse of hell.

There were two fire engines still in attendance, men and women inside, still damping down.

The last vestiges of smoke in the air.

Bunches of flowers, a few, clustering along the pavement to either side.

'When did it happen?' Karen asked. Vestiges of smoke catching at her throat, smarting her eyes.

'Two in the morning, give or take. Petrol bombs through both downstairs windows. Some kind of accelerant through the front door. Poor bastards inside never stood a chance.'

'Payback.'

'Without a doubt.'

Three young men, aged between fifteen and seventeen.

A girl of sixteen; another just twelve.

One thing to withhold names from public scrutiny, maintain reporting restrictions in place; another within the world in which they lived: holding them back for further questioning, even if they were later released, like painting a target on their backs.

'Witnesses?' Karen asked.

Ramsden laughed and shook his head.

There had been a fire in New Cross, Karen knew, some thirty years before. Thirteen young black people killed. Part of her history. A racist attack? An accident? Revenge for some uncharted wrong? At the inquests an open verdict was twice returned. To this day, no charge in relation to the fire had been brought.

And if those lives lost had been white . . . ?

She remembered her father driving her past the spot when she would have been no more than seven or eight years old.

'Remember what happened here,' he had said, removing his hat. 'Don't forget.'

She did remember, a small part of her, every day. And if ever it looked as if she might forget, there was something like this.

Or this . . .

Just five days later, what had happened in Wood Green and the events that had led up to it faded from the news, the head of the Trident independent advisory group issued a statement proclaiming a very real fear that, due to further government cuts, the unit, despite its successful record of building trust and solving gun and violent crime within the

black community, was, as previously rumoured, facing immi-
nent disbandment.

Sure, Karen thought, why not? Just a few black kids, capping
one another for fun, why not put the money where it's really
needed? Where the votes are.

59

She hadn't meant to be back again, but there she was. Almost a habit, but not quite. Not yet summer but the trees in full leaf, or so it seemed. Karen wearing no topcoat today, just a light jacket, sweater, jeans. Swimmers at the far end of the pond, a few; one lowering himself from the board before striking out, arms carving the water with ease.

This time, the young woman was standing just a short way along the path, and without her hood now, easy to recognise.

Karen waited for her to come closer.

'Sasha.'

A nervous smile.

'That was you, before?'

The girl nodded.

'How did you know I'd be here today?'

'I didn't. Not really. But I'd seen you here, a couple of times. I don't think you saw me.'

'Just the once.'

'Yes.'

'You come here a lot?'

Sasha pulled at a stray length of hair. 'More and more.' She shook her head. 'I don't even want to. I just . . .'

Karen nodded. 'I understand.'

'Do you?'

'I think so.'

Sasha waited a moment longer, then reached out towards Karen, and when she opened her fingers slowly, there in the palm of her hand was a ring.

'What's that?' Karen asked.

But, of course, she knew.

'That's the ring he was wearing,' Karen said. 'Petru, the night he was killed.'

'Yes.' A breath more than a word.

'You've had it all along?'

Sasha gave a fierce shake of the head.

'Tell me,' Karen said.

'My dad, we was having this row. A few nights back. Awful. I'd come in late. A party. Just friends, that's all. But he started calling me these names. Bitch and whore and all of that and then he . . . he took this from one of his pockets, like he'd been keeping it there special, and threw it in my face and said, "Don't think I won't fuckin' do it again, 'cause I will."'

Her hand was shaking now and Karen reached out and covered it with her own, feeling between them the small hardness of the ring.

'I just need to ask you, Sasha – there's no doubt in your mind what he meant by that, is there?'

'No.' Sobbing. 'No.'

'And you'd be willing to make a statement, repeat what you just told me?'

'Yes.' The word barely heard.

Karen moved closer and held her tight, for those short moments a bulwark against her tears.

ACKNOWLEDGEMENTS

Apropos a list of some three or four years' reading towards the back of his excellent little book, *On Writing: A Memoir of the Craft*, Stephen King says he suspects most of those books noted had some kind of influence on the novels he was writing at the time. In which case, glancing back through the last twelve or more months of my own reading during the course of writing this book, and seizing on authors whose names reappear several times, there should be traces here of, in no particular order, John le Carré, John McGahern, Willy Vlautin, Kate Atkinson, Horace McCoy and Colm Tóibín. More specifically, I reread with intent Peter Temple's *The Broken Shore* and *Truth*, because they seem to me to exemplify the very best of the kind of novel I'm trying to write, and Brian Thompson's *Ladder of Angels*, which is, for me, the great unsung British crime novel of the last few decades, rivalled only by his own *Bad to the Bone*.

In common with two of my characters, I read and was gripped by Attica Locke's *Black Water Rising*, dealing with civil rights, racism and political chicanery in the state of Texas, and

Oakley Hall's *Separations,* which, like *Ladder of Angels,* revolves around the search for a missing woman – just find the girl!

Peter Coles, formerly a detective superintendent with the Nottinghamshire police, was of great help, as usual, in the early stages of writing this book, answering my often hapless and naive questions with patience and attention to detail.

My thanks, also, to Mark Gardner of *Jazz Journal,* who, when he learned the title I was intending to use, went out of his way to acquaint me with as many recorded versions of the Tadd Dameron composition 'Good Bait' as exist.

My editor at Random House, Susan Sandon, in addition to her usual good advice and accurate eye, has shown patience almost beyond the call of duty in the, for me, unusually lengthy gestation of this book, as has my agent, Sarah Lutyens. What my partner and our daughter have had to contend with during this time is best left undocumented, but they did and I love them all the more for it.

John Harvey, London, June 2011